BABY DOLL

THEA LAWRENCE

Edited by Ben Browning

Cover design by Covers By Jules

@coversbyjule.s on Instagram

ISBN

Print: 978-1-7388810-1-7

Kindle: B0BM74DTKK

Author Note

Babydoll is **book one** in the Revolver Duet. This is an interconnected duet and the books **must be read in order.**

This book contains content and themes that are not suitable for readers under the age of 18, including: Drug and alcohol use, smoking, misogynistic characters and views, self-doubt and anxiety, explicit sexual scenes (condoms are used in this book as it is set in 1986 at the height of the AIDS epidemic), masturbation, mentions of vomit/vomiting. dirty talk, kink and dom/sub dynamics (while these have been written with care and attention, please remember that this book is fiction, and therefore not an entirely accurate depiction of reality and those relationships), praise kink, bondage (belts and ropes), biting, impact play, choking/hand necklaces.

Dicktionary

For those who want to dive right in to the spice, or avoid it, here are the chapters with spice:

Playlist

Maroon - *Taylor Swift*

Band of Skulls - *Fires*

The Strokes - *Under Control*

Lana Del Rey - *Norman Fucking Rockwell*

Motley Crue - *Girls, Girls, Girls*

Queen - *Good Old Fashioned Loverboy*

Stevie Nicks - *Edge of Seventeen*

David Bowie - *Modern Love*

Taylor Swift - *Delicate*

Incubus - *Anna Molly*

Ari Abdul - *Babydoll*

Bush - *Mouth (Stingray Mix)*

Cigarettes After Sex - *Affection*

Cavale - *Burst Into Flames*

The Lumineers - *Ophelia*

Vance Joy - *Riptide*

Billy Joel - *Vienna*

The Beach Boys - *God Only Knows*

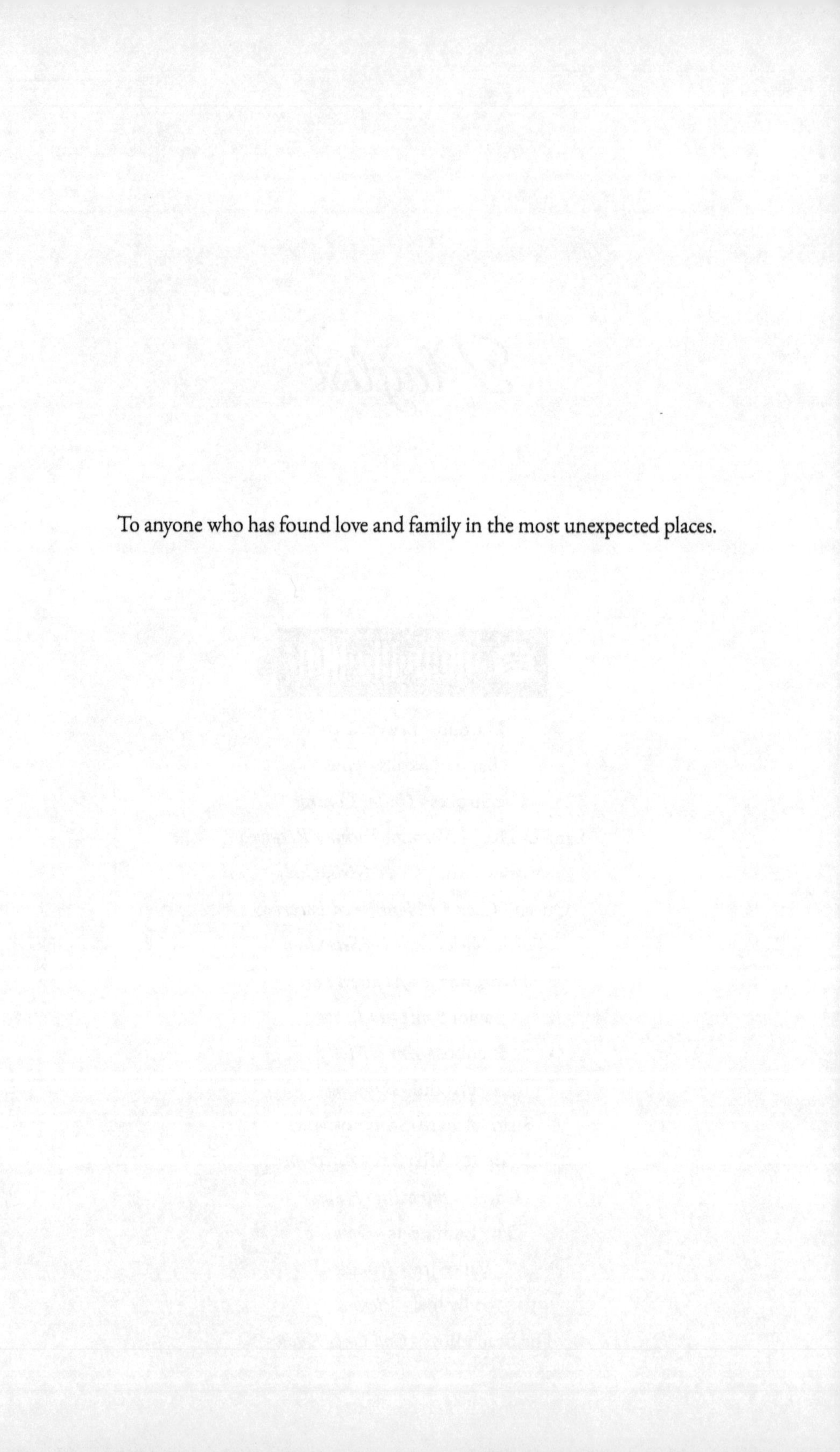

To anyone who has found love and family in the most unexpected places.

Contents

Once in a Lifetime

WILLIAMSBURG, NEW YORK

"I don't know if you know this, Phoebe, but I've heard, traditionally, most people start packing at least a few days before they leave for a big two month trip."

Phoebe Miller grits her teeth, desperately shoving clothes into her suitcase as she cradles the phone against her ear. She's been avoiding the clock for as long as possible, what you can't see can't hurt you after all.

"You know what, Brian? Right now, I need a supportive boss. How about you say things like, 'You'll make your flight, Phoebe!' and 'I believe in your ability to pack two months worth of shit in...'" She glances up, wincing. "Forty minutes? Jesus..."

"You're a disaster." Even on the other end of the line, she can practically see him shaking with laughter. *"Even without heavy traffic, you might still be fucked."*

Phoebe sighs as she shoves a pair of underwear into her suitcase.

"Listen, Brian, I feel like we're not communicating properly. Remember how encouraging and life-affirming you used to be? I need that Brian with me right now. Come on, give me a solid 'You can do it, Miller!'"

"Listen, as long as you have your notes, you can pick up the rest on the road. You do have your notes, right? All that prep-work?"

She grunts as she crams everything into her suitcase, praying that she doesn't damage anything in the process.

"I've got my tape recorder, typewriter, extra paper, three notebooks, pens, camera, and ten rolls of film... all the work stuff. Did that all last night while I was on the phone with Mr. Sullivan."

Now, if only she could close the damn suitcase and get it zipped up.

"Perfect," Brian replies. *"Look Phoebe, I'm just really happy you took this assignment. It's a great fit, and I think you'll knock it out of the park."*

"Well, I must admit, it's better than album reviews, which… you've kept me on for a whole year."

"I know," Brian sighs. *"I know. But hey, this is an opportunity for you to show us all what you can do. You really are the best person for the job, Phoebe."*

"Right, right, not because Sullivan didn't want Chris anywhere near the coverage?"

"Actually, I believe the words were 'fuck no' followed by a quick and concise 'fuck off.'"

Phoebe smiles. She wouldn't necessarily call Chris her work nemesis, but he's a real asshole. It also doesn't help that he has a bit of a bias against the band, a bias he made very evident in his review of their first album. There's no way they'd drag him along on a two month tour.

"I'll let you go, just pack the rest of your stuff and call me if you need anything, okay? I've got your itinerary and the hotels, so I'll be checking in periodically to see how things are going. And watch yourself around Bell. He's got a… reputation."

She scoffs. Her goal is to be invisible, a fly on the wall. These people are her job, not her friends.

"I got it, Brian. Thanks."

"Great– oh, and don't let them pay for anything. I'll reimburse you for whatever you need."

"Absolutely, I'm looking forward to the best champagne each place has to offer."

"Don't push it, kid."

She can't help but laugh a little. He's such a dad.

"Yeah yeah, I promise. I'll update you in a week. Should give me time to do a couple interviews at least."

"Sounds good. Good luck, Phoebe, and take care."

"You too, Brian."

She hangs up the phone, grabbing the rest of her belongings and desperately shoving them into her bag.

"Come on, please! I need this!" Finally, it gives and zips all the way up. She lets out a sigh of relief and steps back, her hands on her hips. "That's the first thing to go right all day."

She practically *begged* Brian for this story. In fact, she knocked on his office door every day asking him to put her on this assignment. She even snuck notes into his lunches. Co-workers called her desperate, but she called it determination.

Hurriedly she shrugs on a leather jacket, one she bought specifically for the tour. She fluffs up her hair to make herself look a little more unkempt, double-checking to make sure that the circles around her eyes aren't too noticeable. She's trying to mold her look, to fit in with a rock band.

Her long brown hair frames her naturally soft features, with some baby fat still lingering on her cheeks, all topped off by warm honey-colored eyes. It all combined to make her look a little younger than she is, and the jacket was supposed to add some sharper edges; make her look a little tougher. Somehow, after all that, she's *still* not sure about it.

Fuck it. No time for that. She grabs her bags and rushes to the stairwell, but before she's even a few feet away, she doubles back to check the lock. Maybe she's a little paranoid, but she'll be gone two whole months. Then again, what the fuck is someone going to steal? Her coffee pot and record player? She chuckles to herself, before pausing and jiggling the handle a third and final time. She really would miss that coffee pot.

Checking her watch, Phoebe curses under her breath; she grabs her suitcase and runs as fast as she can down some stairs and straight out the front door of the lobby, managing to flag down a big yellow taxi in moments. She flings her suitcase into the trunk with wild abandon and slides into the back seat, shocked at how lucky she got.

"Where to?" The driver asks. He's a little past middle-aged, maybe a bit younger than her dad. Nothing about him screams secret serial killer, so that's a win.

"JFK, please!"

The driver nods and takes off. It looks like she's going to make it, if just barely. She sighs as she gazes out the window. After a couple minutes the driver catches her eye in the rearview mirror.

"You headin' home?"

"Actually I'm going on a work trip."

"Ah. Where to?"

"Everywhere," she laughs. "I'm actually covering a band for the last leg of their North American Tour." She pauses for a moment. "Revolver, heard of them?"

"Oh, yeah. My kid listens to them. Pretty good."

"Yeah," Phoebe murmurs. "They are."

He's trying to get a better look at her in the mirror, shifting in his seat a little as the ride continues.

"So, you a journalist or somethin'?"

"Yeah, I used to freelance but now I write for a magazine. Titanium."

"Don't know it. I pretty much just listen to Neil Diamond these days."

"Neil Diamond is cool," Phoebe chuckles.

"Hey, can you write that in an article or somethin'? My son really needs to hear someone other than me say it."

Phoebe smiles as he speeds through the city. She catches whirring scenery as they pass by apartments and storefronts. She's going to miss New York. Mostly she'll miss the chaos, the unexpected, but she's certain she'll encounter a new breed of it on the tour. It's not long before they pull up to the departures terminal at JFK, cutting it closer than she'd like, but still not late.

"Fifteen," the driver tells her.

Phoebe hands him a twenty.

"Here, keep it."

"Thanks, toots."

She manages to check herself and her luggage just in time to sprint to her gate, covered in sweat. The attendant glances at her ticket and flashes a curt smile.

"You're fine, miss," she laughs. "We're not even close to being finished boarding."

"Oh, thank God," Phoebe breathes.

Boarding is simple enough, and she slides into her seat in the smoking section, stretching out her legs and relaxing as she digs her notebook out of her bag. There are four members of Revolver: Damien Bell, Shaun Slater, Johnny Reed, and Ophelia Powell. Brian wanted her to start with Bell for this piece, mostly because there's so little information about him out there. What is public knowledge is that he's notoriously... Well, media shy isn't exactly the phrasing she'd use. Every week, there's a new story about him getting thrown out of a bar, smashing a guitar through a car window, or hurling beer bottles off a balcony at random passerby. Just last week, there was footage of him being arrested after punching a paparazzi. He smirked and flipped off the cameras before being taken down to the police station.

Phoebe lights a cigarette, going over the information that Bell has reluctantly given to the press while the in-flight safety announcements are playing. Revolver's frontman is 26 years old, born and raised in Brooklyn. He's the primary lyricist of the group, and for someone the media's labeled a 'bad boy,' his songs are surprisingly poetic. Nothing he writes feels disingenuous or recycled, despite the subject matter, and that's about all she has. At least the rest of the group has been a little more open over the years.

Johnny Reed, also 26, played bass guitar in high school but stopped after he decided to pivot and study law. He's been Damien's best friend since they were kids. Johnny is probably the least complicated of the bandmates. He doesn't speak to the press often, nor is he known for his antics. As far as she can gather, he's more of a studious musician who fell into it somewhat accidentally. Ultimately he made it a year into law school before he quit that and started the band with the others.

Shaun Slater, 25, is a classically trained guitarist with a degree in music theory, and the only member who didn't spend his whole youth in New York. His mother, Gabrielle, teaches piano while his father, Max, started out playing the standup bass before swapping those skills to guitar. Max toured with Ella Fitzgerald, Miles Davis, and played on a Frank Zappa album before he started releasing solo work. Shaun obviously inherited his parents' love for music. He writes with Bell, playing perfectly off of his lyrics, and often improvises onstage when the situation calls for it.

Phoebe is jolted from her notes as the plane lurches into take-off. Her stomach flips and she takes a deep breath, swallowing over and over in the hopes her ears will pop. When she was a kid, this was the part of flying she dreaded the most. Her older brother used to hold her hand, a little to keep her calm, but mostly because he was anxious too.

She glances to her right, looking for anything to distract her, and sees a nervous-looking girl with a face full of soft freckles and thick glasses. Phoebe offers a reassuring smile, and the girl smiles back, her fingers digging into the arm rest.

You'll be okay, she mouths, and the two exchange one more quick smile before Phoebe digs into her bag for her Walkman, rewinding the cassette: Revolver's debut album. She slides her headphones over her ears and smashes the play button a little too hard. She's quickly met with the electric whine of Shaun Slater's guitar sending shivers all the way down her spine, followed by the crash of drums as the plane continues to ascend.

"Okay," she whispers. "Who's next?"

Ophelia Powell, 26, has been playing the drums since she was five years old. She grew up in Brooklyn with Damien and Johnny, and the three shared quite a few classes in their highschool days. Her influences lie in the likes of other female drummers: particularly Bobbye Hall, famous for her work on *Lean on Me*, and Maureen Tucker, who played drums for the Velvet Underground. In one of the few public interviews Damien's done, he called her the beating heart at the center of the group. A little cheesy, but still.

Ultimately, It wasn't too long until Revolver shot to the top of the charts and, more importantly, managed to stay there for much longer than most newcomers to the rock scene. The problem, or more accurately the opportunity in front of her: no magazine has been able to get a good sit-down interview with any of them. Bell both basks in, and loathes the press.

He pretty much rejects every interview, and has been known to explode during the few he's taken part in. He just seems to really love telling journalists to go fuck themselves. As a result they've been wildly speculating about him, whether or not he's actually writing these songs, if and when he's going to burn out, standard stuff.

Now, the band is in the midst of one final North American tour before they head back into the studio to put out a second album. The kind of success that they've had is lightning in a bottle, and it's extremely difficult to replicate. There really is a whole lot to think about, but what worries her is getting Bell to open up.

"Miss?" Phoebe jumps as the flight attendant leans in. "Would you like something to drink?"

She takes her pen out of her mouth and flashes a sweet smile.

"Champagne, please. My boss is covering it."

A voice cuts through Phoebe's dreamless sleep, and she feels a gentle hand on her shoulder. She jolts awake, her eyes meeting a pair of soft hazel ones, along with a big smile. The flight attendant chuckles softly as Phoebe gets her bearings. She doesn't remember falling asleep.

"We're going to start landing, if you could put your tray table back into the upright position and put your bag under your seat, that would be great."

"Y– yeah," Phoebe mutters. "Sure, no problem."

"Thank you."

She cleans everything up and tucks her bag beneath her seat, keeping her Walkman with her and rewinding the tape to start it all over again. When she looks to her right, the girl has her headphones on, too. Phoebe focuses on the music as she closes her eyes, feeling the plane begin to make the slow descent toward the tarmac. It's a bit of a bumpy landing, jostling her a few times as she white-knuckles the armrest until the plane comes to a complete stop. She checks her watch: Right on time.

As she makes her way toward baggage claim, she sees a man holding a sign with her name all in caps. Troy Sullivan, Revolver's manager. He's wearing a pair of tinted blue sunglasses, a black t-shirt underneath a dark red and gold leather jacket, and black jeans. His facial hair is neatly trimmed into a goatee, and his hair is wild, yet Phoebe can't help but think that he deliberately styled it that way. It looks almost too perfect.

She might not have recognized him right away, he's rarely in any of the pictures, but there's something about his ostentatious ensemble that screams 'management.'

"Phoebe Miller, I presume?"

"That's me!" She chirps. "Pleasure to meet you in person, Mr. Sullivan."

"Please," he laughs, "call me Troy. Mr. Sullivan makes me sound like I'm some geriatric, and I already feel like an ass standing here with this sign."

"Got it," she chuckles as he bends the cardboard in half and jams it in the trash can.

First impressions? Troy is much less uptight than she expected, but he's still a little intimidating. She can tell that he's sizing her up just by the way he's looking at her as she adjusts the bag on her shoulder.

"Sure you're up for this?"

"Absolutely. I'm a professional," Phoebe assures him.

"Of course you are," Troy replies. "Well, there's a car waiting outside. We'll take you to the hotel and introduce you to the band."

She has to jog a little to keep up with his long stride as they make their way to the parking lot.

"So, just a hunch, but I take it Bell isn't too excited to meet me?"

Troy laughs, glancing back over his shoulder.

"Wasn't at first, but he changed his tune once I mentioned you're a woman."

She sighs, and Troy laughs as he slows his pace and squeezes her shoulder.

"Relax, Miller. It's a joke! Look. I'll be honest, he's not thrilled at the idea of a journalist following him around for two months." He lights a cigarette and takes a quick drag. "I'm sure you've heard some... less than great things about him, but I promise you're not walking into the lion's den."

It's a small comfort coming from his manager, but it's better than nothing, and Phoebe gives him a curt smile as he takes her suitcase. She stuffs her own cigarette between her lips and climbs into the car next to Troy, who flashes her a toothy grin.

"Welcome to the next two months of your life, Miller. Let's make them count."

20th Century Boy

LOS ANGELES, CALIFORNIA

After being bombarded by music blaring from the car stereo and Troy's war stories from deep in the rockstar trenches, Phoebe's more than happy to see the hotel pull into view.

"They had a late show last night and went a little too hard, but they're in good spirits, so you should be fine."

"You know I don't have any questions prepared, right?" She asks him. "I'm planning on observing first and then–"

He cuts her off with a wave of his hand.

"I don't need your process, sweetheart, I'm just letting you know what you're walking into."

"Got it."

"They have another show tonight, and then we leave for San Jose tomorrow, and we'll be pretty much hitting a different city each night."

He looks over at her with a smirk as they walk into the hotel.

"Hope you like bus rides."

"Does anyone?"

"I'll take that as an enthusiastic yes!"

As they walk past the front desk toward the elevators, Phoebe's stomach is in knots. She'd been at this job for three years but still got starstruck sometimes. It's hard not to when you've grown up listening to Bowie and suddenly he's sitting right in front of you; at least he'd been sweet.

The elevator stops at the fifteenth floor and Phoebe takes a deep breath as Troy leads her toward the hotel room.

"We rented out the entire floor, not a big deal, we just want some privacy."

He hands her a set of keys.

"You're across the hall from Bell. I apologize in advance for what you're going to see and hear."

Before she has a chance to respond, Troy opens the door, and she's quickly ushered inside. Johnny and Shaun are sitting on the floor, guitars in hand, jamming together quietly while Ophelia nods along, tapping her drumsticks on her thighs. To be honest, Phoebe expected the room to be filled with half-naked groupies given the band's reputation. Instead, she has a quiet moment to observe them on their own turf.

First is Johnny, wearing blue jeans and a white t-shirt that's a little too tight on his torso, a tan line peeking out from beneath his shirt sleeve, exposing paler skin. She studies the sharp slope of his jawline and the way the light makes his cheekbones a little more sculpted than in the pictures. His brow is knit together in concentration, long tattooed fingers dancing along the bass strings. There are remnants of eyeliner, smudged beneath his vibrant blue-green eyes, visible only because his blonde hair is held back by the bandana tied around his head.

Next to him is Shaun, with curly black hair that's cropped close to his head, high cheekbones, and stubble dusted across an angular jaw. He's in black jeans with holes in the knees, and a blue tank top that shows off dark brown skin and muscular shoulders. Shaun looks just as focused as Johnny while he plays, his fingers wiggling against the fretboard, trying to perfect a riff. When the instrument doesn't produce the sound he wants, he huffs and looks up at her, flashing a thousand-watt smile. His warm brown eyes glitter in the sunlight that pours through the curtains, and Phoebe smiles right back.

"That was good," Ophelia offers.

"Don't patronize me," Shaun laughs.

"I mean, it'll sound better when it's plugged in."

She cackles as he elbows her, almost teetering over before shoving him back. Ophelia's fiery red hair flows down her back in large waves that contrasts her pale, freckled skin. She has delicate features: round cheeks that dimple when she smiles, a small upturned nose decorated with a silver ring through her right nostril, and topping it all off are sparkling olive-green eyes. She's leaning heavily into a casual look, sporting an oversized black NYU sweater and bicycle shorts. Her vibrant-blue painted toenails stand out against the carpet as she twirls her drumsticks between her fingers. She smirks when she sees Troy at the door.

"Lookin' good today, Sullivan!" She shouts.

"Very professional," Shaun agrees. "Can't even see the mustard stains on that suit."

"Where's Bell?" Troy asks, trying to overlook the fact that the three bandmates have collapsed into laughter.

"Shower."

"He alone?"

Ophelia nods and Troy lets out a long sigh, clearly a little relieved.

"We'll wait for him to finish before we make introductions."

Phoebe stands with her hands stuffed in her pockets, trying her best to maintain a relaxed posture as she smiles at the group. Ophelia emphatically returns the gesture. Phoebe doesn't have to imagine working with this much testosterone, as rock journalism isn't exactly a diverse career either. It's a lot of over-confident men masturbating intellectually in the form of 3,000-word essays on the death rattle of American rock music. They've been writing the same think pieces since the '60s.

As if on cue the bathroom door swings open, and Damien emerges in a pair of black jeans that hang low on his hips, steam billowing out around him like an exclamation point on his entrance. His hair is wild and long, only half-dry and still dripping water down his torso. He's wearing a pair of dog tags around his neck, framed perfectly by his open dress shirt.

She's scoured hundreds of pictures of him, but he's somehow even more handsome in person, with rock-solid abs, chiseled cheekbones, and a razor sharp jaw dusted with stubble. He pushes his dark hair out of his face, sizing Phoebe up like a predator as his bright blue-gray eyes cut right into her. Her heart pounds and she feels butterflies tormenting her stomach.

This is new.

Troy clears his throat, only slightly undermining the almost comically perfect entrance with an off-handed wave of his wrist.

"Kids, this is Phoebe Miller from Titanium. She's going to be with us for the next two months, so play nice and I'm sure she'll give us some good publicity. I think we could all use it right about now."

Damien lingers by the bathroom door, watching her intently while Troy goes through introductions with the rest of the band. He grabs a pack of cigarettes off the table as Troy reaches the end of the formalities, lighting one and letting it hang lazily from his mouth as he struts straight toward her.

"And of course this peacock's Damien Bell. You can't miss him."

He sticks out a large hand, his left wrist adorned with silver bracelets and his fingernails painted black. Even more silver decorates his fingers. Skulls, crosses, and something that looks like an old wedding band conspicuously placed on the wrong finger.

Damien is intimidating, much taller than she thought he would be. He must be at least 6'3". She grasps his hand confidently, trying to stand up as straight as possible, and he smiles. It's cautious, but not malicious, as though he's sizing her up. She breathes a sigh of relief. She'd heard some horror stories.

"Phoebe, right?"

His voice is soft and a little gravelly, sending a shiver up her spine.

"That's me," she replies. Something about his voice changes the entire dynamic in the room, with her own words almost crushed under the weight of her spreading anxiety.

He looks her up and down, his eyes lingering for a little too long on her hips and breasts before he struts past. Her cheeks must have gone from a light pink to a deep crimson in a matter of seconds. She didn't even blush this much when she met Bowie.

Shaun motions for Phoebe to take a seat, but the only place left is the edge of the bed that Damien is currently occupying. She sits down, quickly tucking her bag between her knees. Rock stars have big personalities and sometimes an even bigger physical presence. Already, she's beginning to feel caged.

"What do you wanna play tonight, Damien?" Johnny asks him.

It's already as if she's not in the room, and that's exactly how she likes it.

"The new one I wrote," Damien replies. "We'll open with it."

"Automatic?" Shaun asks.

"Yeah,"

"I still gotta learn the solo on that,"

"Well, figure it out, dude," Damien mumbles, blowing a huge plume of smoke into the air.

"I've figured it out, *asshole*," Shaun bites back with a grin. Damien snickers. "I just need a little more practice."

Damien sits up, turning his attention back to Phoebe.

He's studying her, trying to figure her out. She swallows hard and looks around.

"Is this what you guys typically do before a show?"

"Well, I usually drink more," Damien snarks.

Troy rolls his eyes.

"Or he's balls deep in some groupie," Shaun replies.

Damien crushes his cigarette out in the ashtray next to the bed.

"I'm going to the bar to write," Damien grumbles. "There's some chick in my room. I can't fuckin' concentrate in there."

"Oh, so that's why you used my shower," Shaun laughs.

"Nah, I just missed your musk."

"Aww, isn't that sweet?" Shaun pulls a face at Johnny, who chuckles and shakes his head.

"Don't get too loaded!" Troy shouts as Damien gets to his feet, grabbing a notebook and pen off of the nightstand.

"Yeah, yeah."

"I'm serious, Bell."

Damien shuffles out the door, letting it shut behind him. The others shrug. They've clearly been dealing with this for a long time now, and barely miss a beat as Johnny and Shaun transition into working on the new song. Phoebe listens for a few moments before grabbing her bags, suddenly a little more self-conscious.

"I'll let you guys practice. I'm pretty exhausted from the trip."

"Sure," Troy replies. "We're leaving for the venue in a few hours for soundcheck. Show is at the Whisky. I'll wake you up, or just swing by here around 7:00."

"Got it," Phoebe replies, turning back to the others. "It was nice to meet you. I'm really looking forward to the next two months."

"Us too," Johnny says, showing off a big beaming smile.

"Well, some of us," Ophelia replies. "Damien will come around. He's just a little rough around the edges."

That feels like the understatement of the century given everything Phoebe's read.

"And you seem cool," Shaun adds, like a little consolation prize.

"Thanks," Phoebe laughs. "I appreciate that."

She digs her room key out of her pocket. 1507, just down the hall. As she reaches her room she can't help but glance across the way. Bell has a ***Do Not Disturb*** sign on the door, because of course he does. Suddenly the handle wiggles, and Phoebe steps back in surprise.

A petite girl with short dark hair pokes her head out. Her mascara is smeared underneath her eyes, her body covered only by a white bed sheet. She glances around the hall frantically before noticing Phoebe.

"Hey!" The girl hisses. "Are you with the band? Revolver?"

"Uh, sort of?"

"Do you know where Damien is?"

Phoebe shakes her head. She knows better than to get involved in this shit.

"No. Sorry."

The girl rolls her eyes.

"Jesus, what an asshole."

"You could rack up the room service bill while he's gone," Phoebe suggests.

Bedsheet girl raises her eyebrows and nods vigorously.

"You know what? That's not a bad idea. Thanks, babe!"

Phoebe smiles to herself as she enters her room, her good deed done for the day, but her jaw drops as she takes in the sheer size of it. A king size bed, a bathroom with a tub bigger than anything she could possibly imagine, *and* a shower?!

She whistles to herself.

"You're living the high life now, kiddo."

She kicks off her shoes and throws her bags onto a chair before beelining for the bed, flopping down on it face-first. It's soft, so much softer than the one back home in Williamsburg. By this point, the compounded anxiety and excitement had pushed her exhaustion all the way into her bones, and seconds after she sinks into the mattress, she's asleep.

Phoebe jolts awake, feeling even worse than before. The clock on the nightstand shows 4:00PM. Rolling onto her back, she briefly contemplates trying to get a little more sleep before the inevitable reality takes hold: she's going to feel like shit no matter what. Instead, she decides to go down to the hotel bar, peeling off her t-shirt and throwing on a fresh tank top. Maybe she can score an interview with Bell if he's still there, or at the very least, get a drink.

As she goes to retrieve her bag, the phone rings. She just stares at it for a moment, confused and a little scared. Phoebe's mind always goes to the worst case scenario: maybe she's getting fired, or maybe Bell decided he didn't like her, and he wants her off of the tour. She gulps as she picks up the receiver.

"Hello?"

"Miss Miller, we have a call on the line from a Samantha Miller?"

Phoebe sighs. She forgot that she had told her mom where she was staying. Despite trying to keep her work life very separate from her personal one, her mother has always had a tendency to insert herself where she isn't wanted. She loves to give feedback; it's her true passion, and a general pain in Phoebe's ass.

"Miss Miller?" The concierge's voice snaps her back to reality.

"Uh, yeah— yeah, send her through... or patch her through or whatever you guys do."

The concierge laughs.

"I'll transfer the call."

There's a clicking noise and Phoebe sucks in a deep breath.

"Phoebe?"

"Hi, mom."

"I'm just checking in to make sure you landed safely." Her voice is tight, but relieved. *"So how is your big cover story for Rolling Stone?"*

"You mean Titanium."

"What's that?"

Phoebe rolls her eyes.

"It's the magazine I've been working for? For two years?"

"I thought you were with Rolling Stone."

"No, mom."

"Oh, Phoebe, I just don't understand it! You were smart enough to get into Stanford with your brother–"

"Mom–"

"Are they at least paying you well? Maybe I could call Brian..."

"Stop it," Phoebe warns.

"I just want what's best for you, sweetheart."

Phoebe begins to tune out as her mother drones on and on about the same things as always: how her brother, Michael, found a respectable job as a doctor and Phoebe should think about settling down and having kids. It's the exact fight they get into every holiday, birthday, or any other time her mother calls.

Phoebe begins to make a distinct crackling noise.

"Mom— breaking— up— ca— he—"

"Phoebe?!"

She hangs up the phone, quickly slinging her bag over her shoulder and scurrying out the door before her mother can call back. She heads straight to the front desk. The concierge smiles at her as she approaches.

"What can I help you with?" She asks.

"Can you tell me where the lounge is?"

"Just down that hallway and to the right."

"Great, thanks– oh, um, I'm in 1507... if a woman named Samantha calls again, can you just tell her that the phone is on the fritz or something? She's kind of a lot to deal with."

The concierge smiles.

"I'll pass the message along."

"Thanks."

The lounge is packed, and as she's moving towards a small booth near the back, Phoebe spots Bell sitting at the bar. He's nursing a glass of whiskey, rhythmically tapping his fingers against it as though he's trying to capture whatever's playing in his head.

Phoebe takes a seat in an empty booth in view of the bar, waiting for somebody to come by to take her order. Occasionally, someone stops to try and talk to Bell or ask for an autograph. He indulges them, but only for a moment, before turning back to his work. The bartender tells the ones who linger too long to get lost. Bell seems to appreciate the privacy, even if nobody else does.

Phoebe orders a whiskey sour, flips open her notebook, and begins to write about her first meeting with the band. Occasionally her eyes flick up at Bell, who is lost in his own writing. She makes notes on his posture, those rings that adorn his hands, his quiet dedication to his craft– even the way his fingers wrap around that whiskey glass.

As she's working, she suddenly feels a presence, looking up to see him towering above her with a smirk on his face. His shirt is half buttoned up in accordance with the rules of the lounge, but she can still see the dog tags hanging from his neck, along with the requisite bit of skin he loves to flaunt.

"You could have said hi."

Phoebe's a little taken aback.

"I didn't want to bug you."

Damien nods slowly, staring at her just long enough that it nearly makes her want to escape into the crowd, before he gestures to the seat across from her.

"Can I sit?"

Her heart pounds against her chest.

"Sure. Yeah."

He slides into the booth, his notebook tucked underneath his arm and a full glass of whiskey in his hand. She can smell the alcohol on him, but he seems sober outside of the slight drooping of his eyes.

He reaches into the pocket of his jeans and pulls out a pack of cigarettes. She watches him closely, resisting the urge to take notes on the exact way he taps one out of the pack before handing it to her. Phoebe whispers a small thank you as he lights it, the two of them exhaling slowly. The nicotine does absolutely nothing to calm her nerves. Bell, on the other hand, looks relaxed. One arm drifts up to rest on the top of his seat as he leans back, tilting his head to the side. His movements are almost cat-like, so fluid that she can't tell if he's been practicing them for years, or if this kind of sensuality has just come naturally to him his whole life.

"Were you... observing me, Phoebe?" His voice is calm but pointed.

Is he flirting, or just being a dick?

"Was I what?"

His lips curl into a smile and his eyes twinkle.

"Back there at the bar. Were you watching me? Taking notes?"

"Uh... n– no."

He leans forward and chuckles, his rock star façade fading just a bit. It doesn't make her feel any less nervous, though.

"It's cool, Miller. You don't have to hide anything, I know what journalists do. You're just writers. Writers observe. It's like half of your job."

"Do you observe?" She asks, regaining some confidence along with the territory.

"Every minute of every day," he replies.

Phoebe's quiet as she watches the ash collect on the tip of his cigarette. She's very good at awkward silences, but she figures this might be her one shot to sit down and have a real conversation with him, and she doesn't want to bore him into leaving.

"Do you only write lyrics?" She asks, gesturing to the notebook.

He perks up at the question.

"There's some prose in here," he offers, picking up his book. "But poetry is just easier. It flows better."

She nods, once again resisting the urge to reach for her notebook and write down a quote. It's hard to repress instinct, but she has a feeling that if she started to treat this like a formal interview, he'd shut it down immediately. Brian made it clear he wanted sound bites. Snippets that give the reader insight into the artist and how their mind works. Anything and everything that falls from Bell's mouth is fair game. That's what he told her, at least.

Damien catches the twitch of her fingers and laughs softly.

"Do you only write articles?"

The tone is a little aggressive. She shifts in her seat and taps her cigarette against the ashtray. He's watching her just as much as she's watching him.

"I used to write fiction when I was a kid."

"What kind?" He asks.

"Science fiction, mostly."

His eyes light up. That's good, they can talk about something other than his antics; something more personal. It's boring to write about a stereotypical bad boy. Why not bond a little over art?

"You ever read Huxley?"

"Yeah. I prefer Asimov, though. I like robots."

He smiles and blows a cloud of smoke out of the side of his mouth.

"Robots, huh?"

"Yeah."

"Who else do you like?"

"William Gibson."

"He wrote, uh... Neuromancer, right?"

She chuckles.

"You know your science fiction."

"A little bit. I like fantasy books."

She feels like she's getting somewhere with him. Normally, her tactic is to observe and keep her distance; to be professional. She has a feeling that isn't going to work with Bell. He seems to like it up close and personal, and she's willing to let him in a little, if it means getting a good story.

His eyes dart around the bar, taking in his surroundings before he leans over, as though he's about to tell her a secret. Phoebe mirrors him, her hand inadvertently sliding her notebook forward a little. She has to glance down to make sure that it's closed.

"Can I ask you something?"

"Sure."

"When you write this thing, can you just make us look cool? Like real artists?"

She laughs awkwardly.

"That's not really my job. These tour assignments are supposed to give the public an insight on the inner workings of the band."

"What do you mean?" He asks, his brows knitting together.

"You know, just what you guys fight about, what holds you together, what inspires you." She draws in a breath as he stares her down, almost glowering at her. It makes her chest squeeze a little tighter. "Even if a piece is unflattering, it's still attention."

"Is that what you were hired for?" Damien asks, a snarl stitched into his voice. "To give us attention?"

Her eyes bounce from his fingers drumming gently on the table to his eyes, and back again.

"Damien, I don't want to be enemies."

He chuckles.

"I'm just fucking with you. It's just with that whole media frenzy around the bouncer I hit…" he whirls his hand vaguely in the air and rolls his eyes.

Phoebe flashes him a big, confident smile that she's certain he can see right through.

"Understood," she replies.

"I hope so." Damien stands up and tosses back the last of his whiskey, "I'll see you tonight, Phoebe."

She's surprised to find she likes the way that her name sounds on his lips, but hopes she won't get used to it. That would make things difficult.

"Yeah. See you."

Her voice is a little pinched as she watches him strut away. There's a bit of pride rising in her chest as she realizes that she's survived her first encounter with the infamous Damien Bell.

He signs a few autographs on his way out the door, and shakes some hands. Just before he vanishes, he turns back and winks at her. She blushes and writes a note to herself, underlining it three times.

They're your job, not your friends.

L.A. Woman

BEVERLY HILLS, CALIFORNIA

Phoebe's head is buzzing as she takes the elevator back up to her room. It was the look in his eyes that really set her teeth on edge. Is he going to try and control what she writes? Worse yet, is he going to try and get Troy to read her fucking drafts? This whole thing is starting to make her nervous. Her job isn't to write a fluff piece, it's to give the public a good insight into how Revolver works.

Phoebe breathes through her anxiety, digging her keys out of her pocket as the elevator doors open. Stepping into the hall, she barely avoids Ophelia as she comes barrelling around the corner, stopping just short of a full collision.

"Just the person I was looking for! I was going to go to Beverly Hills to grab something to wear before the show. You wanna come with?"

She was planning to prep her gear, make sure there's film in her camera, that her batteries were charged; god, she still had to check in with Brian. She was pretty certain how that call was going to go. If she asked for his advice, he'd tell her what he always did, "It's business, kid, you're not out there to make friends." Still, this could be a good chance to get to know the band one on one before they get on the road.

Ophelia seems to sense her hesitation.

"Don't worry about money. I'll buy you whatever you want."

"Oh, I'm not supposed to—"

Ophelia's sudden laughter cuts Phoebe off completely.

"If we all did what we were supposed to do, nobody would ever have any fun. Come on. It's been a sausage fest in this fucking hotel, and I wanna go clothes shopping!"

Phoebe runs a hand through her hair, a little smile forming on her lips.

"Sure, you know what? That sounds fun."

Ophelia pumps her fist and takes her hand, and in only a few minutes they're in a taxi on the way to Beverly Hills.

"You know, when Troy told us that you were going to be writing an article and following us around, we were all pretty skeptical."

"Yeah?"

"Yeah!" She laughs, briefly meeting Phoebe's eyes before continuing. "We've had this kind of thing happen before, without Troy's permission of course. Journalists try to sneak backstage, follow us from city to city. Damien usually shuts it down fast."

"Well, I'm grateful to be on tour with you guys. I know Damien doesn't really like... well, my whole occupation."

Ophelia laughs again, before taking on a slightly more serious tone.

"Well, he's been pretty burned by the press. Photographers invading his privacy, all of the headlines, it's a lot for him to deal with. Actually, he's surprisingly sensitive, but don't tell him I told you that."

Phoebe picks at the peeling polish on her nails, before suddenly speaking up.

"Can I ask you something?"

"Sure— Oh! Stop here!" Ophelia squeals, tapping the back of the passenger seat. The car comes to a halt and she hands a wad of cash to the driver as the two get out.

"What was your question?"

"Is he really as bad as people say? With journalists, I mean."

"Depends on the journalist."

"I'll make sure to stay on his good side."

"I'm sure you'll be fine. It might be a little easier for you given, you know..." she gestures to Phoebe.

"What?"

"You're a woman. He's a little softer with us." She leans over toward Phoebe, comically glancing to both sides before locking eyes. "Can I tell you a secret? Off the record?"

"Uh, Sure."

She cups her hand over her mouth and whispers even though they're alone outside of the boutique.

"He's actually kind of a big teddy bear once you get to know him. The whole rock star thing? It's an act. It's not easy to break through all that ice, but I wouldn't have been his friend for this long if I didn't like him."

Phoebe nods. She feels a sense of relief knowing that underneath the swagger, there's a real person.

"I'll keep that in mind."

Ophelia throws the door to the boutique open and practically yanks Phoebe's arm out of the socket as they step inside.

"I can't tell you how much of a relief it is to have another girl on this tour."

She waves at two of the sales girls.

"The only person I can convince to come clothes shopping with me is Johnny, but he wanted to go for a run before the show. 15 miles! Can you believe it?"

"He runs?"

"Every day. He's the only one in the band who doesn't smoke. He's tried to get Damien to quit at least a hundred times, but..."

"It's hard to get him to do anything?" Phoebe jokes.

Ophelia laughs and nods her head.

"You got it."

The two of them browse through the racks, and within a couple minutes Phoebe's holding a pair of bright red leather pants. She almost chokes when she sees the price tag.

"What's wrong?"

"Nothing, just... two hundred for a pair of pants?"

"I know, it's ridiculous. But it's *Chanel*, so..." She pauses and tilts her head, grabbing the pants from Phoebe and holding them up. "You're getting these right? And don't say you don't have money because I have a credit card. And then *another* credit card if the first one doesn't work."

Phoebe laughs.

"I don't know."

"Do you like them?" Ophelia asks.

"Yeah."

"Then why are you worried?"

"I promised my boss—"

Ophelia scoffs.

"I promise Troy things all the time. Live a little, Pheebs."

Phoebe grins. She likes Ophelia. The girl has a magnetic sort of presence that draws people in, and Phoebe feels instantly at ease the second she smiles at her.

"Okay, okay. You twisted my arm."

Ophelia's eyes sparkle, her nose scrunching up.

"Cool. You're getting these, and I saw some cute black dresses over here– oh, and a mini skirt! I saw a pink one over here that would look amazing on you!"

Ophelia takes her hand and drags her toward some more racks. She has great taste, and they spend the next hour grabbing as much clothing as they can. It's fun, and it makes Phoebe feel a little less like a fish out of water.

In the changing room, things are much the same, with Ophelia consistently bringing her items of clothing faster than Phoebe can try them on.

"Found these for you, too!" Ophelia's ethereal voice floats toward her from the outside, as two black dresses are draped over the door.

Phoebe grabs them and pulls them down. One is a soft, stretchy spandex that's probably going to be incredibly tight when she puts it on, and the other is almost a snakeskin pattern. She runs her fingers over the scales and looks at the price tag. Four hundred dollars.

"Jesus," she breathes.

"You good, babe?" Ophelia calls.

"Yeah," she laughs. "Just checking the prices."

"Well, cut it out! Just try one of them on!"

Phoebe grabs the snakeskin one first, removing her jeans and kicking them aside, tugging the dress up over her hips. It's a stretchy material, but there's a little bit of room for her to breathe, which is always very nice of a clothing designer to do. She turns to the side, striking a pose and biting her lip, her stomach sticking out just a little. Phoebe smiles to herself, liking what she sees in the mirror.

Ophelia's jaw drops when Phoebe steps out of the room, doing a little twirl.

"Holy shit!"

"You like it? I don't know where I'm gonna wear this thing," Phoebe chuckles.

"Breakfast? Church? Who cares, you look amazing!" Ophelia gushes.

Phoebe feels her cheeks redden and she looks down at her bare feet. The boots she was trying on are still in the change room.

"Thanks."

"You feel good?"

Phoebe nods.

"Well, you look great."

Ophelia checks her watch, cursing at her wrist like it personally offended her. Phoebe is a little surprised that she even has a watch, considering her general chaotic state of being.

"Shit, we gotta be back to the hotel soon. If you wanna try on that other dress, do it now, but I think this one is the winner unless you want both."

"I'll just take the one," Phoebe whispers. "You really don't have to–"

"I do." She nibbles a little at her thumb nail. "I don't get to spend a lot of time with girls on the tour, Pheebs. And you seem cool."

It's a brief moment of vulnerability that she seems to shake off immediately, but Phoebe takes it to heart. It's not easy being surrounded by men all the time. Phoebe sympathizes in a lot of ways.

"I think you're cool, too," Phoebe replies. "Thanks for taking me out today."

"You looked like you needed it when you walked out of that elevator."

Phoebe chuckles.

"That obvious, huh?"

"Well, it's your first day, you don't know anybody and I know how lonely that can be sometimes. Not that I felt sorry for you or anything–" Ophelia holds out her hands. "God, please don't think that."

"No," Phoebe replies. "Not at all. Everyone's been really nice so far. I mean, Bell's given me a bit of a hard time, but I kinda saw that coming."

"Don't read too much into it." Ophelia pats her on the shoulder. "It's like I said, he's a teddy bear once you get to know him. It's just getting over that hurdle that's the hard part, but if he says anything mean to you, tell me and I'll smack him."

For her sake, Phoebe hopes that whole teddy bear thing is actually true. The last thing she needs is Bell breathing down her neck and "approving" whatever she chooses to write. He's not her editor, and he never will be.

Ophelia pays for everything, as promised, and they walk out of the store, massive shopping bags hanging from their arms. Phoebe wouldn't tell Brian anything about this shopping expedition. Ever. For the rest of her life.

"You wanna get ready for the show in my room?" Ophelia offers. "I could do your makeup."

"Okay!" Phoebe chirps.

Ophelia hails a cab and Phoebe can't help but smile as she gazes out the window, the sun just beginning to set as people stroll down the sidewalk. It's nice to be around Ophelia. She didn't grow up with sisters, so she's always cherished her female friendships. At the very least, she's grateful not to be shut away in her hotel room by herself her first day on the job. A gentle elbow from Ophelia pulls Phoebe from her thoughts, and she turns to see the girl beaming at her.

"I'm gonna make you look cool, Miller. By the time we leave, you'll be one of us."

City of Angels

THE WHISKY A GO GO

"So where did you grow up?"

Ophelia pulls out her enormous makeup bag, dozens of little plastic containers clattering around as she plunks it down on the bathroom counter

"Brooklyn."

"Cool! We're all from there too, except Shaun but he moved in pretty quick."

Ophelia's hotel room is filled with so much hairspray that Phoebe finds it a little hard to breathe.

"Okay, so how old are you?"

"Twenty-three," Phoebe replies.

Ophelia narrows her eyes.

"For real?"

Phoebe laughs.

"You wanna see my ID?"

"Sorry, most people lie. At least the first time. I'm twenty-six."

"You all went to the same prep school, right? Upstate?"

"Yeah. We were all in marching band together. It's how the group got started."

"Marching band, seriously?" Phoebe asks, barely stifling a giggle.

She should be writing this down, but her notebook is sitting on Ophelia's bed.

"Yeah. Don't tell Damien I told you, 'kay? He played the trombone." Ophelia shakes her head. "He called it the tromboner."

"Of course he did."

Fuck the notebook, there's no way she'd forget something like that.

"Boys, right?" Ophelia shrugs.

"I don't know how you put up with them on your own."

"Sometimes they bring girls with them on the road. That helps. I've gotten to know a few of Damien's girlfriends, or... whatever he calls them. They don't usually last more than a few cities, though. Sometimes Johnny brings Erin, that's his girlfriend– they're engaged!" She frowns. "Oh, don't put that in the article. They're both real private about that stuff."

Phoebe watches as Ophelia teases her fiery red hair to the point where it looks like flames licking the sky, stumbling a little as she's half focused on the conversation at hand.

"Noted."

With a quick hand, Ophelia swipes black eyeliner over her eyelids, pushing it out with a Q-Tip until it forms a thick, smokey wing. She completes the look with red lipstick and a ton of blush on her temples. She does Phoebe's makeup next, toning down her signature eyeliner look just a bit since she won't have the stage lights on her. Phoebe teases her hair up to the height she likes. It's not quite as dramatic as Ophelia's, but enough to stand out. She pulls her brand new leather pants over her hips and grabs a halter top to go with her leather jacket. Ophelia nods in approval.

"You look cool," She pauses for a moment, "Professional-cool."

Phoebe laughs.

"Thanks, Ophelia."

Suddenly, there's a pounding at the door.

"Ophelia! Where's our journalist?!" It's Troy, of course.

She yanks it open, hands on her hips.

"Calm down man, she's with me!"

"Thank God," Troy sighs, visibly relieved.

Where did he think she was?

"You look good," he says offhandedly as his eyes bounce between the two of them, before snapping back into manager-mode. "Alright, get your shit, kids. We've gotta go."

Phoebe rushes back to her room, grabbing both of her cameras, a notebook, and her tape recorder. She shoves them haphazardly into her bag before darting out the door. The band is already waiting at the elevator.

Bell is in a leather jacket, tank top, and leather pants. He has black eyeliner smeared beneath his eyes, smirking at her as she tries to run in her new boots, which of course have not been broken in. She winces with every step, only slightly out of breath when she reaches them.

"You look nice," he says softly.

"Thanks."

"You could almost pass for one of us."

"Is that an insult, or..." Phoebe mutters as she adjusts her bag on her shoulder.

"I barely know you," Damien laughs. "Why would I insult you?"

She swallows, feeling his stare burning into her, but keeping her eyes fixed on the elevator door for the whole ride.

When they get to the lobby, the concierge quickly ushers them toward the back of the hotel, and Phoebe takes up the rear as they slip into a limo prepped to take them to the venue. A bunch of groupies rush up just before the car can pull away, screeching and banging on the windows. A few of them lift their shirts, pressing their bare tits against the glass, and she can hear some errant chuckles as the driver gets clear of them, but not from Damien. His eyes are on her the whole time.

"Nothing you haven't seen before, huh, Miller?" He teases.

"Comes with the territory," she mutters, staring out the window in hopes of avoiding his gaze for the rest of the trip.

Thankfully the drive is quick, and soon they're parked behind the Whisky a Go Go. She's never actually been inside the Whisky before, only read about it. Anyone who grew up reading Rolling Stone or any kind of unauthorized rock autobiography knows the Whisky. Everyone who's anyone has played here. The Doors, Steppenwolf, Zeppelin, The Beach Boys. It's legendary.

The dressing room is stocked with food and booze; bottles of champagne, water, burgers, candy, you name it. Damien is wandering around, fingers lightly grazing the walls as he soaks in the ambience. He's transfixed, basking in the glory of playing here, of sitting in the same room as his heroes. The rest of the band isn't so awestruck, all moving to different spots to do their own prep for the show.

Phoebe pulls out her camera, taking her first few candid shots of the group. First is Ophelia, who's touching up her makeup. She's gorgeous, and it's hard not to waste all her film just taking pictures of her. Johnny and Shaun are working on riffs and basslines. They're covered in glitter, eyeliner smeared all over their lids. They look up at her every so often to throw up metal horns or pose for the camera. She smiles back, finding herself surprisingly at ease.

When she turns to Damien, it's immediately clear that he's more focused on his appearance than he lets on. She gets a few photos of him leaning into the mirror and examining his face, but he hears the shutter click from her last shot and glides toward her.

"So, you're the photographer *and* the journalist for this story?"

"They couldn't afford a photographer," she tells him, taking another photo as he looms over her. That'll be a good one. "I took some classes in school, though."

Brian didn't have the budget for more than one person on this assignment. He was already paying Phoebe a lot more than usual just to follow Revolver. She's not a professional photographer, but she likes candid shots, and they seem to work with most of her articles.

Damien smiles and reaches for her camera. Phoebe laughs nervously and pulls away, raising an eyebrow.

"What are you doing?"

"It's only fair," he says.

"I'm supposed to be the one observing you guys."

"Come oooonnn," he whines, more demanding than anything else.

The others are watching, probably waiting for him to pull something, but Phoebe hands him the camera anyway. He picks it up, leaning towards her as he stares at her through the viewfinder. She can smell him. Cigarettes, cologne, and leather. The shutter clicks and he pulls the camera away from his face, handing it back to her with his first sincere smile.

"That was a good one."

Phoebe can feel herself sweat as he walks away, but thankfully Troy breaks the tension by calling the band to the stage for soundcheck, leaving the two of them to watch from backstage. As the band runs through the show, Phoebe can tell that Bell is saving his voice for the crowd. He's holding back on the big screeches and screams that he's known for. He's going to be on his A game tonight.

Once they're all warmed up and ready, soundcheck turns into a game of tag on the stage, with Troy immediately cupping his hands over his mouth.

"We're rock stars, ladies and gentlemen! Not five-year-olds!"

"What's the difference?" Ophelia yells.

"Hey!" Troy shouts. "This is a big show, so it's important that you don't suck!"

"Oh no," Shaun suddenly cops an expression of terror, "guys what if we suck?!"

Troy rolls his eyes.

"Every day with these idiots," he mumbles to Phoebe.

She laughs as she scribbles in her notebook.

"How long have you been their tour manager?"

"The whole time. They're good kids. Dumb as hell, but good kids."

"I get a very protective vibe from you," Phoebe says.

"Well, someone's gotta be the den dad around here, or Bell would self-destruct. Not on purpose but, you know, he's just–"

"Reckless," Phoebe finishes.

"That's a nice way of putting it," Troy quips, gesturing to the stage where Damien and Shaun are deep into a wrestling match. Ophelia and Johnny are cheering them on as they almost knock, well, pretty much everything over.

"Okay! Okay!" Troy yells. "Enough! Backstage, now!"

Back in the dressing room, Troy plies the group with beer in an attempt to keep from too much mayhem. Through the thin walls Phoebe can clearly hear the Whisky a Go Go fill up with patrons as Shaun pulls up a chair and sits beside her.

"You wanna interview me?"

"Sure!" Phoebe says enthusiastically, pulling out her recorder.

She was going to wait until they were on the road to start shoving a microphone in their faces, but now is as good a time as any. Normally, she prefers to do interviews when she already has questions on hand, but something in her gut is telling her to embrace the chaos of the tour. It'll probably do her a lot of good.

"Shaun, the guitar on this album is..." She trails off and bites her lip as she tries to find the perfect word. Finally, she settles on: "Wicked."

"Wicked?!" Johnny asks from the back of the room. "What about me? I've practically got flames shooting out of my fingers on stage! Hendrix style!"

"He set a guitar on fire," Damien reminds Johnny. "Not the same thing. And you play bass, bro."

"Hey, I am the backbone of this band!"

"Uh, that's me, dickweed," Ophelia retorts. "And don't you fuckers forget it!"

"Hey, easy!" Shaun shouts over his shoulder. "She's complimenting *me* right now! So shut the hell up!"

Damien's sitting casually on top of the dressing room counter with his legs extended. The weight of his gaze continues to make her nervous, but she has a job to do.

"Who inspired your sound?" Phoebe asks Shaun, turning her back to Damien once again.

He nods to himself, taking a deep breath before diving in.

"My dad, mostly. When I was a kid, he used to take me with him when he'd play in the studio with all these legends. And I would sit there and watch him. I wanted to be just like that. So I went out and got a degree in music theory, learned everything there is to know about composition and how to craft a really good song. It all came from my dad, but I fucking *love* music."

"What's your favorite thing about it?" Phoebe asks.

"I like music that sounds like I'm listening to something I shouldn't be listening to, you know? Almost like a confession. So, anyone who makes that kind of music, I'm into it. You should put a little piece of yourself in everything you do. There's so much manufactured shit out there now. So many people have sold out. But the thing is, it's not about money, or fame or any of that bullshit."

"The paychecks are killer, though," Ophelia chimes in.

"Who's getting paychecks?" Johnny asks, glancing around in mock panic.

Revolver, despite their success, has had some critics rag on them for being a Mötley Crüe knock-off, or a bunch of Duran Duran wannabes, or chastising Bell for drawing too much inspiration from the rock stars of the '60s, most of whom are washed up or dead by now. These critics call them hacks, but Phoebe disagrees. Their sound is inspired, sure, but it's still all their own.

She leans a little closer, holding the microphone out so that she can capture everything: "You mentioned the manufactured nature of rock. Over-producing. Stuff like that. Do you think rock is dead, or dying?"

Shaun laughs, and Phoebe can hear Damien snicker from off to the side.

"I don't even know what rock was to begin with. Some people say it's a lifestyle." He points at Damien who throws up metal horns. "Some people say it's a mindset, some people say it's a very specific type of music. I'm kinda between those last two. But rock is always changing, because that's what art does. So, I don't think rock is dead. I don't think you can kill a genre of music. Styles are gonna change, we'll fade into obscurity and someone else'll take our place. It happens, man. I think rock 'n' roll is just trying to survive, like all of us."

"That's a good quote," Phoebe chuckles.

Shaun leans back in his chair, craning his neck so he can look directly at Bell.

"Well, I am the resident genius."

"It's true," Damien confirms.

Troy pokes his head in, and Phoebe pauses the recording.

"You're on in five. Oh, and Miller? You're with me. We'll watch from the back."

"Got it," she replies, snatching up her gear and getting to her feet. "Thanks Shaun, we can pick this up next time."

"No problem, you know where to find me!"

As she moves for the door she feels a hand on her arm. Her heart jumps as she whips around to see Damien smiling at her.

"Whoa, whoa, calm down. Just wanted to say those were some good questions."

"Thanks," she laughs awkwardly.

"How long have you been a journalist?"

She blinks, and stares at him a little perplexed.

"Uh, a few years."

Phoebe's heart is in her throat and the feeling is starting to make her nauseous. He looks her up and down.

"You might just last the whole two months."

She scoffs, suddenly less enthralled.

"Thanks...?"

"See you after the show."

He rips off his shirt and tosses it onto the floor as he steps out of the dressing room. Her jaw falls slack as she watches him leave, even his back is toned. It's going to be a very long two months if he keeps pulling shit like this.

"Miller!" Troy yells from outside. "Two minutes!"

She skitters out of the room, shutting the door behind her.

Voices Carry

The Whisky a Go Go

The Whisky is packed tonight. Phoebe and Troy sit in the back while Ophelia, Johnny, and Shaun set up. The crowd screams as the lights get low and Damien steps out from backstage. He's in shredded black jeans, boots, and nothing else, his arms outstretched as he takes in the crowd.

"Good evening, Los Angeles!" He booms.

The screams intensify; women are already throwing things onto the stage.

"We're Revolver, and we have a couple of songs to play for you tonight. We're going to open with a new one just for you, because we love you that much. This is called Automatic."

He looks over his shoulder at Ophelia, and the song begins with a crash. Guitars scream and wail, and Bell slips deeper into his stage persona. Or is it even a persona? She watches him gyrate and writhe around as he howls into the microphone. The lyrics are a little sadder than most of Revolver's tracks. Still, the crowd is gobbling up every note. Phoebe scribbles down small descriptions of the way he moves as fast as she can, not wanting to miss a moment of the performance. She tries to stick to animal imagery at first; snake, cat, feral, before immediately moving into something more elemental: "Bell is Electric." She circles those words ferociously on the page as Troy leans over.

"He's totally on tonight."

She nods, speaking without turning away from the show.

"Any reason why?"

"The fact that they're playing here. He told me he wanted to turn over a new leaf. I told him to behave himself in front of the journalist."

"Interesting."

The rest of the show is fantastic. Easily one of the best she's ever seen. The band looks like they're having the most fun they've had in a long time. Bell, of course, pulls his signature stunt of pouring half a bottle of whiskey down his torso before beckoning a woman onstage. She's a petite redhead with a big, beaming smile. She runs her tongue up and down his chest and Damien laughs, grabbing her face and placing a bruising kiss against her lips while the crowd roars. Damien turns to Troy and motions at her with a flick of his head.

The band launches into their another song as Troy brings the woman offstage, whispering into her ear before some roadies show her down the hall. Damien drains the rest of the bottle, chucking it into the crowd, clearly not caring where it lands. Phoebe just barely makes out a smash of glass near the door but the audience is pulsing with the music, not a care in the world.

As the show reaches its conclusion, Troy gestures at Phoebe to follow him back to the dressing room. The redhead from before is waiting, seated in one of the little plastic chairs near the wall. Troy whistles and makes a motion for her to leave.

"Uh, I'm waiting for Damien?"

"What's your name, sweetheart?"

"Trish."

Troy nods his head and strokes his beard, looking her up and down. Phoebe can see that Trish is getting nervous.

"Okay Trish, my name is Troy, and I'm waiting for you to leave. You can see the boy-toy after we're done."

Phoebe can barely stop herself from laughing as Trish opens her mouth to protest, but Troy cuts her off immediately.

"Out, princess! Move it!"

"Geez," she hisses. "Fucking uptight."

"And don't you forget it, sweetheart!" He shouts as she struts out the door. Troy turns to Phoebe. "Some of them really bug me."

"No shit?" she laughs.

She takes a seat as the band walks in. Damien is hanging back, his body half leaning out the door as he chats up Trish.

Troy claps his hands.

"Bell!" He barks. "You can waste time with groupies later!"

Damien rolls his eyes and closes the door behind him. As he slides past Phoebe, she feels his fingers brush the back of her neck. The sensation sends a jolt of electricity through her body, even though it only lasts for a nanosecond.

"Your shirt tag is sticking out," he tells her with a smirk.

Her hands fly to the back of her neck to make sure he's not messing with her.

"I got it," Damien laughs.

She doesn't look up at him, trying to play the situation off as best she can.

"Yep. Thanks."

"No problem, I'm here to help." He grabs a bottle of water and downs the entire thing in a few gulps. He passes one to Johnny and Ophelia, tossing another across the room to Shaun, before holding the last bottle up for Phoebe. As she prepares to catch it, he quickly closes the distance between them instead. Their fingers brush together as he carefully places it in her hands, and she feels those same sparks again.

"All right, we leave tomorrow. Bright and early at 11:00am," Troy announces.

"That's not early," Johnny corrects him.

Troy raises an eyebrow, glancing over at Damien who has returned to his corner to light a cigarette.

"It's early for at least three of you."

Damien grumbles softly as Troy stares up at the ceiling deep in thought.

"Alright, so next we're hitting San Jose. Venue's the good ol' Ritz, and then it's right back on the bus. So, Bell? No girls."

"Yessir," he mumbles with a small salute.

Troy pulls the tour itinerary from his pocket, his finger tracing along it.

"Oakland after that, and from there we drive straight to Portland." He looks around the room. "Are we all on the same page?"

There's a collective yes mumbled amongst the group, and Troy looks relatively satisfied.

"Good. Now, get something to eat, and get back to the hotel ASAP. We've got a big day tomorrow." Troy pauses, halfway out the door before swinging back in, "you kids were great tonight. Let's keep that energy up for the rest of the tour."

In the aftermath of the evening, Johnny and Damien chat quietly in the corner, laughing and occasionally trading barbs and light blows. Shaun sits on top of the dressing room table, munching on a burger. Ophelia pulls up a seat next to Phoebe, handing her a burger and beer.

"Hungry?"

"Yeah, thanks." She unwraps the burger, glancing over at Ophelia who is already deep into hers. "You guys were fantastic."

Ophelia takes a sip of beer to clear her throat and smiles.

"Thanks! It felt good. It always helps when the crowd is really into it too."

"I got some good notes," Phoebe says softly.

Ophelia grins.

"Look, I know you're worried about that one." She gestures to Damien. "But I really think this is going to be a good two months."

"What makes you say that?"

It was a level of optimism that Phoebe hasn't quite reached herself

"Just a feeling," she replies, gesturing with her beer can.

Phoebe raises her own beer and smiles.

"Cheers to that."

She's up late again, hunched over her typewriter, her headphones covering her ears. The music is cranked as loud as it can go, trying to drown out the noise that inevitably leaks in from Damien's room across the hall. It's mostly laughter, but there's the odd moan and that recognizable clatter of a headboard against the wall.

How the hell can she hear it from all the way across the hallway?

Phoebe makes a mental note to ask Troy to get her a room further away when they hit the next city. She's used to hearing people go at it, she's had a few roommates over the years, and she currently lives in an apartment with very thin walls. But it's 4:00AM and she just wants to write in silence, or maybe even get an hour or two of sleep.

In all fairness, Troy did warn her, but come on, 4 in the morning?

She stands up, her Walkman attached to her hip, and rips the cork off a bottle of champagne that she lifted from backstage after the show. It explodes instantly, foam pouring out from the mouth of the bottle, and Phoebe swears, putting her lips over the top. She tries to tilt it back to drink some, but she chokes, spitting the liquid onto the floor.

"Shitshitshit! Fuckfuckfuck!" She yelps, running into the bathroom to grab a water glass.

She begins to pour what's left of the champagne and fills the glass to the brim, downing the whole thing in a few gulps before pouring herself another. The moans across the hall increase in volume, overwhelming both the Huey Lewis and the News performance, and her calm.

She walks back to her typewriter and wills herself to get back to work. After a few surprisingly productive minutes, she realizes the noise has died down. She sighs in relief, removing her headphones tentatively, and relaxing into her chair. Unfortunately, there's only a couple moments of peace before a knock at her door makes her jump.

With the champagne bottle still clutched between her fingers, she curses under her breath as she walks toward the door, peeking through the peephole. Damien is standing outside, shirtless, his hair completely disheveled as he wobbles in place.

Forgetting that she's in nothing but a baggy t-shirt filled with a million holes and a pair of shorts, Phoebe swings the door open. His eyes are bloodshot and rimmed red. He immediately flashes her a big smile, and Phoebe raises a brow.

"Heyyyyy, Phoebe, you got any smokes? My... lady friend is out, and I think I left mine back at the Whisky."

He's absolutely wasted.

"Hang on a second."

She walks to the desk and hears him push the door open, stepping inside behind her. *Make yourself at home, why don't you?* She mouths with her back to him, before turning back to see that he's barefoot, swaying slightly as he looks aimlessly around the room.

"Are you writing?" He asks, gesturing to the typewriter and the piles of crumpled notes she has next to it.

"Yeah. Just some notes from Shaun's interview."

"Cool." He pauses and pushes his hand through his hair. "Hey, uh, sorry to bother you so late. Just... nobody else was awake. I'd bug Ophelia, but she likes her beauty sleep."

"You don't?" She asks.

"I'll sleep when I'm dead," he chuckles, before looking at the ground. "Sorry about the noise, too. We'll keep it down."

Phoebe can't tell if it's the booze, or if almost everything she's read about Damien is a mild to moderate fabrication. He's kind of sweet, and seems a bit nervous. Maybe Ophelia was right about him being a teddy bear. Sure, he's intimidating, but he hasn't told her to go fuck herself all night.

Certainly a little more bark than bite.

"It's really not a problem," she whispers, handing him the pack. "Here. Keep 'em."

"Really?"

"Yeah."

Damien fishes out three cigarettes before pressing the pack back into her hand. Their fingers brush against one another, lingering a little too long; it's the most contact they've had.

She looks down to see a small tattoo near his thumb that she's never noticed before. It's a tiny heart that looks like it was done rough, with a sewing needle and a pen. Otherwise, there's not a single tattoo on his body, at least not that she can see. His whole cock could be tattooed and she'd never know.

He smirks at her, and she blushes at the image she's conjured into her head.

"I only need three," he says, cutting through her thoughts. "I can grab another pack before we leave tomorrow. Thanks, Miller."

He glances at the champagne bottle in her hand and snatches it up, a little splashing on the carpet.

"I *will* be taking this, though." He uses the bottle to point at her as he stuffs a cigarette between his pillowy lips.

"Write sober, edit drunk."

"It's the..."

He whirls around and skips outside, shutting the door behind him before she can correct him.

"...other way around, actually," Phoebe whispers quietly.

She looks around and exhales, locking the door and settling back into her chair.

She can still feel Damien's delicate touch against her hand.

"Goddammit, Bell, that was the last of my booze."

Hanging on the Telephone

THE BEVERLY HILTON

"We're leaving in twenty, Miller!" .

Phoebe's head snaps up to find daylight pouring in through the window. She doesn't remember falling asleep, but everything hurts, and she has post-it notes stuck to her cheek. A cigarette butt falls from behind her ear as she stands, the irritation of an unresolved hangover only intensifying as she pulls the champagne cork out from her mess of hair.

How the fuck did that get in there?

"I'm up!" She barks, her words tasting like an ashtray.

Her room looks like a hurricane's hit it and she moves like it's coming back for a second pass, dressing faster than she ever has before. Tossing on her jeans and t-shirt, all while hurriedly brushing her teeth, she barely manages to stuff her gear into her suitcase. There was no way she's going to slow them down on her first real day of the tour.

As she steps outside, she sees Damien's door is wide open. He's fully dressed in a leather jacket and black jeans, leaning against the wall with one hand as he lazily dangles the hotel phone from his other, the handset cradled between his shoulder and ear.

She glances back at him as she finishes locking up, prompted by a surprisingly soft laugh.

"I'm fine, Ava! I am, really! Yeah. We're leaving for San Jose, and then Oakland... yeah, and Oregon after that. I'll be fine, I promise. Look, I get that you're worried but I've been doing this for a long time– Oh, fuck off!"

Phoebe smiles despite herself.

"Okay, okay. Tell mom and dad I love them. And Merlin. And thank them for looking after her– Oh, you're looking after her? Did you buy her that food she likes? Yeah, the Fancy Feast stuff."

He pauses, and there's that laugh again. It feels strange to see him as anything other than the brooding bad boy.

"No, I don't spoil her!" More laughter. "Yeah, I'll bring you a present. I always do. Okay. I love you too. I'll see you in a couple months. Later!"

He's silent as they take the elevator down together, seemingly lost in thought. Phoebe wonders what he's thinking about, maybe this Ava person, perhaps the tour... but she doesn't ask. It's none of her business after all, really she's just thankful for the quiet.

After all of their bags and equipment are loaded, Phoebe's the last to board the bus. As she goes to sit in an empty spot near the front, she's startled by a shrill whistle; Damien is sitting alone. He raises his eyebrows and tilts his head to the side, motioning for her to come join him at the back. It sort of feels like the high school bully beckoning her to come and sit with him so that he can make her life a living hell. Phoebe hesitates for a moment. It wasn't highschool anymore, and does she really want to deal with him for the whole ride?

He holds up a pack of cigarettes, gesturing to them like some used car salesman. *I owe you,* he mouths, *come on.*

Glancing around the bus, she can find practically no outs. Shaun is focused on playing his guitar, Johnny is reading a book, and Ophelia is already asleep, half-pressed against her window with a big floppy hat pulled down over her face.

She lets out a barely audible sigh and walks toward Damien, giving him an awkward smile as she takes a seat.

"Relax, Miller. I don't bite–" He pauses and shifts forward to catch her eye, "Unless you're into that."

Phoebe scoffs, not 10 seconds and already he's back on this bullshit. She stands, angling for the front seat she left behind, but Damien leaps up and grabs the back of her jacket.

"It's a joke!" He laughs. "I'm sorry. I'm sorry, okay? No more funny stuff. I promise."

"That was supposed to be a joke?"

She doesn't even turn around, content to leave him hanging, but he quickly pivots and pulls out the big guns.

"I thought you wanted an interview?"

She turns back to him, perplexed.

"Now?"

"Nah," he replies. "I'm not ready yet. But, I think it's only fair that if you get to know all of us, we get to know you. Ophelia told me you had some one-on-one time, so I figured it's my turn."

"You wanna know stuff about me?" She asks.

Usually, musicians don't care to delve into her personal life. They like to talk about themselves, their art, their process, and that's fine by her.

"I do," Damien replies. He leans over with a big grin on his face. "I'm *obnoxiously* curious."

Phoebe laughs. All of this goes against her personal rules, not to mention Brian's, but playing along here is probably her best bet at a good story. A real story. If he asks her anything that hits too close to home, she can always lie. It's not like she's going to see him after this anyway. He might be fucking with her, sure, but he could give her the interview that every journalist's failed to get since the band burst onto the scene. He could open up and give her something real, on purpose or not.

She slides back down into the seat, taking a deep breath.

"Okay. Ask away."

He grins.

"Where were you born?"

"Brooklyn."

"Really?" He asks.

"Yeah."

"Did you grow up there?"

"Yep."

His eyes glide over her, and he bites his lip.

Damn that's hot. Her lips part just a little.

"Who was your best friend growing up?" He asks.

She snaps herself back into gear, hoping he didn't notice.

"Her name's Janis. Still my best friend, actually."

Shit, she meant to call her this morning. It'll have to wait until Oregon.

"Mine's *that* guy," Damien says, pointing at Johnny. "We've got each other's backs 'til the day we die."

She feels that itch, Brian calls it the writer's itch– to scrawl, scribble, and take notes, even if they feel utterly meaningless. It's a reflex, and every time she gets a new piece of information she can barely help but indulge.

Damien sees her fingers twitch and he grins.

"Don't think you can turn this into my interview, Miller. I told you I wasn't ready."

"Sorry," Phoebe replies, smiling. "I guess I'm just obnoxiously curious."

Damien laughs.

"You're funny. I like that."

Could that be the first genuine compliment he's given her?

He rips a piece of paper out of his notebook, balls it up, and throws it at Johnny, who raises his middle finger before it even hits, letting it bounce off him with barely any other reaction. He's dealt with this before.

Damien cackles.

"Moving on, what are your parents like?"

"Normal," she replies, trying not to laugh at the overtly dull question.

"Elaborate," he demands. "So are mine and look what they made!"

He really is cute when he's not trying so hard.

"My mom's an interior designer, dad was in the military. He's retired now."

"Military huh?"

"Yeah."

"Mine too," Damien tells her. "Wanted me to follow in his footsteps. Johnny's dad was the same. It's probably one of the reasons we get along so well."

"Mine just ran a strict household," Phoebe replies. "No boys, homework got done the minute I got home from school, home by 9:00PM–"

"Wait, even when you were 18?"

"Yep."

He's clearly a little taken aback.

"Jesus, sounds like prison."

She shrugs.

"I never went out much anyway."

"Never went out much? You?" He scoffs. "I find that hard to believe."

"Why?"

"Just look at you."

Phoebe takes another deep breath as she feels blood rushing to her ears. He probably does this all the time, to so many women. It shouldn't matter, but it does. She has to keep it professional.

"Damien, if this is–"

"Phoebe, chill out. I think that you're insightful, and you're clearly good at your job, and I..." He looks a little frustrated, struggling to find the right words. "Look, I'm sorry. You can sit up at the front with Troy. I just– I think you're cool, and I'd like to get to know you."

She frowns.

"*You* want to get to know *me*?"

"Yeah. I mean, we're going to be on tour together, crammed into this bus and stuck in hotels for two months. I might as well, right?"

Phoebe nods. She can't deny the logic.

"Okay, so anything else you want to ask?"

He smiles, his confidence returning quickly.

"Who's your favorite band? Of all time?"

It's a tough question. She runs through a few options in her head before finally landing on...

"Queen."

"Really?" He asks.

"Yeah. Mercury's vocals are beautiful. He's absolutely magnetic, even on a record."

"I had a big Queen poster in my bedroom for years." He grins. "My sister stole it for me, from a show I didn't get to go to. I was grounded." He fiddles with one of the rings on his hand, twisting it back and forth before glancing back up at her. "You have siblings?"

She nods.

"A brother. He's older. In his thirties. He's a doctor; runs marathons, has a wife and two kids."

Damien lets out an emphatic whistle.

"Yeah," she grumbles. "So, you can imagine me being the disappointment of the family."

"Why would anyone think that? Not a lot of people get to write for a living."

"Well, let's see," Phoebe mutters. "I live in a closet in Williamsburg, I make no money, I'm not married, don't have any kids... I don't even date anymore because dating in New York is impossible, and every time I *do* find a nice guy, all he wants to do is tell me about this *cool band* he's thinking of starting– and that's best-case. Most of them are just dicks."

"Anything else?" Damien chuckles.

"Oh, yeah, my parents say that this isn't a real job. I'm just playing rock star or whatever. So that's great, lots of respect and admiration from that part of the family."

She huffs, immediately regretting the vent session. That kind of thing always opens you up, puts you way too close. In the end it just makes the job harder.

"Well, maybe you don't need their approval, but I imagine some respect would be nice. You seem to be doing fine without it though, for what it's worth."

She nods her head as they both let the conversation trail off naturally into silence, and it's not too long before Damien's staring out the window, humming to himself while Phoebe writes in her notebook. Every so often he shifts in his seat, their arms or knees touching briefly, and each time she can feel her breath hitch in her chest. It's agonizing.

Drawn out over a couple hours, she's stuck somewhere between annoyed and overstimulated, with an inkling of something she'd rather not address keeping her from getting much work done. Just as it reaches the point where she can't take it anymore, Phoebe notices the bus swerve, glancing up in time to see them come to a stop in front of another extravagant hotel.

"We're here for the night!" Troy announces, quickly ushering them off of the bus. "Soundcheck is in six hours, so take a nice nap."

He turns sharply, towards Damien, his tone shifting.

"Or do whatever deranged stuff you're going to do, Bell."

Shaun and Johnny help a somewhat grumpy Ophelia off the bus, still exhausted from the night before. Outside, Phoebe moves to grab her suitcase, but Bell stops her, shaking his head and dragging her toward the hotel.

"You're not a roadie, Miller. You're with us now!"

Inside the hotel, Phoebe takes in her surroundings. This interior is even more lavish than the last, and while it's clear the band has long since gotten over it all, she still finds it impressive. It is, unfortunately, also busier than their previous hotel and there's a lot of sitting around in the lobby while they check in. After a good 15 minutes, Johnny's head suddenly whips around.

"Where's Damien?"

Ophelia shrugs, just as they hear the crash of piano keys from an adjacent room. At first it's just noise but then there's a melody. It's Elton John. "Saturday Night's Alright for Fighting."

Shaun and Johnny laugh, getting to their feet and following the sound. Phoebe can't help her natural curiosity, turning all the way around in her seat to see what's going on. Ophelia smacks her on the thigh.

"Go!"

Phoebe rushes into the room, finding Damien sat at the piano. She didn't know he played; it never came up anywhere in her research. He's missing some notes here and there, but he's pretty solid, and when he gets to a particularly difficult part, his nose scrunches up like a kid focused on a math problem.

The boys are singing along, with Johnny drumming on the piano to keep time.

"You're off beat!" Shaun yells over the music. "Go get Ophelia!"

"I am not! Fuck you, dude!"

"It's in 4/4!"

"This *is* 4/4!"

"It's not!" Shaun shouts. "I thought you had rhythm!"

Damien sings overtop of their screaming match, his long hair falling over his face, and Phoebe smiles as she leans against the doorframe. She pulls her notebook out of her pocket ready to write, just as she sees a very angry looking man make a beeline toward them. He's definitely some sort of management judging by the stiff-looking suit and slicked back hair.

Johnny whacks Shaun on the arm, and motions to Damien to stop playing.

"Excuse me, gentlemen, the lounge is booked for a wedding this afternoon. You can't be playing here."

Damien looks up at him, smiling.

"What if we replace the musical act? Can we stay then?"

"I'm afraid not, sir."

"Come ooooon!" Damien whines.

The man frowns.

"Sir. Please."

"Come on dude," Johnny laughs. "Let's go."

Phoebe catches Damien's eye as the three of them walk out of the lounge.

"I didn't know you played piano," she says softly.

"My mom made me take lessons when I was a kid. I suck."

"If you can play Elton John, I don't think you suck," she laughs.

Damien grins.

"Thanks, Miller. That's the nicest thing your magazine has said about me."

Her stomach drops as she follows them back. Troy waves at them from the front desk, with Ophelia standing beside him.

"I hear you're giving free concerts in there," Troy teases as he ruffles Damien's hair.

"Ha-ha," Damien mumbles as Troy hands out their room keys.

It's at that moment Phoebe realizes that she forgot to ask Troy for a room further away from Bell. Maybe she'll get lucky.

Damien grabs the key out of her hand and glances at it.

"Hey, Miller! Look at that! We're neighbors again, what are the chances!"

He holds up his own key in front of her and her heart sinks.

Fantastic, another sleepless night.

Phoebe sits hunched over her desk, the phone ringing in her hand. It had been a bit of a chore to figure out how to get a long distance call through, but the concierge had been helpful enough.

Janis was born in Tokyo to a Japanese artist and an American architect, with the family ultimately settling in the U.S. when she was four years old. The two friends had been inseparable all the way from childhood through university. They used to pull all-nighters finishing assignments while they listened to records and dreamed about being famous journalists, ones who didn't take shit from anyone. In the end, Phoebe went to Titanium and Janis got a gig writing for the New Yorker, neither quite as free as they originally hoped.

"Hello?"

"Hey!" Phoebe hisses. "It's me!"

Janis gasps.

"Holy shit! I thought Bell might have killed you."

"Unfortunately, no," Phoebe laughs. "Although, if I do die on this tour, it'll be from sleep deprivation courtesy of him."

"Wow... you two are already going at it, huh?"

"Oh shut up!" Phoebe whines, flopping onto the bed. "He was in the room across the hall from me last night and brought some girl up. I passed out at my desk with my headphones on because of the noise."

"Comes with the territory, right?"

"Does it ever."

Janis chuckles.

"Well, other than that, how's the chaos?"

"The chaos is... chaotic?"

Phoebe sighs, she really isn't sure how things are going quite yet.

"I'm surprised you're not crying, actually," Janis teases. *"I read some of the shit he's said in interviews. He's vicious. I'd be scared of him for sure."*

"No tears yet. You know, he's…" She pauses for a moment, choosing her words carefully. "He's not what I expected."

"So it is all an act!"

"Not exactly?" Phoebe replies. "I don't know why, but I get the feeling he might like me." She frowns, scrunching up her nose. "Maybe. I don't know, it's weird."

"Well, how's everything otherwise?"

"Good. The hotels are great," Phoebe takes a moment to really take in her room for the first time, "Speaking of which, this is the biggest fucking bed I've ever seen in my life."

Janis laughs.

"Well, I'm glad you called. Oh, hey! I got another assignment! I wanted to call so that I could brag about it, but I didn't know where you were staying."

"Don't worry, I'll pretend not to be jealous," Phoebe laughs. "What is it?"

"The Reykjavík Summit."

"Damn, for real, Reykjavík? That's a really big deal, Jan."

"Crazy, right? They're flying me out to Iceland, but first I'm going to Tokyo for a few days to visit my grandma."

"Well, you deserve it. You're an amazing writer, Jan."

"Hey, you are too! Don't go selling yourself short! I'm excited to read your article."

Phoebe can hear Janis start to laugh on the other end of the line.

"Oh, and I broke up with Jeremy."

"Finally!" Phoebe exclaims, not missing a beat. "God, he was a dick."

"He really was, wasn't he?"

"What was the nail in the coffin?"

"Total lack of commitment. He said he wanted to be free to take his career to the next level."

"Right, right… because competitive surfing is a great job for a guy who doesn't know how to surf."

Janis howls with laughter.

"At least he's better than that ex of yours who found his life's purpose driving an old pizza delivery van around for no reason."

"Uhhh, it's called 'finding yourself,' Janis. Don't crush his dreams."

Phoebe feels like Janis is right beside her, and they effortlessly slide back into their old dynamic, talking until she can feel her ear beginning to ache.

Suddenly, she hears a knock at the door.

"Miller! There's a car downstairs! Five minutes!"

"Shit. Jan, I gotta go."

"Okay. Have fun! Be safe! And tell Bell if he says anything mean to you, I'll kick him in the fucking dick."

All the Young Dudes

THE RITZ, SAN JOSE

Phoebe has always been anxious to be late to pretty much anything, everyone moves too slow and talks too much about shit that doesn't matter. She's stuck in the elevator listening to some stockbroker drone on and on into his massive brick of a cellular phone. The antenna's almost hit her in the face a couple times and she's had to bite her tongue to keep from smacking him while he paces around the small box like he's the only one there.

Outside, Damien is standing in front of the car talking to a girl Phoebe doesn't recognize. She's fawning all over him, of course, and he's lapping it all up.

"You're late, Miller," Damien quips as he catches her eye. "What's the matter, can't keep up with the big kids?"

"Fuck off, *Bell*," she mutters under her breath, heading straight for the car. She doesn't need to put up with his bullshit right now.

He looks surprised, blinking a couple times as a small smile creeps across his face, immediately losing interest in his new friend.

"Whoa! What's with the hostility?" He laughs as he climbs in after her.

"Aren't you supposed to ride with the band?"

Her tone is clipped and cold, a combination of nerves and irritation.

"I can do whatever I want," he replies. "And I want to figure out what crawled up your ass and died. You were so sweet back on the bus."

"Nothing's wrong." Her voice is all sharp edges as she buckles her seatbelt. "I just don't like wasting my time."

Damien grins and lights a joint as the car with the rest of the band in it pulls out in front of them.

"Oh, so you're saying that lovely conversation we had on the bus was a waste?" He teases, his smile growing, along with her irritation. "That's hurtful, Miller."

Phoebe stares straight ahead, trying as hard as possible not to meet his gaze.

"Wow, that's exactly right. It must be tough having *so* much empathy."

Damien leans over, narrowing his eyes as he gets right in her face. She isn't short by any means, but he seems fucking enormous with the two of them crammed into back seat, and there's nowhere for her to go. Nothing about this man is small.

"Maybe this could mellow you out."

He lights a joint and blows the smoke out of the side of his mouth, handing it to her. Phoebe stares back at him and blinks. She can smell his cologne, woodsy with a hint of spice, now blended with the heavy aroma from the smoke.

She plucks the joint from his fingers and takes a drag, holding it in for a few seconds before she rolls down the window and exhales, valiantly resisting the urge to blow it right in his face. Honestly, he'd probably be into that.

Damien chuckles.

"Atta girl."

Immediately her cheeks grow hot. She's unsure exactly what about him keeps setting her off, but it's adding to her ever-mounting pile of frustrations.

He eases back into his seat and pulls a notebook out of his bag while Phoebe looks out the window, trying to distract herself. After a few minutes, she feels his pinky brushing against hers and turns her head. He holds up the remnants of their shared joint, offering it to her.

"Peace offering?"

"For what?"

He grins.

"You tell me."

She stares at the joint, wondering if she should accept his half-baked apology before she inevitably takes the final drag and tosses it out the window. Damien looks pleased with himself. He clearly likes to get under peoples' skin.

As they arrive at the venue Damien leaves her in the car without a word, moving through the crowd and signing a few autographs along the way. Phoebe sighs and heads in toward the back, carefully making her way around the sea of women that surround Damien. He's basking in it all as he poses for photos, probably promising dozens of girls that they can come backstage when he knows damn well that Troy will blow a gasket if he hears word one about it.

"He's not your problem," she whispers under her breath as she pushes the door open. "You're just here to observe."

Damien trails in about ten minutes after her with lipstick smeared on his face, strolling past her as she's loading film into her camera.

"Lighting's shit out there," he tells her.

"I'll take some pictures during soundcheck."

He chuckles.

"Guess you want the real inside scoop, huh?"

"That's my job. Gotta keep up with the big kids."

Damien snorts.

"You still want that interview?"

"Not if you're going to dangle it in front of me like a carrot."

He claps her on the shoulder, leaning in with a big smile.

"You've gotta chill out, girl." All she can smell is that mix of cologne and pot as Damien stares at her. "I don't know what the hell happened to you in the hotel room, but it's gonna be a *long* two months on the road. You'll want me at my best, and you'll want to make friends."

"I can make friends."

"Look, I don't wanna tell you how to do your job or anything–"

She meets his eyes, fully for the first time since the car, glaring.

"Except you are."

He smirks, his eyes bloodshot.

"You're feisty, Miller. I like that in a woman."

Phoebe struggles to keep composed, but luckily Damien heads for the door. At the last minute he spins around dramatically with his arms out.

"Gotcha!"

He disappears around the corner and Phoebe takes a deep breath, finally able to relax again.

"Fuck."

She grabs a beer from the table filled with amenities, and guzzles half of it in one go before heading outside with her camera and her notebook. She's here to do her job, but she'd rather focus on anything but Damien Bell.

Soundcheck is a breeze. The band is tight, and they're playing well. Damien is still relatively sober, but Phoebe catches him intermittently swigging from a bottle of whiskey between songs when he thinks no one's looking.

She doesn't really know what his deal is. One minute he's curious about her, asking her questions about her life and where she grew up, and then the next he's berating her, telling her she can't keep up with him and his stupid antics. Was he just fucking with her back on the bus? Really though, it's probably a waste of time thinking so much about some asshole in tight leather pants.

The turnaround from the soundcheck to the show is surprisingly quick, and soon Phoebe is feeling a little excited again. The Ritz is sold out, and there's only standing room left when Troy calls them up to perform. As they're walking down the hall toward the stage, Johnny wraps an arm around Phoebe.

"You can't let him get to you."

"Damien? I'm not."

"You sure? Because you two seemed pretty chummy on the bus, and now you're avoiding him."

"I'm not avoiding him."

Johnny snickers.

"Look, Damien's mostly a good guy, he just tends to, you know..." Johnny's struggling a little with his words. Even he has a bit of trouble talking Damien up sometimes. "Oh, like on the playground! When a boy would pull your pigtails to tell you he liked you?"

"That's not a great analogy. Those boys were just dicks."

He sighs, his face slightly pained.

"But, you know what I mean, right?"

"Not really, what exactly are you trying to say?"

"I'm saying that Damien's not as bad or annoying as you might think he is. You've just gotta give him a chance," He glances toward the stage, shaking his head a little, "or, how about two chances?"

"Or three?"

"Hey, you're getting it!" Johnny laughs, patting her on the back.

As they reach the stage, Johnny runs up the stairs backwards, pointing dramatically at Phoebe.

"Remember what I said!"

Over the course of the night, Phoebe takes far too many pictures despite the terrible lighting. Occasionally, she creeps out onto the stage to crouch down and grab some more candid shots of the band, each one of them completely focused on their own instruments. It's chaotic to be in the thick of it all, the music almost swallowing her as she takes shot after shot. She doesn't even really care if the pictures are good, she just likes to capture the band in their element.

She stays low, trying to keep out of everyone's way, and crouches beneath Shaun while he's in the middle of a guitar solo. He winks at her right as she clicks the shutter, giving her just enough time to turn and catch a shot of Ophelia wailing on the drums, a wildfire of red hair surrounding her. As she shifts around the stage, her viewfinder falls on Johnny, his smile bright and warm in the midst of a dueling duet with Damien. As he breaks away and heads to the front of the stage, she slips as close to the floor as possible, catching Bell in profile as he screams at the crowd. There's something mesmerizing about the way they reach up toward him, practically worshiping him from below, and she can't help but get caught up in it all for a moment before rushing back off stage.

At the start of their last song, Ophelia pours a bottle of beer onto the snare. She twirls her sticks above her head and smashes them down as the liquid splashes all over, gleaming in the stage lights. It's a clever trick played perfectly to the crowd, and they love it. Before long, they're screaming for an encore.

And then another.

And another.

The band plays four more songs before Troy pulls them offstage for good, congratulating them all on a show well done. They're covered in sweat, beer, and smeared makeup, and Phoebe can feel the adrenaline in the air as they whoop and holler all the way to the dressing room. Damien is so euphoric that he slams the door to the dressing room open with his boot heel, throws his head back, and howls like a wolf.

"THAT. WAS. FUCKING. AWESOME!"

He grabs Phoebe by the shoulders and shakes her gently, making her laugh. Honestly, it's infectious. When he's like this, everything about him is.

"It was, wasn't it?!" His eyes are wild, pure electricity.

"It was!" She giggles.

"I knew it!"

The band cheers, and even Troy is in on the fun. Their debriefing session is even shorter than it was at the Whisky; Troy seems relaxed for the first time in ages, with Bell leaving soon after to head to the bar.

"We have booze here!" Shaun calls after him.

"Yeah, but I'm here for the girls!"

He points directly at Troy, full of confident swagger before he heads out the door.

"Don't wait up for me old man, it'll be way past your bedtime!"

"You'd have to be worth waiting for, kid."

Phoebe sighs. It looks like Bell was going to be the cause of yet another sleepless night. Maybe she could sleep in the lobby if she told the hotel manager the guy who commandeered his piano was causing a racket. Maybe he'd throw Bell out. Even better.

The rest of the night is all beers and burgers with a little light conversation, but without Bell in the picture there's a distinct lack of drama. By the time they make it back to the hotel, Phoebe's too exhausted to worry about the potential sleepless night that awaits her, just excited to feel her body hit the mattress.

As she approaches her door, digging in her bag for her room key, she's surprised by some slight movement out of the corner of her eye. It's him, just sitting in the hall, his back pressed up against his hotel room door. His eyes are closed, and he looks absolutely wasted, shifting slightly once in a while with a light groan.

Phoebe's brow furrows.

"Bell?"

There's no response, and she walks a little closer.

"Damien?"

"Hmm?" He raises his eyebrows, but doesn't open his eyes.

"What are you doing?" Phoebe chuckles nervously.

"I'unnowherrreee my roomkey is."

"Ah."

"ThinkIiii leftitin the…"

He thumps on the door with the back of his hand.

"The bar, you mean?"

"Thassit."

"I can get Troy."

"Naaaaaahhhhhh!"

She has no idea what rooms any of the others are in, and they might not answer anyway. She looks around the empty hall and sighs. She can't just leave him out here. He's way too drunk to be by himself. She crouches down and taps his face. Damien grunts, his eyes only opening for a moment, and all she sees is bright red surrounding a gray iris.

"Damien, do you want to sleep in my room?"

His eyes slowly flutter back open at the question. He stares at her– well, not at her, more like through her. It's that kind of vacant stare that she's seen many times after a long night out with friends.

"Yes," he whispers. "Iwouldlike... yep."

"All right." She extends her hand. "Come on."

Damien reaches up and grabs her wrist. He's so strong that he almost pulls her to the ground, and she yelps.

"S'rry," he mumbles as they struggle to get him to his feet.

"It's okay."

Phoebe has to carry him inside, his feet practically dragging on the floor, and Damien flops face first onto the bed immediately after they reach it. She grabs a pillow and tosses it onto the couch near the window, ready to lay down herself before she stops, looking back at him. He's rolled onto his side, staring at her.

This man is completely helpless.

Phoebe grabs an ice bucket off of the dresser and puts it on the floor.

"Just in case you need to puke."

Damien reaches up and grabs her forearm, staring up at her with a big smile.

"Thanks Feeeebeeee," he slurs, giggling to himself.

"No problem," she whispers.

Helpless Damien is surprisingly adorable.

When she wakes up the next morning, Damien's spot on the bed is vacant. The mystery is quickly solved, however, with the sound of violent retching from the bathroom. Her head is pounding from a kink in her neck, compounded on top of an already wretched night, and the sound certainly doesn't make it any better. She grabs a bottle of water from the mini fridge, some painkillers from her bag, and knocks on the door.

"Yeah?"

"Can I come in?"

"Sure."

He's still wearing clothes from last night, but his jacket is on the floor and his shirt is stained with vomit. Phoebe taps him on the shoulder as he sticks his head back into the toilet and vomits again. She waits, covering her face and setting the water and pills down beside him.

"Got you some stuff to help with that."

"Thanks."

He looks up at her. All of the bravado and arrogance has disappeared. He's probably too hung over to even pretend. He looks soft and vulnerable. She swallows the impulse to reach out and run her fingers through the dark waves that frame his face.

"You should have just left me in the hall," he mumbles.

"I'm surprised you remember that," she laughs. "You were fucking gone."

"Yeah," he chuckles. "Sorry."

"It happens to the best of us."

Phoebe leans up against the counter, her vision still blurry from the lack of sleep as Damien sits back on his haunches and takes a few deep breaths.

"Found my room key," he mumbles, a hint of shame in his voice.

Phoebe laughs.

"That's great, I'm so proud of you."

He looks around and sighs.

"I'll get out of your hair. I'm gonna try and sleep this off before we drive to Oakland later."

"Sure."

She follows him out into the hallway, and Damien reaches out to grab her hand, trying to shake it but only manages to briefly grasp her fingers. He holds them awkwardly for a moment before leaning over and kissing her on the cheek. It's featherlight, but it makes her heart jump.

"Thanks again, Miller. You're good people."

"It's really not a problem," she manages to mumble.

He squeezes her fingers gently one last time, before letting go and walking back to his room. Phoebe closes the door, sighing as she leans against it. She gazes up at the ceiling as she draws in what may have been the deepest breath of her life, trying to ignore the fire that's beginning to burn in the pit of her stomach.

"Girl," she says, shaking her head. "You have got to get your shit together."

One Way or Another

The Four Points Hotel

Phoebe groans, rubbing her eyes as she rolls onto her back. It was happening all over again. She never told Brian, he'd absolutely have freaked out, but there was a vocalist on a previous assignment who she fell for. Hard. The band was much smaller than Revolver, struggling to really get their name out into the world, but they were good. Much more important than the band, though, was Alex. He was tall, with long blonde hair and warm brown eyes. Alex was charming, outrageous, untamed, and she was stupid enough to get involved with him. She had a type, sure, but he made her feel alive.

There was no explosive ending to their relationship, no big fights, no lingering anger. The tour ended, and they followed quickly after; he promised to call like they always do, but that phone never rang. That's how things like this go. That's what she told herself. Still hurt like a bitch though. Back then she handled it by swallowing the pain and diving into her work, and eventually the memory of Alex stopped stinging so much. She was ready to tackle the Revolver assignment when it got pitched; she'd be professional this time, removed. He could literally be prince fucking charming right out of a storybook and she'd brush him off, that's what she told herself. It wouldn't happen again. But what's the harm in a little fantasy?

His hands... the way they wrap so effortlessly around the microphone as he sings. Phoebe stares up at the ceiling and she can practically see the long line of silver bangles that cascade down his wrist, hearing the sound they make as he gyrates, and glides across the stage. And his body? Now that she's seen those abs in person, they make her angry, viscerally angry. Who gave him the right to just walk around with his shirt off? Or open? It's not fair.

Then there's his lips. Full and soft– well, she assumes as much. She pictures what it would feel like to kiss him, or feel his mouth trailing down her neck. His breath on her skin. If she closes her eyes and thinks hard enough, she can feel it, his voice rumbling in her ear, moaning her name. Her skin is on fire, and a deep, familiar ache floods her body, vibrating within her so violently that she begins to sweat as she lets her mind wander.

They're just thoughts, right? She doesn't have to act on them, and she won't. She's a professional. Damien understands the nature of their relationship. He has to. Besides, he doesn't even like journalists. It's all a game to him. That's the part that actually makes her angry, but she pushes it out of her mind for now; reality is only so useful in moments like these.

Her hand slides into her jeans, popping open buttons and slipping beneath the hem of her underwear. She gasps in quiet surprise at the wetness that greets her. Her fingers circle her clit and some of the tension that's coiled throughout her body begins to melt away as she imagines it's Damien and his deliciously talented tongue down there. She can almost feel his head buried between her thighs, the feeling of his stubble scratching at her skin.

Her back arches, and she reaches up to grab her breast, teasing her nipple through her shirt. A vivid memory suddenly shakes her imagination: her first time with Alex. He fucked her senseless in a filthy bathroom stall, hiking her skirt up over her hips, nipping at her neck and moaning in her ear.

But now it's all Damien, his voice filling her ears, telling her how beautiful she is... how well she takes his cock. Her body tingles, fingers desperately flicking her clit faster and faster while she whimpers.

Her eyes slide shut, picturing Damien slamming her up against a wall, his mouth on hers. Phoebe can practically hear his moans, swallowing her own just in time when she remembers he's only one room over. She can't help the odd few noises that slip out, but as long as she doesn't get too loud it should be fine. Her clit pulses beneath her touch, breath quickening as she pushes herself right to the edge. A soft groan spills from inside her and within seconds, she's coming – muscles quiver and twitch as she bites down on her knuckles, holding back another gravelly moan.

Her eyes pop open, fixed on the ceiling, lust and arousal quickly replaced by a flood of guilt.

"What the hell are you doing, you idiot?" She whispers.

It must be the smell of his cologne on her pillow. That's it, it's making her crazy. Rolling off of the bed, she rushes to the shower before more thoughts of him can invade her mind.

The scalding hot water cascades down her body, bringing her back to her senses, as she scrubs herself down.

"This is not happening again. You can't do this again," she repeats, as though it's some kind of affirmation; a mantra. "Be objective. Be reasonable," she tells herself. This is just a crush. Hormones. Brain chemistry. It'll go away.

It.

Will.

Go.

Away.

Phoebe sighs, turning off the shower and wrapping herself up with a big fluffy towel. She pulls some clothes out of her suitcase, tugging on a fresh pair of jeans and a t-shirt. As she's running a brush through her hair, trying to figure out how the hell she's going to handle the Damien problem, the phone rings. The receiver may as well be electrified the way she hesitates before finally lifting it to her ear.

"Hello?"

"Downstairs," Troy growls. "Restaurant. Five minutes."

Before she can answer, the line goes dead. Phoebe's guts twist. Does Troy know Bell was in her room last night? They didn't do anything. Surely he would back that up. He wouldn't stab her in the back like that. Would he?

When she gets down to the restaurant, she's surprised to find Damien alone, nursing a glass of whiskey. As Phoebe pulls up a chair, he grimaces at the sound of it squeaking against the linoleum, glaring as their eyes meet. He looks pale, and he's covered in sweat.

She keeps her voice low.

"How're you feeling?"

"Like shit," he grumbles, "Thanks for asking."

Well, so much for the vulnerable guy who was in her hotel room earlier. To be fair to him, she's had pretty serious hangovers in her time. She knows what it's like.

"Bell, you have got to be fucking kidding me!" Troy isn't holding anything back as he storms in, slamming a newspaper on the table; Damien and Phoebe both flinch in unison.

The rest of the band follow behind him, quietly taking their seats while Troy looms over Damien. He's furious. Beyond furious, actually. If flames could shoot out of his eyeballs and burn Bell alive, she's pretty sure he'd be a scorched pile of ash right about now.

Troy points at the paper, stabbing at it aggressively with this index finger.

"Take a look at this shit!"

Phoebe leans in to get a better look, one headline immediately catching her eye.

REVOLVER'S LEAD SINGER UP TO HIS OLD TRICKS

Accompanying the less than ideal headline are a slew of photos: a very drunk-looking Damien getting thrown out of The Ritz, and another of him taking a terrible swing at the bouncer. In the third photo, he's splayed out on the ground on his back. Looks like he must have missed.

Damien frowns, his expression grim.

"I was hoping nobody caught that," he mutters, avoiding Troy's gaze.

"Well they did, Karate Kid! Shall I regale the rest of the band with the story?"

Damien shrugs.

"Last night a bouncer kicked the door to the women's bathroom open to find Bell and some girl goin' at it. Of course, she had his dick in her mouth. Apparently, she was very enthusiastic, and our perfect gentleman here became enraged and started a fight." Troy leans in toward Damien. "You're lucky you were too drunk to land a punch on anyone, and that he's not pressing charges. Hope it was worth it."

"Jesus, Damien," Shaun whispers.

Troy runs his hand through his hair, pacing around the table.

"We talked about this, the whole point of this tour is to finally get some good publicity!"

"That's rock 'n' roll, baby," Damien mumbles halfheartedly.

"It's a goddamn circus," Troy snaps. "And you know it."

Phoebe jumps as Damien slams his hands down on the table.

"Because that's what people fucking pay to see!"

"Kid, they're sure as hell not paying to see your drunk ass getting tossed onto the sidewalk like garbage!"

"Lay off him, Troy!" Johnny exclaims. "This isn't going to get us anywhere."

Troy rolls his eyes

"And what if he got up to something else last night? Something that just hasn't come out yet?"

Phoebe clears her throat.

"If it's any consolation, he probably didn't cause any more damage after that," she says softly. "He slept in my room last night."

Damien shoots her a surprised look, and she shrugs.

"Oh, great!" Troy throws his hands up in exasperation. "Now you're fucking the journalist!"

"It's not like that!" Damien and Phoebe say in unison.

"You know what? It better fucking not be. Any funny business between the two of you and I'm calling your editor, Miller."

Phoebe locks eyes with Damien whose mouth curls into a small smile. It only lasts for a second before he leans back and lights a cigarette, looking her up and down.

"It's strictly platonic," Phoebe says. Troy has to believe it. She almost believes it herself.

Troy drums his fingers on the table, his head tilted up in thought.

"Actually, if you two were fucking we might get a better article."

"Come on, Troy!" Ophelia sighs, smacking him on the shoulder. "A little respect, Jesus..."

"Not cool, man," Johnny mumbles while Shaun shakes his head.

Phoebe can't read Damien's expression at all.

"I'm sorry, Miller. That was out of line. I apologize."

"It's okay," Phoebe whispers.

It's not really, but Troy sounds sincere, and she doesn't feel like starting anything else right now. It's tense enough at the table already.

Troy turns his attention back to Damien. He's clearly still on edge, but his tone's a little softer already.

"Alright, how hungover are you?"

"Extremely."

"Have you eaten?"

Damien shakes his head.

"Well, that's probably why you feel so shitty," Troy grumbles as the waitress comes over.

By the time their food arrives, Troy and the others are busy chatting about the rest of the tour. Damien pushes a basket of fries to Phoebe.

"I have pizza," she tells him, gesturing at the slices on her plate as if he could have missed them.

"Yeah, sure, but you didn't eat anything all morning."

She raises an eyebrow.

"And how *exactly* do you know that?"

"Because you didn't leave your room *all morning*," he says playfully.

Her heart beats a little faster.

"And how do you know *that*?"

He stares her dead in the eye, a smirk tugging at the corners of his mouth. She watches as he leans forward in what feels like slow motion, his lips brushing lightly against her ear as he whispers.

"Thin walls."

Suddenly, the slice of pizza in her hand is the most unappetizing thing in the world. She thought she had been so quiet, except for that single moan, but even that had been... sort of quiet? Hadn't it?

Mercifully, Damien turns and stares out the window, and the extended bout of teasing that Phoebe expects never comes. His expression is totally unreadable as they finish their meal, and even after Troy sends them away to pack, he says nothing for the entire trip back to their rooms. With a door finally between the two of them again, the next hour is devoted solely to washing away pure humiliation. Damien heard her masturbating, to fantasies of him, right next door. The thought makes her want to crawl into a hole and die.

"God? If you exist, please just hit me with lightning, or a rocket, or a whole other bus while we're loading up today? That'd be really great."

Once she's thoroughly rinsed off the embarrassment of the afternoon, Phoebe preps for the upcoming bus ride. Hopefully she won't have to sit with Damien again; no doubt he'd spend the entire time trying to get a rise out of her. As she's loading some more film into her camera, she hears a soft knock on the door.

"Yeah?"

"Troy said the bus is ready to go."

It's Damien. Of course it is.

"Oh– uh, yeah, cool. I'll be down in a minute."

"I'll hold the elevator for you."

She glowers at the door.

"Sure."

She grabs her stuff, hauling her suitcase and bag behind her. Damien is at the elevator, still holding the door for her as promised. So far so good. Maybe he just won't bring it up.

"You look better."

"Finally got some beauty sleep," he replies.

"Me too," she laughs.

"I'll bet you did," he whispers under his breath.

The slightest smile lingers on his lips before it slips away without a trace, and he doesn't say another word to her all the way out to the bus. Damien climbs on first, taking a seat beside his bandmates, thankfully leaving Phoebe to take the free seat beside Troy.

She turns to him, trying her best not to catch Damien's eye.

"So, how's it going?" She asks.

"Fine. Just putting out fires left and right thanks to that one." He gestures at Bell who's listening intently to one of Shaun's new riffs. "Thanks for taking care of him last night, by the way."

"No problem," Phoebe replies. "Figured I'd give you the night off."

Troy laughs.

"I appreciate it, but you don't have to take on that responsibility you know."

"I just didn't want to leave him out there all night when he was that far gone. I've lost friends that way."

There's a poignant pause before Troy pats her on the shoulder.

"Me too," he replies. "Listen. I know you've probably been told not to accept money from any of us, but I owe you one for saving his ass, so your drinks are on me tonight."

"It's really okay, Mr. Sullivan–"

"Don't 'Mr. Sullivan' me. They're just drinks. Besides, you're one of us for two whole months. No fly on the wall shit. It's just not how we do things."

While the band gets ready in the dressing room, Phoebe scribbles feverishly in her notebook. Often, when she's unsure exactly how to start a piece, she'll lay out a bunch of little details, one quickly cascading into another. Before long she's filled the page with a sort of mood-map for the venue or show, or whatever the focus of the night is. It's a little chaotic, but it helps tie the entire thing together, at least as long as she can remember what she was thinking at the time. As she's circling the big bolded 'Oakland' in the center of the page, she feels someone looming over her and winces.

Anyone but Damien.

Luckily, her prayers are answered, and she's relieved to see Johnny's dazzling smile. He stands awkwardly for a moment, seemingly not quite sure how to start the conversation, running a hand through his hair before he crouches down beside her.

"Hey, I was wondering if you maybe wanted to interview me before the show tonight? Or something?"

Good material *and* a distraction from Bell? Her eyes light up and she smiles.

"Yeah. Yeah, absolutely! Anything off-limits?"

He frowns quizzically, not quite sure what she's asking.

"Ophelia mentioned... a fiancée?"

"Ah, I see what you mean. Yeah, that'd probably be best to avoid," Johnny tells her. "It's not that I'm ashamed, Erin's great, but I don't want fans speculating and digging things up about her, you know? Things can get crazy."

"Understood," Phoebe replies, putting on her professional face. "Completely."

"Cool. Thank you," he whispers, clearly relieved. "I just like to keep some parts of my life separated from all this."

Johnny seems to have a good head on his shoulders, probably does him a lot of good in this industry. More importantly, he provides balance to Bell's wilder nature, grounding the band just a little bit. Phoebe casually points the microphone in his direction, giving him the heads up that they're starting with a little nod.

"So, I read that you originally intended to be a lawyer."

"Yeah," he laughs, rubbing the back of his neck. "I'm a better bass player than I was a student."

"What made you want to run away and join a rock band?"

Johnny lets out a gentle laugh.

"I'd always wanted to be a musician. I mean, I've loved playing bass since I was a kid. We were in the school's marching band together, way back in– actually, can you not put that in the article?"

Phoebe laughs.

"That part about marching band? I think it makes you relatable, but I can leave it out if you'd like."

"It just sounds so dorky." He lets out an awkward laugh. "I'm sure you've heard, we have an image to maintain."

She nods, a mock somber look on her face.

"Consider it stricken from the record. Actually, I won't even transcribe it, nothing to strike."

"Thanks," He smiles warmly, lost in a moment of introspection. "I remember when we were all hanging out in school together, I know it's a cliché but it really was one of the best times of my life. And leaving it all was hard. You know, when you get out of school, most of those friendships don't last, right? I never wanted that to happen. So, when Damien suggested that we start a band, I was all in. He'd been writing for forever since we were kids, and his poetry was always just a cut above. Of course he's my best friend too, but that's not— look, he really is just one of the most talented people I know. It was kind of a no-brainer. It really wasn't hard to get Shaun and Ophelia to join either, not once I was all-in."

A sheepish smile plays on his lips.

"Although, I think it's fair to say I just wanted to avoid responsibility for a little while longer and *maybe* make a shitload of money doing it. I know that doesn't sound particularly artistic or anything."

Phoebe shrugs, she's definitely heard worse.

"People get into art for all kinds of reasons."

"Very true, very true," Johnny laughs.

"So the connection between the band members is what's most important to you? Do you feel like that comes through in your music?"

"Definitely. We're like a well-oiled machine: If one part isn't working, it all falls apart." He leans back in his chair for a moment, looking down at his hands. "It's funny, most people think that Damien is the leader of the band, but it's really not like that. We all get a say in what goes into each song and we all put a little piece of ourselves into every one."

Johnny's passion is obvious, for the band but also for art in general. It clearly bothers him, at least a little bit, that everything written about them is focused on Damien. And why wouldn't it, if they all put in so much work? She smiles, gearing up for her favorite question.

"What's your favorite thing about music?"

It's simple, to the point, but it always works.

"Wow, uh, honestly everything. Fuckin' everything!"

Johnny leans toward her, grinning.

"You want me to elaborate?"

Phoebe laughs. He knows it's a cheesy answer, but it works for him.

"That'd be nice."

"I love the way it feels when you play it, the way it connects people from all different backgrounds and walks of life. I love the way that people can take a song that we've written and have it mean something to them. It's just beautiful, man, all of it. Just beautiful."

His sincerity is infectious, and the openness almost shocking next to Damien's carefully curated rock-star persona.

"I always worry about answering these questions because I'm afraid I'm gonna sound like a complete asshole."

"You don't. Trust me."

The sound of the door swinging shut grabs her attention, briefly distracting from the interview. It's Bell, of course, sauntering around in the same tight leather pants that he had on during their San Jose show and, of course, no shirt.

Speak of the Devil and he shall appear...

He's barely paying her any mind, carrying on a conversation with Ophelia about the night's set. Phoebe feels some measure of relief as he passes, perfectly content to be ignored, but the subtle brush of his fingers against her shoulder puts her right back on edge. What's less subtle, and what grabs her attention immediately, is the very clear outline of his cock through his pants. Her eyes bounce back to Johnny, hoping they didn't linger long enough to be noticed. She can feel Damien staring at her. He's doing this shit on purpose.

It's like he's trying to get her to break.

"So, uh, did you have any more questions?"

"Oh! Um, not at the moment. That was great." At least it doesn't seem like Johnny's noticed, thank god.

"Hey no problem! We can always do another one if the ol' muse hits!"

Before she can respond the door slams open as Troy leans in to scan the room. He smiles, looking a little surprised when he sees Damien where he should be for once.

"On in ten, children, let's make it a good one!"

"Shit. I've gotta call Erin," Johnny mumbles, sliding out of his chair. "Thanks for the interview, Miller."

"No problem," she mutters.

Ophelia and Shaun are already halfway out the door as well. Phoebe shoves her recorder into her bag, struggling to be as quick as possible. She'd rather not be alone with cocksure Damien Bell right now.

"When do I get my interview?" Damien purrs, pushing himself off of the wall and walking casually past her. She swallows hard and turns her head, forcing a smile past the adrenaline pulsing through her body.

"Any time you want. I mean... that's what I'm here for."

He's holding the door, casually waiting for her by the only exit.

"I'll keep that in mind," he says sardonically.

He nods toward the door, waiting for her. Phoebe shoulders her bag and moves quickly for the exit before he slides effortlessly in her way, almost causing a full on collision.

"I like the outfit tonight," he says softly, reaching out to brush away one of the strings of her halter top. She stumbles back slightly, it's hard to meet his gaze when they're so close. The eyeliner makes him look even more intense.

"Ophelia picked out the shirt."

"She's got great taste."

His gaze lingeres just long enough to make her squirm before he turns, walking off like it was a completely normal interaction.

"I'll see you out there, Miller."

Completely and totally normal.

She waits for him to turn the corner before she collapses against the wall and rubs her face.

"This couldn't have waited until there was a week left on the tour, could it?" She mumbles to herself.

No. Of course not.

"You good, Miller?"

It's Troy, his neck craned around the corner. He definitely didn't see any of that nightmare because he still looks like he's in a pretty good mood.

"Yeah," she laughs. "Sorry, just cleaning up my stuff."

"Oh, hey, did you get your camera off the bus?"

"Yep," she mutters, pulling it out of her bag.

"Good, good! Bell wants more pictures; saw you the other night and thought it was a great idea."

"Of course he does."

Troy cups his hand over his ear.

"What?!"

He's only half paying attention.

"I said I'll be right out!"

He gives her the thumbs up and disappears.

Phoebe takes a long breath, thinking back on the mess of the last couple days. Fly on the wall? Objectivity? Why was it suddenly so impossible to just do the job without all this extra shit?

Maybe she'll just get extremely drunk tonight.

Seems to always work out for Damien fucking Bell.

Kids in America

Fox Theater

Phoebe watches from the sidelines, her notebook in hand and camera around her neck as the music guides the crowd to pulse like a beating heart. The band has a good rhythm with one another, with Shaun improvising riffs, Johnny doing his best to keep up, and Ophelia holding it all together. Damien seems just as enraptured with the audience as they are with him, howling into the mic as he leans down, his fingertips just barely brushing against theirs. Before long he's on his knees, eyes locked with a girl at the front of the crowd who's practically screaming every word back to Bell.

Phoebe had been planning to stay off the stage this time, as far away from Damien as possible, but the scene is so raw that she can't help herself. It would be an amazing shot for the article, impossible to pass up. She tosses her notebook onto a nearby amp and slowly creeps out onto the stage, getting right down to Damien's level to capture the moment. With the two caught in profile, and Damien howling like a wolf, Phoebe snaps a photo. She can already tell it's going to look incredible on film, glancing down at the camera for a moment to advance the roll. Suddenly there's a fingertip beneath her chin, tilting her head upward.

Damien.

He's covered in sweat, his long hair sticking to his face, staring at her like he wants to eat her alive. His finger trails down the length of her throat before he withdraws his hand, leaning in close. She instinctively holds up her camera like a shield to stop him from making eye contact. It's all too much; the proximity alone is enough to make her feel faint.

She snaps another photo, unwilling to miss the peak of this performance, before Damien winks and glides away from her, still howling into the mic. Free from Bell's gaze, she scrambles back to the wings where Troy is waiting with a double gin and tonic. She plucks the straw from the glass and tosses it to the ground, gulping down the whole thing in one go. He looks surprised, and a little impressed.

"You good, Miller?"

"Uh-huh. Just thirsty."

Troy grins.

"Those shots out there, you think they'll be good?"

"Yeah," she replies, almost gasping for breath. "Definitely."

Troy gestures to Damien, who has one arm slung around Johnny's shoulder while he sings.

"Just... be careful around him."

Her eyes slide over to Troy, and she purses her lips.

"I'm always careful."

"You're a smart girl, I'd hate to see you get hurt."

The last thing she needs is for Troy to think that there's something going on between her and Damien. That it's affecting her work.

"Don't worry, I know how to deal with children."

Troy snorts, calling for another round as they watch the rest of the show in silence. No matter how much alcohol she puts away, she can't stop thinking about being down on her knees looking up at him, and by the time the band gets off stage Phoebe is swaying.

Ophelia walks up, grabbing her shoulder and shaking her lightly.

"You good?"

"Yep."

Ophelia giggles.

"Are you sure?"

"I had some drinks," Phoebe confesses, pressing a finger to her lips. "Troy is a bad influence."

"Well, I can't have him take that title away from me. I want to go dancing. You in?"

Phoebe claps her hands together.

"*Hell* yes!"

She has to get this crush out of her system and blow off some steam. Clearly her hotel room isn't working in that regard because a certain *someone* is, how did he put it? Obnoxiously curious.

Ophelia wraps her arm around Phoebe's shoulder and leans over to whisper in her ear.

"You look like you need to get laid, Phoebe."

Honestly? A great idea. Perfect, no notes.

"And you're gonna help me with that?"

The drummer smiles.

"I'll be your wing woman, Pheebs. Guaranteed success."

Ophelia grabs her hand, and leads her back to the dressing room. As the two girls stumble inside, Phoebe immediately makes an effort to act as sober as she possibly can, casually flopping into a chair.

Damien turns to her and grins.

"Looks like Miller's wasted."

"I'm not!" She exclaims, beginning to pout. "I'm not..."

"Leave her alone," Ophelia tells him before looking over to Troy. "Need us for anything?"

He shakes his head.

"Not tonight, you were all solid as a rock, so go and have some fun." He points at Damien. "No fun for you tonight, though, you're on probation. Johnny? Keep an eye on him."

Damien rolls his eyes.

"I was going to go back to the bus," Johnny whines. "I don't want to Damie-sit!"

"Too bad, Reed," Troy replies. "I've done enough of that shit for the last two years. It's someone else's turn tonight. You can call your girlfriend later."

Johnny sighs dramatically.

"Fine."

"We're still sleeping on the bus tonight, right?" Shaun asks.

"Yeah, but the driver is getting some shuteye so it's off limits right now. We leave at 5:00AM *sharp*, so go and blow off some steam if you want, just be back in time for us to hit the road. You can be as hungover as you like on the bus, I don't care."

Damien's face lights up.

"Except for you, Bell."

"Oh, I can't even have a drink now?"

"Okay sure, since you asked so nicely, you can have *a* drink, but I will smack you upside the head if you get your ass kicked by another bouncer."

Damien scoffs and lights a cigarette as Ophelia looks around the room.

"Phoebe and I are going to the club next door. Open invitation."

"Yes," Damien answers immediately.

Phoebe's stomach turns. He's staring directly at her.

"I'm in," Shaun says.

"Sure, I am on Damie-Duty after all," Johnny replies. "As long as I don't have to dance."

"Not even one?" Ophelia asks.

"I'm saving it for someone back home."

Damien and Shaun gag, and Johnny throws some empty water bottles at them.

"You're so old fashioned," Ophelia chuckles.

"Someone's gotta be."

Ophelia claps her hands together.

"Okay, no time to waste. Let's party!"

The bar is filled with smoke and the music pounds as Phoebe and Ophelia move their bodies along with the beat, the drinks in their hands sloshing all over the floor. Phoebe feels a little tipsy, but nothing she can't handle. Eventually, Ophelia leans over, shouting into Phoebe's ear.

"I have to pee! If any creeps show up, call Johnny! He'll deal with 'em!"

"Yep. Perfect. Got it!"

The words fly right by her, barely registering as Phoebe keeps dancing. She feels herself slipping away into whatever force is powering the most magical dance floor she's ever been on; the music in the air and the slight buzz from the alcohol create the perfect distraction from her own brain. From thoughts of Damien Bell, and his stupid fucking face.

But, it's not stupid. It's beautiful. Maybe she's the stupid one? Well, who cares. As she throws her hands above her head, getting lost in the music once more, she feels someone bump into her. A very handsome man with short dark hair and a gorgeous smile is dancing beside her. Well, dancing is a strong word. He has no rhythm, but he's very cute.

"Hi!" He shouts over the music.

"Hey!"

"I'm Jake!"

"Phoebe!"

He sticks his hand out and she laughs, shaking it clumsily.

"Do you always do such formal introductions on the dance floor?"

"My mom raised me to be polite!" He leans in closer, alcohol on his breath. "You're really pretty!"

"Thank you!" She laughs. "Do you want to dance?"

"Yeah, I mean we're already dancing... but together right?"

She looks over at the bar. Damien is watching them as Johnny talks his ear off. He's smiling, but there's something about his eyes that makes her heart beat a little faster. She can't tell if it's jealousy, or if he's planning something as he suddenly slams a drink back and puts it on the counter. The bartender pours him another.

She turns back to the new guy and smiles, wrapping her arms around his neck. They get very close very quickly.

"Together," she mutters. "Jake, right?"

"Yeah, yeah, that's me!"

The two sway together in silence for a bit, until halfway through the song, Jake leans closer, his lips brushing her ear.

"Do you maybe... wanna make out?"

Phoebe pulls back, laughing.

"Yeah, sure, why not?"

A huge grin spreads across his face.

"Cool!"

He presses his lips to hers and Phoebe leans in, her fingers swimming through his hair. It's soft and curly, and he's a pretty good kisser, gentle, sweet, and playful. His tongue flicks her bottom lip, as if he's asking for permission or guidance, and Phoebe amps up the intensity. He kisses like Alex, close enough to make her ache.

Jake tears his mouth away from hers, kissing up and down her neck and biting into her skin as they move to the music. Phoebe's head rolls back, spotting Damien from across the bar with a glass of whiskey in his hand. She lets out another moan and he drains his drink, disappearing into the crowd. Good riddance. When the song ends and they finally get a look at each other again, Jake has lipstick smeared all over his mouth. She giggles, moving to wipe it off.

"You're a good kisser."

"Oh wow, thanks! I'm thinking of getting another drink. Do you want one?"

Phoebe pauses for a moment, realizing for the first time just how hot she's feeling without any distractions.

"Can I meet you back here? I wanna get some fresh air, and I can grab some water on the way back. Five minutes or something, sound good?"

"Sure!" He only gets a couple steps away before he turns back around. "Hey, we can make out more when you get back, right?"

She gives him an enthusiastic nod.

"Definitely."

"Cool," he breathes as he bolts for the bar.

Phoebe walks through the crowd and slips out the back door, leaning against the building as she taps her pockets. She lets out a frustrated sigh. Wrong coat. Suddenly, the back door to the club opens and Damien steps out, a cigarette between his lips. He seems surprised to see her, nodding as he pulls out his lighter. Her heart begins to thump faster. Her mouth is dry.

"Thought I'd be alone out here," he mutters.

So did she.

"I can leave," Phoebe offers.

"It's fine," he laughs. "I could use the company."

She bites her lip and shoves her hands deep in her pockets, standing awkwardly for a few moments before he breaks the silence.

"I thought you'd be back in there with your friend."

She shrugs, pulling her pockets inside-out.

"Came out here for a smoke, but no dice."

Damien takes a long pull before passing his cigarette over.

"Split my last one with you?"

"Nah, that's okay."

"What?" He laughs. That gorgeous laugh. "You think I have cooties?"

"No, it's just..."

He leans in a little closer. Too close.

"Take it."

His voice is low and raspy, and the wording flips some switch in her brain. It was almost a command.

Damien raises an eyebrow. Maybe she's just that obvious, but sometimes it feels like he can read her mind. She reaches for the cigarette, trying to control the tremor in her hand as she takes a drag.

"Thanks," she mumbles, passing it back.

His fingers brush against hers and she tries not to gasp. It's so pathetic. She's pathetic, doing this all over again. A thousand thoughts run through her mind. Her, pressed up against the wall, fingers digging into her thighs and squeezing them so tight they leave bruises. His lips pressed against hers.

She thinks about the way he lifted her chin at the concert and stared into her eyes like he wanted to devour her right there onstage. She doesn't make eye contact with him for fear that she'll spontaneously combust. She can feel him studying her every move.

"I didn't know you could let loose like that, by the way. Back in the club." He says it softly, but there's something else behind the words.

She shrugs.

"When you spend your whole life doing everything right, you tend to take the shots you can get once you're free from all of that."

"Amen to that," he mumbles.

She sighs, staring up into the sky.

"Back then, whenever I could have done something bad, I'd feel too guilty. I still do sometimes."

"But it's fun, yeah?"

"Yeah," she giggles, looking back down at her boots, kicking playfully at the ground. "It is."

Damien exhales, a cloud of smoke slowly escaping his lips.

"Well, rebellion looks good on you. Keep it up."

He hands her the rest of the cigarette.

"And thanks for the show."

Watching him walk away, Phoebe feels a sudden surge of unexpected confidence.

"Damien, what are we doing?"

He chuckles.

"What do you mean?"

"This whole thing. What is it?"

He closes the gap between them, reaching out to brush a strand of hair from her face.

"I believe you've already defined it."

"How?" She shoots back.

He leans in, his mouth just inches from hers. She can smell the whiskey on his breath mingling with his cologne; his classic mix. All she has to do is lean forward and take what she wants. He grins, and his tongue slides across his bottom lip. It's almost a sneer, mocking her and testing every boundary she's built up until this point. They're going to play this game until one of them breaks, and she has a feeling that Damien is very, very good at this.

Phoebe fights the urge to close her eyes and enjoy the moment as he gently caresses her cheek with his thumb.

"Strictly. Platonic."

His words are like a gut punch, and he leaves Phoebe standing alone in the alleyway, the sound of the heavy door ringing through the air like a bell.

She tosses the cigarette on the ground and stomps on it. Once, twice, three fucking times. Anything to drown out how much she wants him to slam her against the wall and fuck her brains out.

"Thanks for the show?" she growls. "Motherfucker…"

Phoebe storms back into the club, passing right by Damien who shoots her a little wink. It just makes her more angry. She finds Jake on the dance floor and immediately grabs him by the shoulder.

"Oh hey, I thought you left!" He shouts.

She grabs his face, pulling him in for a rough, desperate kiss, and he lets out a squeak of surprise.

"Look. I can't go back to your place or anything, but I want to fuck you."

Jake's eyes go wide.

"Here, in the club. Would you be into that?"

"I – ye – yeah. I mean, yeah. Yeah! Super into that. You're, like, incredibly hot." He gulps. "It would be an honor to do sex with you."

She giggles.

"So, what do you think, bathroom?"

Jake frowns.

"There's a huge line, last I checked."

"Alleyway?"

"Great idea!" He chirps, enthusiastically. "I've always been a fan of alleyways, unsung heroes in a world of streets."

She beams. Finally, a nice guy without an attitude or ridiculous leather pants.

"Shit," Jake mumbles as he roots through his wallet. "I didn't bring a condom– you know what? I'll go ask someone!"

Before she can even say anything, he's disappeared into the crowd, and then someone's tapping her on the shoulder. It's Johnny.

"Time to go."

Her mouth hangs open, eyes wide as saucers.

"But, I was gonna... me and that guy were–"

Johnny waves a hand, cutting her off.

"Sorry, it's almost 5:00. You're done, Pheebs."

He gestures toward the exit where the others are standing.

Phoebe lets out a long whine of frustration, and Johnny chuckles, wrapping an arm around her shoulder.

"There will be plenty of others on the road, princess," he assures her.

"Yeah, yeah," she mumbles as they walk toward the rest of the band.

Damien grins at her as she approaches.

"Cockblocked, huh?" He teases.

Phoebe sneers at him.

"Shut. The fuck. Up."

"Heyyyy!" Damien laughs. "What's with the hostility?"

She's ready to jump down his throat, but Johnny looks over at him, scowling.

"Leave her alone, man."

"Yeah, you don't want to piss her off," Shaun tells him.

"That's riiiiight," Damien drawls, taking a step so that he's in front of her. He continues to walk backwards toward the bus with his arms out wide. "She's dangerous. Aren't you, Miller?"

"Dangerous is my middle name," she grumbles.

The rest of the band heads onto the bus, with only Damien sticking around outside, keeping a close eye on Phoebe. When she finally moves to board, he stops her with a large hand on her shoulder.

"I don't think you're dangerous."

She looks up at him. Somehow she feels even smaller in his presence. Or he's gotten bigger? Or it's the booze? It must be the booze.

"No?"

"No," Damien rumbles.

He brushes her cheek again, the back of his fingers making her shiver. Despite her better judgment, she leans into his touch, moaning softly. Damien's eyes shine and a devilish grin spreads across his face.

"You know what I think you are?"

"What?"

"Just a little pussycat."

Her eyes snap open. She feels her chest growing tight.

"And I think you're a condescending asshole!"

As soon as the words fly out of her mouth, she regrets them. He really can be an asshole, but she doesn't need to make an enemy. Judging by the way his eyes narrow, she thinks he might explode. Instead, he laughs, his shoulders shaking.

"Okay Miller," he chuckles. "Maybe you've got a little bit of bite to you."

What's this guy's deal? Hot one minute, cold the next. She wants to tell him what she really thinks of him, ask him what he really wants, but before she has a chance to react, the driver sticks his head out of the door.

"You kids coming or what?"

Damien steps aside, gesturing for Phoebe to board the bus.

"After you, babydoll."

Stuck in the Middle

CALIFORNIA-OREGON BORDER

Someone is calling her name. Phoebe grimaces and reaches out to swat the sound away, but they catch her hand. It's Johnny, and he's crouched down in front of her, laughing softly. She struggles to lift herself into an upright position, immediately regretting the choice as her head begins to pound. Johnny quickly places something greasy in her hand, she can smell the food through the paper wrapper. And then there's the nausea.

"Morning, sunshine!"

"Noooooo!" She whines, covering her face with her hair, her ears ringing from the sound of his voice.

"Aww, Johnny, let the little princess sleep."

Damien's voice floats in from somewhere beside her just as they hit a bump in the road. Her stomach flutters and she gags, followed by more laughter from the two of them; it's like they're taking a cheese grater to her senses.

"You should eat," Johnny tells her. "Got you a breakfast sandwich."

"Thanks," Phoebe mumbles, pushing herself upright, her eyes finally adjusting to her surroundings as she claws the wrapper open. Johnny smiles, patting her on the shoulder before heading back to his seat near the front of the bus, and leaving her alone with Damien.

"Those are good," he tells her, gesturing offhandedly at the sandwich.

"Hope so," Phoebe mutters.

She takes a bite. Bacon, egg, cheese, and hot sauce. It's incredible, lighting up every single one of her taste buds. Even so, she still has to suppress the urge to immediately wretch– the bumpy road encouraging her. She fights back the feeling, and Damien watches with a smile on his face as she gorges herself. Within seconds, she's devoured the entire thing and sits licking her fingers in the aftermath. It's exactly what she needed.

He hands her a bottle of water from a compartment beside him, which she gratefully accepts, guzzling it down like she hasn't touched a drop in a week.

"You're a trooper, Miller."

"Hmmph."

Damien is– God, why is he always shirtless? Practically all he's wearing is a pair of denim shorts cut off just above the knee. His legs are stretched out, propped up on the empty seat in front of him. She's never realized how long they actually are. Muscular, too. There are rips in the denim that look strategic and her eyes trail up his thigh until they land safely on the book that's cradled in his hands.

"What the fuck happened last night?"

Damien grins as he pulls his sunglasses down his nose.

"You don't remember?"

She shakes her head.

"Bits and pieces."

"Well, first off you and Ophelia drank the *entire* bar–"

"It wasn't *that* much."

"Fine, fine. You danced a lot, pretty well honestly," he pauses for dramatic effect, his smile widening just a bit, "oh, and of course you had your tongue down some guy's throat for... well pretty much the entire night."

She groans, rubbing her eyes. Yep. Of course.

"It happens, Miller. You were having a good time. There's nothing wrong with that."

"Well, if that's all I did, it's not so bad. Definitely could have been worse."

He raises his eyebrows.

"So I guess you don't remember either of our conversations then, huh?"

She feels like she might really be sick this time, unsure if it's the dread or just the hangover, but she's praying the bus doesn't go over another bump either way.

"Our wha?"

Damien snickers.

"Well, first off we shared a cigarette in the alley."

She struggles to pull the sharp little snippets of memory from her aching head: the cool brick of the alleyway bathed in smoke, soft words too muffled to understand... his face just inches from hers.

Her eyes widen.

"We didn't…"

"No," his head dips slightly to the side, fully taking in her reaction. "No, you don't have to worry about that. But you asked me something interesting. Do you remember?"

She's drawing a blank.

"You asked me what we're doing, the two of us."

She winces, covering her face.

"Oh, God."

"You asked me what our *whole thing* is, our deal."

Face in hands, Phoebe lets out a wail that's a mix of agony and annoyance. She feels like she's forcing every gear in her brain to turn in order to fully process what's going on. Why can't she just go back to sleep? Damien chuckles, and she instinctively lifts her head, finding him right in front of her. His palms are pressed into her seat taking up the empty space on either side of her body. Her heart leaps into her throat as he stares at her.

She sort of remembers the conversation. Mostly, she remembers the way he smelled and how little effort it would take to lean in and kiss him.

"Strictly platonic," she mutters back, disappointment and relief filling her in equal measure.

"Asked and answered," he whispers.

She wanted to kiss him so badly last night, but he kept opening his fucking mouth.

"That's what you said back when Troy asked us at the hotel, but that's not what I get when I look at you. When we *really* talk. Can you tell me I'm wrong?"

She swallows, her throat raw.

"It's unprofessional."

He nods.

"I get it, Phoebe, you have a job to do and I respect that."

The use of her first name throws her off a bit, it sounds strange coming from him, and stranger still as he shifts into a more serious tone.

"Contrary to what you might believe, I respect you too."

She quirks an eyebrow.

"Do you?"

He nods.

"You do great work." He pauses. "Like your Van Halen piece from last month for example."

It was just an album review, nothing special, but she's shocked he'd read it.

"You make all of these cool connections and really personal observations. You let your readers know a little something about you through your relationship with the music. It's personal, a little like reading a diary."

Phoebe glances down at her fingernails, picking the dirt out of them. Janis told her the same thing once.

"I didn't know you read my stuff."

"I've been reading your work for a while," he confesses. "I think I have every copy of Titanium back at my place."

"Does Troy know?"

"Nope. He didn't tell me anything other than the fact that you were a woman, so it never came up. He didn't even tell me what magazine you were from. When he introduced us, I finally got to put a face to the work I'd been reading for six months."

Her entire body is vibrating. She thought he was just bluffing when he told her that he'd read her stuff. If he has the whole run of Titanium though... they had covered Revolver before, and it wasn't pretty. She thought Chris's review was unfair. He called Damien 'a drunken clown who thinks he's Aldous Huxley.' She wonders if he has that copy in his apartment too. Maybe he uses it for dart practice.

"Okay, sure, so you respect me."

He nods.

"So you get how this has to go from now on, totally professional."

"Right," he whispers, a microscopic smile still clinging to his lips.

Damien stands, towering over her. His bare torso glistens with a thin sheen of sweat as the afternoon light is magnified by the windows of the bus. She wants to reach up and run her fingers along his skin.

No. Professional.

Fuck.

His confession should bring her some comfort, but it just increases the tension between the two of them, complicating things further. She thinks back to Troy's threat to call Brian if he even got an inkling that something's happening between them. Her job is literally on the line.

Damien leans forward placing both hands on her knees, his dog tags dangling in front of her face.

"If you're ever interested in changing up our *thing,* just know that I'm not opposed."

Without another word, he stands up and casually saunters down the aisle to sit with Johnny; he doesn't even look back at her. Phoebe buries her head in her hands and groans softly, flopping even further into the seat as she preps to spend the next hour or so fighting through her hangover. Unfortunately, she barely gets a few minutes of shuteye before she feels someone drop down onto the seat right next to her.

"You look like shit," Shaun's voice cuts straight through the silence.

She's surprised to find herself laughing, relieved to be talking to anyone other than Damien.

"Thanks for noticing."

"You and Ophelia both, actually." He elbows her gently. "You guys were drinking like it was your last night on earth."

"Hey, so were you!" Phoebe chuckles. "I saw you and Johnny trying to race those whiskey shots."

Shaun shrugs his shoulders.

"I'm a rockstar, what's your excuse? You've been Miss Professional up until last night."

"I needed to blow off some steam," Phoebe sighs. "Clearly."

"It was just a bit surprising. You *are* kind of a square, Phoebe, can't deny it."

He's right, she even surprised herself. Last night was ridiculous, at least from what she can piece together. And now she's paying for it.

"Nah, honestly it was good to see you having fun, gotta let loose once in a while, right?"

She chuckles, nodding along with his words. Something about Shaun always puts her in a better mood.

"Hey, I was gonna ask you, if you're feeling up to it... Ophelia and I are playing cards, but Go Fish is boring with two people, and *Troy* cheats, so he's out–"

"I do not cheat!" Troy bellows from the front.

"You're a cheater, man!" Shaun yells back. "Accept your flaws, learn from them and grow!"

"Don't make me come back there!"

"And do what, dude?" Shaun laughs. "Shake your fist at me? Brag about walking to school uphill both ways back in 1917?"

Phoebe's shoulders shake from laughter as Troy flips Shaun off from the front seat. Her headache's getting worse, but it's worth it.

"How 'bout it, Miller? You wanna play with us?"

"Yeah, totally. Do you mind if I ask you two a few questions while we play?"

"Always on the clock, huh?" He flashes her a warm smile. "No problem at all."

Phoebe grabs her notepad and recorder from her bag and they make their way to the front. As she passes Damien, he glances up at her.

"Careful, Miller. Don't ralph."

She scrunches up her nose and sneers at him.

"I'll be sure to do it *on you* if I need to."

Shaun and Johnny snort with laughter, but Damien only tosses her a cocky wink in response. She can't tell if it's the movement of the bus or just being around him that's making her hangover even worse.

When they make it over to Ophelia, they find her tucked in at a small table sticking out from the wall. She's already shuffling a deck of cards, clearly ready to go, and her eyes sparkle as she sees them approach.

"You got her!" She chirps. She passes Phoebe her second breakfast sandwich of the day. "We were gonna bribe you with this, pretty smart, right?"

"You don't need to bribe me," she laughs. "Actually, the idea of more food is making me feel a little queasy."

"I'll take that, then," Shaun replies, snatching it from Ophelia's hand. "I'm still starving."

"We've got lots of water," Ophelia offers, handing her a bottle as they settle into their seats. "I have some painkillers somewhere in my purse too, hang on."

She roots through her bag, pulling out makeup brushes, a Tootsie Roll, a can of soda, tampons, a few tubes of lipsticks, and a wallet that's covered in stickers and sharpie marks before she finds the little bottle of pills.

"She's got a whole convenience store in there," Shaun teases.

"I never hear you complaining when you need something!"

Ophelia tosses Phoebe the bottle and she rips the cap off, tossing back two pills and guzzling the water. Once she's settled and a little more hydrated, Phoebe switches on the recorder, glancing over to Shaun while Ophelia deals cards.

"The last time we talked, you told me that rock 'n' roll was changing, do you see yourselves changing with it and switching up your style for the next album?"

Shaun chuckles to himself.

"Straight to business, huh? Well, yeah, I mean, Damien and I have talked a lot about that. We're not sure how we're going to approach it, but I'd like to experiment with some softer stuff, just to switch things up. Biggest thing we're worried about is putting out a bunch of albums that sound the same. His lyrics are getting better, and the more the four of us play together, the more seamless it all gets. But even seamless can get boring if you're just doing the same shit over and over again. Ophelia's worried about that, says it all the time."

"Definitely," she agrees as she looks at her cards. "We don't want to be a one trick pony. I mean, just look at Bowie. He went from Ziggy Stardust to really embracing synth. He moved away from glam rock and that whole persona he had built without a second thought."

They're clearly in this for the long-haul.

"So, it sounds like longevity is important to you guys?"

"I think it should be important to every artist," Shaun replies. "You got any 3's, Phi?"

Ophelia grimaces and passes him a 3 of diamonds.

"Like, my dad's a career musician, right? He makes solo albums, but he works on other peoples' projects, too. He told me it's not about getting rich, it's about balancing making art with making a living. I wanted to make sure that I surrounded myself with people who understood that."

"Your dad made a big impact on you."

She can see how much Shaun loves his dad, how his eyes light up when he talks about him.

"Yeah. I'm always learning from him. He taught me everything I know about showmanship and music, and then my mom taught me what matters most: never lose sight of what you love." Shaun taps his cards against the table. "So I combine the two. Like, I *love* getting up on that stage every night, the adrenaline rush of not knowing what's going to happen, feeling that energy from the crowd, but that's just a part of it. We're grateful to be where we are. But eventually, we're gonna get older and we're not gonna be cool anymore. So I'd like to be able to support a family doing this, just like my parents did for me and my sister."

Ophelia beams at him and Phoebe can feel her chest fill with warmth. Something about his expression and the softness of his voice made the whole thing feel so personal, like he's telling her a secret, and she has a sudden pang of guilt that she's recording. Shaun pipes up, easily reading her expression.

"Oh, don't worry, you can print all that. I don't mind."

"Thank you," Phoebe says softly.

"You got any 7's?"

"Go fish," Phoebe replies.

"Should've asked Ophelia," he sighs as he reaches for the deck and tucks a card into his hand. "She has a terrible poker face, just look. Ask her for a 7 when your turn comes around, you'll see."

She punches his shoulder.

"Fuck you, dude, I have a great poker face!"

Phoebe considers waiting, but decides to keep the questions up. They'd reached a really natural rhythm and she'd hate to lose it.

"Your mom's a piano teacher, right?"

"That's right, yeah," Shaun laughs, still taking a punch here and there from Ophelia. "You did your research."

"I'd be a bad journalist if I came into this unprepared."

"Yeah, well being a bad journalist is pretty normal as far as I can tell," Ophelia quips, finally leaning back into her seat. "A lot of them come in asking really boring shit, and that's usually the best case."

Shaun scoffs.

"Yeah, and people wonder why we don't talk to the press. I remember, we did an interview where one of these dudes kept calling her Olivia. We all kept trying to correct him, and he just kept doing it. He didn't even care."

"Asshole," Ophelia mutters. "He didn't even want to talk to me, you could tell he wasn't interested. He just zoned in on Damien the entire time, and of course Damien felt terrible. He kept trying to steer the interviewer to ask questions about the band instead of only him, but this dude just wouldn't stop."

Phoebe cringes.

"I've seen too many journos like that. They think the frontman is the heart of the band and the other members just fade away. It's bad practice."

"I mean fuck, if the Doors didn't have John Densmore, Robby Krieger, and Ray Manzarek, it would just be some dude onstage in leather pants rambling on about death and mescaline. Nobody would want to pay for that," Shaun replies.

Ophelia shakes her head and sighs.

"God, that's every frat party at NYU a couple hours in. Anyway, Shaun, you got any aces?"

"Go fish."

She crinkles up her nose and grabs another card.

Phoebe smiles.

"So, I know you guys are recording after the tour, but will you have any time to decompress? This stuff must be intense for you, being on the road so much."

Shaun nods.

"Sometimes, yeah. I mean, with these guys it's kinda like being on vacation, but it's still isolating in a way, you know? We've all got other friends back home who we miss, and family. It's hard being away from them. Whenever we're done I mostly just can't wait to get back and see my parents and my friends. God, I miss hanging out with my dog."

Ophelia pouts.

"I miss Duke!"

"Me too," Shaun sighs. He looks up at Phoebe. "He's a golden retriever. My dad found him, said I needed someone to play for who'd appreciate my sound."

Ophelia giggles.

"Now he just howls along whenever we jam at Shaun's place."

"Duke can belt those high notes. I keep telling Damien he's got competition."

The interview descends into friendly conversation, and Phoebe soon forgets the recorder is even running. She feels a sense of ease overtake her, just asking them both normal questions: their favorite bars, spots in New York, records. This is the part of her job that she loves the most, so much more than getting the perfect sound bite. She could write for hours, all just about their time playing cards.

If only she were this comfortable around Damien, able to just talk like people instead of sniping at each other. How much longer will she be able to put up with his condescending attitude before she explodes? How many more times can he invade her thoughts before she's forced to give in?

Hello, I Love You

PORTLAND, OREGON

"Okay! Welcome to Portland, ladies and germs! Everyone up and off the bus!"

Phoebe lifts her head and blinks as Troy's booming voice pulls her from her hungover slumber. For a moment, she's a little confused, but quickly puts things together. After a few rounds of cards with Ophelia and Shaun, she'd returned to her seat, intent on adding some new pages to her growing pile of notes. Less than 10 minutes in, however, she quickly found herself nodding off. It wasn't long before she was fast asleep and, judging from the state of things, drooling on her notebook.

"Well, so much for that," She grumbles.

Glancing out the window, Phoebe sees some massive hotel she can't immediately place. It's not quite as nice as the ones in California, but it'll have a shower and a bed, and that's all she needs. She's the last one off the bus, stumbling a little on her way down the stairs, and finding Troy waiting with her suitcase in hand. He smiles.

"How're you feeling, Miller?"

"A little less like death warmed over. But still pretty bad."

"Well, get as much rest as you can, the show is a little earlier tonight."

She frowns. She wanted to nap in a real bed, at least for a while. Something about the bus made it impossible to relax.

"What time is the show?"

"Starting right at 8. We're here for three days, playing two shows, and you guys get one day off, so if you want to do some touristy stuff, that'll be tomorrow."

Phoebe nods. It'll be nice to actually have a day specifically for R&R, or at least some focused writing time.

In the lobby, Troy makes a beeline for the front desk as Phoebe wanders off to the side, finding Damien silently reading alone. As she sits down next to him, he holds out a pack of cigarettes without even looking up.

"I'm fine," she murmurs.

"You sure?"

"Yeah." She smiles awkwardly. "Thanks, though."

He lights one up before stuffing them back into his jeans and quietly returns to his book. Maybe it's the exhaustion, or just the silence, but she feels a little more comfortable around him. Maybe they still had a shot, to be friends at least.

Off in the corner of the lobby she spots Ophelia giggling as Shaun whispers something in her ear. They're both very... engaged in the moment.

"Wait, are they together?" She asks offhandedly.

Damien looks up.

"Oh, those two? Hard to say, really. They had a thing when we were all teenagers, and sometimes when we're on the road it sparks up again. Pretty sure it's mostly casual, though, and it's kind of a secret."

"Does it affect the band?"

He shrugs, clearly not too worried about the subject.

"If it ever does, we could just pull a Fleetwood Mac and write our version of Rumours. Maybe win a fuckin' Grammy."

Phoebe chuckles, but the conversation is cut short by the sound of a clearly aggravated Troy struggling to keep calm.

"That's impossible, we booked the whole floor!"

"I'm sorry, sir, but there are renovations... we've had to shut down all access to the tenth floor."

"You've gotta be kidding me," Troy mumbles.

Phoebe can almost see the vein in the side of his neck pulsing as he glares at the concierge. There's a moment where she thinks he's going to jump the desk, but thankfully he relents, sighing and shaking his head. The man hands him a few room keys, giving him yet another apology which Troy ignores as he gathers everyone together.

"Alright kids, I have good news and bad news."

"Do the bad news first," Shaun tells him.

"Yeah, just kick us right in the balls," Ophelia says wryly.

Troy chuckles and takes his sunglasses off, hanging them on the collar of his t-shirt.

"The bad news is, there are renovations on the tenth floor. The whole thing. Said renos, *apparently*, won't be finished until the day after we leave." He pointedly turns back towards the concierge, who takes the opportunity to busy himself with the phone. "The good news is that you're all about to get a lot closer. Literally. Because we only have two rooms."

"You're holding three keys," Ophelia points out, raising her eyebrows.

Troy looks around sheepishly.

"Am I?" He laughs. "Right. Sorry. I have my own room. The five of you can fight for who gets to sleep where."

"Wait, what about the bus?" Johnny asks.

"Like I told you before, we can't be on that bus unsupervised, liability and all that. Anyway, that poor man's earned a break from you lunatics."

"What about another hotel?" Phoebe asks, her voice a little desperate. The logistics are starting to dawn on all of them.

"Pre-paid, little lady," Troy replies. "Besides, most of them are booked up. Some conference or something. But like I said, it's a good thing! It's bonding! Builds character, you know, all that shit."

Troy slips his key in his pocket and walks straight to the elevator.

"Shit," Johnny mumbles.

"This is fine," Shaun laughs. "We did this a bunch in the early days, remember?"

"Yeah, it was for a month, and then we all decided to pay for our own rooms," Ophelia remarks. "Because this one –" she points at Damien, "is so goddamn loud."

Damien smirks and wiggles his eyebrows.

"Alright, alright, stop living in the past. How's this, Johnny and I can take a room and the three of you can have the other one. Simple."

"Nope," Johnny says, shaking his head. "Not happening. I love you, dude, but I'd actually like to get some sleep after the show tonight."

"I'll behave," Damien tells him.

Johnny rolls his eyes.

"Heard that before."

"Why doesn't Damien just take one room and the rest of us can split the other one?" Phoebe asks.

"Fuck no!" Shaun exclaims. "You give Bell a room of his own and his ego will get even bigger. Someone has to suffer to keep him in check."

"What do you mean?" Damien asks, batting his eyelashes. "I'm the lead singer. don't I deserve my own room?"

"Guys, come on. Not now," Ophelia mumbles.

"Okay, okay!" Shaun exclaims. "I got an idea. We play odds and evens. One round. Odd numbers split a room, even numbers split the other one. Where we end up is where we end up. Sound fair?"

Everyone nods and Phoebe feels a surge of anxiety. Her hands begin to sweat.

"Okay." Shaun sticks his fist out. "And we're agreed we're sticking with the outcome, right?"

"Right," they all say in unison. It's like the playground all over again.

"One... two... three... shoot!"

Phoebe looks around the circle. She's holding out two fingers, and so is Damien. Her heart racing, she glances around at the others. Ophelia's showing three, Johnny's showing one, and Shaun's flipping everyone off.

He snickers.

"Just for the record, it still counts."

"Oooooh!" Damien chuckles. "Tough luck, Miller."

"Best two out of three?" Phoebe asks, hoping against hope.

"'Fraid not," Shaun says before his face turns solemn and serious. "We all agreed to abide by these rules, and by these rules we shall abide." He pats her on the shoulder, handing her the key with a big goofy smile.

"Don't worry, you'll survive. And remember, it builds character!"

As the rest of the band heads off to the elevator, Damien wraps an arm around her shoulder, grinning from ear to ear.

"What are the odds, huh?"

"You planned this," Phoebe mumbles. "I don't know how, but–"

"How could I have planned this? It's nothing but a lovely coincidence, Miller!"

He steps back and extends his hand. She can hear his bracelets jingling softly.

"Look, I promise, I will be a perfect gentleman for three whole days. No girls, no sex, no bullshit. You can work on your article, and I'll work on my music."

She stares at him, eyes narrowed in suspicion.

"Really?"

"Absolutely! Hell, I might even give you that interview you want so badly."

She sighs.

"Fine."

He flashes her an enormous smile, taking her hand in his.

"Friends?"

Even as almost every fiber of her being screams at her to not trust him, a little hope pushes through. Maybe they can make the best of a shitty situation.

"Friends."

Damien seems pleased with himself as they head upstairs. His hands are full, carrying her bags along with his own. It's a perfect addition to his newfound chivalry. As Phoebe swings the door open, and Damien saunters in, she pauses for a moment, as if entering the room could have some sort of lasting consequence. Damien drops their bags at the front door and collapses onto the couch. He looks up at her standing still in the doorway as she nervously glances around.

"I'll take the couch, don't worry."

"Oh, uh... we can swap one of the nights," she offers.

"Sure."

Phoebe gets to work setting up her typewriter and her notes. She was planning to call Janis, but that seems to be off the table with Damien here for three days.

"How's the hangover?" Damien asks. He's on the couch, stretching himself out like a cat as he reads his book.

"Fine."

He nods, seemingly content with her curt response, but it's only a minute or two before he pipes up again.

"You wanna get something to eat?"

After the conversation this morning, she seriously considers saying no. They shouldn't be pushing this boundary. But the reality is that they're already going to be in close quarters for three days. How much worse could dinner make it?

"Did you have something in mind?" Phoebe asks, the words falling out along with a soft sigh.

Damien smiles mischievously.

"Room service, compliments of Mr. Sullivan."

She shakes her head. She's barely spent a dime since she's been with them.

"I'll pay for my half."

"Nope," he replies.

"You can't be serious."

He stares at her.

"I said no."

"Fine," she counters, a hand on her hip. She might as well get something out of this arrangement. "Then I get that interview, you said it was on the table."

He sticks out his hand without any hesitation.

"Deal."

Phoebe smiles as they shake, relieved to have gained at least a little bit of ground. When the food arrives he places the conspicuous bottle of wine off to the side before diving into a fresh burger.

"Alright," his mouth is so full she can barely make out the words. "Feel free to ask me anything you like."

She sighs, pulling out her recorder. He's sitting on the couch, practically half the room away.

"I don't think it's going to pick up the audio, you're too far."

He shrugs.

"You could just say you want to get closer to me, Miller. We should be honest with each other."

She stares at him silently, an unimpressed expression painting her face.

He swallows his food and nods to himself.

"Right. Professional."

"I'd appreciate it."

She'd rather not spend the entire time keeping him in line, they'd never get anything done that way. He plops down next to her on the bed, burger in hand, and Phoebe presses the record button. Damien looks down at his food with a profound look of sadness on his face.

She snorts.

"You know you can eat while we talk, it's not a radio show."

He brightens up immediately.

"You sure?"

"Yeah," she laughs. "Transcription's easy, won't be a problem."

"Good, I'm still fuckin' starving," he growls, taking a big chunk out of the second burger before motioning for her to begin.

She'll give him an easy one to start, something to warm him up a little. When she was formulating these questions, she wanted to steer clear of his image. She's curious about him as an artist, his writing process, not the media circus that surrounds him.

"So, Damien, you write a lot of love songs, or at least ones that could be interpreted as love songs."

He barely looks up from his burger, just a quick glance.

"Uh-huh."

"Is that a topic you're particularly interested in exploring through your writing?"

"It is."

She's got to dig into him a little, make him want to respond with more than a couple words.

"Why?" She asks pointedly. "Nothing wrong with it, but some people could call the subject cliché."

He laughs, wiping the burger grease onto his shorts and leaving a dark stain behind on the denim.

"Look, being in love is the best part of being human. It's a rush, like getting high on another person. Their mind, their soul, what makes them angry, what makes them passionate. You get to know what's in their mind: their hopes, their fears, what turns them off and on..."

He bites his lip as he stares at her. He looks hungry, and the burger's not long for this world. Phoebe's eyes flick toward the window, trying to ignore the heat growing under her skin.

Mercifully, he looks away.

"Being in love is one of the best things in the world."

Time to change the subject.

"What's the *best* thing in the world, then?"

He leans back in, a little closer than before, eyes sparkling.

"I don't think you could write my answer in a magazine. Not the one you work for at least."

Phoebe almost bursts out laughing from the bluntness. He's so brazen about it. God, maybe they should just deal with the tension that's clearly mounting between them. It could be a one-time thing. The others are way down the hall. Troy is God knows where. They could just... do it.

And then what would happen? Would things get even more awkward than they already are? She's already been forced to abandon the "don't get too close" rule. It's just not working.

Even Troy said that's not how they operate. They're like a family and, in the few days she's been with them, they made her a part of it.

"Have you ever been in love?" He asks, cutting right to the center of it.

"I'm asking the questions."

But she wants to tell him.

"Come on. Just gimme this one."

She sighs, practically whispering the word.

"Yes."

He stares at her, frowning slightly.

"You're still raw about it."

Phoebe scoffs. She finally unwraps her burger, taking a bite.

"You can't tell that from a look."

Damien flashes a cheeky grin.

"Miller, I don't need to look at you to know what you're about."

"Oh really, I'm just an open book, huh?"

Damien nods.

He's bluffing, pushing her to break first. So much of this feels like him playing some kind of long game.

"Alright, moving on," He straightens up, striking a professional pose. "Ask me another one."

She sighs.

"Why are you so open with me? I've read the other interviews you've done and you barely ever say anything that isn't a joke or an insult."

He raises his eyebrows, chuckling.

"Like I said back on the bus, I respect you as a journalist, but I really do hate most of them."

"Why?"

"Too many asinine questions about stupid bullshit that doesn't matter. Who I'm fucking, how much I'm drinking, my antics, you know the type. They think my life is a fucking circus, and so I've embraced it. That's all they care about, but it's probably the least interesting thing about me."

Damien reaches over, plucking a french fry off of the plate that sits between them.

"I just appreciate you asking about shit that matters."

She grins.

"Don't worry, even if you *were* nothing but a circus, I could still say some nice things about the other guys."

Over the next half hour of shooting questions back and forth at each other, the interview shifts into something else entirely. They're just talking, about anything and everything, and she's amazed by how effortless it all is.

They talk about their favorite bars.

They talk about their favorite bands and albums.

They even talk about their friends back home.

"Is Janis as uptight as you?" Damien teases.

Phoebe laughs.

"Hey, I'm not that bad."

"I dunno, you're a little bit of a square, Miller," he tells her, scrunching up his nose.

She shrugs.

"Honestly, I think you might have to be in this line of work. It's so easy to get wrapped up in all the stuff that's going on, better to just avoid it entirely."

"Hey, I didn't say it was a bad thing. We need people like you to balance shit out. What would the world be like if everyone was as cool as me?"

"I don't like to think of a world without a future."

Damien's jaw falls open, his eyes wide.

"What?! Miller's got *jokes*!"

She smiles to herself, internally putting another mark in the 'wins' column.

"Circling back, no, Janis is not as *uptight* as I am. She does have her shit together, though."

Damien rolls onto his back and stares up at the ceiling.

"Where's the fun in having it all together?"

"I think stability can be good."

"Yeah, if you're 80," he laughs. "That's not what I'm looking for at all."

He shifts onto his side, looking up at her from the bed.

"How about you, Miller, what are you looking for?"

"I don't know," she whispers. "I thought I'd have it all figured out by now."

She stares into his eyes for a few moments too long before looking away. Damien seems like he's about to say something, but he's cut off by a loud knock at the door.

"Shit," he groans. "5 bucks says I know who that is."

He rolls off the bed and heads to the door, cracking it open slightly, and Troy immediately pushes his way in, craning his neck to see inside.

"Where's Miller?"

"Here!" Phoebe calls out, nervously raising her hand like she's back in grade school. This could look *very* bad.

Troy's eyes bounce suspiciously between the two of them as Damien stands in his way.

"So, you two are sharing a room?"

"We got screwed in a game of odds and evens," Damien replies.

Troy's stare is suffocating, but Phoebe keeps her expression as neutral as possible. Damien drums his fingers along his crossed arms, still markedly placing himself between Troy and the rest of the room.

"Anything else we can do for you?"

Troy huffs.

"Be downstairs in an hour to head to sound check."

His eyes linger on them, as though he's trying to gather as much information as possible before he turns and leaves. This could be annoying. She thought she left her overprotective dad at home for this assignment.

Damien shuts the door, chuckling to himself before turning back to Phoebe.

"He's a real pain sometimes." He shakes his head and sighs. "Anyway, you wanna shower first?"

She blinks.

"Uh, shower...?"

"Yeah, do you wanna use the shower first, or second?"

She turns her head slightly with a little smile to herself. Of course he didn't mean together. Even he's not that brazen.

"Oh, yeah, that'd be great. I won't be too long."

Phoebe heads into the bathroom with an armful of clothes. She showers, mulling over the afternoon as she shampoos her hair. It went better than she expected, and so far this whole sharing a room thing isn't so bad. She's getting somewhere with him, or at the very least she's getting more comfortable.

She quickly towels off, drying her hair and pulling it back into a ponytail. She throws together a casual look for the show: black jeans with the knees blown out and a Queen t-shirt that she's cut off to expose a bit of skin.

She takes a moment to look at herself in the mirror, smiling at the result.

Maybe the next three days will be okay after all.

Phoebe steps out into the main room, gesturing to the open door.

"Bathroom's all yours."

He nods, looking her up and down as he moves by.

"Cool look, Miller."

He takes much longer than she did, but when he emerges she can't help but stare. His hair is blow-dried, and his eyes are perfectly smeared with that black eyeliner. He's sporting a combo of black jeans and a leather jacket, his dog tags twinkling underneath the lights, offset by his bare chest.

"How do I look?"

Delicious, she thinks.

"Like a rock star."

"Perfect," he replies as he slides his feet into his boots. "You ready?"

She nods and he pushes the door open.

"Après-vous, Madame Miller."

Except he butchers the pronunciation, and it comes out as 'aprezz-voooz.'

At least he tried.

"Your French is atrocious," she laughs. She's feeling more and more at ease with him. He raises his arms, shouting as he runs ahead to the elevator.

"What the hell d'you expect, babydoll? I'm from Brooklyn!"

Her stomach flutters at the affectionate nickname, it's more comfortable now, somehow warmer.

"Hey so, thanks for taking a chance on me today," he mumbles as he looks up at the floors counting down.

God, he's cute.

"Well, thanks for the interview," she just barely manages to get out.

His smile is enough to make her knees wobble.

"Any time. Just for you, though." He winks. "Can't let the rest of the journos realize I'm not just a walking train-wreck."

The energy at Satyricon is electric, and Phoebe can almost feel the pulse of the crowd as they drive around the back. On the ride over Troy had told them it was one of the most popular punk venues in the city, a real up-and-comer, and Damien ate that shit up. The band is in high spirits as they reach the hall to the dressing room, just in time to see a man exit from a room across the way. He has short blonde hair and stands slightly taller than Phoebe, smiling politely as the rowdy group passes by before frowning quizzically at the sight of her. He looks as if he's trying to solve a little puzzle, and Phoebe places the final piece as her jaw drops.

"Oh my god, Lukas?"

His face lights up in recognition and his smile returns.

"Mouse?"

"*Mouse?*" Damien whispers. "The fuck?"

"Lukas, what the hell are you doing here?!" Phoebe squeals, rushing toward him as he wraps her in a gentle hug and kisses her cheek.

It had been six months ago in London, a week-long festival. He was a concert promoter and she was there as press. She immediately noticed his long fur coat and ridiculous choice in shoes, and they quickly hit it off, sharing a few drinks throughout the week. They had planned to go out for a real date following the end of the show, but a last minute adjustment meant she had to fly back to New York a day early. She was the mouse that scurried away.

"I'm here managing the opening act," he says, glancing around, "and you are here with..."

Troy steps forward, cutting right through their conversation.

"Troy Sullivan, Revolver. You manage Soldat, right?"

"That is correct," Lukas replies. "It's a pleasure to meet you, Mr. Sullivan."

As Troy introduces each member of the band, Damien's expression is almost unreadable. His jaw is slightly clenched, his mouth in a firm line. The only thing Phoebe can detect is the smallest flicker of jealousy in his eyes.

"It is lovely to meet you all." He smiles. "We are just now finished with soundcheck, and so the stage is ready for you."

She had forgotten how quirky his English was, his phrasing too proper, all with his noticeable German accent punching through.

"Great," Troy replies. "Well, we should get to it."

He ushers the band into the dressing room, but Lukas grabs Phoebe's hand before she can follow them in. She whirls around, almost bumping right into his chest. His soft amber eyes twinkle under the lights of the hallway, contrasting his high cheekbones that lend a certain sharpness to his face. His beard, slightly darker than his blonde hair, offsets his full lips, which curl into a smile that could make her melt. Nothing about him has really changed in their time apart. He's even still dressed in that same outrageous coat with the fur lining on the collar. Always dressed for winter, even when it's only fall.

"It is good to see you, Phoebe."

"Good to see you too, Lukas."

He smiles softly.

"I should ask again, what are you doing here?"

"Oh, I'm on assignment for Titanium."

"Very exciting," he purrs. "How long will you be staying?"

"Three days."

He smiles.

"Would you like to get a drink, perhaps after the show? To catch up?"

The perfect distraction from Damien.

"It's a date."

He reaches out to brush away a piece of lint from her jacket and gently caresses her arm in the process.

"I am looking forward to it."

She blushes.

"Me too."

"Lukas!" Someone calls from the dressing room behind him.

He laughs, shaking his head in mild exasperation.

"Duty calls. I will see you after the show, Mouse."

"Yeah, see you," she breathes.

Phoebe watches as he disappears around the corner, lingering a little before turning back to the dressing room to find Damien standing in the doorway.

"Jesus!" She hisses, jumping back and laughing. "You scared me."

"Sorry." His voice is curt.

"I thought you were all on stage for soundcheck."

He shakes his head in response, saying nothing as Phoebe walks past him and into the dressing room. She can see him watching from his spot in the doorway as she hangs up her coat and fishes through her bag for her camera and notebook. She can hear the band yelling for him from the stage.

"You'd better get out there."

"In a minute," he says softly.

"What?" She laughs. "Don't tell me you've got stage fright now."

He walks toward her slowly, his gaze so intense she starts to feel that familiar fire in the pit of her stomach. He towers over her, staring her down.

"Something like that," he breathes.

In an instant, his hands are grasping the sides of her face, the pad of his thumb gliding along her lip. Her heart hammers against her ribs and she can barely breathe as he leans in a little closer. She's wanted this, pictured it for days now, and her single squeak of surprise when their lips meet quickly turns into a moan as a thousand watts of electricity shoot through her body. He tastes like menthol and a hint of tobacco.

One of his hands wraps around the back of her neck while the other swims through her hair, her own hand coming to rest on his bare chest, fingernails clawing softly at the skin. Damien pushes her backward so that she's pressed up against a countertop. His body is flush with hers and she can feel a distinct pressure against her thigh. Phoebe groans, letting the sheer pleasure of the moment overwhelm her until suddenly she realizes what the fuck she's doing – what they're doing. She breaks the kiss and pushes him backward causing Damien to stumble, his lips pink and swollen as his body is forced away from hers.

"We promised," she hisses.

Keep it professional. Just friends.

He stares at her, pupils blown out from the intensity of the moment.

"Guess we lied."

"BELL!" Troy's voice bellows through the halls, furious. "Soundcheck! *Now!*"

Damien walks out the door, leaving her alone in the dim light of the dressing room with her head in her hands, wanting to scream at him almost as much as she wants more.

Light My Fire

SATYRICON

"What the fuck?"

Phoebe slams her fist into the table. They had a deal. Friends. Now she has to go back to that godforsaken hotel tonight and sleep in the same room with him after the best kiss of her stupid fucking life.

"What the fuck?!"

Paranoia is already digging its claws into any sense of calm she still had a grasp on; he planned this, all of it. She shouldn't have had dinner with him, should have kept the interview brief. It's all fucked.

Tears of frustration sting her eyes as she looks for something, anything to distract her from this mess. Her eyes fall on a phone, off on the other side of the dressing room, and she slams the door shut, swearing at the lack of a lock. She crosses the room and dials the first number that comes to mind.

The phone rings.

It rings, and rings, and rings, and rings.

"Come on, Jan. Pick up."

She's got to be awake, it's only 11:00pm back in New York. Phoebe taps her foot impatiently, glancing over her shoulder every few seconds to that bastard of a door with no lock. She quickly loses track of the rings, staring blankly into the distance while trying to stop her mind from spinning out of control. She sighs and slams her palm against the wall.

"Come on, Jan! Fuck!"

Finally, there's a click, followed by an intake of breath. Please don't be her machine.

"Hullo?" Janis's voice sounds rough.

"Jan! It's me!"

"Ugh. Phoebe. What the hell do you want?"

"Crap, were you asleep?"

"Yeah," she groans. *"I leave for my trip tomorrow, remember?"*

"Shit," she whispers. "Sorry."

"No, no. What's up? You sound tense."

"I'm fucked!" Phoebe hisses, unable to hold back everything that's bubbling in her chest.

His lips were softer than she ever dreamt them. His kiss was gentle yet commanding, so fucking intense that it took her breath away. She felt safe even though her heart was thumping ten thousand beats per minute.

"What do you mean?" Janis asks. *"What's wrong?"*

"We kissed."

"What?"

"Yeah, me and Bell."

"When?"

"I dunno, like five minutes ago?"

Janis lets out a deep sigh.

"Pheebs, you can't do this again."

"I know!" She hisses, holding the receiver like she was choking the life out of it. "You don't think I know that?! *He* kissed *me–* well, he started– and I didn't– Do you hear what I'm saying to you?!"

"I don't even think you're hearing what you're saying."

Phoebe groans.

"You just got so bent out of shape last time."

"I know."

She didn't tell her just how hurt she was after things ended with Alex, but Janis knew just the same. She could always read Phoebe better than anyone.

"Well, was he at least a bad kisser? That would make me feel better."

Phoebe snorts and twirls the phone cord in her fingers.

"No. Fuck, Jan, it was amazing."

Janis lets out another long sigh.

"Well shit, Pheebs, you might be fucked."

She wants to be angry, but all she can do is laugh.

"Damnit, this sucks so much. I have no idea what to do and–" Phoebe shakes her head, still having a hard time processing everything. "I just wish you were here."

"Me too, someone needs to give him a smack upside the head."

Oh shit.

"Troy said if he found out anything was going on, he'd call Brian."

"Well fuck."

"Yeah."

"Do you think he knows? Or... is Damien going to tell him?"

The thought makes her queasy.

"I don't know, I– No I don't think so."

"So, okay, just assuming everything is fine for a moment, can I ask you something?"

"Yeah."

"Do you like him?"

No hesitation. It just comes out.

"I do."

"I mean for real, not just you like that he's extremely hot."

Phoebe sighs, remembering their conversation in the hotel room; how it made her feel when they opened up to each other.

"Earth to Phoebe! Look, I'm going to hang up this phone if you don't say something in 3, 2—"

"Yeah, it's real."

She starts running the whole thing back in her head.

"There's been some tension, not just the kiss. It definitely goes both ways."

"Sure. The guy practically drips sex. And you? You're cute, funny, smart, and you've got a little bit of that girl next door thing going on."

"The... girl next door thing?"

"Yeah," Janis laughs. *"You're an all-American girl! At least when you're not smoking, swearing, or drinking your face off."*

"That's just teenage rebellion," Phoebe replies.

"At twenty-three?"

"I'm a late bloomer."

Janis laughs.

"The way I see it, you have two options. One is the professional thing to do, and the other is a little more complicated."

"Lay 'em on me." She'll take anything that's not a whirlpool of angst at this point.

"Okay, option one: you could confront him. Lay out clear boundaries, only go to the shows and then go straight back to the bus or hotel once they're over."

Phoebe fiddles with the phone cord. It's good advice, but she's tried that one already.

"What's option two?"

"You could see where it goes."

Phoebe groans.

"I was hoping you'd have better suggestions."

"Unfortunately, I only have about two brain cells left right now and they both want to go to sleep. For the record, though, my money's on option two."

Phoebe's startled as the dressing room door swings open and Damien steps inside. She watches in silence as he saunters past her to a row of coats.

"I gotta go, Jan."

"Just fuck him, Pheebs. Get it out of your system."

She flushes, eyes darting between Damien and the floor. He couldn't have heard it, but...

"Okay, great, thanks! Call me when you land! Loveyoubye!"

She slams the receiver down far too hard and grimaces at the sound before turning back toward Damien. His eyes are already burning a hole right through her.

"Hey."

"Hi."

She braces, expecting him to move in on her, but he stands still by the coats.

"Smokes," he says, pulling them from a pocket and smiling halfheartedly. "Thought you'd be gone."

She shakes her head.

"I've got a job to do."

Her voice is hardened and icy.

Damien nods. He doesn't move.

"Can we talk after the show?"

There's a little waver in his voice. He's lost some of his confidence from before, and the awkwardness between them makes everything feel heavy.

"I'm having a drink with Lukas."

"After that then," he insists. "Back at the hotel."

She can sense the urgency in his voice, along with something new. It makes her even more nervous.

"No problem. We're in the same room anyway."

"Why does he call you Mouse?" He cuts in too quickly, barely letting her finish.

"Because I tend to be quiet and *mind my business*." There's more venom in the words than she intends, but maybe that's the kind of thing he needs to hear.

He clearly wants to retort, but stops himself, and Phoebe hears the whine of guitars from the stage. The pre-show's starting.

"You should get going," Phoebe says, with a coolness she isn't quite expecting.

Damien stands stock-still for an agonizingly long moment, before finally moving to the door.

"I'll see you out there?" He's waiting in the doorway, his back to her. There's that little waver in his voice, like he's a little nervous for the first time in a long while.

"It's my job."

Damien leaves without another word, and Phoebe finally lets herself relax, waiting a few minutes before heading out into the venue. This time, instead of watching from the side of the stage, she'll be watching from the audience. She tells herself it'll allow her to get new angles, shots that relay the real experience of being in the crowd. It's a lie, but it sounds great. As she settles in for the pre-show, she feels someone climb onto the bar-stool beside her.

"I think perhaps we don't have to wait." Lukas' voice catches her off guard. "Shall we grab that drink here?"

She smiles. Maybe this will help.

"Sounds great."

Soldat's lead singer is a woman with wild pink hair that's teased to high heaven, wearing big streaks of matching blush on her cheeks. Phoebe can't help but be impressed as she screams into the microphone. Their sound isn't particularly unique, but it's been well cultivated, and they put on a solid show. After listening to a couple songs in relative silence, she looks over to her new companion, who's proudly sipping his whisky as the crowd eats the band up.

"How have you been since we last talked?"

He was clearly waiting until she was ready. She'd forgotten how observant he was.

"Pretty good," she replies, grateful for the distraction. She finds herself quickly focusing in on his warm whiskey-colored eyes as he studies her face in turn. "Finally got out of writing album reviews."

"Good for you. You're building a more diverse portfolio."

She smiles. Talking to him was always so effortless.

"What about you? I thought you'd be promoting bands in London or Paris or something."

He shrugs.

"For them, the label came to me. I believe they have a good sound, but more importantly, it's been a long time since I've had a vacation." He laughs and shakes his head. "Of course this is still work, but it's at least a vacation away from the same old places."

"Well, I'm glad you decided to take the job."

"I am as well. I must admit, I wasn't expecting to see you here, but I'm glad we finally had the chance to get that drink."

Soldat's set is relatively short. They only play six songs, but they leave the crowd in high spirits, chanting for the main attraction. Phoebe takes a deep breath and Lukas elbows her gently.

"What is this, are you nervous for them?"

"No, why would I be–"

"I'm sorry Mouse, but you are a terrible liar."

Suddenly, Damien's voice cuts through everything.

"Hello, Portland. We're Revolver, and we'd like to play you some songs tonight."

He's sitting at a keyboard, looking melancholic. It's a little odd, as far as she knows, he's never played keyboard or piano on stage before.

"We never do this, but we're going to open with a cover, so enjoy the treat! He turns to Ophelia with a grin. "It's all you, baby."

The song begins with a snare drum hit, followed by a keyboard introduction that she recognizes instantly. They're playing Light My Fire by The Doors. The cover is wailing and beautiful, and all their own. Phoebe watches with bated breath as Damien begins to sing, his eyes locking with hers the moment the first words leave his lips. She drains her drink, and Lukas leans toward her.

"Can I get you another?"

"Please," she rasps.

He studies her for a moment, brushing a stray bit of hair behind her ear.

"You seem preoccupied."

"I'm sorry," she breathes. "I promise I'm not."

He grins.

"The look in your eyes says otherwise."

Phoebe stares at Lukas. She needs someone, anyone, to take her mind off of him, off the way she can feel him staring at her right now. He's ignoring every single person in the crowd, every screaming fan throwing their clothing on the stage, just to capture her attention.

"Kiss me."

He tilts his head.

"Am I kissing you because you want *me*, or am I kissing you to distract you from something else?"

"A bit of both," she confesses.

Lukas brushes her cheek.

"I do not think that a kiss right now would be appropriate, Mouse. As much as I would like to."

"Not even a little one?" she asks, half joking at this point.

He leans over, laying a single kiss on her cheek.

"I think your mind is on someone else."

Phoebe looks up at the stage, and sure enough Damien's eyes haven't left her.

"It's that obvious, huh?" she laughs.

"He seems very protective of you."

Subtlety is not his strong suit.

"Well, he doesn't own me."

Lukas smiles.

"A real kiss then."

He gently presses his lips to hers. They're so soft, almost silky. When she opens her mouth for more, he pulls away.

"Teasing," she giggles.

"That's the goal," he purrs. "But I think it will not work, even if you liked it."

"Why not?"

"Because your mind is clearly elsewhere, Mouse. You're only half here with me tonight." He smiles wryly. "But also, and perhaps equally importantly, because Damien Bell looks like he wants to punch a hole through my skull."

"Are you sure you don't want to just fuck me against the wall of this bar?" She asks. "Take my mind off of him?"

He throws his head back and laughs.

"I would love to, Phoebe," he replies. "But it's not the right thing to do, not tonight."

The rest of the night is a mix of pleasantries and work, all intermingled with drinks and Damien's constant stare. Finally the band finishes up their set, and Phoebe is able to turn back to Lukas uninterrupted. As the crowd disperses, she half expects Damien to storm out, or to call her backstage. But the moment never comes.

The two of them share a few more drinks, until eventually she spots Damien and the rest of the band leaving the bar. He waves, raising his eyebrows as if he's beckoning her to follow. She holds up her half-full drink in answer.

"Do you have to go?" Lukas asks.

"No, not yet."

Damien can sweat it out a little longer.

They linger until the bartender announces last call. She'd loved chatting with Lukas, but there was also something appealing about ignoring a problem and just hoping it would go away.

"Scheisse." Lukas flinches as he glances at his watch. "Ah, Mouse, maybe in a different time or place, we could have been something."

She smiles, a little sadly.

"Do we really have to close that door?"

He kisses her on the cheek.

"I'll see you on the next tour."

The cab ride is a blur, but she manages to hold it together, reaching the hotel sometime around 3AM. Things are a little hazy, and she has to dig out her room key to confirm she's on the 11th floor, testing a few of the locks before she gets the right one.

As she walks in, she finds Damien at the desk with her typewriter, a bottle of whiskey clutched in his fist.

"Damien?"

He lifts his head and scowls at her.

"Didn't think you'd be home."

Phoebe frowns, she finds something about the word *home* unsettling.

"You wanted to talk?"

"Yeah."

He stands, stumbling immediately as he tries to take a step toward her.

She might not be in the best shape, but he's barely functioning.

"And you're wasted."

She crosses her arms over her chest and he laughs.

"Well, you were gone for like five hours, what was I supposed to do?"

Phoebe scoffs.

"I had drinks with Lukas for *a couple of* hours, and now we can't even talk. I mean look at you."

"We can talk."

Maybe they should. He's probably not going to remember this in the morning, but this might be her only chance.

"Why did you kiss me?"

"I wanted to," he replies, taking another swig from the bottle. "That was easy, come on, ask me more."

"No, that's not it. Tell me the truth."

"Because I saw his fucking hands on you, and I–" Damien cuts himself off and shakes his head. "And you kissed me back."

"Damien, you're really drunk. I don't think–"

"Fine!" He exclaims, throwing his hands in the air. "I'll go fuck off to the other room!"

If they end the night mad, there's a chance they never fix things. Maybe he pulls away and she never gets another interview. Maybe they never get to really talk again. But she was getting somewhere. *They* were getting somewhere.

She puts a hand on his arm as he grasps the door handle.

"Wait."

He turns around, his usually bright eyes dulled by melancholy.

"You're right. I did kiss you back."

He blinks a few times, not fully there.

"Could you stay? We can talk more in the morning, when we're both less fucked up?"

"You want me to stay?"

"Please."

He stares at her in silence for a while.

Maybe it's too late. Maybe he's done with her.

Maybe–

"Okay. I'll stay."

He walks past her toward the couch.

"Mind if I take one of the pillows?" He asks.

"Oh! Uh, yeah, yeah that's fine."

Damien smiles as she hands him one, along with a blanket. He gets comfortable, stretching himself out as she heads to the bathroom. Shutting the door behind her, she breathes a small sigh of... relief? Exhaustion? Both feel pretty appropriate right now. As she brushes her teeth she tries not to think too hard about the conversation she knows is coming in the morning.

Stepping back out into the dim light of the main room, she can see Damien's dragged the couch just a few inches away from the bed.

"Felt kinda lonely over there."

She smiles, saying nothing as she climbs into bed, turning to face him. He's already looking at her, the normal shine returned to his eyes.

"Thanks, Phoebe."

As his eyelids flutter closed, she can't help but ask the question that's been lingering in her mind for days now.

"Damien?"

"Hmm?"

"What are we doing?"

He smiles.

"I have no fucking idea."

Dream a Little Dream of Me

PORTLAND, OREGON

Sun spills in through the crack in the curtain, filling the room with a beautiful golden hue. Phoebe opens her eyes cautiously, ready for the sharp pain of a hangover, but only finds the empty couch beside her. She groans.

There's pressure on her body. It takes her a few seconds to realize there's an arm wrapped around her waist and warm breath on the back of her neck. She's struggling to take in her surroundings. She's definitely still in the hotel room, but her vision is blurry. Must be the booze. When she looks down, she sees a small black elastic band wrapped around a thick wrist, and attached to a large hand. She smells his cologne as she breathes softly, turning her head as silently as possible just in time to find Damien already waking up.

"Hi," he mutters, rubbing his eyes.

Phoebe rolls over to face him. His arm doesn't leave its place around her waist. He has a sleepy expression, a half-smile covering his face.

"I thought we were going to talk," she whispers.

"We can't talk like this?"

"It's a little closer than I would have liked," Phoebe replies.

Damien leans in, his lips hovering over hers.

"How's this?"

"It's–"

His mouth cuts off the rest of her sentence and she moans, her hands roaming all over his body with a mind of their own. Damien tugs on her bottom lip with his teeth and fireworks go off in the back of her brain. It's like he's flipped a switch, and she's instantly transformed into an insatiable beast.

She gasps, and he immediately takes the opportunity to slide his tongue against hers, pulling her on top of him in a single motion so that she's straddling his hips. He's rock-hard, and she absolutely doesn't need a visual to know he's huge. She pulls her mouth away from his, moaning at the pressure of his cock rocking against her clit. Even through two layers of fabric, it feels incredible. Damien looks up at her with a devilish expression on his face, his eyes flickering.

"Go on, babydoll," he purrs. "Grind on my cock."

She groans, trying to hold herself back.

He arches an eyebrow.

"You do want to, don't you? It's all you've been thinking about. Letting me touch you, fuck you, lick that gorgeous little pussy..."

She can't stop the moan that escapes her lips; why would she even want to anymore? He reaches up, grabbing the back of her neck and pulling her close, nipping at her ear.

"Show me what a dirty fuckin' girl you are."

Her eyes roll back at the gravel in his voice, all logic has gone out the window. Her hips move slowly at first, then wildly as if her body is completely beyond her control. Damien grips her waist with one hand while the other reaches up to pinch her nipples through the thin fabric of her shirt.

"You like that?"

She nods.

"You're soakin' wet, aren't you?"

"Yes," she breathes.

"Just for me, huh?"

She nods again, eyes closed, struggling to keep some measure of control. Her hips grind against him a little harder and she can't help but wish he was inside her. She's so close.

"I want you to say it," he demands.

"Yes, Damien!" She cries. "It's just for you!"

"Good girl."

Phoebe begins to shake, her orgasm just out of reach. She hears Damien groan as she rocks her hips faster and faster.

"Fuck, sweetheart, you look so good doing that. I can't wait to bend you over that desk and fuck you nice and slow." Phoebe gasps as he begins to take control, gripping her ass and guiding her movements. "Until tears stream down that pretty little face of yours and you can't fuckin' take it anymore."

"Damien," she breathes.

"You'd like that, wouldn't you?"

A jolt of electricity shoots down her spine and she feels herself tumbling over the edge. She didn't even realize she was this sensitive.

"Yes. Oh, God, Damien! I'm coming!"

"Atta girl," he growls.

She arches her back, completely losing herself in the moment, but suddenly there's a voice. Disembodied. Familiar. She can't tell where it's coming from, but it's calling her name.

It sounds like Damien, but when she looks down at him, he's gone.

Phoebe gasps as she feels something brush her arm, and the next thing she knows she's back in the hotel bed with nothing but the blankets wrapped around her.

"Phoebe?" The voice asks, slightly muffled. "You good?"

She blinks, adjusting to both the violent light and the agonizing change of pace. Damien is towering over her, his toothbrush in his mouth. She stares at him in confusion for a few moments, and then it hits her.

"M'good," she mumbles.

It was a fucking dream.

"You were tossing and turning. I was gonna let you sleep, but it looked like you were having a nightmare."

Her face reddens as she looks up at him, trying to force a laugh.

"Something like that."

"There's breakfast," he says, gesturing to the room service cart. "They're not New York bagels, but they're pretty good."

Phoebe sighs, sitting up and stretching her arms as she takes stock of the situation. Does he even remember last night? He was drunk as hell. They both were. As she shifts a little she realizes the underwear she wore to bed is soaked from her dream. It felt so real. His hands, his lips, his... everything. It was all so perfect. She grabs a bagel and finds herself lost in thought as Damien strolls back into the bathroom. Why is her brain doing this to her? Maybe Janis was right, just fuck him and get it over with.

Damien's voice echoes out from the bathroom.

"You wanna go for a walk? There's a park near here, uh, Tabor or something? It looked pretty nice on the brochures downstairs. There's a mountain and shit."

She chews her bagel. Maybe he doesn't remember what he said, or what they fought about. Or maybe he just wants to forget about the whole thing.

"Sure. I just have to get ready."

"Take your time," Damien says softly as he wanders back into the room, dropping down onto the couch in a Led Zeppelin t-shirt and tight blue jeans.

Phoebe escapes to the newly freed-up bathroom to shower and change. It's quick, as she makes absolutely certain to keep focused, snapping herself away from brief moments of wandering thoughts and hands. After only a few minutes she steps back out again in a red t-shirt and a black denim skirt. Damien is standing beside the desk, his fingertips just barely touching it. He glances up at her as she enters, looking like he's working up the courage to say something, but Phoebe's afraid to bring anything up herself. He's being so nice to her, and she kind of doesn't want that to stop. She grabs her camera on the way to the door. Maybe he'll let her snap some photos of him. Harmless.

"Ready to go?"

"Yeah," she replies.

"Cool."

They're both walking on eggshells.

Portland is beautiful, a broad mixture of trees, cityscape, and mountains. The fresh air feels great on her face, and it's probably doing her hangover some good as well. She looks up at the man walking beside her, his perfect hair blowing in the breeze, sunglasses hiding his eyes away from the world. As they walk somewhat aimlessly, his head bobs left and right with quiet curiosity before stopping in front of a thrift store.

"You wanna go in? I need to pick up some new clothes for the show tomorrow."

She tilts her head with a little smile.

"I figured you'd go to a boutique."

"Nah, that ain't me. Come on, these places always have some great stuff."

He takes her hand and leads her inside. Why hasn't he brought up the kiss? Or the million other things that happened last night?

They browse the racks as hair metal crackles of the speakers. The place is cute, and the staff look cool. They're all bored punks with brightly colored hair, patchwork jackets, and dark makeup. The shop isn't very well organized, with different sorts of clothing all mixed together, but Damien doesn't seem to care about that. As he picks out a bunch of clothes, she has to snap herself out of imagining the two of them pressed against each other in one of the tiny changing rooms.

Phoebe pushes a few shirts aside on a rack to reveal a very pretty pale blue sundress with a sweetheart neckline. It's very 1950s, not something she would normally pick, but the color and fabric are gorgeous. She could put her jacket over it and wear her combat boots to make it more her thing, but she has enough clothes. Besides, Brian won't reimburse her for this stuff.

Damien leans over and looks at the dress.

"Pretty."

"Yeah," she sighs. "Unfortunately, I'm not on vacation, so..."

"I'll buy it for you."

He's beaming at her.

"Damien, it's okay. I don't even know what I'd wear it with."

It's a lie, but sometimes those make things easier.

He grabs the dress off the rack and drapes it over his arm, turning in time to stop her before she can protest.

"Please, let me buy it for you."

The unsaid *as an apology* hangs thick in the air between them.

He's trying.

"Okay, sure."

"Now that wasn't so hard, was it?" He teases.

She rolls her eyes, and he struts toward the front counter.

"Aren't you going to try your stuff on?" Phoebe asks.

"I know my measurements," he replies. "Besides, when you look like this everything fits."

"Alright, alright, rein it in hotshot."

Damien dumps the clothes on the counter and grins at two staff members, who stare at him with mild panic in their eyes.

"Hey!" Damien exclaims. "How ya doin'?"

A girl with short green hair pipes up first.

"You're Damien Bell!"

"In the flesh, doll."

The similar nickname gives Phoebe butterflies as she remembers her dream.

"Go on, babydoll. Grind on my cock."

She takes a deep breath, looking down at the floor.

"Hey, you guys fucking killed it last night!" The other punk exclaims. "That set was solid, man!"

"Thanks," he chuckles. "We're playing tomorrow night at the Sapphire Hotel. You should get tickets if you can."

"Already got 'em, man – hey, when's the new album coming?"

Damien digs his wallet out of the back pocket of his jeans.

"We're actually heading into the studio on the back end of this tour, so it won't be too long after that."

The two punks are having the time of their lives, and it's sweet seeing Damien like this, having real and genuine conversations with his fans for the first time the entire tour. As the green-haired girl rings through the clothing, her eyes find Phoebe's every once in a while, filled with curiosity. She's probably trying to work out if they're together, and Phoebe makes sure that there's distance between her and Damien. She doesn't need to spark any rumors.

After signing a few autographs, Damien waves the store a dramatic goodbye and the two of them head back into the street.

They walk a block or so in silence before Phoebe decides to pipe up.

"That was really nice of you."

He nods a little, less a confirmation and more an acknowledgement.

"Well, without the fans, I wouldn't have this job. In my experience, most of them are actually really cool people."

He pauses, smirking.

"And yeah, there are always a few weirdos, but why let them ruin things for everyone else?"

Over the next couple hours they hit a few more stores, with Damien signing autographs here and there. A very starstruck girl on the street gets a kiss on the cheek, blushing furiously before skittering away. Phoebe knows the feeling. Luckily, the fans seem to run out, with nobody around to bother them as they make their way into the park.

It's a gorgeous place, filled with lush trees and a grid of open air reservoirs. Phoebe glances up at the sky to find the sun shining down on them among a few lingering clouds. The walk up to the summit is pleasant enough in the first half, with lovely views and little breaks to snap a picture here and there, but by the final quarter Phoebe is sweating bullets. At first she figures it must be all the cigarettes and beer, but second guesses herself as Damien sprints ahead of her, reaching the top while she's still struggling below.

What in the world is fuelling that monster?

"Come on, Miller! Push it!"

"Go," she heaves. "Fuck. Yourself."

His laughter booms over her and he howls into the sky like a wolf. Phoebe tries to make a face at him as she finally reaches the top, but she doubles over wheezing instead.

Damien smirks.

"Don't worry. Going down will be easier."

She forces herself up just so she can roll her eyes, dropping back down to catch her breath. The view from the summit is beautiful, made even more sweet by the fact that it's just the two of them up there. She can see most of the neighborhood below, with little people milling here and there, and after taking in the view for a while, the two sit on a bench.

Damien pulls out a pack of cigarettes.

"Want one?"

Why not, she's not going to be a mountain climber overnight.

"Sure."

They smoke in silence for a while, taking in the beauty that's stretched out before them. But it's not long before Damien speaks up.

"I'm sorry about last night," he says. His voice is pinched with regret.

She swallows hard.

"You remembered."

"Yeah," he rasps. "I, uh, I regret it."

Her heart sinks a little.

"All of it?"

He smiles, turning to her.

"No, not everything, just—"

"Me neither, not everything."

He stares at her, crushing the cigarette butt with his boot heel. His gaze is magnetic.

"There's something here, Phoebe. Between us. I don't know what it is, but you feel it too, right?"

"Yeah," she whispers, putting her cigarette out on the bench. "I do."

"Doesn't it drive you fucking crazy?"

"It does."

She can't even tell him how true that is.

He sighs.

"Look, when I saw you with that Lukas guy last night, kissing him and flirting with him... and when I saw you dancing with that dude at the bar the night before, I just... I wanted it to be me. And I'm sort of used to getting what I want."

"Perks of being a rock star?"

He laughs.

"It's a bit of a character flaw, actually. Look, I know that you have a job to do. You're not here to fuck around or whatever. I respect that." He puts his head in his hands. "God, I don't even know what I'm trying to say."

She's scared to meet his eyes, but she can't look away.

"You told me if I wanted to change... what we are to each other," she whispers. "That I could do that. That I could choose."

"Yeah. And then I..." he swirls his hand in the air as he lets out a hollow laugh. "Fucked it all up."

She takes a deep breath. She can't believe she's about to do this, all over again, especially understanding the inevitability of what comes in two months at the end of the tour. He'll leave. She'll cry. She'll call Janis, and watch Sixteen Candles on her couch with a pint of ice cream in one hand and a bottle of Jack Daniels in the other. Two weeks later, she'll go out to a bar, find some guy who sort of looks like Damien, and fuck him. It's her best and worst coping mechanism.

"I want to be with you. I want to try."

He perks up, his eyes wide.

"You do?"

"I do."

Damien smiles.

"What about your editor, he's a problem right?"

"I've hid stuff like this from him before. I can do it again."

He elbows her gently in the ribs.

"You sly little minx."

She stifles a giggle. Janis will be thrilled to hear that she was right about this. Then she'll be pissed that she has to listen to Phoebe pine over him once the tour is done. The end of this is going to suck, but she doesn't have to think about that right now.

"Okay, so what do we do about Troy?" He asks.

As much as Damien acts like he doesn't give a shit about Troy's opinion, she can see that deep down there's a mutual respect hidden under a hell of a lot of bullshit. It's almost a father son relationship... if you really squint and you're just a little bit desperate.

"I think he's suspected something since we started sharing a hotel room," Phoebe replies. "He's been pretty grumpy."

Damien sighs, leaning back onto the bench.

"Do you really think he would call your editor if he found out?"

She shakes her head.

"I think he's bluffing. If I get taken off of this assignment, they'll just replace me with Chris, who, if you don't know, is not such a big fan of you guys."

"That's the guy who trashed our album, right?" Damien asks.

"Yep."

He snarls.

"I hate that prick. I'm only a drunken clown *eighty* percent of the time."

She giggles, feeling much more at ease. Damien wraps an arm around her and pulls her close to him, nipping at her jawline.

"So what are we now?" His voice is a soft blanket, wrapping all around her.

"An experiment," she murmurs.

"An experiment?"

She nods, leaning in to kiss him.

"Let's find out what works. Together."

"Okay," he breathes.

A look of realization suddenly dawns on his face.

"Hey, we were all planning on going out for dinner tonight to celebrate. It was just going to be a band thing, but I want you to be there."

She frowns.

"And Troy's gonna to be there?"

"Yeah, of course."

She groans.

"I don't know."

Damien grasps her by the chin and places a chaste kiss on her lips.

"You let me deal with him, okay? I'm an expert."

"Is it really a good idea to rile him up? It feels like that's your area of expertise."

He howls with laughter.

"Fair point. We really do give him a hard time. You know, one time he stepped in dog shit in Rome and couldn't figure out where the smell was coming from. He was flirting with these Italian girls and they looked like they were about to hurl. We all knew why, though. We didn't let it go for weeks. He threatened to run the bus off the road and kill us if we didn't stop talking about it."

Phoebe nearly chokes; it's impossible to remain serious after a story like that.

"That's so mean!"

"I know."

"Did you ever let it go?"

"He thought we did for about a year, but occasionally, one of us will bring it up just to watch him flip out. It never gets old."

After they've both had a good laugh, they find themselves wordlessly staring at each other, his smile softening as she gets lost in the warm glow of his eyes. This is a completely new Damien than the one she met less than a week ago, the side of him that doesn't make it into the papers. Her heart begins to thump wildly as the realization of what they're getting into truly dawns on her.

So much for friends.

It really was a stupid idea anyway.

You Really Got Me

THE WESTIN BENSON

Damien keeps his distance through the whole cab ride back, but every so often she catches him shooting glances at her out of the corner of her eye. And that smile. *Fuck.* It's bright and dazzling, and it makes her palms clammy. Or is that just her anxiety about jumping into this with both feet?

As they pull up to the hotel, Phoebe spots a small crowd of fans and a few scattered photographers. They must have found out where the band is staying. She inhales sharply and he squeezes her hand.

"Hey, can you drive around the back? I don't really want to deal with these vultures."

As the driver pulls around the back of the hotel, Damien hands her one of the shirts he picked up at the thrift store.

"Put this over your head and run as fast as you can."

She grabs it and darts out of the car, making it to the hotel just as a couple of the photographers turn the corner. Damien follows as the cab speeds away, barely escaping the sudden explosion of flashes and a couple hurled questions. She breathes a small sigh of relief, handing the shirt back.

"Is this going to be a regular thing?"

"Afraid so." His face lights up with a cocky smile. "Not gonna back out, are you?"

"Not a chance."

Damien looks around to make sure that they're alone before he captures her lips in a kiss.

"Good, because you'd be breaking my heart if you walked away."

"I thought heartbreak was your bread and butter," she giggles.

"Well, if someone as sweet as you left me, I'd have to write a song about it."

"Ooooh. Me? Immortalized?"

"On vinyl, no less," he purrs, brushing his knuckles over her cheek. "It'll outlive us both."

She runs her fingers through his silky hair as she goes in for another kiss, getting lost in the feeling of his lips against hers. They're still technically in public, and photographers could be anywhere, but Damien is oblivious. Or maybe he just doesn't care as he pulls her closer toward him. To be fair, neither does she. The silver bangles on his wrist jingle as he squeezes her ass.

She moans.

"You ever fucked a rock star in a hotel bathroom?" He asks.

"Yes," she laughs.

He pulls back and stares at her with surprise.

"Wait, seriously?"

"I had a little too much fun on a tour."

"Damn..."

She puts her hand on his chest.

"And, for the record, our first time together is *not* going to be in a hotel bathroom!"

"Why not?" He whines. "It's a nice bathroom. They have embroidered hand towels, and the soap smells like coconut."

"Not happening, Bell."

He presses his lips to her ear.

"Fine, *Miller*. Where would you prefer I fuck you first? The pool? The sauna? How about the front desk, right in front of everyone."

"Don't we have to go get dressed for dinner?" She laughs. "Can't you fantasize about this later?"

"Fine, spoilsport. We'll do it your way."

Damien pretends to mope the entire walk back up to the hotel room, dramatically hanging his head, and once they're inside he quickly makes it his mission to ensure the process is... a bit of a trial. He holds the dress he bought out in front of him, raising his eyebrows in an invitation. She reaches for it, once, twice, even finally getting on top of her tiptoes, but each time he pulls it away, further and further, until he's holding it all the way above his head.

"Jump for it," he teases.

Phoebe scoffs. He's the size of a goddamn oak tree.

"What are you, my high school bully?" She stomps her foot, much to Damien's amusement. "Just give it to me!"

"You're cute when you beg."

Phoebe stops, her skin prickling. Even Damien is blushing, as though he's surprised by his own words. She didn't think that was possible. In the silence, her thoughts begin to wander to her dream, and her eyes dart around nervously. He clears his throat and hands her the dress.

"Thank you," she mumbles, snatching it from his hands. As she walks toward the bathroom, he calls out to her.

"Where are you going?"

"To change?"

He raises an eyebrow.

"Pretty modest for such a supposedly rebellious gal, aren't you?"

Phoebe is already beet red, no use hiding it. She smiles and shakes her head, part of her wondering why in the hell she decided to pursue this.

"You know what you are?"

"What?" He asks, his own smile creeping across his face.

Suddenly she's not quite as confident as a moment before.

"No, it's nothing," she replies as she walks toward the bathroom.

"No!" Damien calls. He slides off of the bed and jogs past her to the bathroom, blocking the doorway. "I'm what? Tell me."

"It's– don't worry about it," she laughs. "I didn't have anything!"

"Really?" Damien asks. "You don't have anything in that big ol' brain of yours? I've read some pretty creative insults from you before."

She puts her hands on her hips.

"Yeah? Like what?"

"I think I remember you writing that a Judas Priest album sounded like Barry Manilow trying metal for the first time." He taps his chin and looks up at the ceiling in thought. "I'd have to look up the exact quote, but..."

She nods, covering her face.

"Yeah, that was me."

Damien grins and pulls her toward him, rubbing his nose against hers.

"Yeah, see? Gimme some of that Phoebe Miller venom."

"I don't want to!"

"Why not, you're so good at it!"

Their eyes meet, and her voice grows soft as she brushes his cheek.

"Because I like you."

"You owe me one, then," he whispers as he releases her.

Phoebe heads for the bathroom, quickly changing into the dress. The way it's cut combined with how the fabric falls on her body creates an overall nice shape, and specifically the illusion of wider hips. She also notices the skirt is much shorter than she originally thought, and as she turns back and forth in the large mirror, she can't help but admire her reflection.

As she steps back out she's immediately hit by the oh-so-glorious sound of an unashamed wolf-whistle.

"Shit, babydoll! You look good."

Phoebe throws on her jacket and laces up her combat boots with a smile. The pet name still makes her a little giddy, and it's all she can think about on their way to the elevator. As they wait for the doors to close, Damien reaches out and links his pinky finger with hers.

"Should we be doing this?" She asks, suddenly a little nervous.

"I don't see anyone around. Do you?"

"No, but–"

"Hey. You can relax a little, you know?"

"I know."

He's right, of course. The elevator is empty, and they're completely alone, but that could change at any moment. Phoebe wonders if she's always going to be like this in public with him, looking around corners and waiting for the other shoe to drop. It is just day one after all, surely she'll get used to it. Still, something about his gung-ho attitude makes her a little more anxious than she expected.

She takes a shaky breath.

"Why don't you seem as worried about this as I am?"

He shrugs.

"I'm just used to keeping things private under the spotlight."

With Alex, the stakes were a little lower. His band wasn't as big as Revolver, so there were pretty much no photographers to worry about. They just had to maintain a little distance when they were partying with the other bands, and be careful with the couple indie mag journos that might show up. But this? Damien is definitely a much bigger reward, and the risk expanded heavily to match.

"Guess I'll follow your expertise."

The elevator dings on the fifth floor, and the two step away from each other as a girl about Phoebe's age steps inside. She gasps the moment her eyes fall on Damien.

"Oh my God!" She squeals. "You're Damien Bell!"

Damien's switch into fan-mode is effortless.

"Sure am, sweetness."

"I'm such a big fan!"

He flashes her a tight smile.

"Hey, thanks, always great to meet you guys."

"No, like, you don't understand. Your posters are everywhere in my dorm room."

Damien chuckles and the girl twirls her hair around her finger, flashing him a flirtatious look.

"We're having a party tonight in my room. Maaaaybe you and the band could join us? Or, if you want, it could be just you."

Phoebe had locked her gaze above the door the second the girl arrived, watching the numbers count down to the lobby. Out of the corner of her eye, she can see Damien rub the back of his neck, and she tries to keep herself from smiling as he struggles to handle the situation.

"Sorry, but I've got dinner and then an important rehearsal tonight. Gotta put the work in, you know how it is."

The girl shrugs; it seems like his dismissal doesn't bother her in the slightest.

"Well, if you change your mind, I'm in 517."

"Got it," he murmurs.

The elevator doors open up to the lobby and the girl steps out ahead of them.

Damien flashes Phoebe a bashful smile.

"Sorry about that."

"Hey, it comes with the territory, right?"

"Yeah, yeah..." He runs a hand through his hair and frowns. "Honestly I thought she'd be a bit more broken up over it."

Phoebe snorts, punching him lightly on the shoulder.

"Buck up, Bell, if she can get over such a horrendous slight, so can you."

When they arrive at the restaurant, the rest of the group is already sitting at their table. Troy glances up as the two of them take their seats, looking particularly grumpy already. Phoebe's stomach drops and she suddenly doesn't feel like eating at all.

"I thought this was a band thing."

"It is, but I decided to extend the invitation out of the kindness of my heart," Damien quips. "Miller's basically one of us anyway."

Troy stares each of them down one after the other.

"So, where exactly were the two of you all day?"

Phoebe's too nervous to open her mouth. Hopefully he planned for this.

"We went for a walk," Damien replies flippantly.

"Just the two of you?" Troy asks.

He nods, grinning from ear to ear. Phoebe's, on the other hand, is burning up. Troy pulls his tinted sunglasses down the bridge of his nose and leans back in his chair.

"What *exactly* is going on?"

"Oh, I think you know what's going on," Damien purrs.

"Oh my god!" Ophelia yells, suddenly perking up. "Yes! I told you when we split up the hotel rooms that this would happen! Come on. Fifty bucks each. Cough it up, morons!"

Shaun and Johnny groan.

"Come on, Ophelia, it was a joke!"

"Gentleman's bet, right?"

She slams her hands on the table.

"Bullshit! You two are just trying to squirm out of this because you lost!" She snaps her fingers a few times in their faces. "Cough it up, losers. I know you're both good for it, we get the same pay!"

Damien snorts as the two grumble, digging around in their pockets.

"So you bet on us to... you know?"

"Duh. The minute I saw you watching her dance with that guy the other night, I knew your fates were sealed. Ophelia's predictions never fail to come true!"

Damien gives a little nod of approval while Phoebe buries her head in her hands, dying a little inside.

"To be fair to the boys, their bet wasn't *too* far off. They thought you guys were gonna hook up in Vegas, but my hook-up senses are unmatched!"

"When are we in Vegas?" Phoebe asks, trying to change the subject.

"Day after tomorrow," she cackles. "So close, but so far, boys!"

"No," Troy sighs, shaking his head. "No, this isn't happening. I'm putting my foot down."

"It is." Damien insists. "And you're not."

"How long has this been going on?!"

Phoebe jumps in, trying to smooth things over as much as she can.

"Just today. We really didn't have any idea..."

"I think we should count the sexual tension, though," Damien quips. "Then we get to say we've been an item this whole time."

Phoebe pinches the bridge of her nose, letting out a long exasperated sigh.

"Jesus, what happened to 'strictly platonic,' Miller?!"

Troy sounds more irate with each passing second. Damien, on the other hand, is practically beaming.

"We decided to go with 'whirlwind romance' instead. I dunno man, I think it's way more interesting, don't you?"

Troy rolls his head back, staring at the ceiling.

"To be fair, Troy, you even said if they were hooking up, we'd probably get a better article written about us," Shaun jabs, flashing Phoebe a thumbs up. "It's a win-win situation as far as I'm concerned."

"*That* was a sexist comment made in the heat of the moment!" Troy exclaims. "It was officially retracted, I will *not* have it dug up and used against me!"

He stands, a bundle of fury, distress, and exhaustion all pointed right at Damien, who has at least four inches on Troy, and twenty more pounds of muscle. It's not like it would be a fair fight. Still, Phoebe doesn't want the first night with her boyfriend to end like this. But that's not right, is it? Not boyfriend. Fuck buddy? That sounds too crass. They never agreed to anything serious, nothing's set in stone. It's an experiment, and so far these are the results.

Troy's eyes suddenly dart away from Damien as he points directly at her.

"I'm calling your editor."

"Nonononono!" She yells, standing up and reaching out to grab his wrist.

He flinches in surprise.

"Troy, please. *Please* do not do this."

Damien steps in, completely calm, the smile never leaving his face.

"Sullivan, let me break this down for you. If you call her editor, she's getting taken off this assignment. If she's taken off the assignment, we'll be stuck with that guy who trashed the first album." Troy swears under his breath. Chris really did leave an impression. "Do we really want a talentless hack like that, one who happens to hate me with a surprising passion considering how charming I am, to be the one writing our big piece?"

Troy glares at Damien for what feels like eternity, his jaw clenched and his teeth grinding, before finally throwing his hands up and dropping back down into his chair.

"Fine. Fine! But you're keeping this a secret. Don't get caught doing anything stupid in front of a camera. You don't even give anyone a reason to think, even for a *single second*, you two have locked lips." He turns to Phoebe. "If your editor finds out, you're dealing with the fallout. It's got nothing to do with me."

"You're not gonna call him?" She asks, relief replacing the dread that was coursing through her veins.

"No, no..." he sighs." You're a good kid, and more importantly you're a great writer. We need this article to sing, Miller, and you're clearly the one to do it. What none of us need, you included, is people to think it's written by some girl who really just likes knocking boots with the frontman."

Phoebe feels the nausea creeping back in, and Troy's expression softens, clearly not wanting to upset her further.

"Look, I trust you. I'm not gonna do anything to ruin... whatever you've got going on, just please be careful, okay?" He suddenly regains a bit of his usual composure. "I wouldn't want to upset the crown jewel in this band, after all."

"Damn right," Damien mutters, raising his glass.

"Wait, wait, I thought I was the crown jewel," Johnny replies, looking around the table. Damien shakes his head.

"Nah, nah, I'm the legendary frontman and you're the bassist with all the mystique."

"Hey, I thought I had mystique!" Shaun butts in.

"You have magic fingers, dude."

Shaun snorts and flips him off.

"What about me?" Ophelia asks.

"You just shred on those drums girl, better than any other." Damien laughs. "The impeccable fashion sense comes extra."

"Hell yeah." She high fives him.

Troy cleans his glasses off on his shirt, looking mostly back to his usual self.

"I don't normally give this talk to Damien, or any of the girls he brings on tour because they're never around for long enough, but I'm just going to reiterate: It's not mine or the other members' job to keep the both of you out of the press. That responsibility has to fall on you. Are we clear?"

"Crystal," Damien replies.

Phoebe nods, breathing slowly.

"Miller, you look like you're dying," Troy laughs. "I said I wouldn't call Brian, and I won't, okay? Everything's good."

She has to say it back to herself a couple times. This can work. It'll be okay. Everything's good. Troy begins to wave his hand sporadically, raising his voice.

"Excuse me! Waitress? Can we get a drink for this one?" Troy gestures back at Phoebe. "What do you want?"

Phoebe blinks, realizing for the first time all night that a drink would, in fact, be amazing right now.

"Whiskey. Double."

"Double whiskey!"

The waitress, who was deep in conversation with another staff member nods to them, looking more than a little annoyed.

Troy sighs.

"She'll get around to it eventually."

The Westin Benson

With the evening effectively salvaged, Troy and the others discuss what the next few weeks are going to look like. This is going to be one of their only full days off for three weeks, with a show scheduled every single night. First, they're in Vegas for a couple days, then Phoenix, Colorado, and so on. Phoebe pulls her camera out of her bag, deciding to take some photos of the band. Conveniently, the perfect cover for her being around Damien is also her job. She snaps a picture as Ophelia leans in with Troy, throwing out the peace sign and making a face.

"Okay, fine, that was cute. You can get off of me now," Troy grumbles.

Ophelia ruffles his hair.

"You're so grouchy all the time, Sullivan."

"I wonder why. You guys take my blood pressure to the damn moon!"

As Phoebe advances the film, looking for another angle or subject, she feels someone tap her on the back.

"Excuse me, are you Phoebe Miller?"

It's the concierge.

"Uh, yeah. What's up?"

"Ma'am, you have a message from a Mr. Brian Gordon. He'd like you to call him as soon as you can."

The man holds out a piece of paper, and Phoebe hesitates before snatching it up, handling it like it's covered in poison ivy.

Brian couldn't have heard something already, could he?

Troy throws his hands up.

"Hey, I didn't say anything. I was here the whole time."

"He's probably just calling to check in," she says, reassuring herself as much as anyone. "I'll call him once we get back up to the room."

The rest of the evening is mostly filled with more tour logistics and cigarettes. Phoebe tunes out a little, the background noise of their jokes and laughter bringing her a small sense of calm as she puts off the phone call. It's a welcome break from the variety of anxieties she's had to deal with all day. Finally Troy calls for the check, putting his hand up as she pulls out her wallet.

"You're not paying tonight."

"Troy, I really have to pay for some stuff on this tour, you can't keep doing this."

"Buy your own drinks tomorrow if you like. I got this one."

"Fine," she grumbles.

As they're standing up to leave, Ophelia excitedly turns to Damien and Phoebe, her face practically glowing.

"There's a beach about a ten-minute walk from here. The boys and I were going to head out there to catch the sunset. We're gonna have a bonfire, get some drinks and all that. You guys wanna come?"

"Sure," Phoebe replies. "I just have to call Brian, and maybe squeeze a bit of work in if I can, but that sounds fun."

"Yeah, I'm definitely in," Damien says.

She beams.

"We'll meet down here in like two hours, sounds good? Awesome."

She's gone before they can even reply.

Back in their room, Phoebe kicks off her boots and tosses her jacket onto the bed. Damien is silent as she sits down at her desk and grabs the phone, dialing Brian's number. She leans back in her chair listening to his line ring.

"Hello?"

"Hey, Brian, it's me."

"Phoebe, hey! How's the tour?"

"It's good," she replies. "I'm getting some great stuff."

"Yeah you are," Damien says softly, a shit-eating grin plastered on his face.

She frowns as she presses her finger to her lips to shush him. He feigns surprise.

"I'm on the phone!" she hisses, exasperated as Brian continues the conversation.

He grins and sits on the edge of the bed, watching her.

Since the park, she's noticed Damien seems to be constantly observing her every chance he can get. Phoebe locks eyes with him and her brows knit together. He shakes his head and shrugs, smiling.

"Bell isn't treating you too badly, is he?"

Her focus snaps back to the call, already having glazed over his last few comments.

"No, no it's fine. He's been very cooperative."

Damien points at himself and gives her the thumbs up. She stifles a laugh.

"Great. Hey, listen, are you able to send me what you have so far?"

She hears the bed creak followed by the feeling of Damien's large hands on her shoulders. They feel nice, strong and warm, melting away knots and she lets out a soft, happy sigh.

"Miller? You still there?"

"Wh – yeah! Yeah. Sorry, I just smoked a joint so I'm a little spacey."

She can hear Damien laughing and tries to reach back to smack his forearm. Complete miss.

"I, uh, only have notes, but I can type them up for you."

He chuckles.

"No problem, kid, you do whatever you need to relax. Can you fax me over what you've got before I leave the office tonight? Say... two hours?"

"Yeah, for sure. I think they have a machine downstairs."

"Great. Listen, Phoebe, I'm glad this is working out. Troy gave me a call this morning and said you were really hitting it off with everyone, that you've been getting some great shots, all that. You're crushing this assignment, kiddo. Clearly the right pick."

She blushes.

"Thanks, Brian."

"Call me if you need anything, all right?"

"Will do."

"And don't get into too much trouble."

Thanks, dad.

"Never do. Talk to you soon!"

"See you, Phoebe."

She hangs up and Damien immediately leans over to kiss her on the cheek.

"Everything cool?"

"Yeah. I just have to get some work done and we can head out."

He groans.

"How long is that gonna take?"

"Probably a couple hours," she laughs. "Why?"

"I was hoping we could fool around."

She tilts her head, moving in closer to give him a long, passionate kiss, before leaning back in her chair.

"Sorry. Duty calls."

He growls and throws himself onto the bed, as though the idea of her working instead of fucking him had sent him into a fainting spell.

"You're so dramatic," she giggles.

"Excuse me, madam. Dramatic is a rockstar's primary condition. I was born to be theatrical!"

"Truly, you're fulfilling your destiny." She grabs her notebook out of her bag. "I just have to type some stuff up for Brian and fax it over, then we can hit the beach."

He lifts his head and smiles mischievously.

"Or, and hear me out, we could forget the beach."

"Aww, I wanted to go!" Phoebe whines.

"Fine," he sighs "We'll go to the stupid beach, but I'm not going to like it!"

"Thank you for your blessing, oh crown-jewel of the band."

Phoebe opens her notebook and gets to work transcribing the hundreds of little sentences and observations she's made over the past few days. She never realizes just how much she's written until she has to pull the article together. Sometimes it feels ridiculous to send it all, most of the notes never actually make it into the final piece, but Brian likes to see the process.

As she's working and typing away, she hears the bed creak again as he stands; looks like he's as restless as ever. Before long, though, it becomes clear this is more than a little restlessness, as Damien crawls under her desk on his hands and knees.

"Damien, what– what are you doing?"

"Playing a game," he replies as he begins to massage her calf muscles.

"What do you mean game?" She stammers.

"I just came up with it, you're gonna love it. It's called *Focus.*"

"What are the rules?" she breathes.

"You focus on your work, and I focus on *you*. It's kind of like a race."

She's flushed, and already a little sweaty at the thought. She breathes slowly, quivering as Damien quirks an eyebrow.

"Ready to play?"

She nods.

"The beauty of this game is that, no matter what, we both win," he whispers as he moves in closer.

Her mouth is a desert, and her throat feels like it's constricting as she feels him place gentle kisses up each of her calves. Phoebe lets her head roll back and the kisses stop.

"Focus," he reminds her. "Or neither of us get what we want."

She feels a shiver run up her spine and straightens up, trying to remain calm and collected.

"That's a good girl," Damien says from below as he returns to the job at hand. Phoebe's surprised to find that the praise alone does a lot of the work.

It's extremely hard to focus on what she's supposed to be doing, but somehow she's managing, at least so far. Even if half of her brain is lit on fire from his touch, she can keep herself in line. Unfortunately, it's not long before the other half starts powering down as well, less inclined to do any work. Some of the 'words' she's typing aren't even really words at this point.

Phoebe feels a little jolt shoot through her with each and every teasing lick he drags up both thighs. He's taking his time, carefully working her into a controlled frenzy, and it's all she can do to simply keep her breathing in check. She can feel the blood rushing to her clit as it pulses, begging to be touched. She wants desperately to squeeze her thighs together to relieve even the tiniest bit of the pressure, but she just keeps typing. The pace is pure agony, but she has to play her part in the game. Soon, the licks become nips and bites, and she starts to feel like she might lose her mind.

"Damien," she moans.

"Keep working, those are the rules." She can feel his breath as he speaks.

"God!"

She hits the desk, half aimed at the man underneath and half a wild thrashing. He laughs as she continues typing literally anything she can manage. Finally she feels him push her soaking wet panties aside and drag a finger between her lips. He flicks her clit playfully. Phoebe's head almost hits the table.

"Fuck you're wet," he breathes.

All she can do is moan in response.

"I don't hear typing," Damien teases in a sing-song voice.

Phoebe tries to work as best she can, but he doesn't make it easy. Occasionally, he'll wrap his lips around her clit and suck until she bucks, but he always pulls away just before her climax hits. She snarls in frustration, hearing his laughter below her.

"It's not funny!" She whines.

"It really is, though."

"You're so fucking cruel."

"Cruel?" Damien inquires as he massages her inner thighs, his hands dangerously close to her aching pussy. "We're playing a game, and games are fun! You know what I think?"

"What?"

He looks up at her, a wicked smile plastered on his face.

"I think if you're busy complaining, you're still not playing by the rules."

He caresses her, as close as he can get before trailing away again.

"Focus."

She nods, returning to the typewriter as Damien buries his face between her legs once more. His tongue is incredible. It might be the best part of his body, at least from what she's seen so far. Phoebe manages to get about halfway through her notes, rough and patchwork as they are, before she can't take it anymore. Without a word, she reaches down and grabs him by the hair and pushes herself against his mouth. His laugh sends waves of pleasure shooting through her body.

"No more focus. You win, you win. Please just make me come."

He pushes her back, looking up at her from under the desk, his chin shining with her slick.

"Well, I'd say we should stop the game, but..."

"Oh god, Damien!" She whines. "I think I'm dying."

He grins and gets back to work, alternating between flicking and sucking on her clit until she's whimpering his name. Her muscles begin to coil and contract, and he's able to hold her there for a few minutes before he goes in for the final push. The wave hits her hard as she comes, and she lets out a howl as her whole body arches. She doesn't care if the rooms next door can hear her, and really, she doesn't even consider it from the throes of complete bliss. It's easily the best orgasm she's had in months, shooting through her body like wildfire as every hair stands on end.

His little "game" leaves her as the human equivalent to a car wreck. Her muscles are jello; she's pretty sure he'll have to carry her to the beach. Damien carefully slides her chair backward so that he can crawl out from beneath the desk, pulling himself on top of her and claiming her mouth with his own. She's still seeing spots, having a difficult time making heads of tails of things, but she can distinctly taste herself on his tongue. As he stands, she can't help but lock eyes with the massive bulge in his pants.

"What about you?" She rasps, her words still a little shaky in the aftermath.

He chuckles, grasping the sides of her face with his hands.

"When we get back from the beach, I'm gonna to give you a night you'll never forget."

"That's a big promise," she laughs, her eyes flashing as she moves in for more.

"Yeah, and I've got a big ego." He says, in between kisses. "Among other things."

Damien helps her to her feet. Her legs shake a little as she grabs some clothes to change into.

"You okay? I thought you might have blacked out for a second."

"Close," Phoebe replies. "Very, *very* close."

He chuckles.

"Well Miller, I'm glad we decided to properly and *professionally* address the tension that was building between us."

She grins.

"Okay, okay, you're hilarious and you know it." She moves to the bathroom door and pauses. "But yeah. Me too."

After her quick change of clothes, Damien seems content to let her finish working on the rest of her notes. Shockingly, there are few spelling mistakes or nonsensical sentences despite his best efforts, and by the 2-hour deadline she's able to drop them off in a big brown envelope at the front desk. She hands over Brian's fax number as Damien and the rest of the band linger by the entrance.

"It might take a little while, we had someone drop something off right before you did," the clerk tells her.

"It's fine. We're heading out to the beach. I can just pick them up later."

As she skips toward the group, Damien shoots her a knowing smile.

"You look a lot more relaxed, Miller. Is there anyone in particular you want to thank for that?"

Shaun and Ophelia gag, Johnny sighs, and Phoebe simply smiles.

Do You Do You Know

CANNON BEACH

There's an understanding in this industry. Relationships of all kinds are explosive, between band mates, managers, and of course the romantic side. In the middle of a tour a groupie had once told Phoebe not to take this stuff too seriously. You're only setting yourself up for heartbreak after all.

They reach the beach just before the sun starts dipping down past the horizon. There are no photographers, and virtually no other people around. Ophelia leads the way as the five of them march to a remote spot, surrounded by rocks right off the water. As Johnny and Shaun unpack the beer, Damien leans over to Phoebe.

"Ophelia would take us to every single beach we pass by if she could. She's obsessed."

"There just aren't a lot of choices in New York." Ophelia pipes up. "Don't make me sound like a freak for liking the outdoors, you shut-in!"

"There so are." Shaun laughs. "New York has tons of beaches, you're just picky."

"Look, I never settle. Only the best for this girl!"

Shaun wraps his arm around her waist and kisses her on the cheek.

"You always pick the best ones."

Johnny walks up beside Damien and Phoebe, handing them each a can of beer.

"It's kind of our chance to unwind during the tour. We went to a lot of beaches in Italy, too."

"They must have been beautiful," Phoebe muses.

Johnny nods, glancing out at the sunset off the water.

"Unforgettable."

They end up settling down near an abandoned bonfire pit just on the other side of the rocks. The boys gather dry pieces of driftwood, tossing them into the pit and using the cardboard from their cases of beer as tinder. Finally, Damien flicks his lighter as they crack into their drinks, and the whole thing goes up. They cheer as the blaze rises quickly before settling, possibly a little lower than they had hoped judging from the reactions.

Phoebe can taste the salt water lingering in the air, mingling with the newly burnt wood and billowing smoke. It's a unique combination, and she savors the sensation as the sun takes its final dive, bathing everything in a warm orange glow. As they all gaze out at the water in silence, Damien sidles closer to Phoebe, pulling her up onto his lap.

"Hi," he whispers.

"Hi."

He kisses her softly, his beer can dangling frivolously from his fingertips. Phoebe giggles.

"You know, before today I didn't realize you were so affectionate."

"Well, to be fair, you don't actually know that much about me."

"Actually, I did research," she says cheekily.

"Yeah? And how reliable were your sources?"

"Fair enough," she chuckles. "Well, with that in mind, thank you for being my primary source back in the hotel room. I'll be sure to credit you."

They're completely alone, save for the band. It's too dark for photographers, and even if someone showed up they'd have no idea who any of them were. A sense of relief washes over her and she leans in for a kiss.

Unfortunately, it's interrupted when out of nowhere, Johnny stands and addresses the group.

"Let's play a game!"

"What kind of game?" Ophelia asks, climbing up onto Shaun's lap. He kisses her on the cheek before pulling out a joint and sparking it. They begin to pass it around the circle as they hear Johnny out.

"It's called Do You Do You Know, Damien and I used to play it all the time."

"Except we had to play it dry 'cause Johnny's parents are total squares," Damien teases. "It's not so much of a game really, you just try to outsmart each other."

Johnny grins.

"Yeah, and I always win."

"Not true!" Damien shouts between sips of his beer.

He slides his free hand beneath Phoebe's shirt, gently rubbing her back. She probably should have brought a thicker jacket, but this is a much nicer alternative. He's so warm, even more in the midst of a cool ocean breeze.

Ophelia cuts in before Johnny can argue his point further.

"Okay, okay, so what are the rules?"

"Very simple," he replies. "You state a fact about anything – a book, a movie, a musician, and if people don't know that fact, they have to drink. So, who wants to go first?"

"I'll go," Phoebe volunteers.

Damien gives her side a quick squeeze before removing his hand.

"All right. Phoebe, kick us off. And remember, you have to start the sentence with 'do you do you know…' or it doesn't count."

"Okay. Uhhhh…"

She's accumulated so many of these little facts over the course of her short career, it's hard to pluck one out of thin air.

"Tick tock, babydoll," Damien teases. "Don't want to get disqualified."

"Shit, is there some kind of time limit?"

"No," Johnny scoffs. "He's just being a dick."

Damien's cackles, his mischievous eyes lit up by the bonfire.

"Oh! I got one!" Phoebe exclaims. "Do you do you know that the Queen song 'Misfire' is actually about premature ejaculation?"

"What?!" Ophelia shouts. "No way!"

"Yep."

"I don't buy it!" She counters. "How do we know if someone's lying?"

"Normally it's a little tough, and you have to go with the honor system, but this one's true," Damien replies. "Come on Ophelia, think about the lyrics!"

She laughs as her gaze trails off into the sky, seemingly going over the lyrics in her head.

"Yeah, okay, that's too perfect to be fake. I give."

She takes a sip of beer, same with Johnny. Shaun smiles proudly.

"I knew that one."

"No way," Johnny counters.

"Okay, okay! My turn," Damien stands, giving Phoebe a congratulatory pat on the back. "Do you do you know that Bob Dylan's first draft of 'Like a Rolling Stone' was six pages long?"

"Jesus," Shaun mumbles. "Dylan's already a snooze fest, but six pages?"

Phoebe's head snaps toward Shaun, a look of disbelief on her face.

"You don't like Dylan?"

He shrugs.

"No, it's just like… Okay, cool, you're deep and shit. I don't need a six-page song to tell me that. There's so much repetition. Why does a song need to be 10 minutes long with the same chorus 30 goddamn times?"

Damien's shoulders shake with laughter.

"See? He knows I'm right."

"I never said you weren't! I'm just waiting for the Dylan super fan to get pissed off."

Johnny shakes his head.

"Wrong. All wrong."

"My dad used to make us listen to 'Blonde on Blonde' on repeat for weeks on end," Phoebe offers. "By the end, I was ready to put a Q-Tip right through my eardrum, so I get it."

Shaun lights up, smiling smugly at Johnny.

"See? I told you!"

"This is a crime. You're all criminals."

Johnny shakes his head, taking a big swig of his beer and standing up.

"Okay, back on track, I have a fact! This is how Damien got me to drain half a bottle of Jack Daniels once, so I memorized it."

Damien snorts.

"I always have a little hope that you'll forget."

Johnny shakes his head and taps his temple.

"Mind like a steel trap."

"A rusted trap maybe," Ophelia teases.

"Hey!" Johnny yelps. "Where's the respect for your peers?"

Ophelia puts her hands up in defense before downing the rest of her beer. She cracks another open.

"Okay, my turn."

"What about me?!" Johnny fires back.

"I've got a good one, I'm cutting in line."

Johnny chuckles, shaking his head as Ophelia stands.

"Do you do you know that Prince played 27 instruments on 'For You?'"

"I knew that!" Phoebe exclaims, louder than she had intended. The alcohol's hitting fast. Or maybe it's the weed. Whatever it is, the combo is strong.

"Well I didn't."

Damien raises his can in salute, draining it completely before tossing it aside, and Phoebe leans over to grab him another. When she turns back to hand it to him a big grin is waiting for her.

"Thanks, doll face."

He leans in for a kiss, and she can't help but get lost in it, dropping the can onto the sand.

"Get a room!" Johnny shouts, throwing a clump of sand at them.

Damien suddenly stops, pulling back from Phoebe with a wicked smile on his face, as if he had been waiting for this exact opportunity.

"Who am I to say no to such a fair request! Phoebe? Let's go find a room."

Damien stands, dipping his arms under her legs and lifting her up with surprising ease. Phoebe giggles like a schoolgirl as Damien carries her off toward the other end of the beach, the rest of the band booing and shouting for them to come back. Before long he sets her down, turning back toward them for a moment before continuing down the beach.

"We'll be back! Chill out and finish your dumb game!"

He takes her hand in his as they walk along the shoreline, the two of them staring out at the moonlit water in silence. The ambience is lovely, and these little moments alone continue to be a blessing, but Phoebe's particularly thankful for the ocean breeze. It sobers her up, at least a little. After a few minutes of silence, she glances up at him, suddenly struck by a jolt of curiosity. He was right, she doesn't really know that much about him.

"What's your relationship with your family like?"

"Where's this coming from?"

"I just– I want to know more about you, and I realized I don't know that much about how you grew up." She pauses. "Off the record, by the way."

He smirks.

"So considerate Miller, I appreciate it."

She punches him in the shoulder.

"I'm serious!"

He laughs, batting back at her a bit before they both calm down.

"I'm really close with my sister, Ava. We're twins, actually, and we always fought like cats and dogs as kids, but she was always there for me when things got bad. Still is. She's the one who pushed me into music, too." Damien pauses, a soft smile on his lips. "She's the one I used to read all my poetry to."

Phoebe can't help but notice that his parents are conspicuously absent from his recounting. The only thing she knows is that his dad was in the military, but she doesn't push. His eyes light up when he talks about his sister, she's extremely important to him.

"Wow."

"Yeah. We're close."

"What does she do?"

"She's an artist. A sculptor."

"Oh, that's awesome!"

"Yeah, her work is in MoMA and shit, so it is pretty impressive. I don't really get her art a lot of the time, but people pay top dollar for an Ava Bell piece, so she must be doing something right. My parents are definitely a lot more into it than what I've got going on."

"Wait, do they know you're selling out venues? This is your second tour, you have a record, it's not some flash-in-the-pan thing."

"Yeah," he laughs sheepishly. "If I'm being honest they're actually really good about the music part. They even play our record when I come back for Christmas. I think it's the lifestyle they're not super into. I know they're never particularly happy to see when I make the news, considering the headlines."

"Ah, I can maybe see their point of view there." She smirks. "Self-awareness is important, I suppose. You're making big steps."

Damien smiles at her, the moonlight carving out his cheekbones and making his gaze more intense. He's not even phased by her playful ribbing.

"What about you?" He asks. "What are things with your brother like?"

"Mostly fine," Phoebe replies. "He's a bit older, that might be one of the reasons we don't have too much in common. Never quite had the same interests at the same time."

She's not being entirely honest with him. They always got along, but it was clear Michael was the golden child. Her parents tried to hide it for a while, but as she got older it became glaringly obvious. And who wouldn't prefer Michael? He's outgoing, pleasant, always cracking jokes at the perfect moment. He got a full track and field scholarship to an Ivy League school and met the perfect girl on his first day of classes. They've been together ever since, of course. Amazing grades took him straight through med school after that, and now he works with kids with cancer. Kids with fucking cancer.

And it's not like Phoebe's parents hate her, they check in sometimes, they worry, it's just that she took a different path. She was drawn to words and poetry at a young age and wanted to follow that; to become a writer, and they were always a little bit disappointed by that. It wasn't their fault she didn't turn out quite as good as her brother. They tried their best.

"You said he's married and has kids, right?"

"Oh, yeah, my nephews! They're actually really cool, three and six. I bought Billy, the older one, a Zeppelin record for his birthday. Michael thought it was hilarious."

"Teach 'em young," Damien says as he grabs her hand.

His grip is firm and soft at the same time.

"Did you always want to be a musician?" She asks.

"Yeah. Well, not *always*. My mom got me piano lessons, for structure and discipline, you know? But uh... well, you can see how that turned out."

She laughs.

"You're really good. At the piano part at least."

"Thanks," he mutters.

He seems almost embarrassed. Maybe playing the piano isn't a very rock 'n' roll thing to do.

"Used to play a lot of classical."

The little bursts of conversation slow as silence falls in between them, and they both return to staring out at the water. They're still new at this, the whole being together thing. No matter how easily it comes one minute, it can get a little awkward the next. After another few minutes of silence, Damien takes her hand and begins to lead her slowly back toward the bonfire.

Suddenly, he speaks up.

"What do you like?"

Phoebe looks up at him and chuckles.

"That's a pretty broad question."

"In bed," Damien says. "What do you want? What do you like?" He meets her gaze, his face once again sporting that devious smile. "Besides me eating you out from under a desk."

She blinks, completely unprepared for the hard left turn this conversation has taken.

"I..."

"You've gotta be into *something*," he laughs, kissing her knuckles one by one. "Come on, tell me. Whatever it is, I'll do it. Hell, I'll buy a clown suit and fuck you on that balcony while I wear it, if that's what you're into."

Her laughter echoes down the beach and she rubs her face. He says it all so casually.

"Do you have this conversation with every girl you sleep with?"

"Well, yeah," he laughs. "Wait, you're not into the clown thing, are you?"

"No, Damien, I am not particularly turned on by the thought of being fucked by a clown, even one as good looking as you."

"Okay, see we're making progress! Seriously though, what's your thing?"

She shrugs.

"I don't really know, not specifics at least. I never thought about it like that before."

"So... you're down to experiment, then? Gotta find out somehow, right?"

"Yeah, I guess I am."

He grins.

"Cool."

"What about you?" She asks.

"I'm so into experimenting I might as well be a scientist."

"Nothing... too crazy, right?" she asks with a quirked brow.

He laughs.

"Phoebe if there's anything you're not into, if you say stop at any point, I stop. I promise. Sex is supposed to be fun, right? If both of us aren't having a good time, what's the point?"

She gets up onto her tiptoes to kiss him on the cheek, and he purrs as he pulls her toward him. This whole day had been so special; intense in ways she wasn't expecting and soft in others. Most of all, it belonged to them. It was theirs.

It's shockingly effortless to rejoin the group, just as easy as becoming a part of it in the first place, and in minutes she's back sitting next to Ophelia and Shaun. The three watch on, whooping and hollering as Damien and Johnny leap from rock to rock, taunting each other with each jump. He looks so free, nothing like the brooding photos that she's poured over in preparation for the tour, with none of the cynicism or vitriol she'd come to expect. In one day, her image of him has completely crumbled away, leaving the man in front of her behind. It was exactly as Ophelia had said that first day, so much of him that people see, the image he projects out into the world, it was an act. Or maybe it was a shield.

A shield he was willing to let down completely, for her.

"Johnny, these boots are two-hundred bucks! If they get wet, you're dead!"

"Don't let me push you in then, pussy!" Johnny shouts back.

The two are right on the edge of the rocks, a spot hanging over the water just enough to induce some anxiety, but not give Phoebe a full on panic attack. She grips her beer tightly as she watches Damien pull off his boots, setting them safely aside.

"Fine. Let's do this!"

Johnny cackles as he kicks his shoes off, the two immediately locking up in a grapple at the edge of the rock. They're even more off-balance now, socks slipping on the smooth rock face, accented by the moonlight and fully backlit by the bonfire.

"This is probably going to be bad," Ophelia sighs, sipping her beer.

"By bad, do you mean hilarious?" Shaun asks. "Watching these two idiots go at it is the highlight of my day."

"Oh, absolutely." She turns to Phoebe, noticing her stiff expression. "Don't worry, they do this every time we go to the beach. Last time they tried to joust with big sticks. They both had welts for weeks, but they ended up fine. They always do."

Before Phoebe can respond there's a loud yelp in the distance, and she looks up just in time to see Damien grabbing Johnny in a headlock as they tumble off of the rock to the water below. They all stand, and Shaun starts to applaud, but Phoebe's nervous. There are a lot of rocks and it's almost pitch black on the other side.

Thankfully, as she rushes around the rocks, the only sound she's met with is laughter. Even in the low light she can see Damien's shirt is sticking tightly to his muscular frame as he pulls himself from the water, his long hair slicked back. Johnny tries to get one last fruitless headlock on Damien before he stumbles past him, out of the water and toward the fire.

"Fuck it's cold!" He shouts as he cozies up next to his bandmates.

"Awww! Poor baby!" Ophelia teases.

"You're dripping all over the seats, dude!" Shaun exclaims.

"I can't stop physics man, trust me, I've tried."

Damien smiles in the midst of the commotion, silently beckoning Phoebe into the water with a single seductive finger.

"Nope," she laughs. "No fucking way."

"Come on, Miller! It's fun! Where's your sense of adventure?"

"If it's so fun why are you shivering like a wet dog?" She laughs.

"I'm just so excited for you to join me, I'm quivering in anticipation!"

She folds her arms and smiles, raising her eyebrows.

He shrugs.

"Okay, okay, maybe I'm just waiting for you to warm me up."

"Not a chance, Bell!"

He's cute, there's no denying it, but the wind is starting to chill her to the bone. She glances back to the bonfire.

"Can't we just go back and–"

She turns to see a devilish smile flicker across Damien's lips before he takes off running for her, water splashing into the air behind him. She turns with a yelp trying to make as much distance between them as possible, but he's too quick for her. She feels him slam against her all at once, tackling her to the ground, and pinning her against the sand. She grunts, struggling to get free, but only shifting the sand around her.

"You okay?" He huffs.

"Yeah, I'm fine." She grins. "You're nothing special or anything. You're just big." She struggles a little more, completely in vain.

"Well, this is just escalation! You wouldn't come in the water, so I had to take drastic measures."

"You're dripping all over me!" She whines, grimacing as the cold water dribbles over her face.

"Oh, so this is the second time I've gotten you wet, or the third?"

"Oh my God!" She flails, trying to hit him.

A soft pink hue dusts Damien's cheeks.

"I know, I know," he chuckles, capturing her lips in a messy kiss.

She can feel something thick and hard pressing against her thigh. He shifts his weight a bit, repositioning himself right between her legs and grinds his hips. She can feel him dragging himself up against her, as if their clothes didn't even exist. Her fingers run through his damp hair as she tries to pull him even closer, but he backs away, grinning as he looms over her.

"I think it's time to head back to the hotel, don't you? I've had enough of the beach."

She exhales, shivering in anticipation as she looks up at him.

"I was never a big fan of beaches anyway."

Gold Dust Woman

THE WESTIN BENSON

The driver is waiting for them in the parking lot, reading a book. Normally he might have bailed, but they promised him 100 bucks to wait around, and he seemed happy enough to take a paid break for a couple hours. Jamming all 5 of them in a single cab is a significantly more obnoxious task when half of them are damp and covered in sand, but the ride is mercifully short. As the driver pulls around the back, Shaun gives a quick look around.

"Coast is clear."

They thank the driver and run into the hotel laughing, all five of them piling into the elevator. Moments after the doors close, Damien pulls Phoebe back so that she's pressed right up against him. He dips his head and sucks on the spot just below her ear, the one that makes her eyes flutter and her heart race. She can feel his cock pressing through his pants and she whimpers, straining to stay as inconspicuous as possible. Thankfully, the rest of the band either doesn't notice, or is polite enough not to humiliate them before they reach their floor. Phoebe's insides swirl with a mix of nerves and a familiar ache as they come across a couple other hotel guests on the way to their door. Just as they pass, Damien squeezes her ass, hard, and it's all she can do not to cry out.

The moment they step inside, his mouth is on hers and everything else falls away. She barely has a chance to kick the door closed as he pulls her toward the bed, the two tearing at each other until they're both stripped down to their underwear.

He breaks the kiss, looking her up and down.

"God, you're beautiful."

The gravel in his voice sends electricity down her spine.

She's rarely felt it, maybe once before, but now it was all Damien. Not just his voice, but the way he looked at her, the way it felt when he grabbed her. It's the same feeling she got when she was kneeling in front of him on stage, her camera clutched in her trembling hands. This time she had nothing to hide behind.

Phoebe's gaze is fixed on his almost-naked body, realizing that she's only ever seen him with his shirt off, and nothing more. He looks like he was cut from fucking marble, with a broad and well-defined chest that's already glistening with a bit of sweat. His arms are toned, the bangles on his left wrist jingling as he runs a hand through his hair. Her lips part as her eyes dip lower, tracing over his chiseled abs, muscular thighs, and the outlines of his hip bones that peek out of the tops of his boxer-briefs. Her real focus, though, is on the large bulge that's being barely contained as it strains against the fabric. He grins and steps toward her, his fingers finding the hem of her underwear and snapping the waistband playfully against her skin.

"Off."

His tone is stuck halfway between excited and commanding, and her body clenches as she slips them down her legs and steps toward him. Damien looks like a starving animal as he wets his lips, towering over her. He cups her cheek, staring into her eyes before his lips claim hers in a slow, teasing kiss. His tongue glides across her lower lip, but he pulls away seconds after she grants him access. Her eyes light up as he nods toward the bed, and she giggles as the two of them stumble over.

Damien sits down and pulls her on top of him so that she's straddling his thigh. Her once-forbidden dream plays in the back of her mind like an old movie, and she begins to grind down on him as she winds her arms around the back of his neck. Damien lets out a soft chuckle as he gently nibbles on her bottom lip. He smells like cologne and salt water.

"So you *do* know what you want."

Phoebe bites down on her lip.

"I had a dream about you," she confesses, looking off to the side.

Her cheeks are hot and pressure builds in her core as she soaks his thigh. He places sloppy kisses up and down her neck, biting down on the areas he thinks will make her moan. He's right every goddamn time. How is he always so right?

He puts a hand on her chin, turning her to face him.

"Tell me everything."

She shudders. He's fully in control. Of her, of everything.

"I woke up this morning and you were beside me, in bed. You started kissing me. Your mouth was– oh god–!"

She can feel herself rocketing toward the edge, and she reaches down without thinking to caress his hardness through his boxers. He's fucking huge.

"Keep talking, sweetheart, it only makes me harder."

She moans, heavy breaths falling between random words as she grinds down into his thigh.

"Your mouth was so soft– and you pulled me– on top of you."

"Did we fuck?" He asks, taking her hand and guiding it to the opening in his boxers.

Her breath catches in her throat as her fingers wrap around his cock. Her hips almost stop as she's a little overwhelmed by the split-focus, but he grabs them and pushes her to keep riding his thigh.

Phoebe strokes him slowly, smiling to herself as his eyes flutter back as he groans.

"We didn't fuck," she continues, stroking slowly up and down his shaft. "Actually, we kind of did what we're doing now."

"Feel good?" He asks.

"So good," she moans, dropping her head again as her hips speed up. It might be too much for her, but there's no world where she'd ever stop.

"Did you come? In your dream?"

It's almost like it's a competition, Dream-Damien against the real one.

She smirks.

"You woke me up and it got... cut off."

"Let me make it up to you," he whispers.

He unclasps her bra, tossing it behind her as his mouth captures her nipple, biting down just hard enough to make her jump a little. It's all the fuel she needs to ramp things up, fucking his thigh with more and more ferocity. It's exactly what she's wanted the whole past week, to be locked in his arms. What drew her to him, or him to her? Is it a good idea? Is any of this right? Those questions she struggled with over the past few days don't matter anymore.

Her skin is all electricity beneath his touch, jolted and burning as her lips part, moaning his name. She's so close to her own release that she can barely focus on stroking him, fumbling around without any real intent, but Damien doesn't seem to mind. His tongue glides over each nipple, alternating between flicking and sucking gently on the hardened buds. His thigh is a riverbed, and every time she drags her clit across it, a new fire ignites inside her.

"I'm– so close," she whines.

"Come on, babydoll. I've got you." He kisses her. "God you're so beautiful."

His final words are such a small thing, soft and kind, but it's all she needs. A week straight of flirtatious glances, burning stares, and taunting words has led to this. All the anxious tension and pure animal energy crashing around inside of her finally gets a release. Fuck objectivity, fuck Brian's rules, fuck her rules for that matter. All she cares about is Damien. His loving lips, his exquisite tongue, and his gentle hands that hold her so effortlessly: the perfect answer to her extended torment.

When she comes, it feels like being swept up in a tidal wave. Her head falls back and a raw, guttural moan springs up from deep inside her as she bucks and writhes. It's overwhelming, and he holds her as she struggles to stay up straight, spasming on top of him. When she finally finds the strength to look up at him again, she finds his eyes almost black and filled with lust. She can feel precum leaking onto her hand as his cock twitches.

"Go sit on the desk."

"On it?" The words are punctuated by deep, labored breaths.

"That's what I said."

Phoebe stands, her legs still shaking as she heads to the desk. She has no idea how her muscles are able to work right now. She's on autopilot, gliding above everything on sheer bliss, but she somehow manages to hoist herself up.

Phoebe looks back in time to catch Damien climbing out of his boxer shorts, and her eyes go wide.

"Oh fuck..."

He grins as he opens his suitcase and pulls out a condom, slowly tearing the package open and making a bit of a show out of rolling it onto his cock. Damien's bedroom and stage personas are similar. Both are arrogant and extremely confident, but even though he's a rockstar, it might be even more well-deserved in here. As he approaches her, he runs his finger through her folds, and he chuckles as she reflexively moans, lifting her hips with a seeming desperation that seems to light a spark in him.

"You're sensitive."

"You think so, Bell? Well after the two mind-blowing orgasms you've given me today–"

He leans forward.

"In the bedroom, it's sir."

She blinks.

"Do you ask all the girls to call you that, *sir*?" Even now, in this compromised state, she feels compelled to bite back a bit. It's exciting.

"Just a couple."

His smile could light up a room.

Damien takes his time, teasing her with his fingers and gently circling her clit until she's a quivering mess again. He makes sure not to linger in one place for too long, and it's killing her. Her cunt clenches around nothing and a deep ache that she hasn't felt in a long time floods her body, making her muscles coil.

"Damien– *sir*," she corrects herself just as he's about to open his mouth, and flushes immediately. It's so humiliating.

"God, just fuck me!"

He hums softly, considering the words as though he's weighing whether or not they're good enough. Phoebe's skin burns, aching for his touch. Slowly, he pushes a finger into her cunt, and then another, but not enough to give her what she needs. She reaches out for his wrist as he teases her, gripping it tightly and trying to force him to fuck her harder. His eyes flick up, lightning flashing in them as he smirks.

"I'll give you what you want..." She smiles, relieved. "But you have to beg."

There's a moment where she thinks about just saying no, not wanting to debase herself just because he said so, but that compulsion fades instantly. She doesn't care anymore, she's too close.

"I need you," she whines as he pushes his fingers a little deeper, just enough to torture her. "Please sir, please just fuck me!"

"How much, sweets?" Phoebe's heart is pounding in her throat and she can barely get a breath in before he speaks again. "Come on. Say it."

She whines, her voice cracking as her head falls back and Damien captures her nipple with his teeth.

"Please, I need you to fuck me so badly. I'll be so good for you, so so good!"

Damien leans back, removing his fingers from her cunt and popping them into his mouth to lick them clean. He casually grabs his cock, placing it right at her entrance, leaning in ever so slightly.

"*That's* what I wanted to hear."

Phoebe whimpers as she watches the head slowly bury itself inside her. He lingers just long enough for her to open her mouth in protest before easing his way in further, stretching her out to accommodate him.

She grimaces.

It's painful at first, but he quickly notices her reaction, slowing himself down further and stopping completely once he bottoms out. He glides his thumb across her bottom lip as he takes a few heavy breaths.

"It's okay," he whispers.

"It's fine, I know," she groans. "You're just…"

He smirks and tilts his head.

"I'm what, babydoll?"

She chuckles and kisses him.

"Such an asshole."

"I really am." He starts to move again, slowly at first. "You like it though, don't you?"

She does. She *really* does.. They stay like this for a few minutes, Damien staring into her eyes, breathing with her as her body relaxes, only shifting ever so slightly inside her. She leans up to kiss him, and even that tiny movement reminds her of his girth.

"You can move a little more."

He grins as his hips begin to roll languidly against her in between heated kisses. His hands wrap around her waist and he tilts her hips up, perfectly positioning her for the tip of his cock to hit her G-spot. She squirms. Phoebe's thighs were already trembling around him before, but the newest thrust makes her slam her hand down on the typewriter keys next to her. They pause as the machine lets out a little ding, laughing as they're both briefly removed from the heat of the moment. She buries her hands in his hair to avoid messing up the rest of her notes, leaving her body fully under his control.

Damien takes full advantage of her self-restraint and begins again, slowly at first before increasing the pace over and over and over, all while staring directly into her eyes. Phoebe is immediately made fully aware of the power he has over her. She can see it in his eyes: he's a god both on stage and off, and he's planning to fuck her senseless until she knows it too. His eyes burn into hers, and all she can do is stare right back as a wanton moan tumbles from her lips. Their bodies move together as though they were made for one another, and while neither of them need any words in this moment, she wouldn't have them even if they did.

And all of the sudden, things are different. His hips begin to snap against her, with vicious echoing slaps. He growls, devouring her whole in a bruising, hungry kiss. She begins to shake as her second orgasm overtakes her in an eruption. Every inch of her skin is hot and she cries out, involuntarily ripping her mouth away from his. The massive pulses of pleasure overtake her, like they're about to liquify every bone in her body; nobody has ever made her come like this. Not any of the shitty dates she's been on, not Kyle, the first guy she fucked in high school. Not even Alex.

Damien's pace becomes animalistic and vicious.

"Fuuuuuuck!" He groans. "You're so tight, I'm—"

"Damien, please!" She practically sobs as she grabs his face and pulls him in for another kiss.

His body stills and she feels every muscle coil. Damien comes with a hoarse, raw moan, bucking against her with even more violent spasms than before. After what feels like eternity, he relaxes, pulling back slightly and pressing his sweaty forehead against hers as they begin their slow descent back to reality.

"Holy shit," he laughs. "Holy fucking shit!"

Phoebe's head falls back as her elbows hit the desk.

"Oh my God..."

Damien taps her on the arm.

"Kiss me?" He sounds surprisingly soft, needy.

They share a final deep kiss before he pulls away. For a second she thinks he could be prepping for round two already, but mercifully he pulls out of her and stumbles backward, collapsing onto the bed. She reclines on the desk, barely holding herself up enough to keep eye contact as he lays there.

"So, hey... you want me to sleep on the couch tonight?" His voice is all raspy, as he chuckles.

Phoebe laughs as she slides off of the desk, her legs almost buckling, and she ends up crawling onto the bed to rest her head on his chest.

"No, Damien. I think I'd like it if you stayed right here."

"Thanks, babydoll," he rumbles as he reaches for a pack of cigarettes and a lighter on the nightstand.

"Those fuckin' springs really dig into my back."

Eternal Flame

ATLAS STUDIOS

Phoebe is pressed up against the hotel room wall, a single leg wound around his waist like a ribbon as he holds her still, fucking her as hard and deep as he can. Her naked back is sure to leave an imprint as Damien controls the pace of his thrusts, a sweaty haze clouding her mind. She can feel herself clenching around him like a vice, raking her fingernails down his back for what feels like the hundredth time.

"Damien!" She whines as he sinks his teeth into her shoulder. "Harder!"

He obliges, speeding up the pace as he bites down, almost breaking the skin. Her body is littered with small constellations of bite marks and bruises, and she loves every single one of them. She knows he won't let her fall, his strong arms secure around her body and pinning her in place, but her feet are still straining to reach the floor as he keeps her steady. Sweat clings to her skin as all of her muscles clench and spasm, the entire room practically a sauna after hours of exertion.

She's trembling, not sure how much more she can take before she loses herself. She's never been fucked like this before. Most of the guys she dated were timid, worried about hurting her and never going far enough. Worse, some of them were only concerned with their own pleasure, completely unable to think even vaguely outside that box. Damien, on the other hand, is finding new ways to make her whimper, whine, and beg every couple minutes.

"You're almost there," he breathes. "I can tell."

She loves the way his voice sounds in her ear, his lips pressed right up behind it. He's got her fully under his control, wrapped up both physically and mentally. She couldn't escape if she wanted to. Pleasure rips through her body like wildfire, fraying her nerve endings and making her sing his name like a hymn. Luckily for her, getting away was the last possible thing on her mind as her whole body clenches and convulses.

He's not far behind, diving deep inside her one final time before his knees finally buckle. In those final moments he almost drops her, just managing to catch himself at the last second. In the end, the two of them lean against each other, barely standing, and not an ounce of energy left between them.

"Sorry, sweets," he chuckles.

"It's okay." She shakes her head, blinking in mild disbelief. "Really."

Out of the corner of her eye, she catches the clock on the nightstand just as it flips over: 2:37AM. How many times had they said they were done, just to start up again? She'd completely lost count. So much for a good night's sleep.

Damien pulls out of her, sliding off the condom and tossing it in the trash can next to her desk. He takes her hand and leads her to the bed where the two of them instantly collapse.

When Damien had said he was open to experimentation, she didn't expect it would be a marathon, and as she looks over the aftermath of their first real night together she can't help but laugh. Despite her best efforts to keep them from harm's way, her notes are strewn all over the floor. Some of the pages are ripped and others simply crumpled or scattered, assuredly all of them completely out of order. Their clothes are all over the room, a piece here or there hanging off some piece of furniture or other, but the rest are scattered with no rhyme or reason.

From her spot on the bed, Phoebe can still see the sweaty outline from where he had her pinned to the wall, the two of them sharing many further mementos of the evening. Simply put, they both look like they'd been mauled by a pack of wild animals.

Damien rolls over beside her, breathing like he's just run a marathon.

"I think... I'm good now."

"Yeah?" She laughs. "You sure? I'm not calling you a liar, but I've heard that before. A couple times actually."

"Yeah, definitely," he grins. "I figure it'd only be polite to give you a bit of a break on our first night."

He lights another cigarette, handing her one of her own before stretching out across the bed.

Phoebe lays beside him, soaking up his look of complete contentment for a few minutes before piping up.

"So, how was that compared to your usual experience?"

He smiles with a slight frown, a little taken aback.

"Are you kidding me? That was crazy!"

"Well, sure but like… it's just a rock star thing, right? A new girl every night, down for anything, ready to please."

He smirks.

"First off, it's really not as good as it sounds."

She snorts, rolling her eyes.

"Right, I'm sure they were all total bores."

"Hey, I didn't say that," he gives her a quick little wink before his expression shifts, becoming a little more serious. "The connection we have, though? None of them came even close."

He's telling the truth. At least she thinks so. Not that there'd be any real reason to lie, but it's so easy to just say whatever you think will make someone happy in the moment.

"Well, how about girlfriends? Any long-lost love you've been pining for all this time?"

He raises his eyebrows.

"Ah, I see what's up, you wanna know if I've ever gone steady with someone before? Ever been super serious about anyone?"

She chuckles. He's always so dramatic.

"Well, have you?"

He nods his head, smiling sadly.

"One or two. Nothing that ended well, mind you."

"So what makes us any different?"

She immediately regrets the question but Damien only shrugs, his expression suddenly much more boyish and shy. He stares straight ahead, taking a drag from his cigarette as if it'll return him that extra veil of confidence she just tore away.

"Look, I like you Phoebe." His voice is soft, a small smile on his face. "And it isn't just because you're hot, or we're amazing at fucking. I just like being around you, talking to you, all of it."

This side of him is beautiful, compelling in a completely different way than his rock persona. It's a side that the public has never seen before, and she's sad that she won't be able to show it to them.

"You talk one hell of a game, Bell."

"I mean it. Every word." He blows a smoke ring, turning to face her. "Does that surprise you?"

"I don't know, a little I guess."

"Is it my *reputation*?" He teases.

She can't really say. He's so clearly not that person, but the stories still make her a little nervous. How long before he finds someone else who piques his interest in the same way she did?

As if to break the tension, the phone rings, making both of them jump.

"What the fuck?!" Phoebe hisses. "It's like 3 in the morning, who the hell could that even *be*?"

"Dunno," Damien grunts, stuffing his cigarette between his lips and flopping on top of her.

"Get off!" She wails.

"Relax. I'm not that heavy!"

"You're huge, Damien!"

He wiggles his eyebrows.

"Thanks, babydoll."

She rolls her eyes, laughing as he finally rolls off of her to grab the phone.

"Yeah? Yeah I'm up. You know it's like– What? A TV interview? Who the fuck is up at 7am? Oh, sure, normal people are up at 7? So you're saying I'm a freak, Sullivan?" He looks at Phoebe with a look of mock-despair. "Yeah, okay, fine. I said yes, we'll be up, Jesus Christ."

There's a moderate pause and a grin quickly forms on Damien's face, widening as he looks back over at Phoebe.

"Oh, what were we doing?"

She holds her breath. Even with Troy knowing about their relationship, she prefers that her private life isn't *constantly* being projected to everyone around them.

"It's like 3 in the morning, man, you woke us up."

She relaxes. Maybe he really was turning over a new leaf.

Suddenly, Damien explodes into laughter putting his hand on the receiver. He struggles to get the words out.

"So, turns out Troy's right below us. He heard everything."

Phoebe puts her head in her hands, groaning as she hears Troy's laughter on the other end of the line. At least they came clean early. It could have been much worse.

"Yeah, yeah, we're done up here. I promise. See you at 7."

Damien hangs up the phone, crushing his cigarette in the ashtray before laying back down beside her, his hands behind his head.

"I'm gonna be on TV tomorrow," he says absentmindedly.

"Oh really?"

The band doesn't typically do television appearances, that much is clear from her research. The couple times it's happened were either not particularly notable, or total disasters.

"Yeah. Good Morning Portland or something like that. Apparently they heard we were in town and called Troy up earlier tonight. I think he was waiting until I was too tired to say no. What a brilliant fuckin' strategist."

Phoebe shakes her head to herself, still reeling from being found out.

"I'm so embarrassed that he heard us," she mumbles. "God, how loud were we?"

He grins, kissing her on the cheek.

"Who cares. You had fun, right?"

"I definitely did."

"Good, 'cause there's plenty more where that came from."

He yawns, stretching his entire body out before fluffing up his pillow.

"Unfortunately, the fun stops here for a little while. We've gotta be up in less than three hours."

"Great," she grumbles, pulling a pillow over her head.

Damien flicks off the lights and the two lay in silence for a while. Even with everything that had happened in the last 24 hours running through her head, Phoebe finds it surprisingly easy to let sleep take her, but just as she's about to drift off, she feels Damien shift and roll toward her. She raises the pillow, and even in the darkness she can make out his shit-eating grin.

"Just to let you know for the record, the way we were going at it? He's not the only one who heard us."

Unfortunately, the next thing she knows the phone is ringing right next to her ear. She groans as she reaches for it blindly, finally getting a handle on it by the 4th ring.

"H-Hello?"

Her voice is full of cracks.

"Yes, hello. This is a wakeup call for Damien Bell?"

"Got it. Thank you."

She hangs up and rolls over. Somehow, the phone had no effect and Damien is still completely asleep. Phoebe shakes him lightly.

"Damien."

He presses his face further into the pillow, and swats her away with one hand. She shoves him harder.

"Damien, come on."

His eyes crack open, only the tiniest sliver of them visible as he grumbles.

"You have to be at the studio in an hour."

"Wha? Studio?"

"You're going to be on TV, remember?"

He sits up and rubs his face.

"Ah shit, right." He takes a deep breath psyching himself up. "Okay, okay. Let's do this!"

It's only a few seconds before he drops back onto the mattress, wailing up at the ceiling.

"Fuck, I'm so tired!"

Phoebe isn't really sure what to do. Is this a supportive girlfriend situation? Is that what they've got going on? Suddenly, and much to her surprise, he hops back up, kissing her on the cheek.

"I had fun last night."

"Oh, um, me too." She smiles, glancing around the room a little. "I mean obviously."

Either he was fucking with her earlier, or the man can just summon energy from out of nowhere, because all of a sudden being up with the sunrise is the easiest thing in the world. He pulls on a pair of black briefs, throwing a shirt and some pants on the bed before swaggering back toward her.

"You gonna come to the studio?"

"Do you *really* want me to come with you?"

She wanted to get some sleep, needed it really, but…

"I do. I really do."

She sighs, bracing herself for the horrors of the waking world.

"Okay."

Damien holds one hand over his heart and the other out flat like he's swearing on the Bible.

"And for my part, I promise I won't do anything to draw attention to us." He hops onto the bed and crawls on top of her, his mouth gliding up toward her neck like a magnet. "Even though all I want to do is stay here all day, and make you come *over* and *over* and *over*."

He punctuates each word with a little bite or kiss, as Phoebe runs her hands through his hair and down his back. As he slows and begins to pull away, she bites down on his shoulder.

She can feel him shiver a little in excitement, clearly a bit surprised by her attentiveness this early in the morning.

"Don't start something you can't finish, babydoll," he purrs.

"Unfortunately, it may be too late for that," she mutters, tracing his chest with her finger, playfully drifting lower and lower until... all of a sudden she hears the familiar click of the door.

"Yeah, man that really is unfortunate!"

Shaun's voice makes them both jump.

"You guys seriously don't lock this thing?"

"Oh my God!" Phoebe yelps, quickly covering her whole body with their sheet as Damien slides off the side of the bed, cackling the whole way down.

"Sorry to interrupt, but Troy's been trying to call you and he can't get through."

Phoebe pulls the sheet down and looks over at the phone. Oh god, she must have left it off the hook after the wakeup call. They reach for it at the same time, but Damien is faster.

"We're meeting downstairs in half an hour," Shaun says. "That should give you two plenty of time to get all those sinful urges out!"

"Get the fuck outta here dude," Damien chortles. "We'll be down in a bit."

Phoebe waits a few moments after the telltale click of the door to finally relax and drop the sheet, standing up to find herself surprisingly sore. The realities of the previous night must be catching up to her, feeling aches and pains in places she never has before. Damien chuckles as she groans, trying in vain to massage her own back.

"You good?"

"Yeah, fine," she mutters, cringing as she takes a couple steps. "What was Troy saying about this whole situation? It builds character."

"Come and shower with me."

He's so blunt it catches her off guard. She raises a brow.

"Are we actually going to shower?"

He does a little salute, making sure to look as serious as he can.

"Scout's honor."

She snorts.

"Well, in that case how could I say no?"

Despite the best intentions, they quickly find they have a hard time keeping their hands to themselves. It all starts innocently enough, but before long he's lathering her up with soap, taking every opportunity to tease her in any way he can.

"You're making this really hard."

Damien slips behind her and gently squeezes her inner thigh as he makes his way further up.

"I'm not the one making it hard."

She can feel his cock pressing against her ass.

"No teasing, we don't have any time," she growls.

"Yeah?" His fingers dance between her legs, slipping over her clit for just long enough to make her body jump. "What are you gonna do about it?"

Just as she's about to respond, he pulls her up right up against him with one hand and dives back in to torment her further with the other. Phoebe stands giddily helpless, as Damien begins to massage her swollen bud, his cock rubbing up against her ass with every shift of his body. It's exciting to be back here again. Phoebe's always been drawn to the initial explosion of a relationship, where everything is a clash of mouths, raw confessions, and solving everything with sex. There's a simplicity there that's horribly appealing in a world of complexities and compromise.

Damien slides his fingers into her cunt, slowly at first, clearly savoring her reactions. He's pushed up behind her so tightly that she can feel every little movement he makes, and hear every little sound. His breathing quickens with each moan or yelp she lets out. As she begins to get comfortable, she can feel him shift his body. He leans his head a little further forward, resting it on her shoulder as he crooks his fingers and presses them right up against her G-spot. Phoebe snarls, muscles trembling like leaves, and from the corner of her eyes she can see the edge of his cocky grin.

"I wanna hear you come."

Phoebe shudders even more, leaning back against him, but he stops, pulling his fingers out and stepping away from her. She turns, a perplexed look on her face.

"What are you–?"

"Had to wait for all the soap to wash off." He smiles, dropping down to his knees. He pulls her closer with one hand cupped around her ass, not wasting a single second diving straight inside her with his tongue.

Only a couple seconds in and Phoebe's letting out a string of breathy moans as his tongue lashes around inside her with quick and practiced motions, but the moment her body stops quivering, he slides his tongue up to her clit and begins fingering her all over again. He's reading her body perfectly, constantly keeping her from finding a rhythm to fall into while setting every one of her nerves on fire. She's overwhelmed as he attacks her from every angle, and all she wants is more. Everything he can possibly give her. She's barely hanging on at the very edge, but she needs him to help her fall, grabbing the back of his head and pushing him as hard as she can into her.

"Oh, God!" She cries.

Her hips roll like waves. She tumbles over and over again as he sucks on her clit, the vibrations of his moans tantalizing her pussy. She flutters around him, her heart pounding and her brain a fuzzy mess. She tries to get a breath in, to get her body under control, but it's impossible as he fucks her straight through her climax and into another. It's a hurricane of spasms and screams, loud and explosive. It's all that and more... until it's not. All at once, everything is soft and gentle as Damien walks her through the final moments of her orgasm, slowly and carefully lapping at her clit.

"Bell! Downstairs!" Troy barks from just outside the bathroom door.

Damien jumps a little, pulling himself away from her and chuckling sheepishly.

"I forgot to lock it again," he laughs. "How long have we been in here?"

"A while," she breathes.

"You're just so distracting, Miller, can't get a thing done when you're around."

"*I'm* distracting *you*?!" Phoebe laughs.

Damien shoots her a quick wink as he turns off the shower, and they go about cleaning up and throwing on some robes as quickly as possible. When he opens the door, Troy is standing there with his arms folded across his chest.

"Wonderful. We've all been waiting for you to finish consummating your relationship for the 100th time so that we can get to work!"

"Good morning to you too, Troy," Damien quips.

"Five minutes!" Troy shouts as he walks back into the hall. "And just so you both know, these doors have locks for a reason!"

The studio is nothing special, just a relatively small building with a couple of rooms for shooting, but Phoebe still finds it pretty exciting. The band is split off early, getting prepped in their own room with a direct connection to the stage, while Phoebe and Troy are taken to The Green Room. As they wait for the show to start, Phoebe nervously munches on the leftover treats as she sits on the couch. Off in the corner, Troy fiddles with the television set, hitting it and adjusting the rabbit ears intermittently.

"You know the problem with going to these smaller news stations is that the technology—

work, you son of a bitch! The technology isn't always up to date."

"Yeah, it looks ancient." She frowns. "Actually, that TV looks like my mom's. She's had it for like a decade."

Troy scoffs and nods in agreement.

Suddenly, he lets out a gasp, rushing over and leaning in to look at her.

"What?" She frowns. Troy looks serious.

"What the hell happened to your neck?" He hisses, tugging at the collar of her jacket. "You look like someone hit you with a bat!"

Phoebe flushes and looks straight ahead.

"I... think you heard what happened."

There's a moment where it looks like he might lose his cool, but Phoebe feels a wave of relief as he heads back to the TV set, shaking his head.

"Christ. Tell him to lay off. You could get a blood clot from those hickeys."

With one final whack from Troy, cheesy music fills the room and the sound of the host's far-too-cheery voice blasts over the television set. She's a petite blonde woman in a bright blue suit jacket with shoulder pads that make her head look microscopic, only made up for by her gigantic hair. The band members all sit beside her together on a couch, giving the entire show a more casual air than Phoebe was expecting.

Of the lot, Ophelia and Johnny are the only ones who don't look hungover; Johnny in particular looks great, like he probably ran 15 miles this morning. He's got a youthful glow and a big, beautiful smile that's perfect for morning television. Whereas Damien... well, he's got some sunglasses on to protect from the harsh lights. Someone backstage in the dressing room definitely made him blow dry his hair at least.

"Good Morning, Portland!" The host exclaims. "This morning, I'm thrilled to have the band Revolver joining me in the studio today. From left to right, we have Johnny Reed, bassist; Shaun Slater, guitar; Ophelia Powell, drums; and Damien Bell on vocals. Welcome to the show!"

"Thanks for having us," Johnny replies, flashing his winning smile.

Damien looks uncomfortable, his head is down and he's picking at his fingernails as though he doesn't want to be here at all. Troy sighs beside her.

"Come on, Bell. Look a bit interested at least."

Luckily, the anchor barely seems to take notice.

"Now, I understand that this is your last tour before you head back into the studio to work on your second album. Are you debuting any new songs on this tour?"

"Yeah, Damien's written a few new songs," Shaun answers. "We like to mix it up, you know? Covers, originals from the first album, and we're really excited about the new stuff he's come up with. The lyrics are amazing."

The host smiles.

"Well, we know your penchant for putting a romantic twist on your music, are they all love songs, Damien?"

He sniffles, barely turning his head to talk to her.

"I think any song can be a love song if you look hard enough," he replies. "So, yeah. They can all be love songs if that's what you dig."

She grins, leaning in closer. It feels like she's taking his lack of interest as a challenge.

"Is there maybe a special someone who's *inspired* your lyrics in the past?"

Phoebe rolls her eyes.

"Of course there is," Damien answers with a smirk, like it's the stupidest question he's heard all day. When he doesn't elaborate further, she doubles down, clearly intent on prying some information out of him.

"How about someone in your life who's inspired a song we haven't heard yet, maybe? Someone our captive audience doesn't know about, give us the juicy details, won't you?"

Phoebe hates the way people like this ask their questions, let alone the questions they ask. She hopes this isn't what she sounds like when she's digging for information.

Damien, on the other hand, seems to find something about her most recent question amusing, sliding down his shades. He bites down gently on the tip of one of the arms, just playfully enough to be noticeable. It's not like he's saying her name, but it makes Phoebe a little nervous. Damien looks directly into the camera and it feels like he's staring at her. She squirms in her seat, but can't pull her eyes away from the television set. Just as quickly as his piercing stare begins, he drops it, turning back to the host with nothing more than a wordless shrug.

"Aww, so disappointing. So no new girlfriends, no one special at all?"

With a huge smile on his face, he shakes his head.

"No comment."

Troy drops his head in his hands and leans forward, rubbing his eyes.

"Well, that went as terribly as anticipated."

"I didn't think it was that bad," Phoebe replies, trying to sound as chipper as possible. "Just that one part."

His head snaps up, his face beet-red as he turns to her.

"No offense, Miller. This is just exactly what I was hoping wouldn't happen today. I even told Johnny to make sure he didn't play around with his answers. He could have just kept saying no! Now people are going to speculate and start making guesses, and with you two doing... whatever it is you're doing—"

Phoebe can't help but laugh. It was such a small little thing, and there's no way anyone could make a connection between them.

"It really isn't that much of a deal, Troy. Besides, he's promised to keep all of this a secret. Everything'll be fine."

"Well, you'll learn pretty fast that Bell has a habit of breaking promises," he grumbles. "Whether you're sleeping with him or not."

Up on the screen the band continues the Q&A through to the end of the segment, all while Damien sits silently on the couch, looking *very* proud of himself.

Listen to Your Heart

THE SAPPHIRE HOTEL

"Damien, I have work to do!"

They're back at the hotel, and Damien's been pulling his normal routine and trying to goad her into his little games. The last 24 hours had been lovely, but his constant attention had put her a little further behind on her article than she'd like.

"Besides, I'll be there for the show. What do you need me at soundcheck for?"

"I need my muse, it gets me in the right mood." He slinks towards her. "If I remember right, you really like me when *I'm inspired.*"

She flushes, turning away.

"You can make googly eyes at me all you want during the show, same as always."

Damien chuckles.

"True, true." He strikes a melodramatic pose before heading to the door. "I suppose I can go without my girl for a couple hours."

Phoebe sighs as the door clicks shut, running her fingers through her hair. She's been struggling to reconcile the two versions of him since she started looking back over her notes. She wants to focus on what he's let shine through since their hike up Mt. Tabor, but it's a side that he's hid away from everyone else, nothing like the version of himself he wears on stage. What would he say if she showed the world how lovely he can be? Would it help more than it hurt? She has to pick an angle, or the article has no pillar to build around. How can she know what to write if she's still not even exactly sure who her subject really is?

She struggles with her outline for a couple of hours before the sudden shrill ring of the phone snaps her out of her funk, and she lunges for it; any excuse to think about anything else.

"Hello?"

"Phoebe?"

"Janis?"

"Hey! I had to jump through hoops to get a hold of you. Your uh, your name wasn't on any of the rooms!"

Phoebe laughs.

"Oh yeah, that was a whole thing, but we got it sorted out."

Janis doesn't take more than a couple seconds to cut straight to the point.

"Are you staying in his room?"

"Oh! Uh, no I'm just in here because– There was a leak or something and I needed a place to–"

Janis sighs, beginning to chuckle.

"I told you!"

Phoebe can almost picture her friend's face on the other end of the line.

"I know."

"Are you sleeping with him?"

She doesn't know what to say, and her silence is only met with more laughter.

"I knew it! I had this feeling in my gut."

"Janis, I don't need you making fun of me. I already feel like a fucking idiot."

"I'm not making fun! I said I wanted you to see where things were going, remember?"

"Yeah, yeah you did."

"So have a little fun with him. What's the harm?"

Phoebe huffs.

"Let's see. Brian finding out and losing all his respect for me? Losing my job? Not being able to finish the stupid article because Damien is latched onto my neck like a vampire?"

Janis cackles.

"Okay, the last one? Sounds like you're bragging a bit. How big are your hickeys? I have to know."

Phoebe glances in the mirror, pushing her hair aside and admiring his handiwork in detail for the first time.

"Damn, wow yeah, they're like the size of silver dollars."

Janis groans.

"Fuuuuuck, that sounds amazing. It's unfair really, we're both out on work trips and you're the only one getting laid."

"So go do it!" Phoebe laughs, tilting back on her chair. "Take your own advice and go find a nice Icelandic hottie and rock their world."

"Girl, I wish. I've been at this summit for two full days, I've barely slept at all, and nothing. The only people hitting on me are a couple guys from CNN and that's a huge no-go. Every time I get near them all I can smell is deli meat and bad cologne. Worst part is I was supposed to be flying back tomorrow but my flight got pushed and I'm probably going to have to sit around the airport all day long."

"Nasty. Well, was Japan any better?"

"Pheebs, it was so good! Grandma says hi by the way, and that she loves you, and she misses you of course. We had a good talk about Jeremy, one that ended with a bunch of words I will not repeat here, and I helped her out with some stuff she needed fixed. She even loaded me up with snacks to take home!" She sighs happily. *"Oh, hey wait a second, where are you guys all gonna be tomorrow?"*

Phoebe flips through her notebook, a quick refresher after the whirlwind of the last few days.

"Looks like Vegas? Two days at Caesar's Palace, and then we're moving on to Phoenix."

"Oh hell yes, Vegas for a couple days? I'm sure I can get a ticket, and it sure beats sitting around in an airport for 24 hours."

"You sure, Jan? That's not a cheap flight."

"I'm serious! I just miss you, Pheebs. We never even got to have drinks before I left, and it's all lining up perfectly. Besides, I'm basically a wizard at charging things to the company."

Phoebe smiles at the thought. They could blow off some steam, get some drinks, and Janis could actually meet the band, really see how great they are. She might even manage to steal Damien's thunder for a couple hours.

"Fuck it, you know what? Let's do it."

"Okay, perfect! Listen. I've gotta go harass a lady about a ticket. I'll see you in Vegas. Ceasar's Palace right?"

"That's the one," Phoebe chuckles. "I'll try and score you a backstage pass."

"Well, I should expect so. What other possible reason could you have for sleeping with the frontman?"

Phoebe snorts.

"Weren't you in a hurry?"

"Right, on my way! Later girl, love ya!"

"Love you too."

As she hangs up, Phoebe's mind is already swirling with possibilities, but she only has a couple seconds to think before the phone's shriek breaks her concentration yet again.

"Janis, if this is–"

"Miller."

It's Troy. She glances over at the clock.

"Oh, sorry, I thought–"

"Show's in an hour. Damien's wondering where you are, keeps bringing it up. Honestly, it's really annoying. Think he might have a crush."

She laughs, picturing a flustered Damien haplessly watching the door for her to arrive.

"Tell him I'll be there in a little bit. I just have to get dressed."

"See you soon, kiddo. And don't worry, it'll probably do him good to stew a little."

She leans back in her chair, glancing over her notes and the almost-zero progress she'd made.

"Fuck it."

Phoebe arrives at the venue in a pink mini skirt, fishnet thigh highs, and a black halter top underneath her leather jacket. She's sporting the boots that Ophelia bought her back in LA to add a little bit to her stature, topping it all off with some liberally applied eyeshadow. Troy is already standing at the bar, at least a couple drinks into his nightly ritual. His jaw drops as he turns.

"Whoa! Miller! I'm not used to seeing you in something so... short." He covers his eyes with one hand, feigning embarrassment. "I feel like I shouldn't be seeing this."

She shrugs.

"Well, when in Rome right?"

"And for a Roman, you look great! Come on."

Troy ushers her toward the back room where the band is rehearsing. She can hear Damien singing lyrics she's never heard before. She pushes the door open and quickly moves to the back of the room, just listening to the richness of his voice as he sings. He's wearing a shirt for once, pure mesh of course, and tight leather pants. He's facing away from her, his head dropped low right next to Shaun who's strumming away on an acoustic guitar. The lyrics are interesting, about a lover long lost to time and space. It's a little bit outside of his usual work. When Shaun plays the final note, Phoebe breaks into enthusiastic applause.

"That was beautiful."

Damien turns around and sees her, and his mouth curls into a mischievous smile.

"Well thank you very much, miss. I do have to ask how you got all the way back here. This is a closed-off area after all."

She chuckles. She can see his chest heaving. From the performance, or something else?

"The song was lovely, Damien, but I don't think you have a career in comedy."

He bites into his lip, his eyes burning into her. He looks like a hungry dog.

"I'm gonna go out for a smoke, you coming?"

Somehow in the couple hours away she forgot just how he made her feel, immediately dropping the playful ribbing.

"I– Yes."

It's practically a whisper.

The band whistles and hollers behind her as Damien takes her hand and leads her outside, but almost none of it registers. She's completely focused on the moment. Once they're out in the fresh air he wastes no time, immediately pinning her against the wall.

"Are you fucking kidding me in this outfit?"

"Thought you might like it."

"Like it? Fuck, I like it so much I'm gonna feel terrible ripping it to shreds."

She brushes her thumb across his bottom lip before grabbing his hand and guiding it between her legs. Damien raises an eyebrow.

"You're not wearing anything."

When in Rome indeed.

"I figured you'd just tear them off," she moans as he massages her clit, making her whole body tighten in response. "Seems like I was right."

He lets out a long, slow breath.

He's trying to keep cool.

"We only have about five minutes before Troy busts through that door and sees something he'll definitely regret."

She arches a brow, grinning.

"Well, if you're as good as you say…" She trails off as Damien gets to work, not wasting any time as he slides first one and then two fingers inside her. She's practically drenched already, just from his presence, from his lips on hers. Not to mention those fucking hands.

Damien fucks her slowly with his fingers, lapping up the moans spilling from her lips like he'll never hear them again. Everything about him is electric and exciting and magical, and every other thing a rock star should be. Damien curls his fingers, pressing against her G-spot. Her head rocks back, slamming into the brick wall as her first orgasm of the night washes over her whole body. She tries to keep from yelling out in pleasure or pain, not wanting to draw any attention, and hisses through her teeth as the waves overwhelm her stinging head. He grins as he unbuckles his belt with one hand, fishing a condom out of his jacket pocket. His fingers fumble as he opens it, swearing softly under his breath. Phoebe kisses him.

"Getting impatient, loverboy?"

"When it comes to you? Always."

He groans as she helps him roll it onto his cock, her fingers sliding down his shaft with just enough pressure to rile him up. She glances up and down the alley, straining her neck a little to be absolutely sure they're alone. When she's finally satisfied, she pinches the hem of her skirt, tilting her head coyly as she slowly lifts it all the way up. She can feel the cool breeze against her newly bare skin as he steps toward her.

"Gonna fuck you now."

A shiver runs up her entire body as he grabs her waist, turning her around and pushing her up against the wall as he gets into position. She bends over, her forearms braced against the wall as his cock presses precariously against her cunt. He plays with her for a couple moments, pressing in just enough to stretch her lips open before pulling back out again. She cranes her neck, looking back at him with desperation in her eyes. It's all she can do to hold herself still.

"Please," she begs. "Damien, please."

The words are clearly enough for him, and Phoebe's initial sharp grunts quickly turn into a singular loud moan as he pushes his way into her. The fit is near-perfect, stretching her to the point where pain just begins to mingle with pleasure, and completely dominates every speck of her attention. Just as she's getting used to the sensation, Damien wraps his arms around her waist, forcing her even closer toward him as he sinks his teeth into her shoulder. Phoebe claps one of her hands over her mouth, barely muffling her scream as she spreads her legs apart. She can feel her labored breaths against her own fingers with each movement, every massive thrust accompanied by the loud slap of his skin against her ass as she struggles to stay up straight.

She can hear him chuckle in her ear, the sound spreading goosebumps across her skin like a storm.

"Well well well, you like it a little rough, huh?"

"Is it that— obvious?" She smirks, craning her neck to look at him.

Even as her words are punctuated by her own grunts, she feels the need to test him. He's at his best when he's trying to make a lasting impression, after all.

He grips her chin, forcing her to look straight ahead as he growls into her ear.

"Now now, you're gonna be a good fuckin' girl for me, aren't you?"

"Yes," she whimpers, his cock slamming into her.

She can feel her thighs clench together as she shudders, dropping down a little bit against the wall. With each sentence he slides himself almost entirely out of her, the head of his cock resting just at her entrance, before slamming himself back in.

"So sweet."

She starts to buckle, her knees quivering as she struggles to hold herself up.

"So soft."

He's relentless, clearly getting more and more turned on the less control she has over herself.

"Fuck, you're gorgeous. You're gonna make me come."

All of a sudden he pulls out of her, helping her back up and turning her around to face him. She stares into his eyes, her heartbeat only just beginning to slow as he lifts her arm up to his shoulder.

"Damien, I–"

He puts a finger on her lips as he gently pushes her against the wall, lining himself up to fuck her face-to-face. She grips his shoulder tightly, as he pushes inside her again, quickly returning to his previous pace.

"Fuck– Damien!" she keens through her teeth.

If they were in a hotel room, she'd be screaming his name, but there has to be some discretion here. As long as she can manage it at least. She's so close, he has to be too. Any second now. Her eyes slam shut as Damien lifts one of her legs further, fully in control as he pins her against the wall. Somehow it feels like he's hitting her G-spot with every thrust.

"You like that?" His breath is heavy in her ear.

She nods, gritting her teeth.

"You love how I fuck you, don't you? Say it."

"Yes! Fuck!" She gasps, barely able to get the words out before holding back another moan.

Damien grabs a handful of her hair and pulls her head back, thrusting ferociously until she's completely lost at the peak of the moment. She can feel herself come, the waves carrying her off the edge of the cliff, but it doesn't seem to end. She doesn't hit the ground, reality doesn't fade back in as she comes down from the orgasmic high. Instead, the wave of liquid fire continues through her over and over again.

"You're fucking beautiful," Damien moans.

Even in her compromised state she can feel his grip tightening, his movements becoming more erratic and strained, until he finally comes with one final thrust.

He leans against her, his weight still pressing her up against the alley wall while the two of them heave in the aftermath. As their ragged breathing slows, Phoebe becomes distinctly aware of her surroundings again, but luckily, as far as she can tell, they're still alone. She can feel his cock recede bit by bit as the two of them fully regain their composure, letting out a little gasp as he finally pulls it all the way out with a satisfyingly sloppy pop. She gazes down as he steps away, the tip of the condom completely filled with his cum. She bites her lip, smirking as he tosses it to the side. Looks like he really was excited to see her.

"What?" He asks, smiling a little himself.

"Nothing, I'm just amazed, that's all. I think we finished in time. There's no Traumatized Troy in sight."

The two start to put themselves back together, with Phoebe having a significantly harder job. As she pulls out her pocket mirror to struggle with the new disaster of her hair, Damien pipes up.

"I was actually just planning to buy you a drink, be all charming and thoughtful, that whole thing. Then I saw you in that outfit, fuck."

She smiles.

"You can buy me one after the show."

Her eyes find his, full of confidence in the afterglow.

"Who knows, if you're charming enough maybe you'll get somewhere."

Damien passes her a cigarette and leans back against the wall.

"You think I have a shot?"

She takes a drag and hands it back before putting the final touches on her salvaged look.

"Anything's possible."

As they ready themselves to head back inside, the sound of voices make them both jump. Panic briefly takes her as Phoebe turns to see someone walking down the alley toward them, but quickly relaxes. It's simple, just act natural. Nothing to see here, after all.

"Phoebe?" A voice calls.

And suddenly, it's not simple anymore.

Phoebe's mind races as the figure gets closer, desperately trying to place the voice, but she doesn't have to wait long. There's a group of them, clearly a band, all hauling their shit to the back door. Her whole body goes on high alert. She hasn't seen him in a year. Over a year now.

"Alex?"

She's still not fully processing the scene that's playing out in front of her. Damien stands beside her, smoking quietly, and perfectly calm. Her heart leaps into her throat as Alex approaches, his arms spread out and going in for a hug.

"Hey! So it is you! How are you Phoebe?"

What the fuck is going on?

"I'm– I– I'm good!"

"It's been a long time!"

She laughs awkwardly as Alex wraps her gently in his arms.

"It– it has, yeah. How are you?"

There's a woman walking up behind him. Redhead, pretty, a baby bundled in her arms. She glances around awkwardly for a bit before Phoebe finally places her. She was a roadie on Alex's last tour. The last tour *they* were together for.

"Good! Great, actually." He glances back at the woman. "Oh, shit, sorry that was rude. This is Emma. Emma, this is Phoebe. You two met once or twice I think?"

Emma waves, forcing a smile. This is clearly as awkward for her as it is for Phoebe.

"And you... have a kid now!" She tries to keep it sounding casual, but she can't wash the surprise from her mouth.

"Yeah," Alex laughs, smooth as always. "That's Krista."

He smiles and offers a half-shrug.

"A year can really change you, huh?"

Her chest aches as she sucks on her cigarette, her mind suddenly flooded with year-old insecurities.

"It really does, yeah," she mutters.

Damien clears his throat, clearly sensing her discomfort, and Alex turns to face him.

"Wow, so you're Damien Bell, right?"

Damien tosses his cigarette on the ground.

"The one and only."

"Alex Ström. We're opening for you tonight. Actually, I've wanted to meet you for a while. Love your stuff."

"Riiiiiight," Damien replies. "And your band is, uh..."

"Delirium."

"Of course." Damien sticks his hand out. "Cool, man. Nice to meet you."

"You too."

Alex glances at Phoebe. He knows. He knows what she's been doing. Because it's the same thing all over again. She's a creature of habit.

"Hey, it's great to see you, Pheebs. You look good."

"Thanks." It's little more than a whisper. "You too."

"Well, see you two inside!" He's almost too jovial as he follows the rest of his band into the building, and Damien scoffs even before the door's fully closed.

"Dude looks like a discount Vince Neil."

Phoebe turns to him, still a little shaky.

"Um, hey, It'll probably be fine but can you keep– I mean, can you maybe ask Troy to keep an eye on him tonight? For me?"

Maybe it's too much to ask. He's not her boyfriend, not really, and this isn't part of his job. Maybe he'll laugh, tell her not to take it so seriously. That she's being ridiculous. She's fun for him now, but once she becomes a chore he'll find someone else.

Damien wraps his arms around her, kissing the tip of her nose. His voice is steady, like he doesn't have a single doubt in the world.

"If he tries anything, I'll kick his fucking teeth in."

She buries her head in his chest as a sense of relief fills her up. It's warm, and she feels a completely unexpected kind of comfort just being close to him. She doesn't even have to look up to know his eyes are only on her.

"You're mine, babydoll."

History Repeating

THE SAPPHIRE HOTEL

S moke and music fill the bar as Phoebe watches Alex strutting around on the stage. He doesn't have Damien's presence, but he has *something*. It's the same thing that pulled her toward him on that tour, probably the same thing that broke her heart. She thanks the bartender and grabs her drinks, heading to a table where Damien is sitting with a few of the roadies. It's a little awkward, but significantly less conspicuous than going at each other in the alley like animals. She slides Damien's whiskey over to him, sipping on her gin and tonic and trying to hide her smile as he shoots her a knowing look. It's impossible, so why even try. She shifts around the table, taking a seat a little closer to him.

"So, when I asked about you being in love before, it was this dude?"

He has an incredulous look on his face, pointing offhandedly at the stage.

"Sure," she laughs. "Make it obvious."

"Don't stress it, he's not looking our way at all."

He's right. As she looks back up at Alex she can tell his attention's split almost evenly between the crowd and someone offstage. Looks like Emma really did make things work for her.

And isn't that exactly how Damien looks at her now?

She takes a big sip of her drink.

The parallel makes her stomach turn. Has she really just fallen for a carbon copy of the same man? What do they say about those who don't learn from history?

"I still can't get over it," Damien continues, sitting back in his chair. "Discount Vince Neil, man that's wild."

"Stop calling him that!" She has to fight back a laughing fit whenever he brings it up. "It's really mean."

"Nah, just honest." He lights a cigarette. "So, how long were you together?"

She sighs. Never the best thing to think back on.

"Four months. It was very hush-hush, but it was intense."

"Like with us?" Damien asks.

"I don't know, would you say we're *together*?" She teases.

He shrugs.

"You're with me the whole tour, Phoebe. What do you think?"

She silently drags a fingertip around the rim of the glass. Not quite the answer she was hoping for, but not a no.

Damien blows a smoke ring.

"How'd it end? You and him."

"The tour ended, and we ended along with it. He said he would call, and I waited by the phone like an idiot."

Something about what she said makes Damien look a little uncomfortable.

"You know how these things usually go, though. Right?"

She bristles at his response. He's worried she doesn't know what's coming.

"I'm painfully aware."

He stares at her intently, and for a moment it seems like he has something he's about to say, but he returns to his drink instead. Phoebe lets out a deep breath, looking straight down at her drink. Why can't they be talking about literally anything else? The silence between them rolls on for a while, punctuated by couple song transitions up on stage, until Damien breaks their awkward stalemate.

"For what it's worth, I'm sorry it went down like that."

"Thanks," she mutters. "Me too."

Yet again, not the feel-good moment she was hoping for.

He sinks down a little in his chair and she can feel his foot tap against hers. He's trying to be cute. To make it better. All she can offer in return is a tight-lipped smile, her mind still swirling.

"Hey."

All of a sudden his face is completely sincere as he looks over at her.

"Hi?" She laughs. There's something particularly funny about how awkward it all is. "What's up?"

"I just– I want you to know, I would have called you."

She laughs even harder. She has to, otherwise she's just setting herself up for heartbreak.

"No Damien, I'm pretty sure you wouldn't have."

Damien leans forward, that confident little smirk finding its way back onto his lips.

"Think you know me that well?"

Her chest feels tight. She really doesn't, but she wants to so badly. She can feel the hair on her neck stand up as his hand ever so slightly brushes her fingers.

Mercifully, Alex's voice breaks them from the moment.

"Thank you, Portland. We're done for the night, but you'd better stay in those seats because coming right up is the band you've all been waiting for!"

The crowd explodes into a chorus of cheers and applause.

Damien leans back in his seat, grinning as he crushes his cigarette in an ashtray. They're clearly not here for Alex, they're here for him. She's here for him, and he loves it.

"You coming?" Damien asks.

Troy is a couple tables away, gesturing for Damien to hurry it up.

"I'm gonna watch from here," she tells him.

"Good. I don't want to look like an asshole singing to someone just off stage." She chuckles, shaking her head as he stands and straightens his outfit. "It's a longshot, but I was hoping there'd be a pretty girl somewhere in the middle of the crowd, a real nerd, maybe with dark hair?" He starts to walk away but stops himself. "Oh, and she absolutely has to be in a bright pink mini skirt, that's the key to this whole 'muse' thing!"

"Careful, don't want to overdo it with all that charm Bell," she quips. "Save some for the stage."

"I'm a generous man, there's enough to go around!" He winks. "Don't worry though, I promise to only ever use my powers for good."

"Okay, alright, let's go, Romeo," Troy grumbles, hooking his fingers into Damien's thin mesh t-shirt and trying to drag him away. "What the hell are you thinking pulling this stuff in public?"

"Troy, anyone ever tell you that you might need something for your blood pressure? Better yet, let's get you checked into an old-folks home so you can finally chill out with your peers."

"Kid, when I die of a heart attack at the age of 40, my tombstone will read: Here lies Troy Sullivan, Fantastic Manager and Cultural Touchstone. At the bottom, an addendum: P.S. It was Bell's fault."

Damien snorts, ruffling Troy's hair.

"I love that even on your tombstone I'm the main attraction. It's just nice to be remembered."

Phoebe watches them leave, a little smile lingering on her face as she flips open her notebook to continue what she started back at the hotel. It's mostly concept words for the article – how she wants to frame it, what it should look like. She's still debating doing the entire piece on Damien's softer side. It might do him some good to abandon the bad boy image for a while. Something about it feels generic, like a cheap halloween costume of a rockstar. A little too much like Alex.

The chair beside her screeches against the floor as someone takes a seat.

"Hey."

She doesn't even need to look up.

"Hi."

"So, you're with Revolver these days?"

"Yeah. It's gonna be a cover story for Titanium."

"Nice," he replies. "Congratulations. You definitely deserve it, your piece on us was great."

"Thanks." Her words are muted. Subdued. "Sorry it didn't get you guys more attention."

He shrugs.

"Sometimes things just don't work out. Besides, I think if we'd gotten bigger, I wouldn't have had as much time to be a dad. Turned out to be a blessing in disguise."

The words feel like a knife right through her chest, but she swallows the pain.

"Congratulations, by the way." She's trying desperately for sincerity. She makes it about halfway. "I'm happy for you."

"Thanks." He pauses for a moment, obviously unsure exactly how to broach the subject. "I, uh, I know it must have been a shock."

"Yeah," she laughs. "Considering you didn't ever call, then you show up a year later with a baby. Jury's still out on the timeline for that one. "

She winces, knowing instantly it was a mistake to say it. Didn't even feel good to get out.

"Sorry," she mumbles.

To her surprise, Alex only laughs.

"It's fine, Phoebe. You have every right to be upset, and, look, I really am sorry that I hurt you."

"You didn't hurt me. I'm fine."

It might be the most obvious lie she's ever told.

She wants to ask him about Emma, what made things work out between the two of them that couldn't have also worked with her, but she decides against purposefully devastating herself today.

Alex just smiles and sips at his beer.

"You're a terrible liar. You always were when we were together, too."

"Fuck you, Alex, I'm a fantastic liar."

He sighs.

"Do you want to know why I didn't call you?"

"Stupidity?" She spits the word out like poison.

Alex drops his head and laughs.

"There's that patented Phoebe Miller razor wit. I missed it."

"Don't get used to it," she mumbles.

When he raises his head again his smile is still there, just a little sadder.

"It's really simple, and it was definitely shitty, but by the end I'd just fallen for Emma."

Phoebe had thought about this day for a whole year, picturing every little thing each of them would say, how she'd storm out and make him regret everything. How she'd feel so much better afterward. Somehow, it was never anything like this. Tears begin to pool in her eyes as her old anger bubbles up, but she does all she can to push it back down and lock it away. It can live in there for the rest of her life, until she dies old and alone for all she cares. She's not going to let him see her like that. She wants to scream, throw her drink in his face, call him every name she can think of. Instead she just turns back to the stage.

Damien is adjusting his mic stand, staring right at her with that big cocky smile. Occasionally he glances over at Alex, but there's not a hint of jealousy. She can see it in his eyes: he's not a threat, he barely even registers on Damien's radar. She sips on her drink, praying that the alcohol will kick in sooner rather than later, and Alex reaches over and taps her hand while he gestures to Damien.

"So, you and Bell?"

She stares straight ahead.

"Just friends."

She has no idea why she lies, but he just laughs.

"There you go again, just terrible." He pauses, taking time to contemplate what he's about to say next before he leans in closer. "Phoebe do– do you still have feelings for me?"

Her head whips around so quickly he leans back a little, and she glares at him. Where is this coming from?

"You have a *girlfriend* and a *baby*, Alex. We're not having this conversation."

He smiles, unfazed by her venom.

"Wife, actually."

She blinks.

"What?"

"She's my wife. Emma and I got married last month."

"Wow. Okay," she breathes. "I..."

It's too much information for her to process at once. She looks for the exit and contemplates fleeing outside for a cigarette before the set, but right on cue the microphone reverberates along with Damien's voice.

"Good evening, Portland! We're Revolver and we want to play you a few songs tonight. Hope you're all into that."

A huge cheer erupts from the crowd, and even Alex lets out a little whoop along with them. She hears Ophelia's drumsticks clack together four times and the music starts, with Damien launching into a classic from their album. Alex gestures to the stage with one hand.

"Man, right out the gate, he's incredible."

Phoebe nods.

"He really is."

Alex watches half of the set with her before Emma approaches the table, clearly a little pissed off. Alex takes the hint, standing up and opening himself up for a hug.

"Well, it was great to see you Phoebe, but we gotta go and put the kid to bed."

She nods, standing and giving the most awkward hug of her life as her whole body rejects the very idea.

"Yeah, it was great," she mutters to no one, watching him vanish into the crowd with his arm slung around Emma's shoulder. In the blink of an eye, they're practically strangers again. Funny how that happens.

That last two weeks of the tour was when the fire between them began to die. She should have suspected something, but she boiled it down to Alex just being bummed out that four months of traveling with zero responsibilities was finally coming to an end. A week before, they were on the tour bus, lying half naked underneath his leather jacket. They'd snuck out to have sex just after sound check while the rest of the band got drinks and relaxed, thinking no one would notice. It was stupid, the whole band knew, but it didn't matter. She was so happy just to be with him. The weight of his "I love you" hit her so hard that she said it back without a thought, and she can still feel the way each word lodged itself in her heart.

And it won't ever happen again.

She looks back up at the stage, giving it all of her attention for the rest of the evening. It feels good to let herself get swept up in Damien's hypnotic stare, or the way his hair falls perfectly over his eyes as he sings. His energy is quieter this evening, no bottle of whiskey prepped at the side of the stage to pour down his chest, no outstretched hands into the crowd. Phoebe drains her drink and makes her way backstage, ultimately standing next to Troy in the wings. He seems surprised to see her.

"Hey, kiddo."

"Hey."

"Everything okay? I saw you talking to that singer from the opening act."

"Yeah," she replies. "All good. Old friend."

"Are we talkin' old friends the way you and Damien are friends?"

"Your deductive skills at work?" she chuckles.

"It's my greatest talent. That, and being extraordinarily handsome, oh and funny. Stylish too…"

"Never forget modest," she adds.

"Yep, that's a good one!" He stretches out his arms. "That'll go to the top of the list."

Phoebe smiles. She was wary of Troy at first, but the more she gets to know him, the more she likes him. Like a discount-dad away from home.

Oh shit. Vegas. Janis.

"Oh hey, Troy, I have a friend from The New Yorker who maybe, just maybe, might be meeting up with us in Vegas. Is that cool?"

"The New Yorker?" Troy asks with a raised brow. "I didn't know we were that high caliber."

"Oh, no, it's– She's a political writer mostly," Phoebe replies. "She's been my best friend since we were kids. We don't get a lot of opportunities to catch up because we're both always away on assignments, so I'm really hoping we can make this happen."

She expects some pushback, more questions, or even a flat-out no, but Troy only has to think for a couple seconds before he responds.

"Sure, so long as she doesn't get in the way of anything, I don't see the harm."

She fights back some tears, the kind that come along with relief in the midst of a disaster, and he gives her a light pat on the shoulder before turning back to the stage. She can tell he's pretending not to notice.

"Thanks, Troy."

After two encores the band is finally free, and Damien immediately grabs her hand as they all head back to the dressing room, his arm quickly finding its way around her waist. He's drenched in sweat, but she doesn't care. As everyone piles into the dressing room to have a few congratulatory beers, Damien pulls her into a half-lit corner. He caresses her face, running the pad of his thumb along her cheekbone. She leans into his touch, humming softly.

She can see the outline of his smile in the darkness as he leans in to kiss her. Phoebe moans, her skin tingling as she runs her hands up and down his chiseled arms. He really is the only man to ever give her full-body goosebumps from just a kiss. Maybe that'll be enough. He leaves her breathless as he pulls away, staring into her eyes for a moment before Phoebe reaches up to touch his face with her trembling fingers. Maybe this time, even when it all ends, it will have been enough.

"What was that for?" She asks.

"You looked sad out there."

She looks away, not wanting to drag down the mood.

"Did you get the answers you were looking for?"

"I definitely got answers," she sighs.

He smiles and leans forward, ready to capture her lips in another kiss, but stops.

"I would have called you," he says firmly. "I would have called every fucking day."

She winces.

"Don't say stuff like that."

He tilts his head.

"Why not?"

"Because I– Look, things are fine. I'm fine."

Don't pull that thread. Please, don't pull at that thread.

"Hey, you two!" Shaun yells from the dressing room. "Your beers are getting warm!"

Damien stares at her, his bright eyes almost glowing in the low light.

"I would have. I promise."

She smiles, a little sadly. Maybe it doesn't matter that it's probably a lie.

"Thank you for saying that."

He frowns, clearly unhappy with how little his charms are perking up her mood, and picks her up in one swoop. She squeals with laughter.

"Damien!"

"Calm down, calm down, I'm just giving you the royal treatment, milady!"

She lets herself relax into his arms as he carries her through the door, and soon she's nestled between his legs on a table at the center of the room. She listens to him joke with Johnny while he runs his fingers through her hair, twisting it into tiny braids and giving her little kisses on the neck here and there. It's lovely being with them, all of them. This little family she's found. For the first time all night, she doesn't think about Alex at all. It will hurt when it's over, the same as it did with him. More.

It'll tear through her like a hail of bullets.

But for now, this is enough.

On the Road Again

The Middle of Nowhere

The bus's engine rumbles through the floor beneath her feet. The band is exhausted, with almost everyone passed out in their seats, swaddled in big blankets. She can hear Troy's snoring from all the way at the front. He's almost louder than the bus. She has no idea what time it is. They're at least a few hours into the 16 hour straight-shot to Vegas, but she's long since buried her watch in her bag to keep from checking it every couple of minutes. Even without that constant distraction it feels impossible to sleep. As she shifts in her seat, tugging at the blanket that she and Damien share, he opens his eyes.

"You good?"

She nods.

"Just tired."

"Me too."

Damien wraps his arms around Phoebe as she rests her face against his chest, listening to the steady sound of his heartbeat. The road is bumpy, and there's something about the eerie silence of the bus that keeps her just on the verge of sleep, even in the comfort of his arms. Damien appears to be having the same issue, grunting and shifting every few minutes. Nobody else on the bus seems to have a problem; it might be funny if it wasn't so frustrating.

Phoebe gives up on trying to sleep for what feels like the 100th time, laying half-awake against him, staring out the window at the blackened sky. He runs his hand gently through her hair and she sighs.

"Hey."

She leans in as he brushes his fingers against her ear.

"I think it's safe to say neither of us is getting to sleep, right?"

She shakes her head, and Damien smiles.

It doesn't take a whole lot more than that to get him going.

Everyone except the driver is asleep, and they're sat far enough back on the bus that they might be able to keep from being heard. Damien dips his head to kiss her. It's intense and a little bit sloppy. She hisses as his fingers begin to find their way up her thigh.

"We can't, what if they wake up?"

He presses his lips to her ear, his voice dropping to a whisper. The sound, combined with the sensation of his fingers carefully gliding under her skirt makes her shudder.

"It's not even daylight out. Everyone's fast asleep. Take a look."

Phoebe glances around the bus. Shaun and Ophelia are passed out on the back bench, turned away with their backs to the rest of the bus. Johnny hasn't moved in hours. Troy's been an unending flow of snores.

"What about the driver?"

She gasps as he flicks her earlobe with his tongue.

"He can't see back here," Damien whispers. His hand stills, waiting for her to make the call. "Whaddya say, sweets? We'll be quiet as mice."

Phoebe sighs. It's this or another dozen hours of sleepless discomfort, and one of those options sounds a lot better than the other.

"We can chalk this up to some more experimentation."

Damien grins, lowering his head to suck on her neck.

"That's my girl."

She shivers as his fingers glide down to play in the growing heat between her thighs, her hand ghosting over the front of his jeans.

"Do you feel how hard you make me?" He growls, pressing himself against her hand.

Her body is blazing-hot, and she can only nod as she bites her lip, terrified to make a sound. His fingers playfully test her limits, in, and out, in and out. With each exit he takes a moment to circle his fingers around her clit, but never close enough to make real contact.

It's driving her mad, but two can play at that game.

Slowly, carefully, she unzips his jeans and wraps her fingers gingerly around his cock. She takes a moment, feeling it twitch in her hand. How many times will she have to see how fucking big it is before she gets used to it? Damien starts to fuck her a little harder with his fingers; she's falling behind in this race. Phoebe begins to stroke his cock, applying enough pressure that it'd be impossible to ignore, only to release the shaft and trace along his tip with a single finger. She smiles to herself as she feels his whole body tighten up. She teases his cock, her lips pressing down on it like she's about to take it all inside her before pulling away with a little flick of her tongue. Her fingers slide up and down its length for just long enough to make it swell even more, all with no sign of release. Serves him right, the arrogant bastard. The incredibly skilled, gorgeous, arrogant bastard.

Keeping the torment up is harder for Phoebe than she thought, though, as the sight of him straining to keep in control lights her up even more. She wets her lips, running them along his perfect jawline. As she nips at the skin, Damien lets out an excited moan. It's enough to put her over the edge. She may have won the battle, but he's winning the war.

"I need you," she whispers.

"Easy, babydoll," he chuckles. "I gotta finish warming you up first."

The moment he curls his fingers she lets out a short, high-pitched squeak of surprise.

Fuck. And they'd been doing so well.

The two of them freeze in their seats, eyes darting quickly around the bus as they listen for any change. Nobody moves, nobody calls out to ask if everything is okay. Thankfully, it seems like the only response to her little outburst is Troy's snoring ramping up in intensity.

Damien's eyes are full of fire, the entire situation seeming to have set him off on another level completely. Before they even have a chance to agree the coast is clear, he starts pumping his fingers into her again. Her body jerks, excitement overlapping fear as he smothers another one of her yelps with his free hand.

"Fuck, you're so wet," he growls. "I think you might be into this, hmm? You're so getting excited, all 'cause we might get caught. Hell, what will they all think when they see what you're like with me?"

She holds back as much as she can, groaning into his hand. Damien, ever the wordsmith, just keeps talking as he plays inside her. So much for staying quiet.

"When we were in California, and I heard you on the other side of the wall, what were you thinking about?"

He moves his hand from her mouth just a little bit.

"You," she whines.

Something about admitting it out loud affects her even more than his fingers, and she gasps as her cunt clenches around him. Damien hums happily to himself, using his thumb to apply the tiniest amount of pressure to her clit. It's enough to almost make her scream, and she has to lean over and bite down on his shoulder to keep from letting it all out.

"It's okay," he whispers as she moans against him. "You can scream my name all you want later. How about tonight? We can take it as slow as you need." Every little sentence is punctuated with his fingers reaching just a little bit deeper. "How's that sound?"

She nods frantically, unable to even whisper as she hurtles towards her climax, but just as she's about to career over the edge he withdraws his hand. Phoebe's eyes snap open wide as she bites back a whine. She gasps for air in mild disbelief, only then realizing that she's been holding his pulsing cock in her hand this whole time, squeezing it like a stress ball every time she got closer to her peak.

Damien smirks, motioning for her to climb on top of him, and she obliges without any words, lining herself up carefully. Luckily, the driver seems like he's turned up the radio a little louder to keep himself from falling asleep and Phoebe sees no signs of movement from anyone else on the bus. Damien shifts himself down on the seat so that Phoebe can easily glide her slippery slit along the underside of his cock. Her cunt aches with pleasure, so close to the release she's been looking for all night.

This version of Damien, this style of lovemaking, it's different from back in the alleyway. It's nice to know that he can be gentle too, but right now she needs more. He was right, though, the thought of being caught right now is the most exciting thing in the world. She glides herself slowly along the length of his cock, enjoying the feeling of it straining against her for as long as she can before she can't take it anymore. Damien is lapping up the attention like a ravenous animal, his hands gripping her ass as he takes some control of the pace, forcing her down against him even harder. After a couple minutes of this agonizing foreplay, he stops, completely still.

"You ready?"

All it takes is a nod and he's pulling a condom from his jeans, sliding it over his cock in a single motion. In the darkness, they work together to line themselves up. Phoebe holds herself precariously above him for a moment, gazing hungrily down at the thing that's about to fill her up. She lowers herself, slowly at first as his cock stretches her lips, but her mouth drops open in a soundless gasp as he grabs her hips and pulls her down in a single motion. She still struggles with his girth, but her cunt engulfs him completely as she shudders, catching her breath.

He strokes her hair, whispering in her ear.

"That's my girl."

Phoebe can't think of anything else as she starts to ride him, her hands on his shoulders and her forehead pressed against his. He starts by just sitting back and letting her do the work, but he doesn't let her lead for long, starting to buck against her as she drops herself down. Every time they meet she can feel his body slap against her clit, and she grinds down on him long enough to get a taste of her oncoming explosive orgasm before sliding back up his cock just in time. The tiny part of her that's still in control doesn't want this to end. She's enjoying herself far too much to let it finish like this.

"Fuck, you feel so good," she moans in his ear. "How can this feel so good?"

"Feeling's mutual, babydoll."

These pet names will be the death of her. Every time one slips out of his mouth, new or old, she feels like she could spontaneously combust.

"Tell me– Tell me I'm a good girl," she whispers, just loud enough for him to hear it. She can feel her whole face go red.

"Oh, you think you've been good? Prove it."

Phoebe lifts herself off him slowly, all the way until the tip of his cock is just barely kissing her cunt. She can feel her legs shaking, her breath ragged as she leans in for a violent kiss right before she drops back down on him in a single motion. He moans against her lips as she bounces up and down the full length of his shaft over and over and over. When she finally breaks the kiss, leaning back for a moment to catch her breath, Damien wraps his arms around her waist and pulls her close. His voice drops low enough that she can barely hear him as he whispers to her, his breath tickling her ear.

"Oh, you've been *such* a good girl."

Every part of Phoebe's body clenches as her cunt quivers around him, and she claps her hand over her mouth to stop her moan from waking the entire bus. Damien quirks an eyebrow.

"Shit, you're really into that, huh?"

"Shut up," she mutters quietly, but she can feel herself grinning ear-to-ear.

Nobody's ever talked to her like this during sex. With Damien it's always something vulgar and nasty, but laced with little bits of praise. She didn't even know it was something she was into until she had that dream, and even then it was more of a far-flung fantasy. With him, it's like music to her ears.

Damien runs his thumb across her bottom lip as he returns to fucking her, his eyes almost black from his blown out pupils. She can see the pink hue that dusts his cheeks in the moonlight, his cherry-red lips glistening with saliva. Phoebe's thighs shake and she feels her cunt clench around him as he captures her lips, swallowing any wanton moans that might threaten to wake up the others. It feels like she's caught in a massive tidal wave, but she's completely content to give in and let herself drown in that ocean of pleasure. He lets her ride it out for a couple minutes before his hands grip her ass and he fully takes over, back to bouncing her up and down on his cock with the perfect rhythm.

She feels like a rag-doll in his arms.

"You ready, babydoll?"

She can only nod her head desperately. Any attempt at words would have her waking the entire bus. Damien reaches up with one hand to grip her chin, forcing her to stare right into his eyes. He's trying to keep cool, but she can see his jaw clenching as he tries to last as long as he possibly can. His eyes slam shut and he pulls her in one last time. Phoebe lets herself go, crashing into the shore.

In a way that has become tradition in their time together, it's another couple minutes before she fully regains her senses. When she comes to, Phoebe finds herself collapsed on top of him, the two heaving in a shared silence.

"Well, you've done it again, Mr. Bell. Congratulations."

He laughs, making a sweeping motion with his arm.

"You know, it's... it's an honor. Thank you so much. First off, I'd like to thank–"

She jams her hand over his mouth to keep him from making too much noise, all while stifling her own laughter. As quietly as possible, she climbs off of him and adjusts her clothes. Damien pulls off the condom and ties it before cracking a window and tossing it onto the highway. He slides himself back into his jeans and zips them up as Phoebe glances around the rest of the bus. It's hard to tell in the low light, but it seems like not a single person's moved a muscle. Damien gestures toward the driver, who's radio gave them the cover they needed.

"The perfect crime."

"Mmm," she hums, adjusting the blankets over them once more. "Looking forward to becoming a career criminal."

As she lays against him, fading quickly into a blissful sleep, there's no restlessness, no anxious tossing and turning. There's nothing else in the world when she's wrapped in his arms.

Viva Las Vegas

CAESAR'S PALACE, LAS VEGAS

"Alright, ladies and germs! We're about fifteen minutes out, and I expect you all to be on your best behavior by the time we arrive. Get all the hijinx and chicanery out of your system!" He looks over at Bell, narrowing his eyes. "That goes double for you."

"I haven't even done anything yet!"

"That's what I'm worried about. You're like a timebomb with no clock, I know you're gonna ruin everything but I have no idea when."

"Why can't you be more like Phoebe?" Johnny chimes in. "*She'd* never single-handedly derail a successful tour in a single night, would you Pheebs?"

Phoebe blinks.

"I've uh, never really had the opportunity."

"Hey!" Damien barks. "Get that narc energy off this bus, Reed!"

He climbs over the seat, flailing his arms at Johnny, who simply leans back a little out of reach. Troy claps his hands together, snapping the two out of their little spat before things can escalate any further.

"See? This is the shit I'm talking about! Bell, you sit the hell down. Reed, you stop antagonizing him. Miller? You just make sure your boy toy doesn't do anything stupid. I've earned my nice Vegas vacation. Capiche?"

Damien sighs, slumping back down in his seat.

For Phoebe, the ride has been surprisingly rejuvenating. She'd had a good number of hours to get some writing done, and was happy enough to just decompress from the last couple days in silence. Damien, on the other hand, was suffering in the few hours before hitting the hotel. Something about the close-quarters and chill atmosphere seemed to make him want to create as much havoc as possible. Maybe he just didn't love being cooped up for long stretches, but Phoebe had a feeling his newfound nervous energy may have had something to do with their little moonlit adventure the night before.

There's a small amount of press at Caesar's Palace when they arrive, and Phoebe instinctually walks a little ways apart from Damien as they drag their suitcases into the lobby. While they wait to be checked in, her mind begins to wander, and those colder thoughts of the tour's conclusion begin to unfurl. In only a couple minutes the inevitable end of their little experiment begins to wrap itself back around her. She stares at Damien as he's goofing around with his friends. How easy will it be for each of them to slide back into their normal lives when it's over? Which one of them will it hurt the most?

"Pheebs!"

The first thing she registers is the big smile spread across Janis' heart-shaped face, her long black hair flying behind her as she frantically dashes toward them. She's in a short green dress with thin straps, probably picked to keep her cool in the Vegas heat while also showing off her tanned skin and intricate half-sleeve tattoo; flowers and birds wrap around her arm with snippets of poetry filling in the blank spaces. The whole look is tied together with a pair of combat boots, her jacket draped casually over her shoulder. Or, it would look casual if she wasn't practically bubbling over with excitement. Phoebe rushes toward her friend, flinging her arms around her and squeezing her tight.

"You're early!"

"What are you talking about? I'm right on time!" Janis steps back, her dark brown eyes filled with joy. Phoebe can't help but notice the purple eyeshadow carefully flicked out in a meticulous wing to make the color pop. She's out to impress.

"How was the flight back?"

"Not as terrible as I expected, and definitely better than waiting for the airline to work it out themselves. I even managed to grab a first class ticket at a reduced rate, last minute dropout or something, so I had some actual leg room for once!"

"Nice," Phoebe replies, looking her up and down. "So, you must be exhausted, do you want to just check into your room, or..."

Janis laughs and rolls her eyes.

"Screw that, I'll sleep when I'm dead. Tons of time for it then."

She glances around, Phoebe following her eye-line as she locks on to Damien and the rest of the band.

"Are you gonna introduce me to these rock stars, and…" She leans, cupping her hand over her mouth. "Your *very* mysterious boyfriend?"

"Wow, amazing, that was very subtle."

"I'm nothing if not extremely inconspicuous."

Phoebe smacks her arm, and Janis hits her right back.

"Well, I don't know about *boyfriend*," Phoebe mutters.

Janis lifts a brow.

"You sure? He's been staring right at you this whole time, seems pretty serious to me."

Janis giggles as Phoebe grabs her hand, pulling her toward the rest of the band.

"Guys, this is Janis. She writes for The New Yorker."

"I'm also her best friend in the entire world," she beams, before turning to Phoebe with what might be the fakest puppy-dog-eyes of all time. "How could you forget that part?"

Damien is the first to offer his hand, a cocky smile on his face.

"Damien Bell, great to meet you. Phoebe has told me absolutely *nothing* about you," he teases.

Janis smiles, taking his hand.

"Well, I guess I'm at an advantage then. She's told me a whole lot about you."

He raises his eyebrows, putting his hand on his chest in mock-surprise as he glances at Phoebe.

"That so?"

"Good things," Janis assures him. "Only good things."

"I should hope so, I've been a *very* good boy lately."

As Janis does introductions with the rest of the band, Damien leans over to Phoebe.

"So, did you tell her I have a huge co–"

"Oh my god, shut up!" Phoebe hisses.

Damien stares at her, shaking his head ever so slightly as he bites down on his lip.

"You have no idea how badly I want to fuck you right now."

Phoebe can feel the heat rising up her neck as Troy returns and begins to hand out their room keys. She busies herself with her bag as the group's attention swings back toward them, hoping to avoid notice.

"Upgraded your room. You now have a king size bed and a balcony, courtesy of my magnetic personality."

Damien slaps him on the shoulder and pockets the key.

"Thanks Troy, you're a real class act."

"Yeah, well don't say I never did anything nice for ya."

Troy turns to Janis without missing a beat.

"Alright, Janis from The New Yorker, got a room yet?"

"Uh, no, I tried calling ahead but things got a bit hectic. I was just about to go and—"

"Here," he replies. "This was gonna be Phoebe's, but since these two can't keep their hands off each other anymore, it's yours."

Janis seems a little taken aback, clearly not expecting the royal treatment.

"Wow, thanks, Mr. Sullivan, that's awesome."

He smiles, tickled that Janis knew his name without having to ask.

"If you already know who I am, you should know my friends call me Troy."

"Well then, thank you very much, Troy."

"Mr. Sullivan makes him feel like an old man," Ophelia quips as she passes Janis, shooting her a playful little wink.

Phoebe can't be sure, but she thinks she can see Janis's cheeks take on a tiny shade of pink. She doesn't really get an opportunity to dwell on it though, as with business concluded, Troy suggests they all head up to their rooms. This time he's made sure to book the entire eighth floor, ostensibly for the roadies and the band to all be able to coordinate if necessary, but with the added benefit of avoiding unwanted press and groupies. As the elevator door opens up to their floor, Damien insists on taking Phoebe's suitcase.

"That seems like a boyfriend duty," Janis teases, carrying her own bag a few doors down.

"Here I thought I was just being a gentleman," he calls back. "There's just something so satisfying about carrying heavy things, it makes me feel so manly!"

Phoebe drags him through the door, cutting off the endless competition of back-and-forth quipping that was sure to break out any second, and gasping the moment she gets to actually survey the room. It's stunning. There's a pristine white L-shaped couch on one end, and a massive king-size bed on the other draped in dark blue fabric that looks like silk. Sliding doors lead out to a stone balcony that overlooks the entire city. Even the bathroom is amazing, almost the size of her apartment back home, with a large open concept shower adorned with bright blue and ivory marble. There's even a large bench for someone to sit on. As she stares at it Phoebe can't shake the feeling that it might be a little *too* big.

Damien gestures at the shower with a flick of his head.

"Very luxurious." He grins. "So much room to really stretch everything out."

"Oh my God, Damien," she whispers.

No matter how shameless he is, she can't deny his words always have the intended effect. She can feel her body lighting up already, prepping for what was becoming a pretty consistent aspect of her daily life.

"Oh, *you're* embarrassed?" He laughs. "You? The girl who eats up my dirty talk while she's riding me like an animal?"

She laughs, whacking him in the arm.

"Would it kill you to have at least a little self-control?"

"Self-control? It's my best quality! Well, top 10 at least."

It's not long into their exploration of the room when Damien finds the mini fridge and immediately grabs a couple beers, gesturing for Phoebe to follow him out to the terrace. As the fresh air hits her face, in the midst of their beautiful new view, two things fully sink in. First off, she's going to fuck the hottest man she's ever met in the nicest hotel room she's ever seen. The thought is enough to make her squirm as he passes her a bottle, and she immediately puts it to her lips for some relief. The second realization, and possibly the more important one, is that the Nevada sun may very well be the literal fucking devil.

To say the heat is stifling would be an understatement, and it's only a couple minutes of sweating under the sun before Phoebe's desperate to return to the pleasures of modern air conditioning. Just as she's about to speak up, however, Damien sheds his shirt, and everything suddenly becomes a lot more tolerable. Phoebe licks her lips as he tosses it to the ground, his body golden and glowing under the rays. The devil's always tempting people after all.

He reaches out with his beer and they clink their bottles together.

"Cheers, Miller."

"Cheers."

For a little while they just sip their drinks in silence, with Phoebe still stuck between ogling and agony when Damien finally speaks up.

"You hungry?" He asks.

Her eyes linger for a moment before she shakes herself out of it.

"Oh, yeah, I could eat. We can try room service if you want."

"No, I want to take you out." He pauses for a moment. "Like, on a date."

"You want to take me on a *date*?" She laughs. "You know Troy said we can't do that stuff. We promised to keep everything behind closed doors, remember?"

"I don't care," he replies bluntly. "I want to take you for dinner. We can get some food and find a spot with a view. Watch the sunset."

"That's strangely romantic for you," she chuckles.

He's not laughing, no smirk or smile on his face. He looks completely sincere.

"Say yes?"

Up until now, even when he's being open and warm, he's usually so in control. Always in charge. But here, if just for a moment, he's completely vulnerable. It's almost like he's afraid. But through it all Phoebe can't help but smile, caught up in the very idea of a real date with Damien Bell.

"I mean... we'll have to sneak out."

He perks up, eyes shining.

"Easy."

She can feel her heart flutter.

"Give me half an hour to shower and change?"

He glances around, frowning just for a second. The look on his face says it all. She knows that he wants her, but that it's probably too risky on the terrace. He's probably also a little nervous, not wanting to ruin things by making a move after suggesting a romantic evening. Phoebe drains the rest of her beer and takes it inside, following her hunch.

She doesn't waste any time as Damien silently follows her back inside, placing her empty bottle on the kitchenette counter before turning around to face him. She leans her back against the counter, staring at him as he cocks his head hopefully. She lifts her skirt just a little, brushing a single finger along her thigh. She can hear his breathing get heavier, his body-language shifting as she brings the finger up to her lips, running her tongue across it playfully. It's all he needs, grinning from ear to ear as he pins her against the table and pulls her hand away, pressing his lips against hers in a lovely kiss.

Slow and steady quickly gives way in the face of passion, however, and less than a minute goes by before he's all over her. Her breathing gets heavier as she lets him take over, one hand caressing her inner thigh as he grabs her hair with the other. She can feel herself letting go as he pulls her head back, just enough to fully expose her, moving in to make a swollen red mess of her neck– Just in time to be interrupted by a sudden knock at the door.

Phoebe groans and Damien curses under his breath as they both struggle for a moment, trying to look as presentable as possible in a half minute or so. When he swings the door open, it's Janis standing in the doorway. She blinks absently for a couple seconds at the sight of a shirtless and clearly sweaty Damien.

"Shit, sorry. I didn't realize I was interrupting something. You guys are really fast."

Phoebe laughs, walking to the door to take over.

"Don't worry, he just walks around like this. What's up?"

"You two wanna grab a drink?" Janis asks, her eyes still wandering around Damien's chest.

Phoebe glances over her shoulder at Damien before leaning in closer to Janis.

"We were sort of planning to go on a date."

"A date?" Janis replies, her eyes bouncing between them. "Like, in public?"

"Not quite," Damien chuckles, walking behind Phoebe and wrapping his arms around her waist.

Janis shifts a little to obscure them from anyone who might be walking down the hallway before shooting them a knowing look.

"How about tomorrow? Think you'll have any energy left over?"

Phoebe can picture Damien's cocky expression behind her.

"Tomorrow will be great, Jan. Drinks before the show sound good?"

"It'll probably be busy with soundcheck, but you two can hang out backstage after you're all done," Damien offers.

Janis beams.

"Alright, it's a date! Bye, lovebirds– and be safe!"

Phoebe closes the door.

"I like her."

"It's hard not to," Phoebe grins. "Alright, I've just got to take a shower and then we can head out."

As she starts to head to the bathroom, he cuts in front of her.

"Damien, get out of the way!" She laughs. "I told you, I need a shower."

"So do I," he says coyly, slipping ahead of her.

Phoebe can feel her body begin to light up again as she hears Damien turn on the shower, and she only manages to wait a couple moments before she gives in, throwing her clothes off and following after him. The second she steps into the giant shower she yelps as he pins her against the wall, wasting no time catching right back up to where they left off. She moans as his hand drifts up her thigh, his fingers quickly finding their target between her legs.

"Now where were we before we were so rudely interrupted?" He purrs.

"We– Oh fuck!"

Any attempt at playful banter on her part is cut off immediately. Damien pumps his fingers inside her, the natural movement of the act intensifying things as the base of his hand presses against the hood of her clit. He's playful but firm, working her expertly until she's dripping all over his hand.

"This is just a teaser, by the way," he whispers. "For what I've got planned for you tonight."

She shudders, her entire body aching. She only registers about half of what he's saying, not yet fully understanding the implications.

"More," she moans. "Fuck me, Damien, I need you!"

"You'll get me," he laughs, giving her a quick bite on the lip. "But not quite yet."

"Make me come," she begs, still lost in the moment.

He shakes his head, slowing his fingers to a much more neutral pace.

"You're gonna ache all night, sweetheart."

The realization hits her like a brick. He's keeping her right there, not letting her get any further, but not letting her cool down. Her mind is on fire. She's close enough that she might be able to push through by force. She begins grinding against his hand, biting his neck, anything to make him take her those extra few final steps to the finish line. But he answers each movement, by pulling a little further away, her bites and moans only making him chuckle softly as he keeps her exactly where he wants her. It's another few minutes of begging and teasing before he pulls his hand out completely and she almost collapses, her body screaming for release.

Damien looks incredibly proud of himself, gazing down at her as she takes some time to recover. Her legs shake as she struggles to regain her composure, leaning against the bench in the corner of the shower. The steam filling the room that would normally help her relax makes everything that much worse, clouding her senses and prickling little beads of sweat across her skin, each one reigniting her need to be touched. After a minute or so, she manages to regain enough control over her body to pull herself up to her full height, meeting his smug grin with a glare.

"Experimentation, remember?"

"This is just mean," she grumbles. "We didn't talk about–"

Before she can finish he's on his knees, his hands latched onto her hips, his face buried between her legs. She buckles, falling forward and using his back to hold herself up as he hops between the devouring strokes of his tongue and the little nips on her thighs. Her fingers bury themselves in his hair as she tries to bend her knees to position him in just the right spot. Cruelly, he pulls away and gazes up at her, the shimmer of his beautiful blue-gray eyes almost making her forget how much he's torturing her.

"You need to learn how to be patient, babydoll."

Phoebe tries a softer approach, running her fingers through his hair, a slow and careful enticement. Seemingly content, Damien returns to sucking gently on her clit. Phoebe's eyes roll into the back of her head; he's so fucking good with his tongue. She grips his hair tighter, trying to hold him against her, but he's too strong and pulls away again just as she's on the edge.

He lays little kisses on her as he stands. Her belly, her breast, her neck, and finally her lips.

"You taste so sweet," he breathes.

"You're so mean!" She laughs, pushing away from him in a mix of delirium and disbelief.

"You really think so?" He rasps.

Damien lifts up her right leg, hooking it around his waist to keep her steady, and slides two fingers back into her. He presses against her G-spot with expert control, his thumb rhythmically circling her clit at the same time. Her hips move along with each plunge, nothing but sharp moans spilling from her lips. All she can do is hope to steal just enough pleasure from him to finish before he plays another one of his dirty tricks. As Damien presses his lips against her neck she does everything she can to focus only on the waves of pleasure.

"Is this mean enough for you?" He smiles as he gazes at her face. She can only imagine the desperate expression she's giving him right now, as little moans escape her lips with every flick of his fingers. "I told you this was just a taste of what I had planned."

"Yes. It's– I mean, no I– I'm so close!"

Just as he sees her about to reach her limit, he pulls his fingers out of her all at once, pressing them up to her already half-open mouth. Phoebe wraps her lips around them without even thinking, sucking away her juices as Damien grins, a new fire in his eyes.

"That's my girl."

She watches as he pulls his fingers away, her body beginning to cool as he presses his lips against hers again. Her tongue plays lazily with his as her body slowly returns to normal. She's disappointed and aching, but at least she's back in control of herself. He breaks the kiss and smiles at her, and she frowns as she feels his hand brush against her waist again, realizing just too late that he's not done with his fun.

As he shoves his fingers back inside her a final time, she almost jumps, her body quickly ramping back up to its over-stimulated state. Phoebe's breath catches in her chest as he continues working her up all over again, thrusting deep inside her while his thumb works her clit, faster and faster. Her fingers wrap around his wrist and she struggles to force him deeper one last time, but he's in full control. It's the same thing all over again as he curls his fingers just enough to drive her crazy before pulling out for the last time.

Phoebe is thoroughly wrecked, gasping for breath in the midst of a string of curses. She was so close, and he just ripped it all away from her.

"You're such a fucking asshole," she whines, hoping beyond hope that he'll show her some mercy. "I was right there."

"My poor baby," he whispers into her ear, shattering her hopes as he pulls away completely.

Her eyes are a mix of anguish and unbridled lust as she stares him down.

"I'm gonna get you back for this, you fucker."

"Fuck, I can't wait for that." He grins.

Her hand begins to wander down her body as she catches her breath, but he steps forward and takes her wrist, as gently as she's ever felt him.

"Don't worry, I'll give you everything you want tonight and more, but you have to wait. No taking care of it yourself, okay?"

She moans, half laughing as everything finally starts returning to normal. Everything but the ache.

"You'd fucking better, you prick, because right now you've got a lot to make up for."

Damien chuckles, giving her a gentle kiss on her cheek.

"Don't worry, I always keep my promises." He stops for a moment, grimacing as he steps out of the shower, his cock still fully erect. "Honestly, given how much you turned *me* on, I'm in pretty rough shape myself."

Back in the main room, Phoebe grabs the blue dress that she wore back in Portland, pairing it with her leather jacket and a pair of sneakers. While her body's calmed down significantly, she does notice that certain movements cause her clothes to ride up in just the right way to light her up again. Hopefully she'll be able to keep it under control.

"How fancy are we going tonight?" She asks, fiddling with her damp hair.

"Not very," Damien replies. "I was thinking we could grab some burgers and head out to Red Rock Canyon and watch the sunset. It's more about the place than the food. No people, just us."

It sounds like a real date. A real date for a real couple.

"I'd love that," she murmurs.

He nods as he throws on a black t-shirt and laces up his boots, his face a mix of excitement and a bit of trepidation. He's nervous again, just like her, and something about that comforts her just a little bit.

Out front of the hotel, Damien hails a cab, standing outside for a moment when the man pops the door open to negotiate.

"Hey, man, we need to hit up a place for food, but after that we're heading to Red Rock Canyon. Any way you can drop us off and pick us up in a couple hours?"

"What's in it for me?" The driver asks flatly.

He's an older man who doesn't seem to have a clue who Damien is.

"How does two hundred bucks sound, my dude?"

"Done," the driver laughs. "You know what? I like you kids. Very generous generation."

Damien grins.

"I am known for my generosity."

Phoebe stares out the window, a familiar warmth growing in the pit of her stomach that gets more intense when Damien reaches over to touch her hand. It's nothing like the shower, not sexual at all, not even really desire. She glances over to find his eyes on her, and quickly turns her gaze out the window instead. The warmth inside her is slowly overtaken by an impossible gravity. She sees Damien's reflection in the window, and he quirks an eyebrow as the crushing sensation inside her grows heavier and heavier.

"Something wrong?" He asks.

"It's nothing," she whispers.

I just think I'm falling in love with you.

Come On, Eileen

RED ROCK CANYON

"Are you sure you don't want me to carry some of that?"

Damien hops across rock after rock with the tray of food and drinks in his hand, the sun setting in front of him and bathing everything in a warm gold and pink glow.

"I got it, sweets. Don't even worry, I'm like a cat!"

He takes another leap and his foot slips, yelping as his body lurches before he barely catches himself. The sharp panic Phoebe feels in the moment fades quickly, and she sighs, shaking her head as Damien turns around. He flashes her a sheepish smile.

"That was close."

"Damien, seriously, come down from there."

"Aww, but it's all part of the show!"

"If you have to stay on the rocks, can you at least walk like a normal person, please? I don't want to have you airlifted out of here."

"Oh, that would be a good story for CNN!" He gestures with his hands and puts on his best newscaster voice. "Impeccable Rock Star, Damien Bell, too cool for Red Rock Canyon!"

Phoebe raises her brow.

"How about: Traveling Idiot Breaks Neck Failing to Impress Girl."

He heaves a dramatic sigh, and his shoulders droop.

"Fiiine, I'll be *normal* if that'll make you happy."

He makes it sound like it's the hardest thing in the world.

"It'll give me less anxiety," she chuckles. "I appreciate the sacrifice."

Their fingers link together and she follows him up the rest of the rocky hill. The ground is loose and dusted at the top, and Damien paces around so much looking for the perfect spot to sit that he kicks up a small cloud. Phoebe grimaces, turning away as she tries to hold in a cough.

"Sorry, sorry... I did *not* think this through. Story of my life, right?" He holds out the tray of food to her. "Hold this for a sec."

She takes the tray while Damien shrugs off his leather jacket, spreading it out on the ground. He gestures toward the impromptu picnic blanket and bows.

"Madam, a plush spread for which to sit."

"Such a gentleman."

"Just for you, gorgeous."

"What about you?"

"Ah, you know me. I'm a dirty boy at heart."

She giggles. He always has a line.

"What if your jacket gets ruined?"

"It's just a little grit," he grunts as she passes him the food, setting it in front of the jacket before plunking himself down. "This thing's seen a lot worse."

Phoebe sits beside him, stretching her legs out in front of her. Damien follows suit, tapping her foot with his own as he passes her a soda.

"You wanna spice it up a little?" He asks, wiggling his eyebrows.

"I'm afraid to ask what that means."

He rests his cup between his legs and digs a flask out of his pocket.

"Why am I not surprised?" She chuckles and pops the lid off of her soda. "Fine, fine, lay it on me."

"Say when."

He tips the flask completely over and Phoebe squeaks as her drink almost immediately starts to overflow.

"When, you maniac!"

He chuckles as she dips her head to take a big gulp of her drink, clearing space to put the lid back on. She quickly recoils from the cup, almost gagging.

"Oh my God, Damien. What the hell *is* that?"

"Just whiskey, I swear! Well, except it's been in that flask for like six months. Alcohol doesn't go bad, right?"

"Not really, but this stuff's definitely taking on some new qualities."

"Ah," he chuckles as he pours some into his own cup. "Aged means it's good shit though. Like wine!"

"Damien, it tastes like it's almost 50% metal at this point. You've drank this before, right? Does your tongue even work anymore?"

He pats her on the back.

"You tell me."

She gags.

"I didn't know I'd be going on a date with such a *wuss*! What about all of those jager-bombs you did back in California, huh?" He elbows her in the ribs. "What happened to that girl, she was so cool!"

"I've got a secret for you, Jagerbombs don't taste like copper and battery acid." She chokes as she takes another sip. "God, why do I keep doing this?!"

His face is red, tears of laughter in his eyes, as he leans up against her.

"You're a trooper, sweetheart."

Damien rewards her with a burger at the end of her coughing fit, and she bites into it without a second thought. Anything to get that horrific burning sensation out of her mouth. He takes a deep breath, sighing softly as he unwraps his own burger.

"You okay, Mister Mysterious?"

"Yeah, I'm good." He smiles, staring into her eyes. "Just thinking a lot lately."

Phoebe's surprised by this quiet little moment free of jokes and repartee. She finds it impossible to focus on anything but the softness of his features as they're bathed in the pink and gold light of the sunset. She studies the slope of his jaw, the little dusting of stubble on his chin, and even the way he furrows his brow as he unwraps his burger. No matter how many times she sees it, she's still blown away how different he is from the man she first met in that California hotel room.

"Can I ask you something?"

Damien is gazing out at the sunset, sitting completely still.

"Off the record, Miss Miller?"

She scoffs. Smartass.

"Seriously, Damien. Why did you bring me here? This is all really lovely, don't get me wrong, but we could have had burgers in the hotel room."

He turns, only looking at her from the corner of her eye, looking almost boyish as he licks some of the grease off of his thumb.

"I wanted this to be special. It's been a long time since I've been on a real date, and I know it's not a fancy dinner, no flowers, no wine, but..."

"Damien, it's not the– this is great, I was just curious is all."

Phoebe finds herself fumbling all of her words. Her mind races, looking for the worst possible reading for what's going on. Does he want to break this thing off before it's even gotten started? Is she about to find out that, oh no, she's great, it's absolutely not her, it's him? Her eyes begin to mist and she reflexively blinks away the tears. She feels like she's hanging on the ledge of a cliff just waiting for him to let her fall.

"Damien, just tell me."

She jerks her head away as he turns back to her, but it's not fast enough. He's obviously seen the tears in her eyes.

"Oh god Phoebe, no, it's not– This isn't anything bad! I'm really fucking into you," he chuckles, chewing on his lip. "Like, *really* fucking into you. I wanted somewhere private, no interruptions, because I wanted to–" he runs his hand through his hair. "This is so embarrassing. I'm usually so much smoother than this."

"Tell me," she whispers.

The tears in her eyes are a distant memory as her heart pounds faster.

"I want to be more. Experiment over, great results. We could publish a fucking paper it went so well."

She can feel the ice-cold anxiety in her veins melt away as his nerve-wracked words replay in her head over and over again.

"You want to be..."

He brushes a strand of hair from her face, his hand coming to rest on her cheek.

"More. I do."

She can tell he's struggling to find the right words.

"Look, I know this is the line you drew, a little experiment to see how things go between us, but I'm going out on a limb to ask you if you want to–" She can feel his warm breath on her face, the smell of cheap whiskey clings to the silence he leaves in the air, but only for a moment.

"I want to be more than that. I think we *are* more than that."

Phoebe feels like she's swallowing wads of cotton. Wasn't this exactly what she'd dreamed about the last few days? Wasn't this the perfect outcome she had hoped for? That line seemed so smart in the beginning, a safety net in case things went sour, but also a shield to protect against a much more frightening possibility.

"Damien, my job–"

"I know. Believe me, I know. And I don't want to fuck things up for you, but it's killing me to not be able to call you my–" he cuts himself off and his voice drops to a whisper as he leans in, his nose pressing against hers. "My girlfriend."

"Bullshit," she giggles as he nuzzles against her. "You're such a liar, you almost had me there."

"I'm not lying!" He insists. "I dig everything about you, your writing, your insight, everything."

She snorts.

"Look, it's all very flattering, but I've seen who you actually *date*. Models, actresses, not nerdy journalists."

He pulls back, his face suddenly completely serious, his eyes digging right into hers.

"Why're you doing that?"

"Doing what?"

"You're tearing yourself down. You're usually so confident with me, funny and clever and cool, but now you're selling yourself short. You're gorgeous, Phoebe. You're kind, you're generous... and sure you might be a bit of a square, but you're the cutest square I know." He places his hand firmly on her leg. "I don't know how many times I can say it, but I won't stop until you believe it."

It's everything, everything she wanted to hear, and it terrifies her.

"Look I– I understand that it's been fun for you, and sure maybe you like spending time with me, and the other stuff is obviously incredible too. I just– I don't think you actually want this."

He reaches over the top of his t-shirt and pulls out his dog tags, slipping them off of his neck and draping them over her head. She shivers as the cool metal touches her skin.

"These were my dad's. I've only ever given them to one other girl, and I never take them off. They're important to me. You're important to me."

She lifts the tags, turning them over in her hand as they shimmer in the low light of the fading sun.

"You want me to wear these?"

"I want you, that's all. Everything else is noise."

Her fingertips tingle as Damien grabs the remnants of her burger and tucks it back into the brown paper bag. She smiles, absentmindedly.

"I was eating that."

"It can wait."

He stares at her for a moment, as if he wants to say something but the words stay caught in his throat, and he moves in for a kiss instead; a kiss for a secret, fair exchange. It's a desperate embrace, smothering everything they want to say with pure passion, neither of them willing to break the kiss for a long while. Phoebe puts her hand against his chest and they part. The smile on her lips says it all, and she curls her fingers around the neck of his shirt, pulling him down with her as she lays down on his jacket. Damien purrs as he climbs over her, pinning her arms to the ground.

"I owe you something, don't I?"

"You made some pretty big promises back in the shower."

She gasps as he caresses the back of her neck, her little hairs standing on end while he undoes the buttons on her dress with ease.

"Don't worry, babydoll," he rumbles. "Like I said, I keep my promises."

He takes his time with the final few buttons, placing soft kisses on each newly bare patch of skin as he works his way down her torso. She slides her arms out of her sleeves as some final rays of sun illuminate her nearly naked body, but all she can feel amidst the sunlight is the softness of his mouth against her hip as it begins to trail lower.

"You're teasing again," she warns.

She's aching with impatience, and he knows it.

Damien's eyes glint with mischief. She can feel the cool metal from his rings and the bracelets pressing against her burning skin as his fingers dance down her body until he reaches her last covered spot. Even with her panties in the way, his control is effortless. His fingers dive into the fabric, pressing just far enough inside her to make an impression before he drags them up, pushing down her clit before circling it playfully. Her muscles tremble, and she swallows hard as she runs her hands through his hair. Her body hasn't forgotten the playful cruelty he unleashed on her in the shower, and it's only brief minutes before she's nearly back in that same state, suspended between the peaks of agony and delight. It does feel different somehow, maybe a little softer, but no less intense.

She's soaking wet, clutching his dog tags absentmindedly in one hand while she grips his hair tightly with the other. His fingers continue to glide slowly up and down her increasingly drenched underwear, clumping the fabric more between her lower lips until her bare pussy is almost entirely in view save for the tiny slit of fabric covering the very middle. Phoebe gasps, a groan escaping her lips as he finally pulls the fabric away from her, plunging a couple fingers inside her. The two of them are bathed in shades of pink and purple, the sunlight dying behind them, soon to be replaced by the gentle twinkle of an endless night sky.

"Good girl," he whispers as his breath tickles her neck.

Her hips shake and wiggle and she presses as hard as she can against his fingers, already desperate for more.

"Such a— t-tease."

She barely manages to get it out.

"Careful, I could do *much* worse."

Her mouth is slightly parted, her tongue just barely visible as she runs it along her lower lip.

"Mmm... You wouldn't dare."

The sensation of his fingers pulling out, followed by the unmistakable ripping of fabric makes her body jump with excitement, his eyes running up and down her as he chews on his lip.

"Were those new?"

She can only nod as he pops his fingers into his mouth and sucks them clean, before flashing her a big, cocky smile.

"Don't worry, I'll buy you a thousand more."

Phoebe stares at him, a sentence lodged so deep in her throat that she doesn't know if she'll ever be able to get it out. These moments of pure intensity are incredible and still so new; she's loved every night of aching lust that's cascaded into release after release, but she wants more. She wants mornings with him, her head resting on his lap while he writes his poetry. She wants to read the paper together the way her parents do.

She wants him to love her.

And wasn't it only a few minutes ago she was fighting against the idea of being a couple? She'd internalized her doubts of his ability to commit to her. All she used to think is that someone like him could never... but now her entire mind is taken up with one question: how much further can they go? Forget the article, forget being found out. She's allowed this man, this gorgeous, intelligent, fiery demi-god of a man, to consume her. And all in a single week. It still doesn't feel real.

"You're shaking." His voice is warm, his hand on her cheek.

"I– what?"

She had no idea just how badly her thighs were trembling until he pointed it out, but she's called back to earth with the first lap of his tongue against her clit. Her back arches and her toes curl as she cries out into the empty sky.

He chuckles, his face lifting up from between her legs as he grips her thighs, giving him full access. She must have been following along to some extent, because she's holding the position herself, straining as she claws against the jacket under her.

"Mmm, you liked that one. Make sure to thank me when we're done."

"F- fuck you," she moans. "Get back to work."

"Oh!" His rumbling laughter reverberates through her entire body. "I like this new take-charge side of you, *Miller*. Let's see how long it lasts."

She growls, lurching forward and pulling his head toward her before clenching it tight between her thighs. She knows what she wants, and she's going to get it. He can't play these games with her forever.

Phoebe tries her best to not sound as desperate as she feels, holding back the heavier moans and carefully letting out smaller grunts and whines when possible. Her entire body tingles, nerves lighting up and jumping with anticipation as she holds him in place. It's all too much: the slick of his tongue and the shockwaves through her entire body as he hums against her cunt. Even the heat of his body as he presses up against her in the cool breeze. It's all she can do not to scream into the canyon as Damien wraps his lips around her clit and begins to suck, his fingers sliding back inside of her at the same time.

Every few moments she tries to speak, but she can't get the words out as her cunt clenches around his fingers and her clit throbs against his lips. Sweat and saliva cling to the insides of her thighs as Damien's stubble stings her skin in the best way possible with every little movement of his head. She's right on the edge, both of her hands grasping his head like she's riding a rollercoaster, climbing and climbing before they inevitably careen down a hill.

"Don't stop," she begs. "Don't you dare fucking stop."

She expects him to try and pull his mouth away to say something clever, to mock her or dole out some punishment, but instead his fingers curl and press into her G-spot, massaging against it rhythmically. A knot forms in the pit of her stomach and she feels like she can't get enough air as the last wisps of sunlight die, and darkness fully unfurls around them. His fingers and his tongue work perfectly in tandem as they dance inside and against her. There are no words, only the soft clink of his rings as he fucks her. No teasing, no mockery, no denial.

His entire mouth engulfs her clit one last time, applying enough pressure to completely overwhelm her as he sucks passionately. She struggles to cover her mouth, reaching out for it once or twice as she tries to hold herself back, but the overwhelming sensations force her to grab back on to him for dear life as she reaches her breaking point. Her voice shakes and catches as she comes hard enough to see stars behind her eyelids, each spasming wave accompanied by a new shriek or wailing moan. It's not too long before she's whimpering quiet profanities as he guides her through the finale, her body singing along.

When he finally pulls his fingers out of her, her body jumps in response. She whimpers, feeling hollow without him inside, but Damien quickly crawls on top of her. His mouth presses up against hers, and she's forced to taste herself on his lips. When he breaks the kiss, he leaves her almost breathless.

"You never answered my question."

She can barely make out his face anymore, but she can feel him pressing down on her, just waiting to plunge inside.

"Forgot what it was," she gasps, each heaving breath an excuse for their bodies to press closer together.

"Be my girl," he whispers, the words causing sparks to rush down her spine. "Fuck this experiment. You and I both know that we don't need that excuse anymore."

He lifts himself up just enough to cage her in between his arms, staring straight down at her.

"Say yes," he murmurs. "I don't want this to stop after the tour."

Her eyes have begun to adjust to the darkness, his outline giving way to the face of the man she loves, looking equal parts hopeful and afraid.

"Damien, I–"

"Please," he begs as he cups her cheek, his thumb stroking her cheek. "Please?"

Here he is, asking for what she's secretly wanted this whole time, soft and vulnerable. Tears pool in her eyes, streaming down the sides of her face. Being with Damien feels like diving into the dark of the ocean, dangerous and exciting. It's consuming every part of her as he imposes himself on each aspect of her life. It could ruin her.

He could ruin her.

"Yes," she rasps, her whole body shaking as a smile takes over her face. "Yes."

He lets out a long breath, pressing his forehead to hers.

"I'll be so good to you, baby. I promise. No matter what."

Phoebe grins and hooks her leg around his waist and twisting, pushing his body so that he's forced to roll back into the dirt. His eyes widen and a big smile spreads across his face as she straddles him, pinning his arms above his head.

"You'd better be," she breathes.

She peels off his shirt, letting his hands free for the moment as she begins to pepper his chest with soft kisses. The dog tags dangling from her neck trail across his skin as she moves. He reaches up to grab onto her, probably without thinking and so used to taking charge, but she quickly pins both his hands back to the ground with her own, their fingers interlocked. In the midst of dragging her tongue along his chest, she bites down on his nipple and tugs, her eyes flashing with a newfound confidence as he yelps.

"Jesus! Where did this come from?"

"Just giving you a little taste of your own medicine, Bell. It sounds like you like it? You can thank me later."

She's still a little nervous to flip their roles like this, but he doesn't need to know that. Besides, it seems like he's definitely not upset about the situation.

"Fuck yeah," he laughs. "Show me what you've got."

Phoebe lets his hands go again, raising her eyebrows to let him know to stay still, before softly stroking his cheek. She smiles playfully, her thumb gliding against the little cleft in his chin, before she pulls it across his lip; his own signature move. Damien sucks gently on the tip, his eyes locked on her, and she can feel her whole body flush. The pressure that's been building against her cunt since she mounted him swells even more, almost pushing into her through his pants as she grinds herself against it. After a few minutes she lays down against his chest, her mouth right up against his ear as she whispers.

"You've been so good tonight, tell me what you want."

His eyes are piercing and his voice is thick with lust.

"I want to feel you around my cock, and I want you to ride it until you're done. I want you to cum as much as you want until you're done fucking me," he begs. "Please."

She blinks, quickly shutting her gaping mouth. She's in charge tonight, and she wants to look that way no matter how much her body screams to slam herself down on his cock and let him destroy her. Instead, she sets the pace. Her fingernails slowly rake his bare chest, ending up resting just at the top of his jeans. She brushes against his cock as she unbuttons them, slowly, letting her fingers run over it through the rough fabric before dragging the jeans down just past his hips in one go.

"Hang on," he laughs.

Damien shifts beneath her and she watches him tear the newly revealed condom wrapper open with his teeth. She helps him roll it over his cock, excitedly wrapping her hand around it.

"Ready?" She asks.

"Yeah."

She lifts herself up and sinks down onto him. That familiar sting comes rushing back, and she breathes slowly to relax her body, carefully sliding up and down a bit of shaft a few times before preparing to go all the way.

"Shit. Atta girl," he whispers as his cock disappears into her swollen cunt. "Take it all, sweetheart."

Phoebe nods, whimpering a little as he takes up every last bit of space inside her. Maybe she sounds a little pathetic, but she doesn't care. She begins to rock her hips back and forth, building up a little friction between them as she sinks her fingernails into his chest, leaving behind tiny red half-moon indents. She can feel him swell inside of her, imagining every little curve and ridge as she throws her head back and starts to move for real. Damien's hands slide up her body, cupping her breasts and pinching her nipples through the thin lace of her bra. Their moans fill the air, and for the first time in days, she's not worried about someone catching them in the act.

This is what she wanted, no matter how much it scared her. This closeness; not just the fun or the fucking, but the promise of more tomorrows after the tour. The more she never thought she could have with this man.

The build to her climax begins to spike dangerously towards its peak, and she feels it coming up faster and faster as she rides him. Damien's hands glide down her waist, gripping her hips. His fingers press into her skin, helping her move as she starts to bounce against him violently, the sound of their bodies slapping against each other melting into the night sky along with her cries. Phoebe's whole body clenches. The beauty of the setting, the feeling of him so impossibly deep inside of her, both paired with the newly christened love blooming in her chest is almost too much to handle. But she can't stop. Not now. She wouldn't dream of it.

"Harder," he groans. "Please, babydoll."

She quivers as she looks down at him.

"Are you close?" She gasps.

He nods, and she smiles through her own waves of pleasure.

"Beg me."

Lightning flashes in his eyes and his breathing gets rapid. He reaches up and wraps his hand around the back of her head, pulling her down so that her ear is right next to his lips.

"*Please*, Phoebe. You know you need this as much as I do," he growls.

She does. She really fucking does.

Phoebe slams herself down on him as hard as she possibly can while he rises up to meet her, over and over. They swallow each other's moans as he wraps his arms around her, holding her in place as he begins to buck like a jackhammer. Sure he's breaking the rules a bit, but she can't bring herself to care when he's fucking her harder than she's ever felt in her life. She breaks their kiss, crying out as he continues to hammer her from below.

"Phoebe, I'm—"

She sinks her teeth into his neck, biting down hard, probably harder than she intended. Damien's body twitches, and for a moment she thinks he's going to flip her over, pinning her down and finishing things his own way, but he doesn't, letting go of her body instead. She can hear his boots dragging along the ground as he shudders, his voice breaking as she feels his cock spasm a final time inside her. It's just the push that Phoebe needs as she smashes into her climax.

Her thighs shake and her cunt clenches around him as she yells his name into the darkness, intermixed with obscenities. The waves rock her body one after another, each one pushing her deeper and deeper into this one single moment, a high she never wants to come down from. Finally, she collapses on top of him, the two of them still twitching and jerking a little every few seconds, Damien's arms wrapped around her waist like ribbons once more.

He recovers first, like he always does, and she finds him playing with her hair when she starts remembering how to think. She's nearly broken, staring at him as exhaustion takes her body. He smiles when he sees her stir, lifting his head and kissing her with so much tenderness that it makes her want to cry all over again.

"You looked so beautiful when you came."

Phoebe's body shakes with giddiness.

"Fuck, Damien, you can't say stuff like that."

"You did though. You always do. I'm almost hard all over again just looking at you."

He's not lying. She can feel it starting to strain inside her already.

Suddenly she's a little bit nervous.

"Oh— I uh... don't think I can go for another round."

He kisses the tip of her nose.

"Not a problem, sweets. There's always tomorrow."

Phoebe climbs off of Damien and stands to button up her dress while he slips off his condom, pulling his jeans back up before tossing it aside. Once she's fully clothed, he reaches up and pulls her back down into his lap, handing her the remains of her burger. They both eat in silence as they stare out at the canyon, still beautiful in the darkness. Phoebe shivers a little, the adrenaline wearing off just enough to realize that the evening cold had crept in, unbidden and unwanted.

Without a word, Damien tucks his jacket around her, and she nestles up against him.

"I guess we didn't really watch the sun do any setting after all, huh?"

"I got a pretty good view actually," she quips.

"Did you? Well, too bad for you I had the best seat in the house."

A horn honks off in the distance, startling them both. Damien curses as he shoves his wrapper back into the bag and they take their final bites.

The driver is waiting, as promised, and Damien fishes out a couple hundred dollar bills from his wallet, handing them over with a big smile on his face.

"Hey, thanks, man."

"Thank *you*, son," the cab driver replies. "Where to?"

"Just back to the hotel, my dude. And take your time."

Damien is good about maintaining his distance in the cab, holding onto her pinky with his own, and shooting warm glances at her every little while. Phoebe's whole body swirls with excitement. She worries that she might not even be able to sleep tonight; all she can think about is tomorrow.

Tomorrow, and tomorrow, and tomorrow.

Just What I Needed

CAESAR'S PALACE

Phoebe rifles through her makeup bag, swearing under her breath while Damien teases his hair in the bathroom mirror.

"What's up, sweets?"

"I can't find my eyeliner," she sighs. "I swear, I saw it yesterday."

He stoops over and picks up a small pencil from the bathroom counter.

"You couldn't mean *this* eyeliner, could you?"

"Thief!" She shouts, snatching it out of his hand.

He holds his hands up in defense, a big grin on his face.

"Hey, whoa! I distinctly remember you saying, 'what's mine is yours!'"

"I never said that!" Phoebe laughs, whacking him in the stomach.

"Well, if you didn't say it, then I made it up and ran with it, so it's real now. No turning back!"

Phoebe snorts and shakes her head.

"You're unbelievable."

Damien steps behind her and wraps his arms around her waist.

"Admit it. You *adore* me."

She bites her lip, her voice almost a whisper as she leans back to meet his eyes, his hot breath peppering her neck.

"I adore you."

Phoebe's hummingbird-heart goes wild as he kisses up and down her neck. He drags his teeth along her skin, his hands drifting down her waist, resting only for a moment before he slips them underneath her dress and stops just short of her underwear.

"Damien," she breathes.

It's an attempt at assertiveness only half realized.

"Just a quickie?"

"I– You have to leave in like five minutes, don't you?"

"Maybe I'll just tease you a little then."

She giggles, lightly struggling against him before her laugh is warped into breathy gasps as he begins to tease her through her panties.

"God, you're such a dick!"

"What did you say, babydoll? Speak up."

She can feel that familiar bulge against her thigh and arches her back, grinding into it. Her body craves more and she can't help herself.

"You want me to say it again? You're acting like a real–"

Phoebe's body responds immediately, leaning into his hand as his fingers slip past her panties and glide against her clit. The pitch of her voice shifts, the final word nothing more than a whine.

"Kiss me," he growls.

Her thoughts are foggy, and it takes her a moment to register the command, but his mouth finds hers the moment she turns her head. Her pulse pounds, and it's as if all the air is sucked out of the room. She grips the marble counter and whimpers as Damien's fingers continue to massage her most sensitive spot as his cock keeps grinding hard against her ass.

"Good girl," he murmurs, ripping his mouth away from hers and sucking another hickey onto her neck. She doesn't give a shit, he could make a hundred more.

She can tell she's starting to lose herself, and it feels like rarely a minute goes by before she has to pull herself back together to keep from ending up as a twitching mess on the floor. She dips her head, trying not to let him see how desperate he's making her, but he lifts her chin up immediately, and she's forced to meet his obnoxiously confident stare in the mirror.

"Beg me for it."

He may as well be reading her mind.

"Please, Damien," she moans. "I–"

She cuts herself off, suddenly embarrassed as her self-consciousness begins to take over. His eyes flash as his fingers speed up, and Phoebe can't help but shiver as electricity shoots up her spine. Her lips part, breath hitching in her chest. She feels like she might just collapse at any second.

"That's all? You can do better than that, babydoll."

"Oh fuck!" She cries out, desperately throwing away any pretense.

What's the point in pretending, anyway?

"Damien– Sir! I need it so bad, I need to come, please!"

Damien immediately increases the pace and pressure of the circles on her swollen clit, as if the words were a trigger phrase that unlocked something inside him. His touch, his warm breath on her neck, the soft rumbling sound of his voice, it's all too overwhelming, and it's placed her right on the edge, frantically moving her body any way that she can to get some relief. As she reaches the verge of coming her breathing becomes more and more erratic, and Damien rips his mouth away from her as he works her to the brink with his fingers. The only release that she can get right now is through him.

"Look at me when you come," he breathes as his other hand moves up to rest gently at the base of her throat.

The touch is tentative, testing her limits. Phoebe's eyes flutter open to meet his gaze, and she fully registers the image reflected in the mirror for the first time: her hair is a mess, haphazardly falling over a face caught in an expression between agony and bliss while Damien towers behind, surrounding her completely. As she watches herself twitch and shudder with each flick and caress from his fingers, it becomes clear just how complete his control is. She can almost hear his husky growl: *You're mine, babydoll.*

Suddenly Damien shifts, sinking his teeth into her shoulder hard enough to make her jump. It's the final jolt she needs, and her whole body shakes violently as the orgasmic waves begin to overtake her. The pressure from his fingers wrapped around her throat increases just a little, sparking something new in her brain as he carries her through her climax. The waves roll over and over as Phoebe lets herself collapse against him, shivering, covered in sweat, but sure in the knowledge that she's safe in his arms. After a few minutes of heavy breathing and quivering muscles she begins to regain her composure, absentmindedly running her hand up the side of his leg and caressing his thigh.

"I thought you said you were just going to tease me," she whispers, still feeling little sparks as his fingers continue idly playing inside her.

He smirks.

"Well, time isn't really a problem when you're as–"

A knock at the hotel room door cuts him off, and Shaun's voice shouts something inaudible.

"Shit." He kisses her one more time on the cheek. "Gotta go."

Phoebe lets out a satisfied sigh as he pulls his fingers out of her, holding herself up against the counter. He even makes a point of licking them clean before washing his hands.

"Don't worry, I'm sure you can finish whatever *hilarious* joke you had prepared when you get back."

He's obviously ready to retort, but the hammering at the door is enough to drag him away.

"Come on, dude! Car's waiting and Troy's dry humping my last nerve!"

Phoebe shoves her eyeliner into her purse, along with a compact, splashing some water on her face and straightening her clothes. She'll have time for more before the show.

"I'll walk with you guys to the lobby. I'm meeting Jan at the bar."

"Are you sure you guys don't want to come to sound check? Real behind the scenes action for your friend."

"We've got a lot to catch up on, besides she'll be excited enough about the–"

"DAMIEN!" Shaun bellows.

"Chill the fuck out Slater, *Jesus!*" Damien roars, grabbing Phoebe's hand.

Stepping out of the bathroom, Phoebe stands back as Damien opens the front door, expecting Shaun to barge right in and the two to go at each other as usual. Instead, she finds him standing calmly in front of them. He's sporting a pair of tight jeans, a mesh shirt, with purple eyeliner smeared over his lids, and doesn't seem even slightly annoyed, leaning casually against the doorway as if he hadn't just been screaming at the top of his lungs.

"So... what were you two up to?"

Damien rolls his eyes.

"Thought you were in a hurry."

Shaun's smile grows. He's clearly enjoying the chance to fuck with Damien a bit.

"I was *urgently* waiting to find out what weird kinky shit you were up to!" He quickly turns his attention to Phoebe, giving her a light pat on the shoulder. "No offense to you, of course. I'm sure if there's anything fucked up going on it's all this guy."

Phoebe smiles, glancing up at Damien whose expression screams that he's about to say something she will absolutely regret. Luckily, just as the color's starting to drain from her face, he's interrupted by the timely arrival of Janis sprinting down the hall.

"Pheebs, Pheebs! I have to tell you something!"

A hurricane of energy, Janis is decked out in a blue mini dress, her dark hair whipping behind her while she runs like a goddamn track star in a pair of stilettos. She stumbles to a halt in front of the three of them, almost bailing but recovering quickly. She nods at Shaun and Damien curtly, as if she just arrived via the most normal entrance in the world.

"Evenin' fellas."

Damien raises his eyebrows, his shoulders shaking with held-back laughter.

"What's up, Janis? You good?"

"Yep," She grins, catching her breath between words. "Just gotta talk to Pheebs. Journalist stuff. You guys wouldn't get it. You're too cool or something, whatever you want the reason to be."

Damien's face is a mixture of bemused and fascinated as Phoebe turns to her friend. Whatever it is, it's *definitely* important, and *definitely* not about work.

"Journalist stuff, suuure," Shaun purrs. "Very believable, good sell."

Janis tucks a strand of dark hair behind her ear while Shaun looks her up and down. She doesn't budge an inch, staring at him straight on without blinking. Phoebe wouldn't have been surprised to discover there was some sort of childhood rivalry between them if she didn't know they'd literally met less than 24 hours ago. She watches as the two continue their standoff, the seconds ticking by in awkward silence, but just as she starts to consider stepping in to break up whatever the hell is going on, Shaun ends the stalemate.

"Come on, Bell," he murmurs, grasping Damien's arm. "I got a cool solo I wanna show you. We're putting it on the new album, no arguments."

"Me? Argue? I never argue, dude!"

Shaun scoffs.

"It's your primary condition, asshole. C'mon, hurry up."

When the two men reach the end of the hall Damien spins around on his toe, a goofy smile on his face as he shoots Phoebe finger guns before backing up into the elevator. Phoebe can't help but chuckle at his antics, still completely befuddled by the whole situation, before turning back to Janis in time to see her take a deep breath.

"Finally."

Phoebe laughs.

"Okay, so what were you yelling about, and what was that with Shaun? Did you guys hook up?"

Janis tilts her head looking unimpressed.

"Look, Pheebs, I can't help it if I'm a total babe, okay? It's my cross to bear." She sighs dramatically. "But no, I did not sleep with some random rocker-dude. That's your thing now."

Phoebe cackles and leans up against her.

"I've missed you."

"Missed you too! Still, gotta tell you something. It's big."

"Big?" Phoebe asks.

"*Huge*. Mega-mall size. Can we talk in your room? I need a drink."

As the two walk back to her room, Janis's eyes land on the dog tags around Phoebe's neck, prodding at them with her finger.

"Ooh, wait a second, who'd you get these from? A *boy* perhaps?"

Phoebe fumbles as she unlocks the door.

"It's a long story, you go first."

Janis cackles.

"Scandalous, Miller! Looks like nothing's changed at all."

The moment they're through the door, Janis rushes to the sofa and throws herself across it. Hoping to prod the subject back in the other direction, Phoebe sits down next to her. Janis was always a fan of long drawn-out stories, so there was a chance that they'd be here for a while.

"So what–"

"I hooked up with Ophelia last night!" She blurts out.

"What?"

Apparently she was also a fan of shorter stories.

"Yeah! It happened! It was awesome!"

Janis lets out a little squeal and dives for the mini bar next to the sofa.

"Wait, but you said you didn't–"

"Pheebs, I said I didn't sleep with a rocker-*dude*," she blushes slightly, "and let me tell you, the way things went I might never want a dude again."

"Wh– Okay, but how did it happen?!"

Janis passes her a beer before cracking into her own and draining a good portion of it in one go.

"Well, I got kind of bored last night while you and Damien were out. So, I wandered down to the bar, and Ophelia was there just sitting by herself. That girl, alone, can you believe it? She recognized me and waved me over, and you know me I'm not turning down a drink, right? So we got to talking, and drinking, and talking, and then we went to a club down the street and danced..." Janis takes a sip of her beer, waving her other hand impatiently at her own delay to the story. "Then we made out in the bathroom. For like 20 minutes. Maybe more, I don't know." Janis starts to laugh, and Phoebe realizes her mouth's been hanging open for at least half of the story.

"And then we wound up back in my room, and we did... you know, stuff. Lots of stuff actually. And she ordered us breakfast before she left this morning and it was the best night of my goddamn life–"

She raises a finger, seeming to anticipate Phoebe's thoughts.

"And before you say anything, I know about her and Shaun and he knows about us. We're not doing anything fucked up. Apparently they have an open relationship."

Phoebe is left practically speechless as Janis finishes, her friend almost gasping for air, due in part to the fact that she told a good chunk of the story in one uninterrupted breath.

"Wow, that's... wow."

Phoebe realizes she hasn't opened her own beer and cracks it as she watches her friend. Her mind is racing with questions. She's known Janis was bisexual since they were teenagers, in fact Phoebe was one of the first people that Janis came out to. She was there when Janis told her parents, who were a little confused at first, but supportive. She'd met a few of her girlfriends over the years, but she doesn't really know how an open relationship works. And wasn't this a little quick to fall head over heels? On the other hand, Janis looked so unbelievably happy. And really, who was Phoebe to criticize a short timeline for falling in love?

"Hey, I have a great idea!"

Janis roots around in the mini fridge, grumbling as she pulls out a couple mini bottles of rum.

"Aw, no lime?"

"You can put that in the suggestion box when we check out tomorrow."

"I just might! What's a Rum and Coke without lime anyway? I tell ya' Pheebs, I could flip this whole damn hotel industry on its head!"

Phoebe gazes at Janis as the two stir their not-quite-rum-and-cokes, the latter clearly off in her own little world of very satisfying memories.

"So, how was it?" She asks coyly.

"You've been waiting to ask that, haven't you?"

"Yes, but I was polite and waited for you to have your little happy-sigh moment. It was just adorable, right out of a cartoon."

Janis sighs again for dramatic effect, leaning back in her seat.

"It was amazing. Ophelia's... She's incredible– and before you ask, no, it's not just the sex. It was everything. We got to talk for hours, talked about pretty much everything. Pheebs, do you even know how funny this girl is? You've been hanging out with her for weeks!"

"Yeah," Phoebe grins. "She's on Troy's ass all the time."

"She's so easy to talk to, looks at you like you're the only person in the room." Janis pauses. "I guess I *was* the only person in the room, but you know what I'm talking about."

Phoebe blushes, her throat tightening as she swallows.

"I know exactly what you're talking about."

She's never seen Janis like this before, absolutely smitten. Normally Phoebe might caution her against this, falling so quickly and so hard, but now... She leans over, wrapping her arm around her friend's shoulder.

"I'm so happy for you, Jan."

"Me too," she chuckles. "I mean obviously I am, but that shit with Jeremy was so rough, you know? I needed the *good* kind of rebound... and maybe this can be more than that? Who knows." She takes a big sip of her drink before slamming it down on the table. "Oh my god, and she was actually interested in my writing! Pheebs, she knows about philosophy and shit! She could actually follow my train of thought, unlike fucking Jeremy who just tuned out of any conversation if it wasn't about him."

"He was a real dick," Phoebe sighs, nodding.

"The worst! I told myself I was just in it for the sex after a while. Just having someone there to be close to, right? Turns out I really need that emotional part too? A dick isn't enough. There's gotta be something deeper."

"It *is* nice when they go a little deeper."

Janis snorts as they clink glasses.

"It's almost embarrassing looking back and thinking that I was even attracted to him to begin with."

Phoebe knows that feeling all too well.

"Well, you know, at the beginning, all of those red flags look green."

Janis scoffs.

"I think I might just be selectively color blind; I just choose to ignore them."

She looks down at her drink, stirring it with her finger.

"I don't really know if anything's gonna happen with Ophelia, but it was just nice to connect with someone who was actually excited to see me again."

Phoebe's ears perk up.

"Oooh, a for-real date?"

"After the show, yeah. I think we're going to go grab a bite."

"Jan!" She cries. "That's awesome! You should come back when you're finished with your article, finish out the tour!"

"Yeah, *if* I finish the article."

Phoebe reaches over and hugs her.

"You will, and it's going to be brilliant as usual. We both know you're going to run that goddamn paper someday."

"Right after I pry that Editor job from Sandra's cold, dead hands."

"Just call me when you're ready and we'll pry together. Take those big rings she wears, too and pawn them for a couple bucks. Teamwork."

Janis giggles and the two lean against each other, shoulder to shoulder.

"I'm so glad we did this."

"Me too," she sighs.

Their brief time together has already reminded Phoebe how much she missed her friend, and how much it'll suck to lose her to the daily grind again in a few more hours. The budding relationship with Ophelia, however, gives her an idea.

"Hang on, let me grab something!"

She gets to her feet and stumbles over to her suitcase, rooting through her bags until she finds her curated copy of the tour itinerary.

"Here. There's a list of hotels and phone numbers."

"Oh, this is great, I can call you both whenever I want! Maybe by the end of the tour my crush on Ophelia will get big enough that I'm hopelessly in love. We'll be twins!"

"Hey, I'm not *hopelessly* in love."

Janis raises her eyebrows to accompany her mocking smile.

"Just make sure you don't pick up the phone while he's fucking your brains out. That's not something I ever need to hear."

The two cackle, taking another couple minutes to finish their drinks before Janis jolts up out of her seat, her eyes full of determination.

"Enough of this love-talk, let's get to that fucking show!"

Life in the Fast Lane

Las Vegas Convention Center

The venue is packed. It's the first show they've played outside of the smaller club and dancehall settings all tour. Vegas is iconic, after all, so it makes sense Troy would book a show like this, one people actually travel to see. It's a test of the band's popularity, of their staying power, and it looks like they've passed.

"I got you a double G&T," Phoebe says as she walks up to Janis, handing her the drink. "And look, real goddamn lime wedges!"

"The lime drought is over!" Janis cheers, putting a hand on her shoulder. "My hero."

"Nothing is too much for the guest of honor."

The lights are low, and the band just finished their little pre-show huddle. As they move to the stage, Phoebe feels Damien quickly pinch her ass and she flinches, hearing him cackle as he runs off. Sighing, Phoebe turns back to find Janis struggling to find the straw with her mouth as her eyes track Ophelia on stage.

She grins.

"Oh my god, Jan. You weren't kidding about the whole crush thing."

"Shut up. I mean, fuck, just look at her!" Janis whispers. "She's so cute!"

She doesn't even break her gaze for a second.

Ophelia's dressed all in black tonight, complete with matching eyeshadow that hits her temples, her flaming red hair pulled back into a high ponytail. She settles down at her kit and spins around a couple times on the stool, twirling her drumstick while Shaun and Johnny ready their guitars.

As the lights adjust and the spotlight hits the stage, an absolutely electric Damien Bell grabs hold of the mic with both hands. The crowd erupts in escalating screams and applause and the grin on his face grows wide.

"LAAAAAS VEGAAAAAS!" He bellows. "How the fuck are ya tonight?!"

The crowd is already deafening, but Damien takes the mic off of the stand and walks toward the edge of the stage, leaning over and cupping his hand around his ear.

"I'm sorry, I didn't *quite* catch that, Vegas! I asked you how the *fuck* you were doing tonight!"

The initial roar is ear-splitting, and further shrieks and whoops are accompanied by dozens of things being thrown onstage, including a slightly shocking amount of underwear. Phoebe and Janis cheer from the sidelines as Damien motions for the crowd to get even louder.

"That's what I wanna hear!" He roars.

Janis snorts.

"God, he's so obnoxiously cocky. Was he just mute the whole first week? How could you fall for him after he opened his mouth?"

"I love it," Phoebe chuckles. "Trust me, he can back it all up."

"Pheebs, you're down so bad, you'd probably think it was hot if he–"

Phoebe tilts her head, pointing onto the stage.

"Hey Jan, check out Ophelia."

The drummer has her stool angled to face them, and as Janis turns and they lock eyes, Ophelia points her drumstick directly at her and slowly drags her tongue across her upper lip. Janis practically melts in her seat.

"Sorry, what were you saying?"

"Shut the fuck up," Janis mutters.

Before Phoebe has any chance for further ribbing, Damien's booming voice takes over the venue once again.

"It's all you, sweetheart, take it away!"

A crash of drums and the whine of guitars launches the band into their first song. Damien's voice is crisp and clear as he howls and shrieks, working the crowd with every movement. Before long he's down on his belly, leaning out over the edge of the stage to hold a girl's hand as he sings directly to her. It's their first really big show, and he knows it. All the more intensity, all the more spectacle. Phoebe sets her drink down a nearby speaker and starts to make some notes, glancing up infrequently at the stage. Janis elbows her in the ribs.

"Jesus, Pheebs, gimme your notebook. You're gonna miss this shot."

She glances up to see Shaun launching into his solo, with Damien pressed against him back-to-back. The two of them move together with confident intensity painted all over their faces, both bathed in the red glow of the spotlights. She watches them for a moment, dumbfounded at the completely uncrafted image just staring her in the face. Janis snatches her notebook out of her hands, slapping her on the wrist.

"Go, go!" She shouts.

Phoebe digs her camera out of her bag, advancing her film as she creeps out onto the stage to get as close to them as she can. The two look directly at her as she starts to snap pictures, both of them with those big, cocky smiles. She crouches down and takes a couple shots from below, the shift in perspective adding that special element of power and proximity. This one was definitely going to be a feature.

As she stands up and Damien winks at her, Shaun leans over, raising his eyebrows and glancing over at Janis, with a look that was practically demanding an answer. Looks like he might have noticed Ophelia's little gesture, or maybe it was Janis's not so subtle ogling. Either way.

"Later, later!" she shrugs, rushing back to Janis in the wings.

"Shaun knows something's up," she mutters as she stuffs her camera back into her bag.

"So?" Janis scoffs. "It's fine, I told you she–"

"Knows what?" Troy asks from behind them.

They both jump.

"What the fuck, dude?!" Janis yelps.

Troy holds his hands up, laughing.

"I'm six foot two, sweetheart. I don't know how you could miss me."

"Damien says you're barely five ten," Phoebe mutters under her breath.

Troy narrows his eyes.

"Tell your boyfriend to keep my measurements out of your pillow talk."

Phoebe grins as Janis cackles.

"So, how do we feel they're doing?" Troy asks, clearly not really bothered by the jab. He plays it up sometimes, but he really does have pretty thick skin.

"Incredible," Janis says. "I mean, from my outsider's perspective at least."

Troy claps her on the back.

"Sweetheart, this is backstage at a sold out show, you're an insider now."

"You hear that Phoebe? It finally happened, I'm cool!"

Phoebe laughs, downing her drink as the three of them huddle together, watching the band through riotous applause, all the way to the finale.

"Okay, you have 20 minutes, tops, before we're heading out!" Troy shouts as the band rushes off stage. Ophelia heads straight for Janis, giving her a big hug without a second thought. Before she can react, Shaun taps Phoebe on the arm and gestures further backstage.

"Hey!" Damien shouts. "Where are you taking my girl?"

"Keep your fucking voice down, Bell!" Troy hisses, smacking him in the arm. "She's not your girl when we're in public, remember?"

"Ow! Watch the merchandise!"

"*What* merchandise?" Troy quips. "Those skinny little arms?"

Damien hits him back, hopping around to dodge any further attacks.

"Stop with the slapping, old man! You're gonna run up your blood pressure!"

"Get back here you little twig!" Troy roars.

He chases Damien around, trying and failing to grab him over and over as Johnny watches on in amused silence. In the chaos, Shaun pulls Phoebe down a hallway, checking over his shoulder to make sure that they're out of earshot.

"Hey, so can we talk real quick?"

He's smiling, at least a little. Looks like Janis might have been right, maybe it really doesn't bother him. Hell, maybe it's even a plus. Phoebe grins back, the alcohol making her a little bolder than she would be normally.

"About Janis and Ophelia, I take it?"

Shaun pulls a wry grin.

"I like your style, Pheebs, you're always on top of shit– can I call you Pheebs, by the way?"

His eyes are warm.

"Totally, all my friends do."

"Cool, cool." He glances over his shoulder, taking a deep breath before he turns back to her. There isn't a hint of jealousy on his face, more a look of curiosity.

"So, Janis said you and Ophelia have an open relationship?"

"Yeah," Shaun replies. "We talked this morning, by the way, it's all cool. I just wanted you to know it's not like Janis is the other woman or anything. I wanna make that clear. Nobody's getting hurt here."

"I understand," Phoebe replies. "I just– what was with that look you gave me back on stage? I thought maybe you were just figuring it all out now."

He laughs, shaking his head.

"Nah, nah, I wasn't sure if you knew about any of this stuff yet. I just want to make sure you know this stuff with Ophelia– it's off the record. We like to keep our private life private, you know? I know the band gets it, and it's great to know you get it, but other people might not. That cool?"

"Scout's honor. I'm only putting your official interviews in the article. Everything else gets locked away in the Phoebe Miller vault."

He beams, and she returns the smile. She's gone from detached onlooker to wanting to maintain friendships with them long-term. Even if she wasn't involved with Damien, the last thing she'd want to do is betray their trust.

"Thanks. You're a doll, Pheebs." He pauses for a moment, quirking his brow. "Just out of curiosity, what other kind of stuff is in the Phoebe Miller Vault?"

She pats him on the shoulder, shaking her head.

"Terrifying stuff. It'll give you nightmares."

"Damien, huh?" Shaun teases.

"ATTENTION: ROWDY CHILDREN!" Troy bellows, jolting everyone from their conversations. "I know Janis is very cool and very fun, but can we actually move *backstage, please*?! You're all shaving years off my life!"

"Hey, maybe try freaking out less, it'll do you wonders," Ophelia quips as she pats Troy on the back. Damien cackles, about to add his own flavor, but flinches when Troy raises his fist.

Shaun glances back to Phoebe.

"Thanks for the talk."

He breaks away from her, following behind Ophelia and Janis while Johnny and Troy bring up the rear, but Damien's eyes are already locked on to Phoebe.

She giggles.

"What?"

He grabs her hand, pulling her back down the hall and away from the dressing room. Phoebe bounces behind him, filled with an excited buzz from her drinks and the night's events. As they turn the corner, he grabs her arm and pulls her inside a dark room, shutting the door. Before she can even blink he's pressing into her, her back against the wall. His lips crash into hers and she immediately wraps her arms around his neck. It's so natural now, she doesn't even need to think. Wherever, whenever, they both know what they want. She briefly wonders if anyone can hear them as his hands slide up her thighs, and her eyes quickly wander to the only light in the small room. It's coming from the hallway, through the crack under the door. A door Damien hasn't locked.

The two of them exchange soft, breathy moans, and his teeth clamp down on her lip, tugging just hard enough to force a whine to escape. She's already wet thinking about what they left unfinished earlier in the bathroom; that they might be caught doing it here. She wraps one of her legs around his waist and she rolls her hips, desperate for friction. Damien releases her lip with a soft pop, breaking the kiss to suck another hickey into the same spot that he did earlier in the evening.

"Damien, you have like ten minutes," she laughs.

"I know." He reaches down, and she can hear him unbuckling and removing his thick leather belt. "Twice as long to finish what I started in the bathroom."

He slides the belt against her skin, slowly, so that she can identify it in the dark. She feels heat spreading from her cheeks all the way down her neck and chest. She swallows hard.

"What's that for?"

He chuckles, his voice like velvet.

"Put your hands out."

A shiver rushes down her spine as she presses her wrists together and he quickly gets started with the belt. She can hear the sound of leather on leather, and the little jingle of the buckle as he works. He holds it in front of her, letting it touch the tips of her fingers.

"Hold onto this."

She takes it in her hands; it feels like he's pushed the belt back through the buckle to make a double loop.

"You know what this is for?"

She pauses, her voice shaking.

"Yes. I think so."

She can feel the warmth of his breath against her face.

"Slide your hands in."

She obeys immediately, and after a moment he tightens it up, pressing her wrists together.

She squeaks in response.

"Too tight?"

She shudders, the darkness hiding the excitement in her eyes from him.

"No."

"Good girl." Damien grabs her by the waist, pulling her toward him a bit before turning her around and gently pushing her up against the wall. "Keep your arms above your head and lean up against this. Don't worry about a thing, I'll keep you up."

Phoebe uses her forearms to brace herself as Damien gets her into position, pulling her hips back. She can feel the anticipation building inside her as he flips her skirt up, slowly sliding her panties halfway down her legs before letting them fall on their own. Gently, he kicks her legs apart. She hears the familiar sound of a zipper behind her, followed by some rustling. She lets out an impatient whine and Damien chuckles.

"Patience is a virtue, babydoll."

Condoms. She almost forgot.

She listens and listens, only hearing something light drop onto the ground followed by slow, calm breathing behind her. As the seconds pass with no movement or sound, she can feel her pulse picking up more and more, her breath getting heavier. Just before she's about to speak, she feels him glide his cock against her, teasing her briefly before pushing the tip in. She lets out a little gasp, but he doesn't move. Again, the seconds pass.

"S-so, how long have you been wanting to tie me up?"

Damien slaps her ass, and her body jumps, pushing his cock a little deeper.

"Since you took control back at the canyon." He leans over. "Do you want me to let you go?"

A nervous chuckle bubbles up from her throat.

"No."

"So, you want us to do something in here... but what?"

Her whole body flushes. She knows he likes to hear her say it out loud. To beg for it.

"I want you to fuck me. Sir."

"Well that sounds fun. So, do you want me to turn on the lights first?"

She pauses, savoring the sound of his voice in the darkness. The feeling of his cock just barely inside her, ready to force its way in. Not knowing what exactly is coming, or even if the door could swing open at any moment.

"No."

She's almost certain she can feel him twitch.

"Well, we're on the same page then. We have to be quick, and you have to be quiet," Damien whispers, leaning over to brush his lips against her ear. "Can you do that for me, babydoll?"

"Yes."

He smacks her ass and she holds back a yelp.

"Yes, what?" He growls.

"Yes, *sir.*"

"That's my girl."

Phoebe melts at the sound of those words, but it's that familiar feeling as his cock begins to fill her up that has the biggest effect, forcing the wind out of her. Maybe she'll never get used to it. All the better.

"Remember to stay quiet," he whispers. His hand glides around her throat and she leans up further against the wall, her hips rocking backward as she takes him deeper.

Damien groans as he finally bottoms out, his hips quickly finding a hard and fast rhythm that forces Phoebe's eyes shut. She swallows moan after moan, biting down to keep herself from screaming when he starts pulling out almost completely before each massive thrust. He's rubbing against that spot deep inside her each time, chasing his own climax while driving her toward her own. Soon, one of his hands slides down her waist, fumbling slightly as he reaches around to play with her clit, snapping her eyes back open. She's adjusted enough to the light to make out small little details, but pushed up against the wall all she can do is look down at her own feet shifting slightly with each impact, the sound of him slapping against her ass filling their tiny surroundings. With nothing else to focus on, the feelings and sounds are amplified. Every slap and every thrust are twice as intense as usual as her mind wraps itself entirely around this tiny little room.

Phoebe feels like she's going to crumble, a fire in her belly and her skin searing from his touch. One of his hands winds up her ponytail and she can feel herself careening closer as he pulls her back by her hair to bite down on her earlobe. Somehow he's both brutal and gentle at the same time.

Suddenly she can hear voices out in the hall. She can't make out the conversation as he continues to relentlessly pound her, but there's unmistakable laughter. There's no way they didn't hear the sounds. Is that what they're laughing about? What if someone saw them head in? She can feel herself tighten up at the thought of what they might saying about her: the girl that lets Damien Bell fuck her wherever he wants. Her breathing gets heavier, more labored. What if they came to check on the noise? What if the door swung open right now and they all saw her like this?

Damien's noticed too.

"Mmm, you really liked it when those folks walked by huh, sweets? You want me to call them back?"

It's all too much, and her hands curl into fists, bone white as she struggles to keep from screaming. She's teetering on the edge, and she can tell by the way that Damien picks up the pace, that he is too.

"Oh yeah, you'd love that, wouldn't you? You want them to watch?"

She's not sure if it's the words, or everything else, but her mouth drops open in a silent cry as her climax overtakes her. Behind, Damien begins to breathe harder as his hips snap faster and faster, finally shuddering as he erupts into a string of grunts and gasps. Her legs shake and she struggles to stay up, her whole body pressing desperately against the wall as he leans into her, still thrusting infrequently as if using her cunt to massage out his last few drops of pleasure. When he finally pulls away, his cock slides out her with a satisfying pop. Warm breath peppers the back of her neck for a moment as he helps her regain her balance before he bends down to slide her panties back up.

"You don't change those," he commands, helping her turn around and beginning to remove the belt. "I want to go through the rest of the show knowing you're wearing them."

She grins in the dark, feeling her wrists come free and listening as he threads his belt back through the loops in his leather pants.

"Lucky for you, I didn't bring an extra pair."

Damien chuckles.

"Someday maybe you won't bring any at all."

From somewhere down the hall, they can hear Troy asking around for Damien, followed quickly by the sound of swearing.

Phoebe laughs as Damien kisses her.

"We'd better go, think you're decent?"

She smooths out her skirt as best she can in the dark.

"Around you? Never."

When Doves Cry

CAESAR'S PALACE

Damien yawns loudly as Johnny leads the two of them to their set of tables, the hotel restaurant already buzzing by the time they hit the floor. They're exhausted from a night of very little sleep, but Janis is catching her cab in the early afternoon and they don't want to miss her.

"Miller, next time he yawns, I dare you to fish hook him."

"Uh, you know, I think he'd be into that," Phoebe mutters.

Johnny smirks.

"Whoa, Miller, you're actually pretty funny! I've gotta let everyone know."

The energy in the restaurant is high, with lots of laughter and boisterous conversations all around them. To Phoebe's mild surprise she spots Janis, Ophelia, and Shaun already tucked away at the second table, laughing and goofing around as they sip their coffee. The three of them together was nothing unexpected, but Janis being up anytime before 10 on a day she wasn't working just felt wrong.

She waves as Phoebe approaches. She looks really fucking happy.

"What the hell?" Damien laughs as sees the inevitable seating arrangement. "I gotta sit at the nerd table with Sullivan?"

Troy's middle finger is raised from behind a newspaper even before Damien finishes his jab, refusing to look up from the business section. It's not his first rodeo.

"We're just worried you'll develop separation anxiety, Bell!" Shaun laughs. "Taking precautions, you get it."

Damien grumbles under his breath as Janis and Shaun collapse into laughter, and Ophelia stirs her coffee in silence, a big grin on her face. Johnny sits next to Phoebe while Damien begrudgingly takes a seat next to Troy, who glances up from his paper in time to catch Damien's eyes.

"Oh, *now* you wanna sit next to me? What happened, figured out you could learn a thing or two from the smartest guy around?" Damien laughs, ruffling his hair, and Troy instinctually rolls up the paper and smacks him on the head. "Watch the hair, clown!"

Johnny sighs and gestures at the two of them.

"They never stop."

"Does it ever get old?"

"Sometimes, but– Hey, can I ask you an honest question?"

"Sure."

"How were we last night?"

Phoebe frowns. That show was fantastic, was he having doubts?

"You guys were amazing!"

He scoffs.

"What, I'm being serious!"

She tears the lid off of one of the little plastic cups of creamer and pours it in her coffee.

"I think you can do better with the superlatives, Phoebe."

She rolls her eyes.

"You want better than amazing?"

"I want better! You're a professional writer! Throw some pizazz at me! There are thousands of words in the English language, show me something I've never seen!"

Phoebe glances around as she racks her brain for the right word. Damien and Troy have fallen into a quieter, less physical conversation, that is to say Damien has stopped behaving like a ten-year-old playground bully now that he has a cup of coffee and a cigarette to keep his hands occupied.

"Okay, okay," she sighs. "What about... Stupendous?"

Johnny nods as he flips through the breakfast menu.

"That's a good one, but we clearly need some more. Keep going."

She grins.

"Marvelous."

"Another winner! I hope they're paying you top-dollar."

"A heart-stopping performance."

Johnny gives an approving nod, his smile getting wider.

"Okay, one more. Hit me."

"Electric– no *Explosive*! The best fucking band I've ever seen in my life. I think my soul left my body at *least* ten times during your set. I know it did, because I met God, Johnny. Capital-G God."

"Wow. Yep. That's more like it." He chuckles, shaking his head as he takes a sip of his coffee. All of a sudden, Johnny begins to gnaw on his thumb nail, the playful energy shifting to a more serious vibe. "We were all so fucking tense about it going in to the show. I've never seen those three that shaken in all the years I've known them. They were terrified. We really needed that show to go off without a hitch."

"And what about you? Were you nervous?"

He blushes, realizing his nervous habit and putting his hands on the table.

"I was a wreck," he admits. "Almost anybody can make a record, y'know? As long as you've got someone who lets you in the door, someone to make it sound good, produce it, make it slick." He sighs. "The hard part is translating that to the shows, doing it live. We're not new at it, we know the ropes, but this was the most legitimate place we've played. They need to remember us for more than a couple days. It's what's going to give us a future. That's what I want at least."

He really cares about this band, that much is obvious. Even if it started as just dicking around with his friends, it's so much more than that now.

"By my count you didn't miss a note last night, Johnny. I think you can sleep soundly in the knowledge that you all gave it 110%."

He perks up a little, that big ray of sunshine returning right on cue.

"You really think so?" He asks.

She nods.

Johnny's a real talent, but he still cares too much about what people think of him. He's humble in a way that Damien probably never was, even when they were kids.

"Yeah, trust me. I've heard a lot of shitty bands, a lot of okay bands, and even a couple *truly* great bands all play live. You guys are in that final category." She pauses for a second, clearing her throat. "And before you say anything, of course I'm completely unbiased here."

"Hey, I'll take it," Johnny laughs. He claps her on the shoulder. "I'm glad you're here, Pheebs, bias or no."

"Hey Reed!" Ophelia barks from her table. "You're bogarting all of the interview time!"

"Alright Pheebs," He sighs, "I guess I don't want to keep you from your extremely important subjects."

Ophelia cackles.

"Just a joke, Johnny-boy. Someone's gotta give our girl an out in case you start to bore her to death!"

Damien leans over as Phoebe gathers up her things.

"Damn, you're popular today. Hope I can schedule a meeting."

She flashes him a coy smile and shrugs.

Ophelia was obviously joking, but thinking about it Phoebe realizes she's been so focused on Damien lately that she hasn't *really* interviewed Ophelia at all. She was there when they were playing go-fish on the bus, but that ended up being almost all about Shaun, and their little shopping spree back in LA was all personal, off the record. There probably wasn't going to be a better time than now.

Ophelia looks up as she walks over, curiosity dancing in her eyes.

"Actually, I've got all my stuff, you wanna do your interview now, for real? We could swap tables, you know, just for a little privacy."

"Hell yeah!" she shouts, turning to Shaun and Janis. "Sorry, lovelies, but I've got a *very* important interview! Can you order for me?"

"I've got you," Shaun replies, tapping his head. "I got all your favorites right up here."

Phoebe follows Ophelia to a back table near the kitchen, digging her notebook and pen out of her bag and setting it all down at the table. Behind them, she can hear Shaun, Damien, and Johnny trading barbs while Janis cheers them all on in unison.

The two women share a knowing smile before Phoebe puts her pen to her notebook, ready to begin.

"Okay, so right off the bat: anything you want off the record, just tell me. I won't write down stuff you're not comfortable with."

"Cool." Ophelia nods. "Actually I'm really excited to do this."

"Oh yeah?"

She's a little stunned. Something about Ophelia always seemed a bit too cool for interviews, and Phoebe figured she'd think they were a little dull.

"Yeah. We don't get a lot of chances to talk to journalists because of Captain Arrogance over there–"

Phoebe snorts.

"Oh right, sorry, I know you two..."

"No, no, it's a fair assessment."

Suddenly Ophelia flinches, and Phoebe hears the smallest sound of something hitting the ground. She glances down to see a sugar packet, looking up again to catch Janis and Shaun trying to stifle their laughter.

Ophelia picks it up and throws it back in one quick motion, hitting Shaun right between the eyes.

"Hey! I'm trying to be professional! Don't make me come over there!" She turns back to Phoebe, smiling as if nothing at all had happened. "Sorry about them. Janis has been riling him up all morning, and you've seen how he can get even without her influence."

"It's okay, but uh…" Phoebe takes a breath and leans forward. "Hey, can I ask you something off the record?"

"Yeah, for sure. I'm an open book."

"So um, Janis told me about the other night."

Ophelia smiles, her eyes lighting up.

"Oooh, care to spill *what* she told you? Any juicy details?"

The color starts to drain from Phoebe's face, but luckily Ophelia cuts her off before she can start stammering.

"It's cool, Pheebs, I'm just fucking with you. The stuff with us, it's all pretty out in the open. Shaun and I aren't big on keeping secrets from each other, let alone anyone else. That kinda stuff makes things messy."

Phoebe nods. Okay, so what Janis said was legit. It's not that she didn't believe it, but it's good to hear directly from everyone involved. It's not her place to intervene like some overprotective parent, but she needs to be sure her friend isn't going to get hurt.

"I talked to Shaun last night too, and he was explaining–"

"Yeah, so you already knew we're a thing, but it's an open relationship. Been like that since way before we started the band, actually. Probably why this whole thing's worked out so well. It gives us the chance to explore different kinds of relationships, have new experiences, stuff like that. A couple of times we've both dated the same person, but that's rare because they need to be cool with the whole package deal. The main thing is that we talk to each other. No secrets, no bullshit, no lies."

"Wow."

She honestly didn't expect that clear an explanation, but it's impressive.

"So, it works?"

"Yep! It's pretty simple really, as long as everyone's onboard. I'm honest with all my partners about Shaun, and he's honest about me. We're both safe, and we tell each other everything. So yeah, yesterday before the show I went to Shaun's room and we hung out and talked about Janis– not explicit details, obviously. Those things are private if the other person isn't in the room. But, I promise, everything's cool." She smiles. "I mean obviously, or we wouldn't all be hanging out."

Phoebe watches Janis and Shaun deep in conversation with one another. It looks intense, but not serious. They're clearly enjoying themselves.

"I've never heard of anything like that before, but if it works and you're all happy, then that's what matters."

Ophelia smiles.

"I think our parents' generation has a lot of hangups about what relationships should look like, the ideal family and all of that shit." Ophelia sips her coffee. "There are different ways to love people. It took Shaun and I a while to figure it out, but I wouldn't trade our situation for anything. As long as everyone is happy, feels heard, and understood, that's what matters to us."

She winks.

"I mean, that, and the amazing sex."

Phoebe smiles sheepishly, trying to figure out how to word her next question.

"And– Okay I'm not trying to be rude, but you guys talked to Janis about it? She understands the whole deal?" It's nothing against Ophelia or Shaun, Phoebe's protective best-friend-instinct just keeps kicking into overdrive.

"Of course! Like I said, I talked to her the other night. After that, the three of us sat down before you guys got here." Ophelia finishes off her coffee, gesturing for the waitress to bring another. "Shaun and I aren't interested in hurting anyone or sneaking around or anything like that just for a little fun. It's best to just lay your cards out on the table. That's how you win big–" She grins. "You like that little Vegas pun? I haven't had a chance to make one this whole time. It's been killing me."

Phoebe snorts.

There's no tension, no jealousy, none of the bullshit that she was afraid of. One less thing to worry about.

"So, you wanna ask me about music? We can keep talking about this if you want, I'm cool with either, but I figure you'll want some stuff that's on the record too."

"Oh, right! Okay, yeah, let's move on to music."

"Cool, cool, ask away."

Phoebe appreciates Ophelia's bluntness, even if it surprises her every so often. She flips through her notebook to a new page, making some quick markings to prep out her questions.

"When did you first realize you wanted to be a drummer for a rock band? I know you mentioned your influences... Bobbye Hall, Karen Carpenter, and Maureen Tucker, right? But was there something specific you heard or saw as a kid that made you think, 'I want to be a drummer'?"

"Damn, good memory Miller!"

Ophelia contemplates the question, her face scrunching up as she stares past Phoebe, but it's only a few moments before she folds her arms across her chest, nodding her head.

"So when I was a kid, I saw a rerun of Karen Carpenter on 'Your All-American College Show,' one from back in 66. It was 'Dancing in the Street,' and that was the first time I ever saw a woman play the drums. She wasn't dainty or shy about it either. She just wailed on those fuckin' things– I dunno, maybe *wailed* is the wrong word, but she sure as shit was proud." Ophelia laughs, her eyes fully lit up. "It was just so awesome to see a woman fully immersed in her own talent, and to be totally unashamed of it. I think we've been taught to downplay stuff like that because we're supposed to be meek or whatever, but I never wanted to be like that. So when I saw Karen thrashing those drums, I immediately knew I wanted to do that too."

She leans back in her chair, stretching her arms out and cracking her neck.

"My sister's a musician too, actually. Concert pianist. She went to Juilliard, has perfect pitch, absolute musical prodigy in every way. The second she sits down at a piano, she dominates that thing. She's more delicate than I am when she plays, but she's not afraid of going hard."

Ophelia smiles when she talks about her sister, but Phoebe can tell there's a little bit of something else behind it too.

"Did your parents put you both in music lessons as kids?"

"Yeah," she laughs. "Piano for the both of us. Yvonne was hooked, like you'd expect. She was really studious and serious about it. I was more interested in smashing the keys than actually sitting down and learning how to play, but there was a drum kit in the music school that we went to. I slipped away to get on that thing whenever I had the chance. Shockingly, our teacher actually told my parents that it would be a better investment to get me some drumming lessons."

"Did they?"

Ophelia snorts.

"Yeah, after I wailed and sobbed the whole car ride home; they weren't happy about it though. I don't think people take drummers seriously, you know? We get forgotten about, but we're basically the beating heart of a band. If they didn't have us, they might as well be a fuckin' folk music act." She pauses, pursing her lips. "No offense to folk-music fans, of course. You got my respect if you can make it work with just a washboard and some spoons."

Phoebe chuckles, scribbling notes like lightning.

"That's a few great quotes in a row."

"Thanks," she laughs. "I can be insightful sometimes."

"I think you undersell yourself in that department," Phoebe replies, twirling the pencil between her fingers. "What do your parents think about this whole rock star thing nowadays? Did they come around to you and the drums when you hit it big?"

Ophelia sighs. There's the tiniest sliver of pain in her expression, but it disappears quickly behind her smile.

"They're... let's call it old fashioned. They definitely love my sister's career. Makes sense, right? It's dignified, very classy." She mimes a gun to her head and Phoebe chuckles. It's something she can definitely relate to. "I think they still see me as some misguided kid who's fucking around with her friends. They don't take it seriously at all, probably because they don't think I do either. I guess they can't see how much it matters to me."

"Are things tense with your sister?" Phoebe asks, "because of the stuff with your parents?"

She shakes her head.

"Nah, Yvonne and I are cool. She actually gets it." Ophelia starts to laugh. "Back when we released our first LP she actually requested a signed record from the band. I told her I could just bring one home but she insisted on paying for it, having it shipped so it could arrive and she could unwrap it and everything. She has it up in her rehearsal studio, in a goddamn frame no less."

"Sounds like you're pretty close," Phoebe says with a smile.

"Yeah. She's younger than me by about two years, but we've almost always gotten along well. There was definitely competition when we were *really* little kids, but I figure that's like any sibling relationship, right?"

Phoebe nods. Sometimes it lasts a lot longer.

"Okay, so we've got your influences, your family... What do you love the most about playing music? Or playing with this band in particular?"

Ophelia leans back again in her chair, staring up at the ceiling.

"It's terrifying," she whispers. She sounds almost reverential.

Phoebe remembers Johnny's words back at the other table. The four of them were scared stiff when they went onstage last night.

"So, you love... that it's terrifying?"

She leans forward on the table again, meeting Phoebe's eyes.

"You never know what's going to happen once you step out on the stage. Maybe someone falls on their face, or we totally bomb. Hell, something could explode!" She pantomimes a big explosion, with sound effects and all. "We don't have a lot of control, we just put as much of ourselves into each show as we can. We could have just as easily stayed totally undiscovered, playing local bars and punk shows, you know? I think success has a lot to do with luck, and sometimes the cards just fall in your favor."

"Would you have been content to keep playing punk shows?"

"Oh yeah, for sure," Ophelia laughs. "So would Damien, honestly. Why do you think we still play so many bars? Troy hates it, says it's money left on the table, but those are our people. We're comfortable there."

Phoebe chews on her pen.

"Do you think that maybe there's an element of being afraid of success?"

"Man, you ask some tough questions."

"Well, we're talking about fear, right?"

She drums her fingers on the table, a mysterious rhythm that she seems to be completely familiar with. It feels like each beat has a purpose, and Phoebe doesn't think she could mimic it if she tried.

"Yeah, yeah, I guess so. We didn't blow up fast, at least not as fast as some people. There are bands that just put out one record, and everything explodes. The industry just expects you to handle it, too. We've had a bit of a slower climb, which I think kept us grounded. By the time we started to really hit we had a few EPs under our belt and a solid fanbase. Hell, I remember Damien and Shaun used to make these shitty t-shirts..." She starts to really laugh, having a bit of trouble getting the words out. "Damien tried to draw a guitar on them, but he doesn't have his sister's refined art skills, so it looked like this weird fucking goose. Oh my *God*, we made fun of him for it forever!"

She grabs Phoebe's notebook, flips to a new page, and draws what really does look like a weird goose.

"Maybe you should use that in your article. Real behind the scenes shit, everyone'll love it."

In less than a minute the two of them are leaning over the table, red in the face over 'Official Damien Bell Weird Goose' merch ideas.

"Hey! Is that joy I hear over there? You know my rules about joy before 10AM!" Troy shouts.

"Mind your business, Sullivan! We're professionals!"

Phoebe wipes away tears of laughter and Ophelia nods her head, forcing herself to focus back up.

"Anyway, what I'm trying to say is I'm glad that we didn't *totally* blow up overnight. Not sure if we would have been able to stay us. Now we're up to that next hurdle and it's coming at us fast so, yeah, to answer your question there's definitely an element of fear to the whole thing."

"I get it," Phoebe chuckles, pulling herself together. "Well that was great, I think I got some really good stuff for the article."

"This was fun, Pheebs. Damien was right, your questions are legit."

She smiles, glancing over her shoulder to find him staring at her, a little twinkle in his eye as he sips his coffee.

After breakfast, Shaun and Ophelia walk Janis to her cab, each of them carrying a suitcase for her while the roadies load up their gear.

"Bell!" Troy barks. "Your shit packed?"

"Yes, *dad!*" Damien groans. He grabs Phoebe's suitcase, using the opportunity to give her a quick kiss on the cheek before handing it off.

Phoebe watches as Ophelia flings her arms around Janis, giving her a quick peck. Janis squeezes her back tightly, both of them giddy as they rock from side to side. Shaun smiles, waving to Janis before heading back to the bus.

"Absolutely smitten," he says as he passes Phoebe by.

"Yeah," she whispers.

"Ophelia talked to you, right?"

"She did. I'm happy things are going so well."

When the two finally let go, Janis takes a notebook out of her purse, rips off a page, and hands it to Ophelia, who takes it, grinning from ear to ear as she runs to the bus.

Phoebe sees her opportunity, moving in for a big hug.

"I'm gonna miss you!" Janis groans. "And not just because I don't want to go back to New York and finish that article."

"Yeah, I bet! No Ophelias in New York, huh?"

"Or Phoebes! You're at least second best now, I promise!"

She breaks the hug and glances up at the tour bus. Shaun and Ophelia are waving at her from a window.

"Ugh, yep, New York is going to *suck* after this."

Phoebe grins.

"Hey, remember what I said, maybe you can swing back when you're done. You won't just be my guest this time."

"Oh, I definitely will," she smirks. "No way I'm missing out on–"

"Hey, lady!" The cab driver calls. "You wanna miss your flight, or what?"

Janis flinches, turning on her toe to sneer at him.

"*Lady*?! I'm paying you, dude. How about you let me say bye to my friend!"

The cab driver mutters something under his breath, rolling up the window as Phoebe roots through her bag.

"Hey, you want my Walkman for the flight?" She leans over and glances at the driver-side window. "And maybe the ride to the airport?"

"Oh! Can I?" Janis asks. "I completely spaced and didn't bring anything distracting. I'm doomed if there's a baby or, oh god, some talkative dude."

Phoebe digs her Walkman out of her purse and hands it to her, along with a couple tapes. Queen and Zeppelin.

"There's fresh batteries in there too."

"You're the best, Pheebs. Thanks." She grins, getting into the car and rolling down the window. "Gives me one more excuse to come back."

Phoebe watches as the car pulls away, smiling as she sees Janis already slipping the headphones onto her ears, the driver visibly annoyed.

"You never need an excuse, Jan."

Don't You Want Me
THE RENAISSANCE HOTEL, PHOENIX

The sound of the door slamming against the wall pulls Phoebe violently from unconsciousness as Johnny barges through the door, half naked and completely wired.

"Guys, Erin's coming! She's gonna be here today!"

They only just arrived in Phoenix at 3:00AM, and Phoebe's body feels like it's been smashed with a meat tenderizer. She's too exhausted to really comprehend what's going on, letting an angry groan slip from her lips as her eyes fall on the bedside clock. It's barely 6 in the morning.

Fuck.

Damien rolls over, groggily giving Johnny the thumbs up.

"Goodferher," Damien grumbles. "And congratulations, man. I know you've been working hard on your fingering skills lately."

Phoebe lets out a muffled laugh from under the pillow, her body rumbling a little as Damien snorts at his own joke.

"Laugh it up, Bell!" Johnny grins. "Not even you can bring down my good mood!"

He grabs Damien's foot and starts to drag him out from under the covers onto the floor. Damien struggles, ending up halfway off the bed as the two throw half-hearted punches and flailing kicks at each other.

"Out!" He roars dramatically. "This is my sanctuary, and you're banished, for all time!"

Phoebe watches in amused silence as Johnny's eyes dart down for the first time, finally realizing that Damien is completely naked. He frowns a little, nodding to himself as Damien lifts his brows.

"So, you've seen enough, or…?"

"Okay, alright, you know what? I'm going to be gracious and call this one a tie," he says as he slowly backs out the door, slamming it behind him.

"How…" Phoebe rubs her eyes, still a little unsure if any of that actually happened. "How did he even get in here?"

Damien shrugs, wandering casually to the other end of the room.

"I might, just *maybe,* have forgotten to lock the door."

She sighs into her pillow.

"Again?"

"It's a bad habit, I'll admit. Everyone's got one right?"

She hears the lock slide closed with a soft click and glances up just in time to brace for impact. Damien lands on the bed with a whoop, grabbing her by the waist and pulling her toward him.

"Alright, maybe I have more than one."

Phoebe giggles as he places gentle kisses up her neck, leaning her head against him. She lets her hands wander down his body, and she can feel him tense up as her fingernails gently graze his abs before she wraps her hand around his slowly rising cock. She wants him, despite the exhaustion. She slides herself all the way down onto the bed, crawling backward until she's directly between his legs. Her heart beats faster and faster as she looks up at him, feeling him getting harder each second as it swells in her hand. She presses her lips against the head of his cock, giving it a soft little kiss.

"Can I?" She asks.

She can feel it strain as he grins.

"Beg for it."

He says it so softly, but the firmness of his words make her shudder. There's a moment of self-doubt; she doesn't want to look foolish or pathetic… maybe she should let him hang there, sliding away and leaving him like this, just like he'd done to her in the past. But the idea of asking, of begging to suck it, it's making her so fucking wet.

She leans forward on bent arms and knees, staring directly at his now raging cock. She's sure he can feel her warm breath against him as she tilts her head, barely an inch away. Her ass is stuck up in the air, swaying playfully for a moment before she tilts her head up to look at him, her eyes wide and reverential.

"Sir, please may I? I promise I'll make you feel *so* good."

His pupils are so big she can't even see the bright blue-gray of his irises anymore. His cheeks flush and his mouth hangs open just a little bit.

"Jesus Christ," he whispers, before regaining his composure. "Yes, you may."

She smiles demurely for a moment before her whole demeanor shifts.

"Jesus is another guy, but I appreciate the compliment."

Phoebe doesn't give him the opportunity to retort, lunging toward him and locking him in a kiss. He moans softly and takes her time with it, letting out little groans as she slowly returns to her initial spot, running her tongue along his perfect abs and leaving sharp little bites on his hips and thighs along the way.

Kneeling directly in front of him, Phoebe grasps it with both hands and starts to stroke it slowly but firmly, from tip to base. She keeps her mouth right next to it the whole time, each hot panting breath from her lips adding to the buildup until it's red and engorged, somehow bulging even more than before.

Damien whimpers.

"You said you thought about my mouth on you," she whispers. "That night back on the bus."

"Yeah," he croaks. "Been thinking about it since the first day you walked into that hotel room, actually."

She smiles.

"So naughty, sir. I thought we were supposed to have a professional relationship back then."

She wets her lips and licks a slow, delicate line up his shaft, his heavy groan music to her ears. She leans in for what seems like the main attraction, only to leave a single tiny kiss. She can feel his greedy eyes burning into her, and she knows he's doing everything in his power not to pin her down and teach her a lesson.

After another round of delicate kisses, she starts massaging his shaft in preparation, her eyes eager as she glances up at him. He nods, and she can feel his whole body shudder as she presses her lips directly down on his tip one last time before she takes him in her mouth. He's so big, and even after some preparation with her tongue, she can only take him so deep so quickly. Damien buries his hands in her hair, raw moans escaping his lips as she struggles with his girth. He lets out a soft whine as the tip of his cock presses into the back of her throat for the first time.

"Don't stop," he whines. "Fuck, you're perfect."

She hums as she slides her mouth up and down his shaft, his body shuddering at the twin sensation as his fingers clench her hair.

Finding a stable rhythm, Phoebe reaches in between her legs to touch herself, keeping the pressure light to mimic her memories of his tongue lapping against her. She hears him chuckle, his confidence clearly returning quickly.

"You were made for this, weren't you?"

She can feel a little shock of electricity jolt through her body as his words land, and she starts to finger herself harder. The two of them have learned a lot about each other over the last few days, the most important being how to drive the other absolutely wild with just a few words. Phoebe lets out a muffled moan of affirmation, and he growls as it reverberates through his cock.

"That's a good girl."

His grip tightens on her hair, and he begins to take just a bit of control from her while she rubs frenzied circles around her clit. The feeling of him forcing himself just that little bit further down her throat before pulling her up for air is exhilarating.

"Don't forget to take care of yourself, sweets. I wanna see you come."

She dives in again, rubbing directly against her clit as she sloppily slides him deeper. Everything about the situation compounds on top of each other: his hands in her hair, his cock twitching in her throat, his confident tone intermixed with moans of sweet abandon, and it piles up until it all comes crashing down. Phoebe feels herself convulsing, choking on him as spittle drips down her knuckles and she struggles to maintain the pace.

"Can you keep going?" He croaks. "I'm–"

"Mmm!" She nods. There's no way she's stopping now.

His grip loosens just a bit as he continues to fuck her throat, fully taking on the more active role he slipped into earlier. She tries her best to match his increasing pace, groaning through her own extended climax as she runs her fingers so fast across her clit she's almost slapping it.

"Fuck, I'm gonna come," he breathes.

He slows himself down as much as possible, giving her time to come up for air as he struggles to hold himself back. She releases him from her mouth with a wet popping sound, a thin line of spit running from the tip of his cock to her bottom lip. Damien groans at the sight.

"H-holy shit, Phoebe."

She can tell by the way he's practically pulsing in her hand that he's right on the edge, his entire body trembling and as he clenches his teeth. The agony in his face, the twitching convulsions of his body... it's so fucking hot.

She dips her head, swirling her tongue around his tip for just a moment before wrapping her lips back around him, her head bobbing quickly up and down. His moans are music to her ears as his breathing quickens, and she feels a swell of gratification when he grabs her head one final time as he shoots it all down her throat.

Phoebe pulls her mouth off his cock as Damien collapses backwards. There's more than she expected and it proves a little difficult to swallow it all, but somehow she manages, gasping briefly for air in the aftermath. She lays down beside him, stroking his slowly shrinking cock daintily as he comes down.

"Where'd you learn to do that?" He laughs.

"College," she says, smiling sheepishly as her chest heaves in the afterglow.

Damien collapses into post-carnal giggles, his nose scrunching up and his cheeks bright pink.

"Thank you for your service, oh educated elite," he replies

Phoebe crawls on top of him, straddling his waist as she leans in for a kiss.

"You're *very* welcome, sir."

His eyes light up.

"Say that again."

She giggles. Something about this kind of play really seems to get him off.

"Which part?"

"Call me sir," he purrs.

She leans in, biting down on his earlobe before whispering in his ear.

"Well, if you're up for it, I was hoping you'd fuck me absolutely senseless after the show tonight, *sir*."

She can already feel herself getting excited again even before the words have left her lips. Looks like he's not the only one who has a trigger.

"Mmm, I think we might be able to arrange *something* like that."

Suddenly, she notices his entire demeanor shift. He opens his mouth to speak, but his breath hitches in his throat. Then, as quickly as the change happened, he's back to normal, smiling happily with a sigh.

"I'm just so glad you're my girlfriend."

Phoebe wonders if the same words that are on the tip of her tongue are also on his. It feels like an unspoken secret lingering between them like a storm cloud, each one of them too scared to be the first to say it, afraid the other might pull away and run.

"Me too," she whispers.

Damien wraps himself around her in their mutual silence. The warmth between them is soothing, and as the sun slowly rises they fall asleep in each other's arms.

The sound of birds outside the hotel window isn't quite as effective an alarm as Johnny crashing through the door, but it does the job. Phoebe crawls out of bed, carefully slipping around a still-sleeping Damien, and makes herself some 1:00PM coffee in the shitty hotel pot. It tastes awful, but it gets the job done. She glances over her shoulder as he lies splayed out on the bed, a sheet draped over his hips at the right angle to pique the imagination. She could watch him for hours.

In fact...

Phoebe roots through her bag and pulls out her polaroid camera, dragging a chair just in front of the bed to get enough elevation for the shot. It'll be a perfect keepsake from the tour. She watches the photo develop as his features take shape: his jawline, the beautiful slope of his nose and the smooth, gentle curve of his plush lips. She feels herself flushing as she remembers his mouth pressed up between her legs. She steps down from the chair, her hand beginning to wander past her waist as her thoughts slip further and further until—

"Whatcha lookin' at, babydoll?"

Her head snaps up. Damien is sitting up in bed, his back resting against the headboard.

"Oh! It's just a picture..." She can feel the heat travel up her neck to her ears. "Of you."

He reaches out for it, a cigarette tucked lazily between his lips. He's lounging so effortlessly, his toned chest bathed in the afternoon sun from the window. She wishes she could take another one.

"Lemme see."

Phoebe hasn't changed out of his t-shirt from the previous night, merely slipping on a pair of his boxers to work in, and she's already regretting it. The room is freezing as she walks over and hands him the photo, her legs sprouting goosebumps as she waits for his reaction. All she can think of is their early morning adventure as she stands there in silence. Her eyes quickly begin to wander, landing on the conspicuously raised segment of the sheets, and she presses her thighs together tightly. She should probably try and find some pants.

"You're good at this! Photography, I mean."

"Oh, thanks," she mutters. "I've been doing it for a while, it's a bit of a hobby."

"Man, I'm even more excited to see the finished shots from our shows now." He frowns for a second, smiling. "You want to take pictures for our second album cover?"

Phoebe blinks a couple times, a little stunned.

"Are you being serious?"

"Yeah." He's gazing intently at the polaroid, turning it a bit here and there. "I like the way you shoot, your composition is interesting. Troy loves that you've been getting stuff from the shows, too."

She's still not sure if he's messing with her, but he looks completely serious.

"Well, yeah. I would love to!"

He grins.

"Great. I'm sure I won't have a problem convincing everyone else, so let's just call it a done deal."

Phoebe watches as he finishes his cigarette and snuffs it out in the ashtray, completely transfixed. Somehow it's still a little hard to believe they're officially a couple, at least as official as people can be behind closed doors. It's what she'd hoped, maybe even more, but it's restricted. The love that's blooming between them is confined to their hotel rooms, to secret dates and furtive glances. It keeps them safe, sure, but it's only a few days in and Phoebe can already sense the inherent problem with their bubble of safety. She's torn between protecting her career and being able to hold his fucking hand any time they step outside.

When Phoebe zones back in, Damien's eyes are on the clock.

"Man, we must have gone pretty hard last night." He grins, sliding to the edge of the bed. "Hey, you wanna come to sound check today?"

He pauses, frowning and putting a hand in the air before she can respond.

"Sorry, no, that wasn't– What I meant to say is I would love it if you came to soundcheck with me. I really want you to be there."

Phoebe lights up, her anxious thoughts pushed aside like they're nothing. The softness of his request, no pretense or bullshit bravado. He just wants her with him. Just her.

"Of course!" She beams. "I love watching you guys."

He smiles, nodding and letting the sheet fall away as he stands. She can feel herself tingle as Damien walks by, his naked body fully lit by the afternoon sun. He gives her a quick brush on the cheek as he passes, and she nearly melts away.

"Awesome. Well, I gotta hit the shower. Something tells me I mighta worked up a bit of a sweat."

It takes all of Phoebe's willpower not to follow him, but she really has been falling behind on her work. She types up a quick new outline that prominently features a much softer side of Damien. All the small things, like the way he talks about his sister with so much love in his eyes, or the way that he and Troy joke around. She even includes some notes on that private version of himself, the one she'd never be allowed to put on the page. The one she fell in love with.

Just for her.

Those painfully unspoken words ring in her ears as she fiddles with his dog tags. She leans over, scooping up his discarded shirt and breathing it in, the light haze of cigarette smoke mingling with his cologne. Her chest tightens like it's locked in a vice-grip, and she feels like she could burst into tears any minute.

She's never had anything like this before, and it's everything.

"Hey, Phoebe!" Damien calls out to her from the bathroom.

She shakes herself, taking a couple deep breaths. Gotta get a grip.

"Yeah. What's up?"

He opens the door, steam billowing as he leans out, hanging casually off the side of the doorframe and still completely nude.

"Got any of that purple eyeliner I can borrow?"

His hair is dried, teased, and perfectly messy. He doesn't even need to try.

"Yeah, hang on. I think there's some in my bag."

She mostly carries black and blue, but she's almost certain she put a purple one in there. She starts walking over to the corner, but he beats her to it, grinning as he roots through her suitcase. It only takes him a couple seconds to find a distraction, and he pulls out a pair of lacy black underwear, holding it up with raised eyebrows.

"Damn Miller, you've been holding out on me?"

She tries to snatch them up but he leans away, keeping them far out of reach from her outstretched hands.

"I was gonna wear them, I just didn't have an occasion yet. Now give them back!"

He tosses them in the air, and in the couple moments it takes her to catch them, he closes the distance between them.

"Tonight," He whispers, his naked body pressed against her.

Phoebe lets out a long, labored breath as she runs her hand down the side of his body, ending just on the inside of his thigh.

"Yes sir."

"Don't go getting me all turned on now, babydoll."

She feels a surge of excitement run through her, suddenly ready to go toe to toe with him again.

"You can't tell me what to do, *sir*."

His mouth twitches and he backs her up into her desk, her fingers fumbling to grasp the wood as he presses his body against her. She can feel his cock pressing up against her, half-erect, glancing down to see it resting just above the waist of her boxers. The heat of his body is driving her wild, even with her own clothes between them, and she can feel her heartbeat quicken as she looks up to find him staring right back down at her.

"I wouldn't advise that sort of behavior," he smirks. "There are rules for this sort of thing, and we all know that when you break rules there are... punishments."

Phoebe feels her heart twist and thud against her ribs as she takes it all in: the smell of his shampoo, his cologne, that fucking stare. The air is filled with his intensity. It's suffocating in the best way.

"Like what, exactly?"

She wants to challenge him. He loves the pushback, and it makes him go even harder, and she can't help but shudder as she tries to maintain a cool demeanor. His hand glides effortlessly up her thigh, and she squirms as he stops just short.

"Well, there are so many options, and the punishment needs to fit the crime. We obviously wouldn't *start* with something as intense as edging you until you're crying, begging me to let you come." He bites his lip. "We're talking *hours*. So that you're *aching*."

His words are practically dripping.

"Oh, you– you're into that, huh?"

She thinks back to the shower, how much they both were desperate for release, and how incredible it felt when they got it, hours later.

"You know I am," he smirks.

He's impossibly confident. Even on her best day she's never felt even half of what he's putting out right now, but she's not giving in. There's something about the whole thing that sparks a sense of excitement in her. Everything with him feels new, forbidden and indulgent.

Damien carefully tugs on the waistband of her boxers, pulling them down just a little past her ass. He takes the lingerie from her, kneeling down and holding them out against her bare skin like she's modeling. His eyes shine as he stands back up, placing them carefully back in her hands.

"Your turn to get ready." His smile is soft and sweet, but the look in his eyes says she could be devoured whole at any moment.

"Oh, and wear those tonight."

Her heart pounds as he places a chaste kiss on her lips, his voice barely a whisper as he leans beside her ear.

"I think I'm going to ruin them."

Baby's On Fire

The Crescent Ballroom

The elevator is empty on the way down to the lobby, but Phoebe stands a couple feet apart from him anyway. It might be stupid, but better safe than sorry.

"You're gonna like Erin," Damien assures her as the floors tick down.

"I've liked everyone else so far."

"Her and Johnny are so in love, it's honestly pretty gross sometimes."

"Is that code for cute?" Phoebe teases.

Damien leans over and squeezes her hand.

"You know me, Miller. Can't stand the sight of people in love."

As they step out of the elevator, Phoebe's gaze falls on a brunette with bright red lipstick dressed in a red tank top and blue jeans. It might normally have been a bit of a stretch to I.D. her so quickly, but the fact that she's sitting in Johnny's lap is some pretty solid evidence.

Erin looks almost statuesque, her strong jaw and full lips drawing the most attention, with rosy cheeks that contrast her pale skin. Her dark hair flows down her back like a waterfall, and Phoebe spots scattered tattoos on her forearms.

"Wow, that's Erin?"

"In the flesh."

"She's beautiful."

"Yeah, she really is. Just in case she tells you, I did try to get in her pants in high school but she punched me in the jaw." He grins. "I was really smooth about it though, I promise."

Phoebe gives him a quick pat on the back.

"I can't imagine it going any other way."

Johnny spots them as they approach, whispering something into Erin's ear that makes her hazel eyes shine with excitement. She hops off his lap and rushes the two of them, stretching her arms out wide.

"Damien! God, I haven't seen you in ages!"

She has a slight Irish lilt to her voice, just shy of sounding like a full-on accent. Phoebe wasn't expecting that, but it fits somehow.

"You saw me three weeks ago!" Damien laughs as she pulls him in for a hug.

"That's ages! So much can happen in a week, let alone three!"

As she steps away she's all smiles, her eyes already on Phoebe.

"And who is this?"

"Phoebe Miller. She's writing an article about us for Titanium."

Erin smiles and lifts a brow, her voice encouraging.

"And?"

Damien sighs, glancing around to make sure that they're out of earshot from anyone.

"Yes, yes, detective, she's also my girlfriend."

"*That's* what I wanted to hear," Erin exclaims, giving him a playful push.

It really does feel like they've known each other forever.

Phoebe smiles and sticks out her hand.

"It's nice to meet you, Johnny talks about you all the time."

"Lovely to meet you too." There's so much warmth in her voice. "And we have that in common, Johnny talks about you all the time as well. He says you're *very* talented."

She's not aggressive, but something about the way Erin talks puts Phoebe on the back foot. Is it her accent? Her confidence? Either way, she can't help but blush a bit.

"Oh! Well, that's very nice of him."

Damien pipes up, ruffling her hair.

"It's true, she's practically a genius!"

"Stop," she whispers, still a little off-kilter.

He gives her a gentle punch on the shoulder in lieu of the kiss they can't share.

"So, how long are you here for?" Damien asks.

"A week. I got some time off from work, and I've been missing that one far too much to ignore." She points at Johnny who tosses her a flirtatious wink.

"So, what do you do, Erin?" Phoebe asks.

"I work for their record label. Johnny got me a job helping out with the production end of things so I could get some experience. It's really just grabbing coffee most days, but I'm

learning the ropes when it comes to sound mixing and all of that. I'm getting a good ear for it
."

"Children!" Troy shouts boisterously as he walks toward the group. "It is time for the much beloved ritual known as sound check! Are we ready?"

The band is a mixture of groans and laughter as they get to their feet. Phoebe and Erin exchange a polite smile as Troy gestures for everyone to follow him to the limo. As they all pile in, Damien pulls Phoebe into his lap while Troy lays into him with an icy glare.

"Relax Sullivan, you see, they invented these-here tinted windows recently, sometime around your 60th birthday I think."

When they get to the venue, photographers are already lingering near the back door. Damien puts on a pair of sunglasses and quickly gives Phoebe a kiss while they still have privacy behind the glass. They hound him all the way to the doors, most of their questions stemming from his comments on that morning show, intermingled with other random gossip they've managed to dig up. All questions without any real intention or meaning. All d ull.

They just want a cheap headline.

The group rushes inside the building without a word as the photographers strain to get that perfect scandalous shot. They'll have to be disappointed this time.

"Can't stand those fuckers, no goddamn class!" Damien swoops in and plants a kiss on Phoebe's forehead, flashing a toothy grin. "No offense to your profession, of course. You're a real gem in a coal mine, Miller."

The band wastes little time sliding into soundcheck, keeping the goofing off to a minimum as Troy sets up some stools for Phoebe and Erin off to the side of the stage. Shaun's guitar whines passionately but is quickly overwhelmed by percussion as Ophelia tests the limits of the drum kit.

And then there's Damien.

Most singers hold back during soundcheck, but not him. Not tonight. He puts his entire being into the song, howling into the mic and writhing around the stage. Phoebe feels goosebumps on her skin, her eyes glued to him as he moves.

Erin chuckles.

"He's only putting this much effort in because you're here, you know."

"I dunno, it feels like he does this all the time."

"You think Bell puts on a show when no one he cares about is watching? I bet if you ask any of the others they'll tell you he started getting a *lot* more enthusiastic the first day you showed up to a pre-show."

She watches Damien strut around the stage, stripping his jacket off and unbuttoning his dress shirt so that it hangs open to reveal his chiseled torso.

"That's all for you, Phoebe. Trust me."

With the final notes of a song ringing through the air, Damien abandons the microphone. He moves toward her and takes her hand, pulling her off to the edge of the stage where even Erin can barely see them. Phoebe giggles as he backs her up against a wall, pressing an urgent kiss against her lips. A beautiful tension lingers between them. It's electric, and more than a little addicting.

Phoebe runs her hand through his messy hair, pulling him back in for another kiss before the two break apart, breathing heavily as they stare at each other. She wants so badly to tell him.

"Damien..."

"Phoebe," he murmurs as he reaches underneath her shirt, tracing tiny circles on her skin. "I..."

His mouth opens and closes a few times before he seems to give up, kissing her again instead. She can almost see the words hanging over his head, and for a second she thinks he still might say it right then and there. Instead, he presses a final gentle kiss to her lips and walks back onto the stage.

Her face is hot, and she notices Troy's eyes on her as she sits back down next to Erin. She leans in close, trying to look as nonchalant as possible.

"Do you think he's mad?"

"No," she laughs. "You're young and in love! Even Troy's been there, he gets it."

"We're not–"

"You know I can hear you two dorks."

Troy's sunglasses are slid down his nose, his eyebrows raised, and Phoebe can feel her soul leave her body as he walks over.

"You're in deep on this one, you can trust me on that, kiddo. I've known Damien for three years and I've only ever seen him act like this once or twice."

"And *I* have known him for most of his life," Erin interjects. "Trust *me* when I say that almost no one gets this far. Most of the time it's not even their fault. Sometimes it's the road, sometimes the press, and sometimes..."

"It's Damien," Troy finishes.

"So don't sell yourself short, kiddo," he says, taking a sip of his beer. "You're smart, you're funny, and most importantly he told me what you called him that night in Oakland. After that, you're aces in my book."

Phoebe blushes as Erin's eyes light up.

"Wait, what did you call him?"

"Nothing, it wasn't–"

Troy laughs like he's remembering the best joke he's ever heard.

"She called that prancing clown a condescending asshole! Right when he was trying his best to hook her!"

Erin lets out a loud cackle, clapping her hands together.

"Ah, Christ, that's beautiful." She wipes a tear from her eye. "That's probably why he likes you so much."

Troy nods in agreement.

"You wouldn't think it to look at him, but he likes people who call him on his bullshit. Why do you think I'm still around after all these years?"

They're right, in more ways than one. Every time she digs at him, or bites back, or takes charge. Every time she pushes back she can see the fire in his eyes burn brighter. He's the kind of man who loves to get bruised in the struggle. Maybe it makes him feel more alive.

Backstage, the band preps for the show in the only way they know how: Beers, pizza, and smokes. Johnny and Erin are trading stories with Shaun and Ophelia as Troy gets a couple jabs in here and there, ensuring none of the boys' egos get too inflated. Phoebe sits on Damien's lap in the furthest corner of the room, purposefully isolated, but still within earshot. He rubs her back as she sips her beer, her shoulders pressing against his fingers as he works out her knots. She takes long euphoric breaths, her mind wandering for a while before she feels a very familiar pressure building against her ass. She freezes in panic for a moment, her eyes flicking across the room, but everyone is busy in their own conversations.

"You okay?" Damien asks.

"Yeah, yeah, fine. You just hit a sensitive spot is all."

"Oh I'll–"

She moves her hips backward, arching her back just a little as she starts grinding against him.

He groans.

"You're being a brat."

"Oh, am I?" she breathes.

He growls, pressing her harder against him as he continues the massage.

"Don't forget about your little punishment later."

"How could I?"

She moves her hips in a sensual circle, enjoying the rumble in his chest as his hands slide down to her waist.

"Are you wearing those panties?"

Phoebe sips her beer casually in an effort to look flirtatious and aloof, craning her neck to look back at him as she does.

"I always do as I'm told."

He smiles, confident.

"They'll look great in your mouth when you're all tied up, just the two of us locked in our room."

She chokes, the beer burning as it nearly shoots out her nose. Erin turns toward them, Ophelia already clued in and holding back laughter. Damien is leaned up against her, his shoulders shaking in suppressed laughter as Phoebe wipes her shirt.

"Wrong pipe," she croaks.

"You can say that again," Damien mutters under his breath.

"Shut up! What is wrong with you?" She hisses as the room's attention shifts away again.

"You don't like my proposal?"

"No, I do, but you could have at least waited until I had swallowed to spring it on me."

"That's what she– Ow!" He laughs as she pinches his thigh.

"Now who's being the brat?"

"Still you."

Damien taps a cigarette out of a pack and hands it to her.

"So, sweets," he lights it up as it hangs from her lips. "You cool with being tied up?"

She takes a drag, thinking for a moment.

"Yeah, I think so. I'm up for pretty much anything as long as we talk about it first. There might be some things I'll want to say no to..."

"That won't be a problem. I like to be in charge, but the most important thing for me is pleasing my partners. I'll definitely come off as a little threatening, but you can say stop at any time. I need you to know that."

She enjoys the danger factor. When he looks at her like a lion about to pounce on a gazelle it sends a rush of pure adrenaline through her body. She likes when he's rough with her, pressing her up against walls, biting into her skin hard enough to leave bruises for days; it's a variety of pain that makes the pleasure all the better.

"Deal." She's excited for him to test her limits.

She continues peeling the label off the bottle as he returns to massaging her shoulders.

"So, what else are you into?" Her voice is a little tentative, still a bit unsure. "In bed, I mean."

"Shit," he laughs. "A lot. Biting, hair pulling–"

"I pull yours, or you pull mine?"

"Both, doesn't matter," he replies. "I love it all."

It's exciting to get to know him like this, it's almost a teaser for what he has in store for her.

"What else?"

"Teasing, obviously," he murmurs. "Maybe a little overstimulation."

His breath on the back of her neck makes her shake. There's something about only hearing his voice, feeling him behind her without seeing him that really turns her on.

"Okay, overstimulation, how does that work?"

"I like to count how many times I can make a girl come, and then I try to beat that record. I'm a real perfectionist."

"Jesus," she breathes.

Phoebe's torn the label right off her beer bottle, and Damien leans in around her side, putting his hand on her chin and turning it just enough that she can see him from the corner of her eye as he speaks.

"When we get back to the hotel room, I'm going to tie you to the bed and mark every inch of your skin so that everyone knows who you belong to."

Warmth rushes down her spine and heat pools between her legs. She squeezes her thighs together as Damien kisses her bare shoulder.

"Then, I'm going to tease you until you're begging me to let you come. You're gonna ache. I want you to soak the sheets because you need me so badly, and just when you think you can't take anymore, I'm going to cut the ropes, pin your arms down, and fuck you until you can't stop screaming."

She's speechless, her jaw hanging open.

"Think you'd like that?"

"Yes," she rasps, her voice barely audible.

"Good," he replies jovially, sliding back behind her and wrapping his arms around her waist.

"Where the hell did you learn about this stuff?"

"Honestly, it's not that weird. When we were in Paris last year I met this woman after one of our shows, told me she was a Dominatrix. We didn't do anything, but I talked to her for like four hours at the bar about her job. It was fascinating, I couldn't stop asking questions. Started to realize that I was into some aspects of it."

She can feel him getting hard again. Opening up about this is exciting to him. Knowing he has someone to play with, and hoping she'll feel the same.

"That said, some girls aren't into it. They want something tamer, which is fine by me. It's like I said before, sex should be fun. If you're not having fun, there's not much point."

She nods in agreement, staring straight ahead as she absorbs everything.

He squeezes her thigh gently, a silent reassurance.

"Again, I'll never push you beyond what you're comfortable with. You say 'stop' and we stop." He snaps his fingers. "Just like that."

She nods again.

"Hey lovebirds?" Troy is at the door. "I hate to break up whatever nasty stuff you're talking about over there, but we've got a show to put on!"

Phoebe was so lost in the moment she didn't realize everyone already cleared out. She slides off the table and Damien gives her a little kiss on the cheek.

"Taking pictures tonight?"

It takes her a second to wrap her head around the question, slow to slide back into the moment.

"Yeah, camera's in my bag. I'll meet you out there."

It's the first time she's seen his face fully since their conversation started. He's beaming.

"Glad to have you here, babydoll."

She watches him strut out of the dressing room, giving her a goofy salute before he disappears around the corner.

Phoebe makes sure that her camera is fully loaded for the show, checking her hair and makeup in the mirror one last time to ensure nothing is out of place before stepping outside and nearly colliding into someone in the hall. She stumbles back, laughing automatically as her elbow bumps against the doorframe.

"Oh! I'm so–"

She looks up to see a man with mousy brown hair, a round face, and a pair of soft dark eyes. He's slight in stature, just a few inches taller than her with gangly arms sticking out of a thin Black Sabbath t-shirt.

"Chris?"

His skin looks unusually pale, dark circles underneath his eyes like he hasn't slept in days. A camera hangs around his neck, and his expression softens into a polite smile when he realizes it's her, his voice light but a little raspy.

"Oh, Phoebe. Hey!"

Her eyes dart back down to the camera hanging off of him and her heart begins to thump. Did he hear them? Did he see Damien?

"Wh– what are you doing here?"

She winces internally. She could have just said hey.

Luckily he keeps on smiling, clearly unfazed.

"Just catching a show. I'm writing a piece on the opening act." His reply comes along with a cocky smirk that makes her want to smack him. Something about him has always driven her crazy, and the worst part is he really is just doing his job.

"Brian mentioned you got the Revolver assignment, that why you're here?"

"Yep," she replies curtly, nervously adjusting her bag on her shoulder.

"Hey, congrats," Chris replies. "Not that many people would want it, but…"

There it is, the barb she was waiting for.

"Are you staying for the whole show?"

"I dunno." He shrugs. "Revolver's not really my style."

"Right," she chuckles nervously. "I think you mentioned you weren't a fan."

He nods, a little distracted as he glances off to the left.

"Yeah, I wasn't ever as into them as you were. I just don't see the appeal, and Bell in particular is just–" He stops, frowning and gesturing with his head. "Looks like someone's waiting for you."

Her heart leaps into her throat and she glances up, relieved to only see Troy's grumpy face approaching. His entire body is coiled, irritation evident in the click of his jaw. At this point she'll take any out she can get.

"Miller, you can talk later!" Troy barks.

She turns back to Chris, flashing him a sheepish smile.

"Gotta go. Sorry."

"It's cool. See ya, Pheebs."

Phoebe heads down the hallway to Troy and he pats her on the shoulder.

"Who was that? Ex boyfriend?"

She balks, mouth agape.

"God, no! I'd rather stick a pen in my eye than date him," Phoebe groans. "That was Chris Meyers, ring a bell?"

Troy's expression darkens and his mouth twitches.

"The Chris Meyers who trashed our album?" He rolls up his sleeves. "I'm gonna say something–"

She grabs his shirt, pulling him back.

"I think you should take the high road on this one, Troy."

"I've never taken the high road in my life," Troy bites back. "Why start now?"

"He's leaving. He was only here for the opening act, anyway."

Troy huffs and she glances over her shoulder just in time to see the fire exit door shut, with Chris nowhere in sight.

"I guess it's his lucky day."

"Phoenix! How the fuck are ya tonight?"

Damien grins as the crowd explodes.

"Awesome. Hey listen, we're gonna play some stuff from the album, some covers, and a couple of songs you might not have heard yet, sound good?

An ear-piercing roar fills the venue and Damien turns and points at Ophelia.

"Sounds like you fuckers are ready for a show! Count it off, fearless leader!"

She salutes with a drumstick and the band crashes into their first song. Damien's on fire, fully engaged with the crowd as Phoebe snaps photos from all around the stage. One shot in particular drives her further out: Damien is howling into the microphone in profile, his teeth bared like a wolf. It might just end up as the featured photo for her article. She advances the film and takes another shot, and his eyes light up like fireworks the moment he sees her. Hidden behind the viewfinder she whispers those few words they've both been struggling to say out loud.

After a couple songs, Phoebe retreats back to the sidelines. She doesn't want to spend too much time in the spotlight, but she also really does enjoy soaking up the performances whenever she gets the chance. Back on stage, Damien puts the mic back on its stand for a moment, leaning in close to make sure he sounds as dramatic as possible.

"Alright Phoenix, we're gonna need your patience for a couple minutes here while we make some quick adjustments."

All at once it feels like a scene from a movie, the band shifting around and rearranging their setup as the crowd's chants get louder and louder with no sign of slowing. Johnny hops up and down a few times, like a boxer preparing for a fight. Shaun gives Ophelia a peck on the cheek, and Damien does a quick jog around the stage before dipping out on her side.

"Troy, we're gonna change it up a bit. That's cool right?"

Troy smiles. Any issues he might have had were washed out the door the moment the crowd erupted the first time.

"Kid, do whatever the hell you want. They're loving you tonight."

Damien grins, his eyes lit up as he runs his fingers against hers.

"Duty calls, babydoll!"

As he walks back onto the stage Damien throws his arms up and down, hyping the crowd up even more. Phoebe furrows her brow as a roadie drags a stool out to the front of the stage and the boys switch over to an acoustic setup.

"We're going to do something a little different for this last chunk of the show. It might not be as rock and roll as you were expecting, but just give us a chance. We know you'll like it."

Once the rest of the band signals that they're ready, they launch into their altered set. It's all acoustic arrangements, both covers and originals. They must have been planning this for days. The crowd clearly finds it a bit unusual to begin with, standing practically still at first, but as the minutes creep on they fall into the more intimate change of pace. Damien looks angelic as the stage lights bathe him in a warm golden glow, and his voice is vibrant throughout the set; you'd be able to hear him clear as day even if you were stuck outside.

As their fifth song fades out to rapturous applause, whistles, and whoops, Damien clears his throat.

"This is gonna be the last number for the night, so please indulge us just a little while longer."

He glances at Johnny, who nods, winking in Phoebe's direction.

Erin turns to her and pats her shoulder.

"Your boy toy has something up his sleeve, it's all over him."

Phoebe's blood chills, remembering the radio show. He wouldn't...

But as the music starts, she recognizes it immediately. It's a cover of Springsteen's "I'm On Fire," the song she said was one of her favorites when she interviewed him way back in Portland. It was just an off-hand comment that she never expected him to remember. But he did. Her eyes well up with tears as Damien's voice mingles with Shaun's guitar. It's such a small gesture, but it overwhelms her just the same.

As the final note echoes through the venue, Phoebe's cheeks are stained with her tears as Erin leans in toward her.

"Told you girl, he's absolutely obsessed with you."

"Thank you, Phoenix!" Damien shouts. "You've been fucking beautiful tonight. We love you!"

The four bandmates exit the stage to thunderous applause, and the moment he sees Phoebe crying, Damien rushes over and wraps her in his arms.

"Hey... hey, what's happened, what's wrong?"

"You remembered," she whispers. "It was just... really sweet."

He holds her tightly as they rock back and forth.

"Anything for my girl."

Love Her Madly

THE RENAISSANCE HOTEL

Phoebe's lost in thought, sitting in the back of the car with the rest of the band, as her stomach swirls with excitement. Damien left the venue early, telling her to stay behind and have a few drinks with Erin while he prepped the hotel room. He wouldn't tell her exactly what he had planned, just that he would walk her through it, and it would be a night she'd never forget. By the time she says her goodnights and makes it to the elevator, she's vibrating with anticipation, so much so that she doesn't notice the two men rushing to make the ride.

"Wait up!" One yelps, just far enough away that he won't quite make it in time.

Phoebe considers letting the doors slide shut, but she thinks better of it, in a good enough mood to begrudgingly hold the door as the two men stumble inside. The first one, a taller pale man with glasses, gives her the once over while his friend slumps against the wall, short of breath as he straightens out his vibrant red shirt.

"Thanks, sweetheart."

Glasses is trying to be slick and cool, but he's barely keeping his breath. Phoebe nods, placing herself off to the side, as far away as possible in the cramped elevator. She watches them from the corner of her eye, only noticing too late that both men have press badges around their necks as the doors slide shut.

Glasses turns his attention to his friend, pushing the button for the 8th floor.

"Okay, so what the hell were you saying in the car? Driver kept interrupting."

"Oh, yeah, right." He's still heaving, taking a moment to catch his breath.

"Remember how I was at the Revolver show tonight? Well the frontman, Bell? He was with some girl. She was up on stage with a camera and they were together after the set."

"Probably just some groupie, right?"

Red shirt shakes his head.

"Didn't look like that to me. They weren't making out. Big long hug, really close. I dunno man, I know it's not his sister. We've seen pictures of her."

"He's a man-whore, dude. He gets with everyone."

"Not with journalists, *dude*. I told you, she was taking pictures and shit. They never let groupies up on stage for stuff like that. It's always some quick flirty bullshit."

The door opens on the 3rd floor and another hotel guest gets on. The two men don't seem to care, continuing the conversation like they're completely alone.

"Okay, whatever, but how do you know she's a journalist?"

"Just a gut feeling!" Red shirt insists. "Anyway, my friend Howie from Kerrang said that he tried to get onstage to snap a photo last year, and Bell threw his goddamn camera into the crowd. They trampled over it like a herd of fuckin' elephants."

Phoebe stares straight ahead, her ears buzzing. Maybe they're just fans. Maybe it's not a big deal. Maybe this is a dream, and if she pinches herself, she'll wake up next to Damien. On a Beach. Somewhere that's not here.

"So what?" Glasses scoffs. "Why do you even care about this shit?"

"Obviously she's not just some random journo! Imagine if I were the guy to break that Revolver's frontman is in a relationship; names, occupation, everything!"

"You can't tell that from a hug," glasses snorts. He looks over at Phoebe as if for confirmation, but she just shrugs her shoulders.

"It wasn't *just* a hug. Look, dude, I'm gonna find out who this chick is. Just need to figure out what floor they're staying on."

The door opens again, 7th floor this time, but the new guest thinks better of walking into the full elevator. God, why can't they just be gone already?

"Why, so you can knock on every door? 'Excuse me, Mr. Bell, do you have a girlfriend in there with you? While you're at it, could you tell me her name, address, social security number?' He'd punch your fucking teeth out."

At this point she'd be happy to help. Mercifully, the elevator stops on their floor and the two get out, Glasses clapping his friend on the shoulder.

"I think you need to go to bed, dude. Maybe work on your plan a little more before you spring into action."

Phoebe closes her eyes and slumps against the wall. She knew this would happen. They weren't careful enough. It was going *too* fucking well.

"Fuck," she whispers to herself. "Fuck fuck fuck."

Someone is going to find out. Everything with Damien, everything she's worked toward could be destroyed in a second. The doors open to her floor and she stumbles out. She has to tell him. She rubs the back of her neck, trying to keep herself calm as the anxiety grows with each step toward their door. She silently steps out of her boots when she makes it inside, the door swinging shut behind her, and she makes doubly sure that it's locked.

Someone has to.

There's a warm, glowing light creeping out around the edge of their small hallway; the butterflies in her stomach slow just a little.

"Damien?"

"In here."

Phoebe wrings her hands as she walks into the room. Two spools of black rope sit in the middle of the ivory duvet, carefully laid out as if they're being presented as a gift. The soft glow comes from the candles he's placed throughout, and the dimmed lights lend everything a reverential feel. Damien is lounging in a chair near the window, dressed only in a pair of black jeans. His eyes follow her as she walks through the room.

He stays completely still.

"Damien, we have to talk."

"Later, sweets."

It has to be now, they need to handle this before it gets out of control. Yet the second they lock eyes, her fear is consumed. His smile, this room... maybe it can wait. Maybe it *should* wait. There's probably not much they can do about it now.

Damien beckons her over with a finger, his silver rings gleaming in the candlelight. She stands in front of him, a little straighter than usual as he gazes up at her from his seat, taking her in like he's observing a curiosity. It's only now that she notices the little strip of fabric dangling lazily from his free hand.

"Kneel," he whispers.

Phoebe drops to her knees in front of him and he reaches out, running a hand through her hair before bringing it to rest just below her chin.

"Nervous?"

"A little."

There's a glint in his eye as a wolfish smile creeps across his face. He leans forward, kissing her, lingering just long enough to draw her in before he pulls away. He reaches down beside the chair and retrieves a black leather paddle, resting what she now realizes must be a blindfold on his knee.

"Now, you're a smart girl. You know what this is for, don't you?"

"Yes sir."

"Is it something you want?"

Phoebe swallows, her heart pounding. Damien gently sets the paddle down in his lap, leaning over to caress her face.

"You can say no, even if you say yes right now, any time you want and we stop. You have my word."

"No, I– I want..." She clears her throat and tries again with more conviction. "I want it, s ir."

He smiles.

"That's my girl. I was thinking we could start with this, and then," he pauses, running the backs of his knuckles along her cheek. "Then I can tie you to the bed. We can see where things go from there."

The hair stands up on the back of her neck in excitement; his words sound so sweet they must taste like honey.

"Yes, sir."

Damien nods.

"Strip for me." He commands, standing and holding out his hand.

Phoebe's fingers slide into his hand as he helps her to her feet. She reaches back, trembling as she grasps at her zipper, tugging it down. It gets stuck halfway, of course it does, but the warm smile on his face is comforting.

"Turn around."

He grabs the zipper, and with a few gentle tugs it gives way. The fabric loosens, and she can feel the soft breeze from the AC brush against her skin, followed by the tantalizing sensation of his fingertip trailing down her spine.

Damien reaches out to help further, but she steps away, sliding the rest of the dress down so that it rests on her hips, leaving her naked back in full view. Using one hand at a time she slips it lower and lower down, until it finally falls away into a puddle of fabric at her feet.

Damien grabs her waist and pulls her into him.

"You look gorgeous," he whispers, before taking a step back and slapping her ass.

Phoebe's body jumps, the cool air stinging her skin as she glances back at him.

"Am I too delicate to use the paddle, *sir*?"

The sound of his hand making contact with her ass a second time echoes through the room. She gasps, trembling as this time real pain shoots through her body, quickly overlapped by a rush of pleasure and adrenaline.

"We don't go harder unless you ask for it. That's how we're going to find your limits."

"Yes, sir."

He circles around in front of her, and for a moment stands in complete silence, staring at her with an intense gaze. His cheekbones and toned shoulders are carved out even more than usual in shadows cast by the candlelight.

"Touch yourself for me."

Without a second thought Phoebe pulls her panties to one side, quickly finding a rhythm as she slides her fingers between her lips and brings them up to rub her clit. She can feel her whole body begin to move, shifting in place to match the pace of her fingers as little moans begin to escape her mouth after a few minutes of fucking herself.

"Now, show me how wet you are."

It takes her a moment to slow down, but when she removes her hand and presents it, Damien takes her fingers gently into his mouth, licking them clean. He leaves the paddle sitting on the chair behind him as he gathers the blindfold in his hands.

"You're going to wear this, alright?"

As he holds the blindfold up in front of her, Phoebe's mind leaps back to the supply closet. The rush she felt at only being able to hear the sound of his voice, how much more intense his touch felt. It was intoxicating, and she wanted as much as he'd give her.

"Anything you want, sir."

Damien walks behind her and secures the blindfold.

"That's a good girl."

She gasps as his lips brush against her earlobe, the sound of his voice making her search for him aimlessly in the dark. His hands gently glide up and down her bare arms, every nerve ending on high alert as goosebumps rise on her skin. She squeezes her thighs together tightly as she feels his fingers trail down to unclasp her bra, letting it fall from her body as he slips his hand in hers.

"I'm going to walk you to the bed. Once we're there, you're going to get on all fours for me." His voice is soft but commanding. It makes her whole head tingle. "Show me you understand."

She nods, squeezing his hand.

He guides her slowly, the two of them laughing awkwardly when she briefly stumbles and he has to catch her, his hand slipping around her waist. She feels his lips press against her neck.

"I've got you, babydoll."

Her fingers sink into the blanket, curling into grasping fists when Damien gives her ass another rough slap. She can hear how his breathing changes, little approving sounds he lets out every time she jumps or shudders at his touch. He's loving her reactions. She readies herself for more, barely hearing his footsteps against the carpet. Her head flicks to the right, eyes wide open in spite of the blindfold and trying to listen as hard as she can. There's a shuffle a few feet behind her, and before long she feels cool firm leather press against her.

"Feel that?"

"Mm..."

She lifts her ass up further in the air for him, resting her head on her arms. He keeps the paddle pressed against her, probably to get her used to the sensation, the texture, the whole idea of it. Phoebe takes a few measured breaths as the adrenaline begins to rush.

"After every hit, I'm going to ask you for a color. Green means go, it's all good. Yellow means you need a moment, and we take a break. Red means we stop. We can start up again if you change your mind later on, but it's a hard stop in the moment, is that all clear?"

Her heart flutters.

"Yes, sir. Very clear."

"We'll be going to five, you'll count each one for me, alright?"

She nods, trying her best not to clench too much in preparation.

"That's my girl." He pauses, pulling the paddle away after a few quick little taps against her. "Deep breath for me."

The only warning is the slightest of grunts before he swings the paddle through the air. The impact against her ass makes her jump, but a split second later her focus is dragged away as she feels her cunt spasm and she lets out a ragged moan.

Suddenly, Damien is pressed up against her, leaning in next to her ear.

"I need to hear you *count*, babydoll."

"O– one!"

"*Atta* girl."

She breathes in and out, steadying herself. Her arms tremble as her eyes take in nothing but the darkness. She feels him slip her panties aside, running his finger between her pussy lips. Phoebe whimpers.

"You liked that," he purrs.

"Yes, sir." The response is reflexive at this point.

"What color?"

"Green, sir."

"Wonderful."

As the paddle strikes her again she lurches forward, biting down on her lip hard enough to taste iron.

"Two!"

Like the last time, as the initial shock fades she can feel her cunt throb. The balance between the sharp impact and aching aftermath has her sticking her ass out more in anticipation. She feels his hand glide down her lower back as he laughs.

"Desperate for more, are you?"

She feels the blood rush up to her chest.

"I'm just doing what I'm told, sir."

"Of course you are. Color?"

Phoebe smiles to herself.

"Mmm, green."

"Such a perfect girl."

Another hit, and her head drops to the bed. She bites down on the sheet as she feels the wave of pleasure rushing through her body, grunting out the count through gritted teeth.

"Three!"

She doesn't know if she can make it through two more, but it's not about the pain. At this point the anticipation is almost as delicious as the outcome, and every moment between the strikes makes the impact so much more intense.

"Tell me what color," he says firmly.

His tone sends sparks shooting through her nerves.

"Green, sir." She pauses, running her fingers over her mouth. " Um, if it's okay, maybe you can go harder this time?"

"You sure?"

She can hear the surprise in his voice.

"Yes, sir. I think... I think I deserve it."

Phoebe smiles to herself as she hears him exhale, slow and heavy. He's just as turned on as she is. The fourth hit forces her to bury her head deep into the bed as she arches her back. Her voice breaks as she groans into the fabric.

"F-four!"

"One more," Damien breathes. Her whole body lights up at the soft rumble of his voice. "Tell me what color."

"Green."

"Harder?" He asks.

"No, it– that was just right."

"You're doing so well, sweets, and remember: deep breath and relax."

She steadies herself, but there's only so much she can do when her whole body is shuddering in anticipation. She hears it coming as the paddle cuts through the air one final time, clenching in preparation. The impact makes her jump and her legs give out as she falls forward onto the bed. Her ass stings in the cool air as waves of pleasure run over her. She can feel her swollen clit throb as she nearly comes, barely holding herself back as she clenches as tightly as possible. She hears something drop to the ground as she groans, slowly getting back up on her knees just in time to feel the mattress dip next to her. Damien unties the knot of her blindfold and the room comes back into view. She can feel sweat all over her body, panting as her eyes adjust to see him sat beside her.

He's beaming.

"Need a break?"

"So sir," she sighs. "Not a chance."

Love My Way

THE RENAISSANCE HOTEL

"On your back. Hands near each bedpost."

Phoebe's whole body is burning, her skin flushed with excitement as she turns herself over, spreading her legs and stretching her arms out to the corners of the bed. Damien grins, nodding in approval as he delicately scoops up his spool of rope. He walks to one side of the bed and begins to gently wrap it around her wrist. It's silky, tight but soft against her skin, and Phoebe is entirely focused on the feeling as she shivers in anticipation.

"Where did you get this stuff? It's so soft."

"Yeah, they don't sell them like this at the hardware store. They're bondage ropes, so they're comfortable for you."

"You just carry it with you?"

He rounds the bed, tying her other wrist and ignoring the question.

"How's that, too tight?"

Phoebe pulls against the bindings, giving a little shake of her head.

"I don't think so. Nothing hurts or feels uncomfortable."

But more than that, there's no way she'd be able to get out on her own. Her mouth parts just a bit as she pictures all the things he could do to her. Anything. Everything.

"Perfect."

Damien walks to the foot of the bed and climbs up on all fours, and Phoebe takes a deep breath as he runs his hands up her legs, eyeing her up like a meal. She begins to wriggle her hips, moaning as he lays the first kiss of many just above her waist. Anticipation flows through her body as blood roars in her ears, but the sound of Damien's laughter cuts through it all.

"Patience."

He pushes her legs further apart, one at a time, and Phoebe strains against the ropes in excitement. Her chest tightens as his fingertips trail gentle pathways along her hips and up her thighs, just close enough to set her off but not for anything more. He begins to nip at her skin, alternating between soft and harder bites. As he works his way up to her breasts, she notices how hard her nipples have already become, so sensitive they're starting to ache. He wraps his lips around one, sucking gently, and that's all it takes to make her cry out. He's put her in a completely different state, her whole body covered in sweat and moments away from a shuddering finish.

"Fuck," she laughs nervously. "I'm gonna come if you keep that up."

His expression shifts, almost menacing as his steely eyes slice into her.

"Don't you *dare*."

His commanding tone snaps her back into their game, the hair on her neck standing up as her eyes widen. Secure in the knowledge that he would never actually harm her, the threat is a tantalizing tool of play.

"Y– Yes sir. Sorry sir."

As he resumes with her breasts, Phoebe can feel herself falling further into her role. She leans into how helpless she feels, into tugging against her restraints and writhing on top of the duvet. Time seems to stretch on forever as her whole body clenches like a fist, desperate for release. She can feel her clit swelling as he clamps his teeth down on a nipple, tugging on it, flicking it with his tongue. When a desperate and aching whine spills from her lips, he leaves her breasts to run his mouth further down her body, stopping to place marks on her most sensitive places. At the end of his journey, Damien nestles himself between her thighs. He gives them a few nips and love bites before he slips her underwear off and crawls on top of her, tracing a finger against her lip.

"Open."

She obeys immediately, and Damien stuffs her panties between her teeth. She groans into the fabric, watching as he slowly slides back down between her legs. She can feel him drag his fingers through her folds, a breathy moan dripping from her lips as he slides one finger inside of her. Phoebe's back arches, and she lets out a muffled curse.

He swirls his tongue around her clit, careful to not touch it directly until the exact right moment. Each brief but calculated flick causes Phoebe to let out another muffled whimper as her body silently screams with desire. It's less than a minute before she's moaning his name into her panties in a desperate attempt to convince him to make her come.

But Damien's resolve is pure steel. He crooks his fingers, pushing up against her G-spot, massaging it slowly as he drags his tongue along her clit. He knows exactly how much she needs, keeping the pressure just low enough and the pauses just long enough that she's always on the edge. After what feels like hours Damien speeds his fingers up, his tongue matching the new pace. Her body begins to spasm and buck, her mind consumed by the impending release. Then, without warning, he pulls his fingers out.

She gasps, letting out a string of stifled moans as her body strains toward him, but the bindings hold her in place. She can feel her abdomen clench and writhe as she watches him step away from the bed and walk slowly over to the dresser.

He lights a cigarette and takes a drag.

A fucking cigarette.

Phoebe lets out a helpless wail, choked back by her makeshift gag which she spits out in desperation.

"Damien!"

"I told you I like to tease," he replies casually.

"No no no, this isn't fair!"

He looks over his shoulder at her, his face completely calm.

"Are you gonna be good?"

Her legs squeeze together as she strains against the mattress, the sheets wet with her arousal and sweat. Her thighs are sticky and her throat is dry.

She nods.

"You need anything?" He asks as he blows a smoke ring.

"You know what I need," she growls.

"If you keep being a brat, I'm going to leave you here while I head downstairs to have a drink."

Her blood goes cold. She would simply die. There's no way she could last alone like this, not in this state. He strides toward her and grasps her chin gently, clearly seeing the anguish in her eyes.

"We both want the same thing here, to get you where you need to be."

She nods, silently.

"Good. I'll ask again, do you need anything?"

Just then she realizes it. He's right, she'd completely ignored everything else her body was telling her.

"Water," she croaks. "My throat kinda hurts."

"I thought so, hang on."

He gives her a quick peck on the cheek before walking off, returning quickly from out of view with a pitcher of water and a glass. He helps her sit up a little before holding the glass to her lips, carefully tipping it as she gulps down the entire thing. He refills the glass and she drains it again.

"Done?" He asks.

"Yeah," she gasps, feeling the effects instantly. "Thank you."

He kisses her on the cheek and takes it away, resting the glass on the nightstand next to the half-full pitcher.

"So, ready for more?"

"Wait, where did you get that pitcher? We don't have a kitchen here."

"All part of the prep. Figured you'd be thirsty at some point, a concierge can get pretty much anything if you ask nicely enough. I guarantee you they were happy that's all I asked for."

He gives her a warm smile.

"So, do you need any more rest?"

She grins.

"No sir, I'm ready for more."

Damien strips out of his jeans, kicking them aside and grabbing a condom off of the dresser before rolling it onto his cock. She pulls against the ropes as he climbs back onto the mattress, letting them dig into her wrists just a little bit as she chews on her lip. She can see his cock twitch, straining the condom as he watches her squirm. She tries her best to hold back a smile. There's some power in being tied to this bed, in playing within the rules. He leans forward, his mouth hovering over her inner thigh for a moment before he bites down. She arches her back and lets out a loud wail.

"Damien– Fuck!"

He soothes the bite, blowing gently against it.

"I'm thinking about rewarding you."

"Yes," her chest is heaving. "Please!"

He smirks.

"I said I was *thinking* about it."

She huffs, grimacing at the thought of him playing with her forever with no release.

"Please, it hurts."

He sticks out his bottom lip in a faux pout.

"Does it?"

"Damien..." she whimpers.

"Well, we don't want that."

He moves back in, gently running the soft pad of his finger over her clit. Phoebe's body twitches and she sucks in a deep breath.

"It looks like I've been neglecting something."

"Please, I've been so good, haven't I?"

"You have. I'm very impressed with how well you're doing."

It's a genuine compliment, and it takes her a little off-guard. She expected more teasing.

"Thank you."

"Still having a good time?"

"Yes, sir." She licks her lips. "Will you please let me come now?"

He grins and drops his head back down. His tongue is like velvet as it glides over her clit ever so slowly. Her whole body relaxes and a series of sinful moans spill out of her mouth, but once again he drives her right to the edge and pulls away. This time, though, things are different. Damien is kneeling on the bed in front of her, his fingers wrapped around his cock as he slowly strokes himself.

"I'm going to fuck you. You're going to feel me so deep inside you that you won't be able to think about anything else, and then you're going to come, and when you do you're going to tell me exactly what you're feeling. All of it."

He leans down on all fours and grabs her waist, pulling her carefully toward him so she's flat on the bed, the ropes still keeping her in place.

"You understand?"

Phoebe nods, breathless.

She watches as he lowers himself on top of her, nestled between her legs. Phoebe's mouth falls open as he leans toward her, placing a soft kiss on her cheek. She cranes her neck, searching for his lips only to let out a loud gasp as the tip of his cock glides across her entrance.

"Damieeennn!" She whines.

"In a second, sweetheart."

Her body is shivering with anticipation. He's always teasing.

She wants to grab him, to force him to commit as he continues to lightly prod her, but the restraints keep her mostly still as she struggles, the feeling of the ropes digging into her wrists driving her even wilder. Luckily, despite all of his posturing, it seems like even Damien has his limits. In the midst of another light glide against her, he suddenly shifts his weight, stretching her out in a single stroke. Her head slams back into the pillow as he buries himself deep inside her.

"Oh my god! Yes, yes!" She moans.

"You're so fucking wet," he laughs. "Jesus Christ."

"You really– turn me on," she groans, wrapping her legs around his back.

"Ditto, darling."

After the intensity of the initial thrust he moves surprisingly slow, taking his time and teasing out as much agony from her as he can. Every thrust and every slap of his skin against hers feels like they're sending pure dopamine to her brain. She can't tell how long he's been fucking her, but it feels like hours have passed and she's still right on the edge. She's tucked in that ideal spot just before the climax hits, like the moment of bliss before the fall has been set on repeat. How he's managing to keep her there, she'll never know, but nothing lasts forever.

"You're mine," he breathes.

"Yes. Yes! I'm only for you," she gasps.

She's starting to lose herself again, drifting away from him despite his masterful control, and he can tell.

"Already? We just got started."

"No, no, no, it's been *so long*. Please let me come. *Please*!"

"Remember the rules," he growls. "Now come for me."

His permission is all she needs to open the floodgates as a powerful, blinding orgasm makes her lose control of her legs. Damien continues to pound her cunt, pulling almost all the way out before dropping back down inside her, practically pressing his entire body weight on top of her with each stroke. It feels like fireworks going off and if she were to die right now, it would be the happiest she's ever felt.

"Oh my god, it's too much! Damien!"

He cries out, quickening the pace.

"Fuck! You're squeezing me so tight!"

"I'm sorry," she whines. She doesn't even know what she's apologizing for.

He laughs as he lowers his arms around her, his muscles straining in preparation.

"I'm gonna fuck you harder now, okay?"

She nods, her eyes wide as she looks up at him, still shaking through the waves of orgasmic bliss. Damien begins to jackhammer into her, moans and yelps escaping her lips with each thrust. She's completely overwhelmed as he slams against her, slapping into her swollen clit as he buries himself as deep as he can. She's not even sure if she's on the second or third climax as everything blurs together. Tears stream down her face and she begins to sob, her cries mixing with moans and grunts into an impossible mess of orgasmic wailing. As he drops down a final time, sliding his hands behind her head to pull her in and complete their embrace, she screams at the top of her lungs.

"Oh, fuck! Oh, fuck–! Damien, I love you!"

He bucks against her cunt, holding her so tightly that she can barely move as the final waves of her multi-part climax run their course. She can feel him spasm on top of her, his cock swelling before he finally begins to slow to a stop. It's a good few minutes of blissful silence, his arms wrapped around her and his head resting against her shoulder, before reality slams into her like a truck.

Love.

Her mind races and she wishes she could reach back in time and smack herself in the face, to take it all back. She said she loved him. She feels him shift on top of her, the two of them seemingly coming to the realization at the exact same time.

"What did you say?"

She studies the ceiling intently. She'd run if she could, but the ropes alone would be enough to keep her, let alone the fact that he's effectively pinned her to the bed. She could lie. She *should* lie. It was too early to say it, it'll be too much for him and he'll leave. She can't even look at him as she utters the next words, too afraid about what's going to happen, but there's no going back now.

"I love you."

He doesn't say anything. All she can feel is his deep breathing against her.

"Damien, I– I think I'm in love with you."

He pulls out of her, staying on all-fours above her and lifting himself up so they see eye-to-eye. She stares up at him, her chin trembling as panic sets in. His eyes are wild, almost completely black in the low light. She can't get enough air into her lungs. He's breathing just as hard as she is.

"You love me?"

"Yes – I mean – I don't–"

She stammers, maybe she can still take it back.

He shakes his head.

"Say it again."

She gulps.

"I love you."

She's on the verge of tears, unsure if this is a sick joke.

His expression is totally unreadable, and he studies her face for what seems like forever. Finally he blinks into a smile.

"I... love you too," he laughs. "Oh God, I'm so fucking in love with you. I've been waiting to tell you for so long."

Phoebe fights back her tears as a huge smile takes over her face.

"I was so scared you wouldn't say it back," she sniffles.

His breath is heavy as he presses his forehead to hers, the two of them grinning giddily at each other.

"Wow. Wow! That didn't exactly go the way I'd expected."

"No?"

"No," he replies. "It was so much better."

Phoebe doesn't quite know what to do with herself, but Damien quickly gets around to carefully untying her wrists, checking to ensure there's no real damage before confidently standing at the foot of the bed.

"So, after such a successful evening, I have *another* great idea. I'm going to run us a bath! I've also taken the liberty to schedule us some room service, just gotta give them a ring and get it sent up."

Phoebe blinks, feeling her stomach rumbling in the absence of more pressing concerns.

"Those both sound amazing right about now."

Damien begins to walk toward the phone before pausing and coming back to stand beside her.

"Hey," he grins and leans over, the tip of his nose touching hers. "I love you, Phoebe Miller."

Her whole body tingles with a newfound joy. She closes her eyes and runs her fingers through his hair, whispering her love back to him in his ear.

It's perfect. He's perfect.

Everything is perfect.

Can't Fight This Feeling

THE RENAISSANCE HOTEL

P hoebe is flabbergasted.

She didn't know what to expect when Damien said he had plans, but whatever it was, she didn't think it would be so... much. The room service cart is almost overflowing as he drags it inside, filled to the brim with food, champagne, and a conspicuous bundle of red roses set off to the side. He grins, pouring two generous glasses of champagne and passing one over to her before toasting the empty room.

"To a fantastic evening!"

She blinks, still a little shocked.

"And the flowers are for...?"

"Your bath, of course. Is it even a romantic bath without rose petals?"

Phoebe feels a hitch in her chest as she fights back the tears welling up in her eyes.

"Damien, it's too much."

"I told you, I want to take care of you. It's a package deal, all part of the Damien Bell Boyfriend Experience."

She laughs softly to herself as he saunters into the bathroom, the muffled sound of running water cascading from beyond the door. The sound is soothing, and she lets it surround her as she takes a few sips of champagne. It's a lovely beginning to the evening, at least until the distinct clatter of something hitting the floor grabs her attention.

"Fuck!"

"Damien? Are you okay?"

"Yeah, yeah I'm fine." He pokes his head out of the doorway, with a goofy look on his face. "Hey, completely unrelated, but do you know how to get oil out of a bath mat?"

She snorts.

"No idea. Strangely, I've never just poured oil all over the floor."

"You're making it sound like I'm doing this on purpose!" He pouts, sliding back into the bathroom.

Phoebe giggles, raising her voice a little so he can hear her over the flowing water.

"Well, I can't see you, so how am I supposed to know that you're not just causing havoc in there on purpose?"

The water stops and Damien pops back out.

"That's a fair point, I am known for my destructive habits," he beckons her over with a wave of the hand, "but we can worry about that later. Come on in, miss Miller."

She pads into the bathroom and is immediately hit with the smell of rich vanilla, purposefully avoiding the conspicuously crumpled bath mat as she moves through the room. Damien has dimmed the lights, the low glow of some candles flickering against a massive tub of white marble. He shuts the door behind her and begins to pluck the petals off of some scattered roses, carefully tossing them into the bath.

"Beautiful," he smiles, taking her hand and guiding her into the water behind him. He wraps his arms around her waist as she sinks in. She loves the feeling of his strong legs pressed against her body, sighing as he kisses her shoulder.

"So, are we going to do this every time we have sex?" A little hope lingers in her voice, no matter how absurd the idea seems.

"Something like it, at least when things are a bit more intense." he tells her. "You've never done this stuff? Nothing after?"

"I mean sure, cuddling sometimes, but in my experience it rarely involves roses and a scented bath."

He leans forward, grabbing a bottle from a side-table and refilling her glass.

"Better get used to it, sweets. It comes with the territory."

A comfortable silence descends on their little paradise as the radiating heat of the water relaxes her body. The heavy air mixes perfectly with the champagne as she lays her head against his chest.

"I wish... I wish we didn't have to hide," he mutters softly.

"We only really have to hide it in public," she chuckles, tilting her head and finding his face unexpectedly somber.

"I don't want to do that," Damien replies. "I want to hold your hand when we walk down the street. I want to go dancing, to kiss you in a crowd of people. I want everyone to know exactly who I'm singing about."

Phoebe's heart flutters at the idea. It all sounds so wonderful.

A smile slides onto his face as he stares down at her.

"Hell, I want you to meet my cat."

"Your cat?" She giggles.

"Her name's Maverick." He runs his hand through her hair "She's really cute, and super smart. She's a little pushy sometimes too; you really have a lot in common."

Phoebe gives him a playful punch before lifting herself up so they can talk face-to-face.

"I know how you feel, but we can still do most of that stuff. We had that lovely hike in Portland, we went to the beach and the canyon. I even get to hear you sing to me at every show."

"I know, I know," he replies with a sigh. "But we're always looking over our shoulders, standing two feet apart in every elevator. How long does that go on for?"

It's what's been dominating her thoughts the last few days.

"Not too long. At least a couple of months after the article is published, but after that I can fudge the timeline a bit with Brian. I'll say that we reconnected while you guys were in the studio, I dunno. I'll figure something out."

He chuckles, pulling her back against him.

"It's gonna make those love songs I'm writing for the new album seem *very* suspicious."

She can feel her body come alive at the words.

"Songs? About me?"

"So far it's just one, but there's always room for more. To be honest I only have two verses and a chorus so far. You're a little tough to put into words."

She racks her brain, struggling with the ridiculously busy days they've had over the last couple weeks.

"God, when did you have time to even think about writing something new?"

"The night I kissed you, the first time I mean." She can feel his heartbeat pick up a little as he holds her close. "It just kind of poured out of me when I got back to the hotel room. I've been chipping away at it since, whenever I get a chance."

She laughs.

"That night feels like such a long time ago."

Her head drops forward as he begins to massage her shoulders.

"May as well have been a lifetime."

She groans as his fingers work out the little kinks and knots.

"A song just for me, this whole romantic evening... I didn't realize you were such a softie, Bell."

He chuckles.

"Not really something I like to let people know about me."

Phoebe was obviously planning to keep their intimacy out of the article, but it's impossible to write about him without mentioning the rest. His sweetness, his passion for his art, the ease with which the whole band gets along. That's the Damien Bell that the public doesn't see, and that's the story. Suddenly, she wonders if he'd even be okay with her telling it.

"I... I wrote a little bit about it in my article."

He doesn't say anything for a moment, but when he does his voice has the tiniest edge to it, just enough that it cuts into her nerve.

"How much did you write?"

"Look, if you really want, I can change it. Fix it."

And there it is. She jumped right to compromising her work. The one thing she didn't want to do. The one thing she promised herself wouldn't happen.

"No, that's..." Damien hums softly as he starts to braid her hair. "Can I ask what's in it?"

"Mostly just the way you are with the band. You're all so sweet together, it's like watching a family. I wrote a little bit about that night at Cannon Beach. You know, when you and Johnny fell in the water?"

He laughs.

"Somehow I already forgot about that. It was a good night."

"Yeah," she whispers. "It was."

He's quiet for a long while, laying the softest kisses on her neck as he plays with her hair. And then, he speaks.

"Keep it in."

She cranes her neck back and frowns, shocked at the response.

"Really?"

He smiles at her, dipping his head slightly to lay a kiss on her lips.

"I trust you, Pheebs. No compromise, just write what you feel. I can't think of anything better for the band than letting the world see us the way you do."

Her whole body relaxes in an instant and she lets out a contented sigh.

"Thank you."

No compromise.

When the water finally begins to cool, the two dry each other off and slide into their fluffy white hotel robes. Damien rolls the room service cart so that it sits close by the side of the bed, perfectly set for them to lounge for the rest of the evening.

A movie hums in the background as he stares at her, chewing on his lip.

"What?" She asks.

"Nothing, you just have the most beautiful eyes."

She scoffs.

"I'm serious, there's all these little flecks of hazel and yellow in there, I don't know how I never noticed until now."

"You're one to talk about beautiful eyes."

He smiles, clearly a little taken aback.

"You like my eyes?"

"Damien, I get lost in them. Like, all the time. How have you not noticed?"

He scrunches up his face, pretending to gag as he bumps his shoulder against her.

"That's so dorky, Miller. God, you're so in love, it's *gross*."

"Shut up! You're just as bad! You make googly eyes at me all day long!"

"Well, *I* thought I was being *romantic*, but it's nice to know that my girlfriend thinks my sensual looks are goofy!"

Phoebe shoves him over playfully, punching him a couple times before finding herself just above him, her face inches away from his.

"I love you," he whispers.

"I love you too…"

She leans in slowly, her lips parting in anticipation before she suddenly stops.

"Oh my god, I just remembered…"

She sits back up on the bed, rubbing her temples in exasperation.

"I can't believe I said it in the middle of sex. Fuck…"

"Aww, don't be embarrassed, Miller. You were really in the moment, and honestly it was really hot."

"But the first time? And I say it when we're fucking?"

"Hey, sometimes sex can release our inhibitions, let us say things we've been holding back for stupid reasons. I'm the same way."

She bites her lip. He might be onto something. It was the second time either of them had confessed something to the other during sex. Is it healthy to rely on all that intensity to make them be honest with each other? Or maybe she's overthinking it. Maybe it was just really fucking hot.

Phoebe nestles into Damien's arms, but as her eyes begin to close and sleep starts to take over, she can't help but think about the real problem. He wants so badly to tell the world about their love, and there's almost nothing she'd enjoy more than to let him. The little crack she saw in his eternal optimism tonight has only strengthened her resolve. If they can ride this out for long enough they'll make it past that hurdle, and finally be free to do all of the things he wants, out in the open without a care in the world. She'll figure it out. She'll make it work. And they'll be happy.

Damien kisses the top of her head, muttering like he's already half-asleep.

"What're you thinking about?"

"Everything," she sighs.

Damien gives her a gentle squeeze as she feels her body relax against his.

"It can wait 'til tomorrow, babydoll."

He smiles.

"I promise."

The next morning, Phoebe is awoken by an unfamiliar noise. She tries to ignore it for a few minutes before she gives up with a groan, opening her eyes to see Damien sat at their desk, pen in hand as he taps out a beat. He's humming quietly to himself, and pausing once in a while to enthusiastically scribble something down in his notebook.

She sits up slowly, watching him for a minute or two before speaking up.

"Did inspiration strike?"

"Had a dream about that song," he tells her without missing a beat. He flips through the pages of his notebook like a mad scientist before he practically leaps out of the chair and dives onto the bed. His hair is all over the place, his beautiful gray eyes shining wildly, and she can't help but think he looks a little manic. He's got to be running on fumes at this point, but this much unfiltered passion is honestly a bit of a turn-on. Phoebe's brain still has to take a moment to kick into gear as he hands her his notebook, and it's a little while before she realizes she can't even make anything out; his handwriting is so messy.

Damien kisses her and flies back off of the bed, grabbing his jeans and pulling them up over his hips in what seems like a single motion.

"I was waiting until you woke up to tell you, I'm heading to Johnny's room to see if we can finish this thing. You wanna come and hang out?"

She smiles. She'd rather give the band the space they need to write, and it might give her the opportunity to actually get some more work done herself.

"Actually, I was going to go down to the restaurant across the street. Can I bring you back something for breakfast?"

"Yeah! Yeah, that'd be great!" He paces back to the bed and leans down, kissing her ferociously on the lips. "Fuck, I love you so much."

With him this full of energy she's almost certain they wouldn't be getting any work done, so it's probably for the best.

"Gotta go!" He shouts. "Loveyoubye!"

"I love you too," she laughs, as he dashes out of the hotel room in nothing but his half buttoned up jeans.

Phoebe grabs her notebook and pen, shoving them into her bag before she locks up. As she walks by she sees the door to Johnny's room wide open and the entire band already set up on and around the bed. There's a moment of brief regret as she walks by, but it passes quickly enough. She really needs to hunker down and get some work done.

Phoebe heads across the street to a small diner she noticed the previous day and grabs a seat at the bar, spending the better part of an hour scribbling in her notebook. She's trying her hardest not to intertwine aspects of her personal relationship with her observations about the band, and it's proving difficult to get more than a few pages in without a rewrite. Everything's so tangled up at this point that it's nearly impossible to separate the objective threads from her heartstrings.

As she takes a momentary break to dive into her pancakes, the bell at the diner door rings out for the first time in quite a while. Phoebe glances up, a little surprised to find Erin standing in the doorway. The two wave, and Erin gestures for Phoebe to join her as she slides into a booth. She puts her notes away and walks over, with Erin looking apologetic as she sits down.

"Oh, shit, am I interrupting? They're deep into it back in Johnny's room and Damien said you were over here so I thought..."

"No, it's totally fine," Phoebe replies. "Just making some quick notes, nothing important."

Erin smiles, the relief on her face obvious.

"Well, how's the article coming? Johnny's really excited about it, said your questions were great."

"It's going… pretty well?" She doesn't sound particularly confident, but she's trying to convince herself more than Erin. "Just hit a few snags here and there. But Johnny's excited, huh?"

"Yeah, he can't stop talking about it."

The waitress comes by to refill Phoebe's coffee and gives Erin a warm smile.

"You want anything, hon?"

"Coffee, and you guys have bagels, right?"

"Yep! Sesame seed okay?"

"Perfect. With cream cheese?"

"Coming right up."

Phoebe leans back as the waitress leaves, tilting her head and studying Erin for a moment.

"What?" Erin laughs.

"Can I ask you something?"

"Sure. So long as it doesn't end up in the article."

Phoebe shakes her head.

"No, this is personal."

"Fire away," Erin replies. She grabs the salt shaker and pours a small pile onto the table, making a circle in it with the tip of her finger.

"How long have you and Johnny been together?"

"Oh, easy question. Ten years. We met at 15, started dating at 16."

"You were high school sweethearts!"

Erin's cheeks dust pink as she smiles.

"He's the love of my life. Has been the whole time."

The way she says it is so full of warmth and love, Phoebe can't help but grin.

"It really shows."

Phoebe takes a breath. It'll be a bit awkward no matter what, so she just bites the bullet.

"So, okay, I just need to ask. How do you guys deal with the whole fame thing?"

Erin sighs.

"By not dealing with it, unfortunately. I pretend that I'm not with him, the fans that know pretend he's single, and everyone that doesn't never finds out. Even the ones who know would rather it wasn't true, so it mostly works."

"Wait, but doesn't that suck? Not being able to do anything together? We're just over a week in and I know it's killing Damien. Honestly it's starting to kill me too."

Erin drums her fingers on the table.

"It does, sometimes, yeah, but it's a bit more complicated. The reason we're not public isn't for the band, it's because he doesn't want me to show up in the paper. It's to protect me."

"So you both just stay quiet about the whole thing? All the time?"

Erin nods as the waitress arrives with her coffee and bagel. She murmurs a soft thank you and immediately takes a big bite, suddenly reminding Phoebe of her pancakes.

"I get it though," Erin mumbles, dabbing at her mouth with a napkin. "The press isn't exactly kind to the partners of rock stars. It's the safest thing we can do right now."

Phoebe's guts twist. She didn't really think about that part. She was mostly just concerned about her job.

"Have you two talked about eventually going public?"

"Yep, every once in a while. I'm the one that's pushing for it, even if it means things are going to change. I think he's just scared about me getting overwhelmed with the attention."

"Yeah, the worst of it always does seem to fall on the women involved, doesn't it?" Phoebe mutters.

"Totally," Erin replies. "It's gross and invasive. The rags think they can just print anything, like we're not even human. Meanwhile, the men are put up on a pedestal, called geniuses. We're either their muses, or we're vilified, or both. No matter what, we're just an accessory at best. I have my own job, my own life, my own hobbies. But they'll never see that, if they even cared to begin with."

Phoebe nods as Erin continues.

"It's more than just that, too, it's the questions about our relationship. Because they're going to dig, and they're going to dig way too deep–" She pauses, taking another bite of her bagel. "No offense to your profession, but it's kind of what you guys do."

Phoebe shrugs. She can't deny it.

"Going public means negotiating what we should and shouldn't talk about, how we should and shouldn't act. I'm an open book, but Johnny's a really private person. There's no way they'd respect that privacy, and he'd rather not give them more strings to tug at."

"There are some things that are special, that you want to keep between the two of you," Phoebe replies.

Erin smiles and nods.

"It's crazy that people don't understand that. They think that just because you're with someone who's in the public eye, or you *are* in the public eye, that gives them the right to pick apart your relationship. Johnny says it comes with the territory, and that's true, but that doesn't mean it should be that way."

Phoebe sips her coffee, trying to get the dry feeling out of her throat.

"Sorry, I'm pretty passionate about this topic, as you can guess. Anyway..." Erin tilts her head a little. "If it's not for the article... this is about you two?"

Phoebe nibbles her fingernail.

"Damien wants to go public."

"Oh, that's— ah, and you don't."

"It's complicated."

"Lay it on me," Erin laughs. "Clearly I get it."

This'll be the first time she's really talked about it with anyone other than him.

"Well, first off I could lose this assignment. Hell, I could lose my whole job. This article is a big deal to me, it's the chance for me to really show that I'm more than just 'that chick who writes album reviews.'" She sighs. "Even if I don't lose my job or the article, will anyone take it seriously when they find out I'm sleeping with the frontman? Would they even take *me* seriously anymore?"

"That's a big risk, then– going public, I mean."

Phoebe looks down at the table as she continues to vent.

"And the stuff you mentioned, the invasiveness and being an accessory, all that shit... that's just the icing on the cake. Really thick, nasty icing."

"So, worst case scenario: your boss finds out and you get fired."

"Right."

"What's best case scenario?"

Phoebe laughs, shaking her head.

"Best case scenario is that my boss suddenly becomes the most understanding man in the world overnight, publishes the article, and it's this huge hit that changes my life. You know he told me I had to be a fly on the wall? That I couldn't get too involved? Really fucked that one up."

"That's impossible with this band," Erin chuckles. "They won't let that happen."

"Yeah, I've noticed."

Erin reaches out and grasps Phoebe's fingers.

"You guys have to talk it out. Really sit down and talk about it all, and it can't be an argument! You have to listen to each other, be open. I know Damien is a lot to handle, but he loves you, he'll hear you out if you do the same."

Phoebe smiles, squeezing her hand back.

"Thanks Erin, really. I don't really have anyone else to talk to about this stuff. It's... a pretty specific issue."

"Well, you have me now," Erin replies warmly. "I've got your back. Promise."

The bell at the door rings violently as Troy barges in, looking around frantically before his eyes land on Phoebe.

"You!" He points at her.

"Seriously? I'm literally just eating!" Phoebe exclaims. "How can I be in trouble?"

"Settle down, Sullivan!" Erin calls over her shoulder. "He's so dramatic. It's like everything is performance art with him."

"We gotta go, ladies. On the bus!" Troy snaps his fingers.

Erin sighs, unimpressed.

"I gotta get my stuff from the room," Phoebe says as he approaches the table.

"Got that covered, Miller. We run a tight ship around here."

"I'm not done with my bagel!" Erin protests.

"Amazing thing about bagels, Erin." Troy grabs her coffee mug, taking a large gulp. "They're portable."

Little Red Corvette

DENVER, COLORADO

They arrive in Denver around noon and it all goes smoothly, only having to wait in the lobby for about 10 minutes as Troy retrieves their room keys.

"Okay. Day off today, show tomorrow night. So get your sightseeing in," he stares directly at Damien. "Or whatever it is you two freaky kids get up to."

Damien looks scandalized as he takes their keys and slides them into his pocket.

"You want us to fly that freak flag out in public? What happened to being inconspicuous, Sullivan? Are you sick? Has the government finally replaced you with one of those body snatchers?"

Troy rolls his eyes.

"Just, keep it down, okay? No matter how far I book my room from you two I always know I'm gonna have something to tell my psychiatrist the following week."

Damien is in a good mood all the way up to their room, clearly very proud of himself, and not a minute after they've begun to settle in, he turns to her with a big grin on his face. "Get dressed," he says, striking a dramatic pose as he throws his bag onto the bed.

"What? Why?"

"Well, I suppose not *everything* has to be a big secret. I'm renting a car and taking you for a lunch date. We're not spending another day cooped up in a hotel, it's time to live a little!"

She stares at him with a frown, mulling it over in her head for a moment. Going out wasn't a problem, they'd done it a few times with no issue, but Damien wasn't particularly skilled at discretion at the best of times, and he looked very excited.

"Come on, babydoll. It'll be fine. We'll take separate exits, we can walk a few feet apart. I won't even grab your ass! Besides, I can get us a corvette. Don't you want to feel the wind in your hair?"

She chews on her lip as Damien's fingers dance up and down her thigh, his big puppy dog eyes demanding her attention. Phoebe sighs, pushing his face away playfully.

"Alright, alright, where are we going, loverboy?"

"I know a good spot, pretty far outside the city. Small place and the guy who runs it was a good dude, no paparazzi and no risk! We can be as cute and googly-eyed as we want, and Troy can save on his therapy bills."

He kneels on the bed, leaning toward her.

"Or should I tie you up first?" he purrs.

She runs her tongue along her lip, her skin turning a soft shade of pink.

"I'd like to do that on a full stomach."

"Mmm, clever girl."

She grins as he kisses her cheek.

"Alright, we're agreed, time to go and get dressed!"

Rooting through her bags, Phoebe finds a black mini skirt and t-shirt that'll do the trick, and takes them into the bathroom as Damien makes a call. She ties off the t-shirt at the front to expose a bit of her belly, teases her hair, and pops on some bright pink lipstick before stepping back out and doing a quick little twirl.

"How's this?"

Damien hangs up the phone immediately, taking a step forward.

"Jesus, maybe we could eat in after all..."

He quickly scoops something up from the ground, and before she can react he snaps a picture of her. Her polaroid camera must have fallen out of her bag when she was grabbing clothes.

"Damien!" She laughs. "I wasn't ready."

"I'm keeping this forever."

"I probably look awful!"

"What are you talking about?" He chuckles as he shakes it. "You look delicious."

Damien lays the picture on the side-table as he gets dressed. He picks out a black button-up shirt and blue jeans, throwing them on quickly before finishing off the look with a pair of sunglasses. The fit is just tight enough to be flattering while leaving a bit to the imagination. His hair is tousled and perfectly frames his sculpted face, accented by the stubble on his chin. She can practically feel it scraping the inside of her thighs.

He glances back over at the nightstand and snaps up the photo, looking at it with a smile before tucking it into his wallet. He walks past her, giving her a quick slap on the ass.

"Time to go!"

She jumps a little trying to hide her grin.

"One minute, I just need my purse."

Damien shakes his head, gesturing into the open door.

"Do what you want, babydoll, but it's my treat."

They pull into a small town about an hour outside of Denver. It's beautiful, with an almost endless blue sky stretching out past snow-capped mountains in the distance. He parks the car and jumps out, rushing over to open the door for her as he bows dramatically.

"Madam."

She grins. He's in a great mood today.

"Such a gentleman."

As they enter the restaurant, the boisterous sound of jovial conversation swells. The host sitting at the front looks up from his book, but there's no recognition in his face, only a curt smile. Phoebe breathes a soft sigh of relief.

"For two?"

"Please," Damien replies. "Somewhere near the back."

The host nods, snatching two menus out of a little pocket on the side of his stand.

"This way please."

Their table is sequestered, tucked in the corner of the restaurant near the bar where a couple staff members are gossiping. It's possible one of them recognizes Damien, but if she does, she doesn't make a move, just smiles at Phoebe and returns to her work. The host gestures to the table, and Damien nods.

"This is perfect, thanks."

They take their seats and he hands them their menus.

"Can I get you anything to drink?"

"Chardonnay, if you have some?" Phoebe asks.

"I'll do a whiskey," Damien smiles.

Their host scribbles in his notebook.

"I'll be right back, take your time looking over the menu."

"Thank you," Damien and Phoebe murmur in unison.

Phoebe lights a cigarette, glancing around as she takes in the charms of the location. It's not grand, but not quaint either. It reminds her of some of the smaller family-owned restaurants back home, the ones you're always happily surprised to find have survived all these years.

"So, how did you find this place? It's really out of the way."

"Ah, yeah. I was dating this girl, Emily, when we first started getting big. Fuck, seems like ages ago now. Long story short, we were up in Denver for four nights. Got sick of eating hotel food after two."

"I can relate," Phoebe laughs.

"So, we went out one day, nowhere particular in mind, just picked a direction and drove. Kinda got lost, but we managed to find this little place. We were starving and would have taken anything, but turns out the food is incredible, and they pointed us back in the right direction. Definitely helped that no one around here's really tuned in to the rock scene. Nobody from the media to think about."

Damien leans in across the table, taking her hand.

"I know you worry a lot about getting caught. I wanted to do something just a little bit special, you know? Not a date with a rockstar, just Damien and Phoebe."

"I love it, Damien, really."

It's a wonderful gesture, touching on each of their biggest wants and fears. Public discovery is a time bomb that ticks away in the background of their day to day, an inevitability that they both try desperately to ignore. Some days it's easier than others, and this is one of them.

"Hey, can I ask you something personal?"

He smirks.

"You can ask me whatever you want, babydoll."

"The sex that we have, the ropes and all that... have you done that with–"

"Just one other girl."

She frowns. It's a little surprising.

"I only ever plan to open that side of myself up for women I feel really compatible with, and even then I sort of have to get a feel for what they like in the bedroom. That first night we fucked, I noticed how you reacted when I pushed you up against the wall."

She blushes, just as a waiter arrives with their drinks. Damien grins as Phoebe tries to avoid the waiter's eye, just in case he had heard anything.

"Yeah, that was... memorable."

"So, I took that as a cue to investigate, see if you wanted to take things further. If you had said no, I would have dropped it completely and just kept it to a little roughness."

She snorts.

"Your version of a little rough had me sweating bullets. I felt like I ran a marathon– in a good way."

"I just like to make sure that the women I'm with are satisfied."

Phoebe raises her glass.

"Mission accomplished. Over and over."

Damien follows suit, and they clink the glasses together.

"I aim to please." He takes a sip of his whiskey, closing his eyes and savoring it for a moment. "Glad you're okay with the ropes and stuff, makes for a really fun time."

She swallows her wine and nods vigorously.

"Okay with it? Damien, are you kidding me? It's fucking euphoric."

He smiles, raising his eyebrows.

"What's your favorite thing about it?"

"I'm not sure really, it's still new, but there's something about being deprived of control that makes me... feel in control, if that makes sense?"

He nods.

"That's the goal. You have all the power when we do that stuff, I'm just there to make it all work."

"I'm still figuring it all out, but I was really surprised by how safe it all felt, even while feeling dangerous at the same time? I don't know how to describe it."

"The most important thing is that we'll always stop the minute you say no." He sighs. "Actually, we should probably come up with some kind of safeword. Needs to be something we wouldn't ever say in the bedroom."

Another little secret just for them. Phoebe taps her chin and looks around for inspiration. People are sipping wine as the sun drips in through the windows, but for some reason the first thing that comes to mind...

"What about narwhal?"

Damien almost chokes on his drink.

"Narwhal?!"

"You don't like it? I think it's cute."

"No, I mean, it works. I guess making me burst out laughing would grind things to a halt, sure."

"Ugh, okay, something less weird." She pauses for a few moments, her brow furrowed. "How about daisy?"

"Yeah, actually that's perfect. Okay, you or I say 'daisy' and whatever we're doing stops immediately. We check in, see how we're feeling, and decompress. If you find that you're not able to verbalize, just tap me three times and I'll stop." His stare is piercing, his expression completely serious. "I *promise*, Phoebe."

"I believe you," she whispers.

He takes her hand, lifting her knuckles to his lips and kisses them softly.

"Thank you."

"For what?" She asks.

"For being so cool with this. All of it."

The deeper they get, the more she finds things out about herself that she never knew before. She wants him to push her to her absolute limit and then bring her back, whispering sweet nothings as he holds her. She feels warm all over, staring into his eyes as they hold hands across the table. She is hopelessly, soul-crushingly in love with this man.

The server returns to take their food orders; it's a quick affair, and this time neither of them is talking about specific moments in their sex life, so Phoebe comes out of it feeling a lot better. Once they're alone again, Damien lets out a long sigh of contentment.

"I'm really glad we got to do this."

Phoebe reaches out again and brushes her fingers against his.

"Me too."

"This is the kind of shit that I want to do with you all the time. I can't wait for the tour to be over, then we can–"

Damien taps his pockets. Probably looking for his cigarettes.

"Fuck, I left 'em in the car."

"Damien–"

She has to tell him about the guy in the elevator, how he saw the two of them together at a show. He needs to know how close they were to disaster.

"Hey Pheebs, you got extra smokes?"

"Oh, yeah in my purse I think."

She digs into the bag, pulling a pack out after a couple seconds and sliding it across the table. He knocks one out quickly, shoving it between his lips and lighting it up.

"The other day–"

"You know, there's this great place in Chelsea I wanna take you to when we get back. They do all of this fancy French food and shit, it's amazing. It's kind of formal, but there's a private room in the back." He smirks. "Maybe we could go once we figure this shit out and go public."

"After the article," she clarifies. "Right?"

"Yeah, of course," he scoffs. "Don't worry. I might be crazy, but I'm not *that* crazy."

He runs his hand through his hair as the server drops off their appetizers and some water. Damien smiles, waiting for her to leave before he continues.

"But hey, I was thinking, if you wanted you could see my place when this is all done. Maybe spend a few nights there, if you, you know..."

Phoebe smiles ear-to-ear. There's something so cute about him when he's like this; his unending confidence is suddenly nowhere to be found.

"Damien, we've been literally living in a hotel room together, I think I'm cool with *seeing* your place."

He throws up his hands.

"Okay, okay! I'm just saying, some people get freaked out about that stuff. On the road is one thing, but when you get home it's different. It's like, you kind of have to start over, you know?"

He might be right. She's barely thought about her apartment back home, or much of anything beyond the trip, really. The road feels like this magical bubble that's completely separate from their real lives. But it's not. There are repercussions. She has to push through and tell him, to make sure they're really on the same page about being more cautious, but he looks so happy in this moment, smiling at her from across the table like everything is perfect and nothing could possibly go wrong.

She can find another opportunity.

They have time.

"If you really want to test the strength of our relationship, you can come stay a couple days at *my* apartment. You'll be able to see such amazing sights as my piles of vinyl, and my one closet with the busted door."

"Oh, hey, I can fix that for you!"

She smirks.

"By 'fix it,' do you mean tear it off the hinges?"

"You *doubt* me, Miller? But, yeah, why not just rip it down and hang one of those beaded curtains in front of it?"

Phoebe rests her chin on the heel of her hand. She can picture the two of them living together in a little apartment in Brooklyn. They both write full-time. She sits on the couch with Damien's little cat in her lap while the band rehearses. Their apartment is filled with books, records, and maybe even some of his sister's art pieces.

"I just realized I never asked, where in the city do you live?"

"SoHo," he replies. "You?"

"Williamsburg, but Janis lives in the East Village, so I'm out there a lot."

"How have we never run into each other?"

"Maybe we did once, it's a huge city, after all."

"Nah, not a chance. I would have stopped dead in my tracks the minute I saw you."

She chuckles. He always has a line.

"You really are too much sometimes, you know that?"

Damien leans forward in his chair, his smile somehow even brighter than before.

"Tell me about the best day of your life."

She takes a sip of wine, blinking.

"The best...?"

"The best day, yeah."

Phoebe sighs, trying to skim over a lifetime's worth of memories as Damien waits patiently.

"I got one. Well, it was more than a day."

"I'll let you break a rule or two, it's your first time."

"Summer break from university, first year. Janis and I took her dad's car on a road trip to Cali. We had no idea how to read a map and no plan for how the fuck to get there, but we were determined to go to Disneyland. By ourselves mind you. Janis had never been before and the last time I went, I was a kid. We slept in the car to save money, and ate shitty gas station food. We even got two flat tires on the way there. Anyway, halfway through the trip, we somehow took a wrong turn and wound up at the border. To Alberta."

"Canada?" Damien's shoulders shake with laughter. "You drove to fucking Canada?"

"Yep."

"How is that even possible?"

"I don't know! Our map was shitty to begin with, then I spilled coffee on it and Janis yelled at me, and the ink on the page blurred so the roads got all fucked up–"

"Oh, so it was *your* fault!"

"I prefer to think of it as a joint failure."

He leans back in his chair.

"I'm gonna double check with Janis on that one when I see her again."

"She'll throw me under the bus! You can't trust a word that girl says!"

Damien chuckles and takes a sip of his water.

He was right, 'just Damien and Phoebe' is nice.

"Did you ever make it to Disneyland?"

"We did, yeah. Those were the two weeks where we realized we were definitely best friends. If you can make it out of Alberta together, you can make it anywhere."

Today might be a close second to her road trip with Janis. Just being able to hold his hand in public with no worries, it means everything.

It still doesn't feel real.

"What about you?" She asks. "Best day of your life."

He takes a quick sip of his whiskey, placing it carefully down on the table.

"When we were kids, Johnny and I went to Coney Island. I stole money from my folks to go, not that they would have missed it anyway. My dad had cash hidden all over the house, still does probably. I think it's a wartime thing. Anyway, we get there, stuff our faces with cotton candy, donuts, hot dogs, all that. Then, the second Johnny sees Erin and her friends show up, he pukes all over the boardwalk." Damien laughs to himself, shaking his head. "It was kind of the last time he got to be a kid, actually."

"What do you mean?"

"Well, his mom died pretty soon after, and he had to grow up fast. Way faster than the rest of us."

"I didn't know that, and his dad?"

"Split when he was a few days old, so really not a thing. 'I'm going for cigarettes; I'll be right back.' The fucker was a real American classic. His mom raised Johnny by herself until he was sixteen."

"How did she die?"

"Car accident. Johnny doesn't like to talk about it." He straightens all of a sudden, looking a little nervous. "Shit, uh, Pheebs you can't put this in the article."

He'd do anything for his bandmates. His second family.

"Of course, all of this is off the record."

"Thanks." He sighs. "He's fine now. He has Erin, and her parents. They kind of helped raise him after his mom died. My parents too, actually."

"That's sweet."

"Nah, it's just what you do when someone needs help."

The server brings their food and refills their waters. Damien declines another drink while Phoebe gets a second glass of chardonnay. He furrows his brow at her as the waitress walks away.

"What?" She laughs.

"I just realized there's a bunch of stuff I don't know about you."

"Like what?"

"When's your birthday?" He asks.

"Next month. October 10th."

His jaw drops and he scoffs.

"You're spending your birthday on tour?!"

"Is there a better way to spend it than with my incredibly talented, incredibly sexy boyfriend?" She asks, a flirtatious smile on her face.

"You lay it on thick, Miller."

"Not as thick as you," she quips. "Pretty impressive how I planned it all out, getting together with a famous rockstar right before my birthday, huh?"

Damien chuckles.

"Well, now I've gotta think of something to get you. You'll be what, 24?"

She blinks.

"I'm surprised you knew that."

"Hey, I know some things, just not everything." He pauses in thought. "24, huh... That's a big deal. You're gonna need something real fucking special."

"Oh, I will?" She laughs.

"Yup, and no arguments."

"What are you thinking?" Phoebe asks as she leans over the table.

Damien only grins.

"Wouldn't *you* like to know?"

Only You

THE CRAWFORD HOTEL

It's nearly 6:00PM when they arrive back at the hotel. Damien parks the corvette a few blocks away, and they walk in separately, even taking different elevators up to their floor.

Phoebe's body tingles with anticipation as she rides her elevator up alone, her mind swimming. As she reaches their floor and steps out, she sees Damien already halfway down the hall, leaning against the wall. It takes her a moment to realize what he's doing, but as she gets closer she can hear the loud moaning emanating from a room she quickly realizes belongs to Shaun and Ophelia. Damien snickers as she reaches his side.

"You think we'll give them a run for their money?"

Phoebe blushes, slipping by him wordlessly and sliding their key into the lock. The moment the door shuts, everything about him shifts. Phoebe squeaks as he grabs her, first stepping back in surprise before leaning into him. It's only seconds before he has her back to the wall, her hands pressed against his chest as he locks her in a passionate kiss. She works the buttons on his dress shirt as his hand slides up her leg, tugging at her skirt.

"Time to get dressed up, pick something you feel beautiful in."

She struts past him to her bags, rooting through them and grabbing a black lace bra, matching underwear, and a pair of heels. He grabs her wrist just as she's walking to the bathroom and fishes something out of his own bag.

"And this."

A red collar, just the right size.

"When did you get this?"

He grins.

"Picked it up for you in Vegas. Figured it was your style."

Phoebe plucks it from his hands and walks into the bathroom, holding up her index finger before locking the door behind her.

"No free previews," she says through the door, grinning ear to ear.

She draws on a thick cat eye that extends to the tip of her eyebrow and swipes on an alluring shade of red lipstick before changing into her underwear. Her chest swells. It's the first time in a while that she's really taken the time to appreciate her own body. The way everything is framed and emphasized... she can't help but turn around and glance over her shoulder and admire her ass.

She slides on her heels, teetering a little at first. She takes a few steps to practice, managing to find a reasonable balance after a minute of pacing. The last thing she'd want to do is fall on her face in the middle of a sexy sashay. With her walk sorted, Phoebe stands in front of the mirror once more, taking a good look at herself in the ensemble as she fastens the collar around her neck. She's gonna blow his mind.

When she steps back into the room, Damien is already lounging on the couch in only a pair of black briefs. Her eyes linger on him, mentally devouring him for a few moments before her attention is grabbed by the small spool of rope on the seat beside him. The lighting is soft and low, and she notices that he's taken the mirror that was hanging on the wall and placed it next to the bed, facing him.

"Now that," he pauses, leaning out toward her, "is what I'm talking about."

Phoebe does a little spin.

"You like it?"

"Like it? You look fucking gorgeous." He takes a deep breath. Phoebe can feel his eyes rake over her body so hard it'd leave a mark.

"How do you feel?"

"Really fucking pretty."

Damien beams.

"You're stunning." He stretches out his arm. "Let me show you."

The hungry look in Damien's eyes makes her tremble as she walks toward him, and he grabs her by the hips, squeezing her ass the moment she's close enough to reach. His eyes trail up and down her body as he licks his lips.

"Sit," he commands, patting a spot on the couch between his legs.

Phoebe slowly lowers herself, and in a moment he's pushing her thighs apart. She breathes steadily as one of Damien's hands reaches around to lift her chin.

"See that mirror?" He asks.

She nods and he places a kiss on her neck.

"I need to hear words, sweets."

"Yes sir, I see it."

"That's my girl." The praise makes her heart flutter. He's still gently gripping her chin with one hand, forcing her to stare at her reflection as his other lands on top of her own, his fingers interlinking with hers. "I want you to guide me, so you can show me how you want to be touched. Can you do that for me?"

"Yes, sir."

He flicks her ear with his tongue and she has to resist the urge to jump him right there, working hard to stay as still as she can.

"Show me how you touched yourself the first time, when I heard you through the wall."

She shudders as Damien chuckles low in her ear, a trail of goosebumps rushing down her spine.

"Don't get shy on me now, babydoll."

Phoebe keeps her fingers linked with his as she guides his hand down her body, over her belly, past her hips, and stopping to hover just between her legs. Gently, she pushes his fingers against her clit and begins to make small, slow circles while the reflection of his rings glitter in the dim light. She whines as he places gentle kisses along the side of her neck, quickly turning to little bites.

"You set the pace," he whispers. "Is this how you did it?"

She nods as the circles speed up. Breath rushes in and out of her chest as Damien begins to suck gently on the newly sensitive spots on her neck. Her clit throbs beneath the variable pressure of his touch and she can feel herself getting wetter, already beginning to soak through the thin layer of fabric. The friction makes her eyelids flutter, but Damien catches them threatening to close and begins to slow his hand.

"Remember the rules: Eyes on the mirror," he commands. "Look at those lips, those beautiful eyes, your whole fucking body."

She forces her eyes back open, guiding his fingers to move faster with hers.

"That's it. I can feel you getting closer. What were you thinking about that day?"

"You," she whispers, her voice shaky.

Phoebe can feel all her muscles tighten as he bites into her shoulder, but she can't stop guiding his fingers in their caress. She can feel Damien's cock start to strain, cradled firmly up against her ass. She begins grinding her hips against him, listening to the low growl that tumbles out from deep within his chest.

"More specific," he breathes. "What *exactly* were you picturing? What did you want?"

A week ago she wouldn't dare even think about it near him, let alone say it out loud, but now...

"You're pushing me up against a bathroom wall, telling me how you're going to fuck me, exactly how I'm going to take your cock."

Her heart pounds and her cunt spasms. Phoebe takes the initiative and guides his hand around her panties. Her hips roll and wiggle, nipples pebbled through the bra as Damien's free hand wraps around her throat. The thin collar presses lightly into her neck, insulating her just a bit from his grasp. He begins by squeezing the sides gently, cutting off the blood flow just enough to make her head feel a bit hazy before releasing.

"You tell me if it's too much, okay? Daisy, remember?"

"I remember," Phoebe breathes.

As her eyes begin to drift closed again, he nips at her earlobe.

"Keep 'em open, sweets, you're gonna watch yourself come." His voice is rough and gravelly.

"Harder," she rasps, using her free hand to put pressure on his grip around her neck.

She whimpers as his grasp tightens, guiding other hand downward and pushing his fingers to plunge inside her. She can feel his rings bumping up against her and gasps, her mouth dropping open as the sound quickly turns into a whine. Damien purrs as Phoebe increases the pace, fucking her with his fingers while she keeps her eyes fixed on her reflection.

Almost without thinking Phoebe lets her hand fall away from her neck, reaching down to pull her underwear fully aside to get a clear view. She watches hungrily as the image of his fingers plunging inside her over and over mixes with the physical sensation, breathing a little heavier. She feels like she's falling apart as the heel of his hand grinds against her clit at the same time as his fingers curl into her G-spot. His grip on her neck makes things blur a little more, like she's suddenly been hit by a strong drink.

"I could watch you do this forever," he groans.

Her hips rock back and forth, her choked down moans getting louder and louder as Damien bites back into her neck. Her legs tremble and her mouth hangs open, sucking in as much air as she can. These small discomforts don't mean a thing, all she can focus on is how good his fingers feel inside her.

Her moans become more raspy and desperate, her hips beginning to buck faster and faster as a sly and cocky smirk forms on Damien's face, reflected in the mirror along with her spasming body. Each stroke feels like heaven, and she's getting closer and closer to the edge. She lets go of Damien's wrist, leaving everything to him as she sinks her fingernails into his thighs. She rolls her head back, straining against his shoulder as she jams her thighs together and tries not to squirm.

"You're close, aren't you?" he whispers into her ear. "You're gonna cum for me."

Phoebe cries out, slamming her eyes shut as he puts a little more pressure on her G-spot, his fingers giving her something to anchor herself to. Suddenly, a tidal wave of bliss comes crashing over her. Damien removes his hand from her throat, placing it on her belly and bracing as he continues to fuck her with his fingers. The rush that comes with the release of her neck brings her back down to earth, and she finds herself gasping as blood rushes through her body.

"Good girl." The sound of his voice brings a smile to her face as his pace slows. "You've been *such* a good girl for me."

Her eyelids flutter open as Damien pulls his fingers from her, holding them up in front of her.

"Open your mouth."

She parts her lips and Damien gently pushes his fingers between them.

"Clean them up."

The command makes her shiver. She watches herself wrap her lips around his fingers, sucking each one individually before moving to the next. The sounds of satisfaction he lets out make her stomach tighten while her tongue swirls around the final finger. She slides off of the couch as she finishes, turning to face him and placing her hands on his knees. Damien tilts his head, an amused look spreading across his face as she reaches out to rub his cock through his briefs.

He licks his lips, his cheeks and neck flushing as Phoebe pulls down his briefs. She wraps her fingers around his cock, sliding them up the shaft with a featherlight grip. She shudders in anticipation as she works the tiniest bit of precum out of the head, slowly dragging her thumb over top and smearing it around before stroking back down his cock. Damien moans, and Phoebe chuckles in reply.

She leans forward, her tongue barely touching the tip and flicking it playfully like it was a dessert worth savoring. His breathing quickens, and she can feel the muscles in his legs clench up, that familiar rush shooting through her body. He can handle a little bit of payback.

Damien has never stopped watching her in the mirror, and as she glances up she can tell she's been pushing all the right buttons.

"You're being a brat again."

"Am I?"

She puts on her most innocent expression.

"Maybe you'll have to punish me, unless of course I can make it up to you."

"We'll see," he smirks.

Damien reaches beside him, grabbing the rope and quickly unspooling it before carefully sliding it through the loop in her collar. He ties a quick knot, looking down at her as he winds the rope gently around his knuckles. Phoebe licks her lips, pressing them against the very tip of his cock before taking him deep into her mouth. One of his hands keeps the rope taut while the other grips the back of her hair, knotting it in his fist as he immediately takes control of everything. He hits the back of her throat and grunts, his whole body tightening in response. She can feel the heat growing between her legs, getting more and more wet as Damien holds her head. The second she begins to gag he releases her, the rope falling slack in his hand as she pulls herself off of him. She coughs, blinking away tears.

"Sorry," she laughs. "It's good, I'm good."

He strokes her head, making no moves to push anything further.

"Don't be sorry. You're fucking amazing." He smiles. "You want me to be gentler?"

"Just a little."

"The rope good though? Remember, you can tap me three times if you need to stop."

"Mmm, thank you sir, but the rope is just right."

She gathers a small amount of saliva and dribbles it from her lips onto his tip. Damien lets out a deep sigh as he strokes himself, spreading it all around his cock to slick it up. She sticks out her tongue to catch the new bead of precum that's threatening to spill out, before repositioning herself for another dive. This time, he gently guides her mouth up and down his shaft, moaning in between words of affirmation as his fingers run through her hair.

"You look so fuckin' hot on your knees."

He slides his cock all the way down her throat again, but this time she relaxes and holds it in, exactly like he wants. As he tugs on the rope just the tiniest bit, a rush of electricity shoots through her veins, her cunt aching. She needs to make him feel as good as she does, but she needs more. He pulls her back up with her hair tangled in his fingers, and she stares at him as she gasps for air, a mess of flaming cheeks and the spittle running down her chin. Damien chuckles.

"Fuck, you look absolutely ruined." He bends down to run his thumb along her lips, surely smearing her lipstick just a bit more to complete the look.

He stands, tugging her toward him with the rope. His eyes are practically on fire, and Phoebe follows his lead, getting shakily to her feet. He turns her around, letting his fingers graze against her waist and the very edges of her panties.

"As good as these look on you, I want them off."

She takes the initiative, sliding them past her hips and letting them fall to the floor. She can see the reflection of his impatience in the mirror as he grabs a condom, rolling it swiftly onto his cock.

He drops to his knees, grasping her waist tightly and pulling her toward him, before sinking his teeth into her supple ass. She lets out a yelp from deep inside her, but it quickly transforms into a full-bodied moan as he squeezes her thigh, running his fingers up between her swollen lips. He still has a firm handle on the makeshift leash, guiding her down slowly with a tug before she's on her hands and knees, her back to him. Damien has one hand wrapped around her waist, positioning his cock right below her as he holds the rope taut in his hand, reminding her who's in control.

He spreads her legs a little wider, one by one, his cock gently kissing up against her with every movement. There's only a moment more of pause before she feels his tip push inside her, followed quickly by his ragged groan. He doesn't waste any time sliding himself further inside, stretching her out to that comfortable level of brief discomfort. The sensation is a little shock and a lot of pleasure every time, and the combination just doesn't get old. Her stomach clenches and she arches her back as a long quivering whine spills from her lips. Damien growls, the sound leaving a trail of goosebumps from the crown of her head all the way down to the tips of her toes.

"That's it, babydoll, right where you belong."

His words drip like honey from his tongue as he continues to slide himself deeper, and her heartbeat quickens as her eyes find him in the mirror. His chest heaves as she takes him further and further in, and she can see his confident smile widen as her face twists from pleasure. The hand that held her by the belly slides up to play with her rock-hard nipples, causing her to twitch and jump until a particularly cruel pinch makes her push back involuntarily against him. He lets out a satisfied grunt, her own yelp clearly goading him on as he finally bottoms out with the help of her little jolt.

This time there's no stillness, no waiting or playful teasing in the moment. This time, they both have an overwhelmingly demanding need. Damien tugs on the leash and smiles as she catches his eye again in the mirror.

"You can pull harder than *that*, can't you sir?"

His expression hardens and he pulls tighter, the collar straining a bit against her neck as she keeps herself steady, dropping onto one forearm while reaching back to brace against his thigh. Muscle ripples beneath her fingers as his hips strain, slapping against her hard enough to almost force her off him. Her skin is flushed, warm with the sweat she can feel forming all over her. She's trembling, her breath rushing so fast she feels like anything more could be the end of her.

"Fuck yourself," he growls, pounding against her like a jackhammer.

Her fingers fumble slightly to reach her clit in the midst of her breathy haze, but she finds it immediately receptive, pulsing under even the lightest touch. She strokes it longingly, in as steady a pace as possible while Damien's rocking her entire body with every single thrust. She can tell she's going to have marks on her neck from the collar, bruises on her skin, but she doesn't give a shit. Maybe she won't be able to walk in the morning, but fuck it. It'll all be a reminder of him. Of them.

The pace quickens even more as she strains against him, and she runs her fingers across her clit so violently she starts to lose her grip on his body. The sound and sensation of their skin slapping together fills her up, mixing with the moans that erupt from both of them. She's making sounds she's never before as she gets lost in bliss, his hot breath burning against the side of her neck.

"I'm gonna come," he manages to grunt out through a clenched jaw.

She tries to speak, muttering some wordless nothing as her body lets go as he pushes past their limits. She feels the rope go slack and he grasps her hips with both hands, fingers digging into her skin. It's only a moment of shuddering reprieve, though, and just as quickly he starts fucking her again, refusing to slow his pace.

"Watch yourself," he groans. "Look how beautiful you are, just like this."

The image of them entwined, his final desperate thrusts punishing her already ravished and aching body, it's all she needs to let the climax ripple through her like a maelstrom. Wave after wave crashes against her like she's a tiny rock on a beach. He has to hold her tight as she quivers and shakes in the aftermath until she finally slumps forward on the ground, nearly breathless.

There are a few minutes of a heavy, comfortable silence as everything resets, their bodies cooling in their bliss.

Damien sighs, leaning forward and kissing her neck.

"You really looked fucking great tonight," he laughs. "You made a good pick."

"Lucky I've got more," she mumbles, looking over to the ruined clump of fabric on the floor.

He strokes her hair playfully.

"You feel beautiful tonight?"

"I did," she whispers. "I do."

"Well, there you go, mission accomplished!" He pulls out of her and stands, clapping his hands together, suddenly full of energy as she stares up at him. "Hey, let me run you a bath."

She smiles as he helps her to her feet.

"Ooh, can we order champagne?"

He chuckles.

"Looks like you're getting used to the good life, Miller."

She grins.

"Well, that's the Damien Bell Boyfriend Experience, right?"

"*Now*, you're getting it."

Dirty Laundry

THE CRAWFORD HOTEL

"So, what do you guys want to do tonight?"

It's just past noon, and the band's on the way to the lobby after finishing a mediocre lunch. Phoebe had been looking forward to an afternoon of relaxation before the trip to their next city, but Erin seems resolved to have some sort of fun.

"It's my last night, and we finally have time to just hang out, no show or anything... I simply won't accept anything less than a beautiful send-off."

Johnny hangs his head as they head toward the elevator. He'd been holding hands with Erin all morning, like he was worried if he let her go she'd just disappear into the air. Phoebe feels a pang of sadness for Johnny. He's been on his game since Erin showed up, even more bright than usual, but it's going to be a rough time once she's gone.

"Why don't we all have dinner?" Shaun suggests.

"Dinner's not really a *beautiful send-off*, is it?"

Shaun rolls his eyes. Damien's usual snark isn't unexpected, but it's certainly not particularly helpful.

"Okay, what the fuck do you have in mind, oh wise one? Putting a guitar through another windshield? That proved extremely memorable, didn't it?"

Damien grins.

"Nah, but you are right, it was cool and I stand by it."

"No one said it was cool, asshole, and it was my guitar!" Johnny exclaims, punching Damien in the shoulder.

"Hey, hey, I bought you a new one, didn't I?" He yelps as they all stumble into the elevator.

As Shaun pries the boys apart, Phoebe's attention is drawn to a man who followed in after them. He has long blonde hair, an angular jaw, and bright blue eyes, matched with an almost sleepy expression that seems like it might have been permanently etched on his face. Almost instantly she has flashbacks to the two men back in Phoenix, her nerves scattering. Her fears abate a little, however, when she realizes the elevator now completely reeks of pot.

"Hey, are you guys, that uh..." He snaps his fingers and looks up at the ceiling while Johnny and Shaun lean forward, waiting for the next words to drop from his mouth. "That uh... Gun band? Think I saw you the other night."

"We are," Ophelia replies with a big Cheshire grin. "We are Gun-Band."

"Right on, man," he laughs, throwing them a thumbs-up. "You guys rock!"

Phoebe chuckles a little nervously, the ride getting only slightly awkward as the man stares off into nothing for a minute before finally pushing the button for his floor.

"I'm Kyle by the way. Here with my brother, in a band together, no big deal. We're playing tonight at a little hole in the wall down the street. For friends and some rad people, and you guys seem like pretty rad people. You should come check us out."

The group exchange apprehensive looks.

"I don't know," Shaun mumbles.

"There's gonna be a party after, and there'll be free beer 'cause the owner kinda skimps on payment. Promise we're not weird or anything, it's all above board."

Shaun raises his eyebrows and glances over at Ophelia, who is clearly considering the offer. Phoebe tries to get Damien's attention, but the look on his face says it's already too late.

"Where's the party at?"

"354 on Main, The Dixon. Show starts at 8, but feel free to show up whenever." He's clearly happy with their response, but his chilled out tone makes for a funny balance with his enthusiasm.

"Cool, sounds good to me," Damien says as the elevator dings on their floor. "I'll be there, don't know about the rest of these clowns though."

"No, I'm *definitely* going," Ophelia replies. "Need to fill the evening with something, after all."

"That goes for me too," Johnny announces, putting his hand on her shoulder.

Ophelia nods, and shrugs into a warm smile, leaning down and wrapping his arms around her.

"Sounds fun! Definitely better than sitting around a hotel room all night."

Phoebe glances up at Damien, anxiety bubbling in her chest, hoping he'll get the message. Going to a dive bar with a bunch of strangers for the night is not what she had in mind. Instead, he just smirks and gestures to her.

"She's coming too."

"Cool! See you guys tonight!" Kyle shouts, as everyone heads out toward their respective rooms.

"Is Troy going to find out?" Phoebe asks as she eyes the other band members nervously. None of them seem concerned, but they almost certainly have far less to be concerned *about*.

"Who cares," Damien shrugs. "He doesn't really have any say. Worst case we get a mean ol' talking to, but even he's pretty chill about our off-time."

Johnny flashes his reassuring smile at her.

"Yeah, our days off are just for us. Besides, he's probably going to spend most of his time in the hot tub downstairs drinking whiskey, maybe reading an old detective novel or something."

Damien lags back a bit, pulling her towards him for a kiss.

"You're not mad, are you?"

"I just don't know if it's a great idea. We're supposed to be careful in public, and we don't know these people… What if there's press there, or someone takes pictures or something?"

"Phoebe, it's not like they're a big band playing a huge venue or anything. Nobody is going to know who we are, let alone you. Besides, people'll be all over getting drinks and letting loose. We'll just be a couple on a fun date!"

"I just don't know if it's worth it. We shouldn't be taking risks."

He pushes their door open, turning to the side to let her into the room.

"You like keeping us a secret?"

She shrugs.

"I mean, sort of, yeah. I like that it keeps us safe."

Damien's expression slips into stony neutrality as she walks past him. The ominous click of the lock echoes through the room, making her heart beat a little faster.

"I don't."

He's leaning against the door, arms crossed.

"You don't what?"

He sighs.

The look in his eyes makes her wince.

"Pheebs, I get why you have to keep us from Brian, but a bunch of fucking stoners in some band aren't gonna say shit when they see us together."

He slinks toward her, sliding his arms around her waist.

"I want to be with you. I want people to know that you're my girl." He squeezes her tighter, and she can feel her pulse racing. "I mean, what's so wrong with that?"

"Like you said, I have to protect my job. But it's not just that, it's my reputation too."

She's just not ready for it yet, for the scrutiny, the fans, or for public opinion on her, all of those things that Erin warned her about. Right now what they have is safe and protected. It's their little version of domesticity, and opening things up doesn't just mean losing a part of that, it means putting all the rest at risk.

But he looks offended and pulls away, something less than anger but just as disconcerting flares in his eyes.

"Am I that bad to be seen with?" His voice cuts back at her like a razor.

"I didn't say that," she whispers. "Don't put words in my mouth."

"You kind of did, though, didn't you?" He shakes his head. "Your reputation, right? And I'm the one hurting it."

Phoebe closes the gap between them and grasps his hands in hers, deciding to take a softer approach. He's upset, she understands that. He's always made it clear he wants more than a secretive little love affair, and maybe he's starting to think that she doesn't.

"Damien, I love you." Her voice is soft, but firm. "I'm trying to protect us, to protect what we have. I couldn't stand it if everything got ruined."

His whole demeanor softens as he stares at her.

"I know, and I'm– I'm sorry, Pheebs. Sometimes I just get all up in my head, and well, everything you're saying–" He sighs. "This is usually the part where girls decide they want out."

Phoebe stands on her tiptoes to kiss him, her hand brushing his cheek.

"I don't."

Maybe he's right. Maybe it won't be so bad. It's just a little dive bar after all, with a nobody band. They can just relax and have another fun night out together.

"Alright, if we're going to this party you have to *promise me* that we keep it low-key. No stunts, nothing that has even the slightest chance of landing us in some local paper tomorrow, alright?"

"It's a promise," he whispers, pulling her in for a tight hug.

Damien gets so much joy out of the little bursts of freedom he creates for them, but it's these small, delicate moments that make her realize just how much she values their bubble of anonymity. It's more than keeping a secret now, it's being allowed to have the space to be sweet and vulnerable without someone shoving a camera in their face. It's not having their whole lives put under a microscope to be dissected.

It's the shield that keeps them whole.

Her typewriter clacks violently as she writes, her fingers moving at a break-neck pace. Inspiration comes in waves and tonight it's all that's carrying her, save for a bit of leftover coffee. She almost started to backslide on the party plans, wanting to stay in and work, but she knows damn well that the rest of the group won't let that happen. Luckily, she's found that rhythm in her work, one that she sometimes only hits late at night when everyone else is asleep.

She turns her head to the open balcony door, taking a small break from her writing as she watches Damien lounge on a patio chair. He's wearing nothing but his boxers and a pair of sunglasses, a cigarette between his lips. The scene may as well have been put together for a magazine cover-shoot, but for now it's just for her. Phoebe smiles as she watches him soak up the last dying rays of sunshine before the evening. This is it. These quiet little moments of togetherness, even apart. Along with everything else, in the midst of all the craziness and fun, this is what she wants the rest of her life to be.

Phoebe shakes herself and turns back to her article. She's working on balance; ensuring each band member gets their moment in the spotlight. It would be so easy for the ensemble to get lost beneath Damien, but she'd lose the full picture. With that in mind, there's so much she wants to write, but all of the off-the-record promises make it complicated to navigate. She has their trust, and she wouldn't break that for anything.

So she writes around their interviews, dissecting their words and intermingling them with process and their time on stage. The parts of them they're willing to share, blended with what they've shown her just by letting her be close. It'll be the first real behind the scenes look at how the band interacts, how they function, and Phoebe chuckles as she thinks back on all the old entertainment-rag speculation. Do they write their own songs? Were they put together by the studio? Do they even *like* each other? At the very least, she'll be able to put all that to rest.

The click-clacking of the typewriter becomes a steady rhythm as she works in between her final sips of coffee. Paragraphs turn to pages, feverishly typed out one after the other, until all of a sudden she feels a warm hand on her shoulder. Damien is hovering over her, and he lays a little kiss on the top of her head. The gesture pulls her smoothly out of her writing groove and into a smile.

"Hey now, I'm still working."

"I know, I know, but it's already 6:00. We gotta leave in an hour."

She blinks and glances up the clock. The last time she checked, it was only 4:00.

"How the fuck did I lose two hours?"

"You were in the zone, babydoll, that place you go when the juices start flowing." He laughs, and his hand slips beneath her chin. "You looked real cute."

"Hah, I doubt it. Probably had a face all scrunched up like this!" She crinkles her nose and glowers, but Damien only smiles back.

"Ah, ah, ah, no doubting me. I have proof."

He walks over to the nightstand and grabs two polaroids, grinning proudly as he hands them to her.

"I pilfered it from your suitcase. Turns out I'm an extremely talented thief as well. Who knew?"

She snorts as he places the photos in her hand.

"I didn't even notice!"

In the first, she's hunched forward in her chair, her nose scrunched up as she's reading over some line or quotation or something. There's a cigarette in her mouth, and her dark hair is a tangled mess around her head. Phoebe begins to laugh as she looks up at Damien.

"You think this is cute? This is literally the face I just made!"

"Hell yeah!" He laughs. "That's Journalist-face. Just means you're working hard."

She giggles, putting it aside to look at the second picture. In it, she's resting her head on her palm with her pile of notes strewn all around her. Her other hand hovers over the typewriter, like she's just figured out exactly what to write. The gentle slope of her nose, the way her lips stick out in a little pout, her brow slightly furrowed and laser-focused eyes... It's a good shot.

"Prettiest damn journalist I know," he murmurs.

He snaps up the photos, tucking them into a page of his own notebook.

"Alright, I'm gonna take a shower," he says, taking a single step away before spinning around and flashing a smile. "Wanna join me?"

She snorts, shaking her head.

"I really want to finish this page. Raincheck?"

"Of course. Everything worth doing is worth waiting for, after all."

A couple seconds into the shower and Damien is already singing to himself. Loudly. She shakes her head, fighting through the distraction, but she's surprised at how easy it is to get back into the groove, words starting to pour onto the page once more. Unfortunately, her focus is shattered again with the shrill ring of the telephone. Of course, there's always another distraction.

"Hello?"

"Miller." Her heart sinks at the sound of her slurred name as it spills out of his mouth. He's breathing heavily on the other end.

"Chris?"

"I figured it out. I figured **you** *out, Pheebs, and this whole thing you've got going on."*

The more he talks, the more drunk he sounds. She looks over her shoulder to make sure that Damien hasn't emerged from the bathroom. The door is still closed, and she can still hear him singing.

"Jesus Chris, you sound awful. Are you wasted?"

He belches. Phoebe feels like she's going to be sick, and not just from the sounds coming through the receiver.

"You– you're fucking Damien Bell. Aren't you?" Her blood runs cold. *"You are. I knew this would happen, y'know. Stuck around after that show, bet you thought I left? Too smart for any of you."*

She can feel the heat rising up under her skin, the sound of the shower thinning into a sharp whine. It's fear, yes, but stitched onto a more powerful rage than she's ever felt.

"Chris, you're going to hang up this fucking phone right now, and you're never going to contact me again. If you do that, and you get a little lucky, you might still have a job tomorrow."

Her voice is almost pure ice, with the tiniest hint of venom coating the edges, but his laughter on the other end of the line makes her dig her fingers into her thigh.

"Come on, Pheebs," he slurs, *"Tell me I'm right. It's gonna get out there, may as well be from me."*

He has no right to be calling her like this– and while he's drunk? Says a whole lot about him as a person, and as a journalist. This is how people destroy their integrity, and their professional relationships. Phoebe may be blurring the lines a bit, but she would never do something like this.

"I could tell Brian, think of that? Blow this whole thing open. People'd go nuts for a story like this. They're all starving for anything to do with Damien after those stupid fucking comments on TV. All anyone's talking about, the wild boy's mystery girl." He pauses, like he's giving her the chance to confess, but she doesn't take the bait. His laughter on the other end makes her skin crawl. *"I know it's you. I know it. That's just who you are."*

Phoebe can feel the air in the room get thick; it's like she's breathing through a straw. She wants to ask him why he's doing this, but that would give him the ammunition he needs. The best thing for her to do is to say nothing, to endure the taunts and figure things out later. She's so angry she can feel her body vibrating. Does he actually have anything? Is this just a drunken threat? Will he even remember this in the morning?

"I don't know what you're talking about. This is over."

She barely manages to spit the words out through clenched teeth.

"Come on, Pheebs! Give me something, for old time's sake! I'll make sure you come out of it looking–"

"Listen to me shitbag, if you *ever* call me again, if there's even a hint of you snooping around, forget about working. I'm going to make sure they won't recognize what's left of you."

"Phoebe–"

She slams the receiver down so hard her ears ring, slumping her head into her hands as the adrenaline pumps through her. Her throat is dry, and she realizes for the first time how hard she must have been holding onto the phone as color begins to return to her white knuckles.

As the sound of the shower stops and Damien's crooning gets a little clearer, she begins to calm herself down. She can't tell him, not yet. Maybe Chris will forget. He was so drunk, could he even string together a coherent pitch? But... did it even matter? Even a mild suggestion that they're together could change everything. It could sink her article if not her whole career, and smash them straight into the public eye. And what if their anonymity is what made it all work?

Maybe they would have to do something, but not tonight. It's Johnny and Erin's time, and she wasn't about to risk ruining their last evening together. Not when something so simple and small can fuck everything up.

Sometimes all it takes is a phone call.

Time After Time

THE DIXON

"Pheebs, I promise, you're gonna have a great time."

Damien's wearing a warm smile, and his voice is so reassuring.

"I know I just–" She sighs. "I dunno, it would have been nice to have a quiet night in."

The call from Chris had really set her off. Damien had coaxed her off the fence about the party before, but now all she can think about is every possible thing that could go wrong. They just need to make it through the night, let Erin and Johnny have their time together without any distractions. Then she can sit him down and have the talk, for real. She's been putting it off for too long.

Damien kisses her cheek.

"We'll have so much time for quiet nights. I really need to blow off some steam," he shoves her shoulder playfully. "We both do."

"Yeah, you're right. I probably only feel off because it's not really my scene, you know?"

"You're a rock journalist," he laughs. "This is a rock show! Besides, I've seen you let loose, so I know that's bullshit."

She purses her lips and stares up at him.

His grin is devilish.

"Just... please, let's have a fun, quiet night. No big stunts or anything, right? We really can't afford to make waves."

He laughs as he holds her, rocking her from side to side.

"You keep saying this stuff like I don't know!" He kisses her temple and then dips his head to nip at her earlobe. "I promise, I will not get *too* wasted, and there will be no incidents."

"Scout's honor?"

"Scout's honor. I'd never lie to you, Troop Leader."

Phoebe takes a look at herself in the mirrored walls of the elevator, and Damien takes the opportunity to pop the collar on her jacket..

"There, now you're fuckin' cool, dude."

Phoebe rolls her eyes, but can't contain her grin.

"Thanks, *dude*."

"You're welcome, *bro*."

Damien is all energy as they walk through the lobby, and she can't deny the mood is infectious. He's a master at getting her to think about anything but the bad stuff.

"You see, the crazy thing about being a lyrical genius with no peers is that it comes so naturally,"

"Sure, sure. So I'll just write down, 'born genius.' Does that work?"

"That's a great title for your article, actually," Damien quips as they meet up with the gang and pile into their limo.

The ride starts out quiet enough, but by the first red light Damien is up to his old antics, poking and prodding at the closest target he can get.

"What the hell, bro?!"

Damien cackles as Johnny tries to punch him in the crotch, the two struggling against their seatbelts.

"Boys!" Erin barks. "Behave yourselves! Damien, no harassment. Not even if it's Johnny."

"Oh, come on!" He groans. "Not even a little brotherly clock on the chin?"

"He couldn't take me," Johnny replies as they begin to settle. "Your hook is weak, Bell."

Damien raises his arm with a shit-eating grin and a maniacal look in his eye.

"Okay, then come and get some!"

Johnny goes to lunge for him, but Erin pulls him back by his hair as Ophelia and Shaun watch the show.

"It's like you don't even try to listen!" Erin barks.

Johnny frowns, exaggerating the forlorn and devastated expression on his face.

"You *know* he started it."

"Aww! Reed, don't take it so personally," Damien teases, flexing his arms. "Gotta listen to the ol' lady after all, she needs to keep you safe from these guns!"

"You'd better cut it out, too," Phoebe mutters.

Damien clutches his metaphorical pearls and scoffs.

"Me? I've been naught but a perfect gentleman, madam." Phoebe rolls her eyes, and Damien leans over, rubbing the tip of his nose against hers. "But even still, for you I'll go the extra mile."

The drive is about fifteen minutes, but it feels much longer, and with each turn or streetlight Phoebe can feel her anxiety balloon more and more. As they stop at yet another red light, she glances out the window to see a couple walk down the street holding hands, leaning up against each other. She lingers on them, somehow unable to look away.

"They're cute, huh?" She feels his arm wrap around her shoulder as his question cuts through her thoughts.

"Yeah," she whispers, letting her body sink into his.

"Maybe that can be us one day. Walking around, hanging out with friends. Just doing normal shit.".

"It will be," she whispers.

They'll make it. They just have to get through these early days. Get her article published then work it all out in the aftermath. They'll be free then, to just be together, with no more professional expectations or fears attached.

Just a little while longer.

People are already lingering around the entrance when they pull up to the bar. It's a dingy place, with a sign that's only partially lit and sagging to one side. A small group of teenagers with half-shaved heads and ratty clothes smash beer bottles a couple doors down, intermittently searching for half-used cigarette butts off of the ground.

Damien whistles.

"Damn, those dudes were right. This place is a shithole."

"Hey, we used to play places like this," Shaun reminds him. "And you still dress just like those kids at least twice a week. Never forget your roots, big guy."

"I've also seen you pick up used cigarettes to smoke." Johnny turns to Phoebe. "He did it like two days ago, you have *got* to fix this man."

Damien chuckles.

"Okay, okay. I made an observation, I didn't sign up for a roast."

"Wait, they canceled the roast?"

Shaun looks devastated as Damien gives him the finger, but Johnny walks right past them; something about this place has its hooks in him.

"Sometimes I miss playing these dive bars," he mutters.

"Yeah, me too dude," Damien sighs, patting Johnny in the back. "Simpler times."

"You guys can say whatever you want, but as for me, I don't miss the pint glasses with the dish soap at the bottom," Ophelia grumbles. "Taking a sip and getting a big hit of Sunlight along with it? It's beer, not a mixed fucking drink."

"God, how about the roaches?" Shaun mumbles.

As they head inside they're met with a crashing of drums and a sound that Phoebe can only describe as the guitar-equivalent of a wailing cat in heat. Shaun looks as if his skeleton is trying to crawl out of his body, like it's a personal attack on him and only him.

The three men on stage are enthusiastic at least, with Kyle and a man Phoebe assumes is his brother totally engrossed in their dueling guitars. The drummer looks entirely lost and is just thrashing against the cymbals.

Ophelia nods slowly, a little bemused by the complete lack of control on display.

"That's one way to do it I guess."

"I'm getting us some drinks!" Johnny shouts, motioning to the group. "Someone find us some seats, maybe somewhere in the back."

"What, you don't want to be up near the stage with the band?" Damien asks with a laugh.

Erin raises her eyebrows as a long feedback squeal makes practically everyone in the bar visibly cringe.

"You guys know what we like, don't fuck it up!" She yells over the noise.

She takes Phoebe's hand and the three of them walk to the back of the crowded room as the boys head to the bar. Despite how rough things are going, the guys on stage don't seem to care, and Phoebe kind of admires that. At the very least there must be something compelling about their energy, because the tiny bar is getting more and more packed by the minute. It's still a small affair, and no one's here looking for them, but Damien knows how to make a scene; with a crowd like this, it'd be easy to make this night all about Damien fucking Bell.

"Come on!" Erin exclaims, pulling on her sleeve. "There's a free table!"

She drags them to the furthest corner of the bar, dodging through small patches of people who are trying to carry on conversations on top of the assault from the stage. The three of them take their seats and Erin lets out a relaxed sigh, scanning the surrounding area with a big smile. Ophelia leans in and raises an inquisitive eyebrow at Erin.

"What?"

"You look really happy for someone who's stuck *here* tonight."

Erin rubs her hands, glancing quickly at Phoebe then down at the table. Phoebe looks back and forth between the two women, completely lost as to what's going on, but Erin doesn't hold out for long. She raises her head, her eyes shining with excitement.

"Well, something *may* have happened–"

"You're engaged?!" Ophelia practically screams, cutting her off.

"We got engaged *last* year," Erin laughs.

"Oh, right," Ophelia sighs. After a moment her eyes widen and she grins. "You're joining the band? Do you have a secret talent we don't know about?"

"Yeah, that's definitely it. I'm gonna play the triangle, right next to you. Better watch out."

Phoebe snickers.

"Great, another one gunning for my job. Well I'm not taking this lying down, you're in for the fight of your life, Campbell!"

Erin chuckles, fiddling with her fingers.

"I want to wait for the boys to get back before we announce the news, so just– oh! Speak of the devil!"

"Fitting," Phoebe chimes in as she spots Damien's grin from the crowd. Johnny and Shaun flank him, the three men clearly very pleased with themselves.

This is it, exactly what she hoped for. They're just a normal group of friends hanging out, and she and Damien are just like any other couple, out for a night on the town. They get to just be themselves, cringing at the noise and laughing at each other's terrible jokes, and not worrying about any of the other bullshit.

"Okay, Johnny, what the hell were you trying to say at the bar? That chick was screaming in my ear. I didn't hear a word."

Damien is drumming his hands on the table, impatiently waiting for an answer as Johnny quickly glances over at Erin, who grins and nods. He wraps his arm around her shoulder and kisses her on the cheek. They're both ecstatic.

"Erin and I have an announcement to make."

Everyone exchanges a look, brains churning with potential theories.

"You eloped," Shaun says.

Damien stands up suddenly, pointing a dramatic finger at the couple.

"No, no, Erin's pregnant!"

"Oh god, no!" Johnny and Erin shout in unison, before giggling at their shared reaction.

"This isn't a guessing game!" Johnny laughs, shaking his head, "and she's drinking. She wouldn't be drinking if she was pregnant. Use your brain, Bell, whatever's left of it at least."

Damien shrugs and lights a cigarette, pouting as it hangs from his lips.

"Okay, fine then, quit being so mysterious about it and spill."

Johnny stands up like he's prepared to make an eloquent speech, his hands waving dramatically.

"I'm an artist, Bell, and so it should be no surprise that I would take my time to tell you all, in the most–"

"We're going public!" Erin blurts out, her face absolutely glowing.

"You're... wait, what?!" Damien exclaims.

Johnny smiles, cupping his hands around Erin's face and giving her a big kiss. A massive cheer erupts from the table as everyone collapses in on the couple in a fit congratulations. Erin looks so happy, and Johnny has to hold back at least a couple tears. Phoebe can't stop smiling.

Witnessing this much joy in their openness gives her hope. Maybe, *maybe* this whole going public thing could work between her and Damien as well. Maybe they don't have to keep waiting. They'd still have to formulate a plan, get ahead of things, but every day increases the chances someone gets proof. The man in the elevator who caught a glimpse of them together, Chris and his not-so-paranoid ravings... but things could work, they could beat them and be free to live their lives.

Phoebe takes another drink, trying to wash down the rage she feels at the memory of Chris's drunken, slurred voice. His arrogance. She never really liked him much, but professional distaste morphed into pure hatred very quickly. He's a threat to everything that she's trying to build. She'll tell Damien tonight. They can start working on a plan right away. Together.

Johnny and Erin giggle, sharing a small moment of intimacy as the group sit back down in their seats. Soft, whispered words of love and affection float between them amidst the chaotic conversations flying across the table, each member of the band claiming they knew it was coming before anyone else. As their eyes meet, Phoebe swallows the urge to climb over it all and throw herself into Damien's arms. It used to be the kind of thing she wouldn't even consider.

And then he walked into her life.

"I believe that it may be time for a toast!" Shaun exclaims, raising his glass.

Damien winks at her as he raises his drink. The smallest gestures in public, even now, still give her butterflies. And there's that anxiety again, dragging itself up from underneath it all. Once they go public, even if they handle it right, will he get bored of her? Or could she get bored of him? Maybe, deep down, it's the secret that's making all this magic between them, the spontaneity and risk. Her smile falters a little.

"To Johnny and Erin!" Shaun shouts. "And, fuck it, to love!"

Phoebe snaps out of her spiral, pulling herself back up to the surface as everyone cheers in agreement. Glasses clink merrily and Damien tosses his whole whiskey back in a second. In that moment, his expression seems to her like one of pure and complete joy. She expected a hint of jealousy, some level of frustration about their own stunted freedom, but it's just not there. He's simply beaming as he glances from person to person around the table.

"I'm getting you guys shots!" He shouts. "Actually, I'm getting *everyone* shots!"

"Damien, we all have drinks!" Phoebe laughs.

"Yeah, but Pheebs, shots and drinks are two entirely different things."

"Oh yeah, professor?" She teases. "Please explain."

"Well, you see, a shot is a drink," he pauses dramatically, "but *smaller!*"

He flashes a toothy grin, laughing at his own terrible joke.

"Besides, who gives a shit! It's our night off, Johnny and Erin are finally free, we have to celebrate!" Damien practically falls out of his seat, rushing over to Johnny to immediately put him in a headlock. "I'm so fuckin' proud of you, dude!"

"Fuck off Bell, Jesus!"

As he holds Johnny with one arm, he points at the table one by one.

"Shots? Yes? Shots?"

"Fuck yeah!" Ophelia shouts. "Get the good shit!"

"I don't think they have the good shit," Johnny grunts, struggling out of Damien's grasp. "My guess is our choices are between battery acid and gasoline."

Damien starts out toward the bar before suddenly spinning around to face them. He throws out some finger guns, trying to moonwalk backward but quickly gives up.

"Battery acid it is!"

If You Leave Me Now

THE DIXON

Four shots in and Damien is still riding a level of high that she's only seen him reach in the aftermath of a sensational show. Not everyone is handling things quite as well, however, and as they all reach the final round of shots Johnny pipes up.

"Jesus, I don't think I can handle any more battery acid."

"Yeah, maybe we should switch to gasoline," Phoebe jokes.

Damien beams, looking around the table. Somehow he's even more ecstatic about the news than Johnny and Erin are. As he slams back his drink, a voice cuts through the crowd directed right at their table.

"Duuuuude!!"

Phoebe looks up to see Kyle stumbling toward them with a can of beer almost half-crushed in his fist. His brother is trailing behind him, both of them drunk off of their asses. Damien flashes them a big, lopsided smile.

"What's up, fellas!" He exclaims as he blows out a cloud of smoke. "Fancy seeing you here!"

"We didn't think you'd show!" Kyle slurs as they sidle up to the table, glancing down at the obscene amount of shot glasses and empty bottles.

"So, what did you guys think?"

"You guys have a... unique sound," Damien offers charitably.

Shaun snorts into his drink and turns around as Ophelia elbows him in the ribs. The brothers don't seem to notice.

"Hey, thanks dude!"

Damien stands up on his seat.

"Bartender! A round for these fine musicians over here!" His voice carries across the bar, despite the newly blaring jukebox.

"Come and get it yourself, big shot!" The bartender shouts.

"You want me to pour my own drinks?! I'm a rockstar, motherfucker!"

Heads begin to turn, along with Phoebe's stomach. The crowd laughs and the bartender grins, shaking his head.

"Yeah, and an asshole to boot!"

"You know what?" Damien shouts as he leaps up onto the table, kicking his empty glass over. "A round on me for everyone!"

Ophelia punches his ankle.

"Get down! You wanna get us kicked out?!"

It doesn't seem like Damien even hears her as his long hair shines beneath the dingy bar light. He made it clear it's not often that they get a day off to really let loose like this, and he seems to be making the most of it.

Phoebe tugs on his pant leg to get his attention.

"Damien, why don't you get down? This is a bad idea!"

He stretches out his arms, his tight black tank top riding up over his abs.

"Live a little, Pheebs!" He points at the bartender. "Hey! Did you hear me? We need those drinks!"

"Yeah, I'm workin' on it, you think I'm a goddamn wizard or somethin'? Now get off my damn table!"

Damien howls with laughter, leaping down as people begin to swarm around them. Phoebe can't help but begin to recede back into herself as he revels in the attention, their little slice of privacy gone for the evening.

It's less than a minute before Revolver's album is blasting from the jukebox, filling the little bar. The band cheers with the start of each song, and the entire bar joins in as everyone gets to their feet. Phoebe calls for Damien vainly over the noise, but he's lost in the moment, surrounded by a slew of newfound fans. After a few minutes of being jostled by the flow of patrons, he finds his way back to her.

"Come on, Phoebe, it's gonna be fine! These are cool people!"

He moves in quickly, clearly intending to kiss her right there, in front of everyone, but she pulls away just in time. The surprise on her face is quickly replaced by a cool glare and she shakes her head silently but firmly. He looks hurt at first, but thankfully, there's still some part of his brain that's working. He holds out his hand in an over-dramatic gesture, and Phoebe shakes it half-heartedly.

"Forgot for a second."

"I could tell," Phoebe replies as her eyes nervously scan the room.

"Don't worry, I got this. I'm a champion of subtlety."

They're pushed apart as more people swarm him, and he's whisked to the other side of the room before she has a chance to slip in another word. She watches as someone hands him another drink, and another, each one making her more and more nervous. Giving up breaking through the impenetrable wall of patrons, Phoebe heads back to their table where she finds Erin alone, waiting for her. She's ordered two glasses of seltzer with lime, handing one to Phoebe as she sits.

"Figured we needed a break from the Revolver circus."

"Thanks," Phoebe murmurs.

The seltzer is a little flat on first inspection, and she squeezes her lime into it in the hopes it'll improve things. People mill all around them, each one bubbling with excitement over the band, or at the very least the free drinks. Erin glances at her, brows knit together.

"You okay?"

"Just a little nervous," Phoebe confesses. "He's pretty drunk."

"I know. He tends to get carried away. It'll be okay though, I've got Johnny watching him."

Erin squeezes her shoulder and motions to the large crowd that's surrounded the band. They're all laughing and accepting drinks from fans. No one's fighting, no one's screaming. It's honestly pretty low-key all things considered.

"You can't be this anxious all the time, Phoebe. It's all just part of the job."

"I know, it's just—"

Erin leans in and gently takes her hand.

"He's got friends to calm him down if he gets out of hand. He's not gonna throw any punches tonight."

"God, a punch is the least of my worries right now."

People orbit around Damien like he's a planet. He's telling stories, knocking back more drinks, and howling with laughter as he smokes cigarette after cigarette.

"You should talk to him," Erin suggests. "You look like you might need to."

"Someone might see us," Phoebe mutters. "I can't risk it. Someone's bound to follow us outside, and the only privacy we can get is in a bathroom."

"Yeah, and that doesn't look too good," Erin chuckles.

And then Phoebe just sort of blurts it out.

"He wants to go public, so badly, and he's been pushing for it so hard– We've talked about being careful but he keeps just... doing shit like this."

"Oh."

Erin's clearly a little surprised, but recovers quickly.

"Well, obviously I get where you're coming from, but you won't be writing that article forever, right? Sooner or later you've got to..."

Phoebe nods, only half listening as she hears a chorus of drunken voices begin to crescendo. Damien leaps up onto a pool table near the back and starts leading a sing-a-long to one of Revolver's songs. His eyes lock with Phoebe's. Her heart is pounding and she can feel her fingernails digging into her palms, her lips pressed into a thin line as anxiety swarms her body.

A couple people turn around, looking for the focus of his attention. A few of them catch her eye. Or do they really? They're so drunk, but all she can think about is the phone call with Chris. What if he's here? What if *anyone* is here? She can already feel the stress rash breaking out on her chest. Her throat is tight, and her head spins. Damien starts to howl drunkenly along to his own voice as it blasts through the speakers. He's pointing right at her. She hides her face, desperate to get the fuck away from here.

"Phoebe, you good?" Erin asks. Her voice is full of concern.

She pulls her hands back and flashes Erin a tight-lipped smile.

"Yeah, totally fine." Phoebe replies. "Just gotta pee. I'll be right back."

She bolts for the back of the bar, cutting her way straight through the crowd like a scalpel. She reaches the bathroom and knocks on the door.

No answer.

She steps inside, locking the deadbolt behind her and taking a deep breath that quickly escalates into panicked gasps. The music outside seems to get louder, somehow making the walls thud like a beating heart. She wiggles her fingers and tries to calm herself down, feeling every part of her body pressing hard against the door just to be sure she's firmly locked in place.

It was a mistake to come here. Damien is pushing boundaries further and further, and the drunker he gets, the worse it's going to get. She puts her head in her hands and rubs her shoe nervously against her leg, her entire body wracked with anxiety.

And then comes the knock against the door.

"Pheebs?" It's his voice. "You in there?"

She steadies herself, taking a deep breath.

"Gimme a second."

Another breath, and another. Anything to slow her heart down.

"Open the dooooor!" He slurs. "There's nobody here!"

He's wasted. She's certain she can smell the alcohol on his breath even with a door between them.

"Please, Pheebs? Let me in?"

She flips the deadbolt. He's alone, leaning against the wall with one hand, a big goofy smile on his face. He probably thinks he looks suave. Any other night she might agree.

"Hey."

Phoebe pulls him inside and shuts the door, locking it.

"What are you doing?!" She hisses.

"Came to find you. Disappeared in the middle of my song. Not very nice." He's stumbling over his words, cheeks flushed.

"What happened to playing it cool, Damien? No big displays in public, remember? And now you're singing to me? Pointing right at me?"

His eyes widen, but he only grins, gesturing toward the door.

"D'you see a photographer out there? It's just the boys!"

"Just the boys? Are you serious? There are a shitload of people out there, and we don't know any of them!"

He sighs and runs a hand through his hair, momentarily dejected.

"Just trying to have a good time, Pheebs."

His face suddenly lights up again, full of enthusiasm.

"But it's a great night! Johnny and Erin? That's us! It could be us!"

"Jesus, Damien, I'm trying to keep my job."

He looks hurt and confused, stepping forward and cupping her face with one hand.

"Hey, hey," he coos. "C'mon, don't do that."

Her eyes sting with tears, feeling the words threatening to explode right out of her chest. Her teeth are clenched so hard that they hurt as he studies her face, his expression softened and sweet. She shakes her head. She has to stand her ground.

"Stop trying to make it into something that isn't a big deal! This isn't okay!" she exclaims, feeling herself start to choke up. "Singing to me? You don't think that tells people that there's something up with us?"

"It's *not* a big deal," he urges. "Phoebe, everyone there is fucking drunk, *I'm* fucking drunk. *You're* fucking drunk."

"Damien, the press is watching you like a hawk! You already dropped a hint on that morning show back in Portland, and now they show up before every gig. Just because you're dodging their questions doesn't mean they're not asking them!" She pauses, catching her breath. "We made a deal tonight, Damien. You promised we'd follow the rules, but you can't seem to even–" She shakes her head. "Do you even respect me?"

His eyes narrow, a storm gathering in them.

"How can you ask me that?"

"Because everything you've done tonight says you don't give a shit!"

The hurt that covers his face makes her heart crack in two.

"And when I gave you my fucking tags? You think that didn't mean anything? All our time together?"

"That's not–"

"Fuck this," he growls. "I'm outta here."

He turns to the door, but as he reaches for the latch he stops. In that moment of pause, she grasps the back of his arm.

"Damien, stop."

"Let me go."

"No, we can't– just not like this, okay?"

As her heart jackhammers against her ribs, threatening to shatter them, she watches him draw in a deep breath. He slumps against the wall.

"Pheebs, I'm sorry, I just– sometimes these parties get kind of crazy and..." He dips toward her, pressing up close to her ear. "...I mess up."

She almost laughs at the contradictions she feels from his mouth against her skin. She wants so badly for this to be over, to fall back into his arms and for it all to be okay. He backs her up against the wall, his arms caging her in.

"I said I was sorry, babydoll."

She wants so badly for this to be the solution, but it's not.

"You just want to fuck and make this go away," she whispers, tears welling up in her eyes.

He chuckles. He hasn't even noticed.

"Best part of a fight is making up," he mutters.

Just as his lips reach hers, she stiffens, turning her head away.

"Daisy," she says softly.

Damien's head snaps up, the immediate recognition of their safeword piercing his drunken haze.

"What?"

She slips under his arm and makes some space between them.

"Fucking in the bathroom isn't fixing this."

Damien's eyes drill into her.

"I'm just trying to make it right, Pheebs!" He's angry, but it might not even be at her. He looks confused, frustrated that he doesn't know how to fix something he didn't know was broken until moments ago. "I love you, I– I can't hide that."

"But you said you could, Damien. Even if it was just for a little while. You *promised*."

"And, what?" He bites back. "Don't you care about what I want?"

She gives his chest a sharp jab with her finger, her eyes blazing and her jaw twitching. Anger bubbles like acid in her chest, threatening to eat her from the inside out. How the fuck can he be so selfish?

"If we fuck this up I lose everything, Damien. My credibility, my job, *everything*."

"No one knows anyth–"

"Chris knows! He fucking thinks he does at least."

He stops, and for the first time all night he actually seems to slow down for more than a second to think.

"Who the fuck– Chris? That garbage writer?"

"Yeah, him."

"How the fuck–"

"He called me when you were in the shower tonight, drunk off his ass. He guessed some of it from that show in Phoenix. He was there, saw me in the dressing room, and we talked for a couple minutes. Guess it got its hooks in him. He stayed around, saw something he couldn't get out of his head. He's obsessed."

Damien's eyes go wide, anger flickering in them like a bonfire.

"You didn't think that was something I should know?"

The sharp edge to his voice makes her fury rear up again. Her teeth clench so hard she feels like they might shatter.

"He called *today*, and I didn't want to fuck up Erin's last night, you fucking asshole!" She's done holding back, he needs to know. "And you know what, honestly? I didn't think you could fucking deal with it! What were you going to do, go find him and beat the shit out of him?"

She's practically spitting at this point.

"That's a low fuckin' blow, Pheebs. You can't just hide shit from me and expect it to go away on its own. You can't lie your way out of this!"

"I'm not lying!"

"Not telling me is fucking lying!" He bites back.

"Well guess what? Some photographer saw us backstage in Vegas. I heard him chatting up his friend in front of me in our hotel elevator. He was talking about breaking a story on us, so thank fucking god he didn't recognize me. What if Chris and this guy meet up? Connect the dots? Damien, we might have been safe, we just had to wait until it was all over, but since you decided to-"

She catches herself and takes a ragged, deep breath.

This isn't a conversation, it's a screaming match.

"Look, okay... I don't want to fight. I know I should have told you about them, I just- there wasn't-"

His head drops and lets out a long shaky sigh.

"I don't want to fight either. It's just... a lot."

They stand facing each other for what feels like an eternity, both unsure what to say to fix things. Phoebe breaks the stalemate.

"Look, Damien, I know that you love me, and I love you. I love you more than anything, but I'm scared."

He tilts his head slightly, his eyes full of sadness.

"I'm scared that any night you could get wasted, have a great time, and the next morning we're in the paper, and that's it."

She can feel his thumb gliding along her cheekbone.

"I'm sorry, Pheebs," he whispers "I don't want to lose you."

"Then just... don't."

Damien nods slowly. He looks exhausted, and so is she. The intensity burned all the anger out of both of them and didn't leave much behind.

"How can I make it up to you?"

She takes a moment, a little dumbfounded with how it all just vaporized in seconds.

"To start off with, you can stop pointing at me while you sing in the damn bar."

"Done. No pointing. I won't even look at you." He salutes her.

She laughs a little, wiping some tears away.

"No, no, I like it when you look at me."

He kisses the tip of her nose. He smells like Jack Daniels and cigarettes.

"You got it, gorgeous. Anything else?"

"We can talk ground rules later. I need you to know, it's not that I don't want to go public with you. I do, it's..."

"Complicated," Damien finishes for her. "I get it. We'll talk about the Chris thing in the morning. We'll figure this all out together."

She nods a little shakily.

"Thanks for giving me another shot." He wraps his arms around her and pulls her in for a hug. "We're good, right Pheebs?"

"Yeah." She mumbles, leaning back into his chest. "Yeah, we're good."

Damien flicks his head toward the door and flashes her a wolfish smile.

"I'll buy you a drink. I can do that, right?"

Phoebe chuckles.

"That's one thing I doubt I could ever stop you from doing."

They head for the door and Damien peeks out.

"Coast is clear," he tells her, slinging his arm around her waist.

They're back to doing this sort of stuff in secret, taking their little moments where they can. She feels a pang of pain alongside the warm glow brought on by his touch. The second they reach the end of the hallway they separate, heading back into the party a couple feet apart. Everything's returned to normal, the patrons split back into little groups concentrated around the bar, or huddled in conversation. People are dancing, drinks are flowing, and the room is filled with smoke.

Damien winks at her over his shoulder.

"Time for that drink," he smiles.

"No strings attached."

In Too Deep

THE CRAWFORD HOTEL

"Oh! There's a cab!" Ophelia bounces up and down on the balls of her feet, waving her arm frantically. Phoebe can't help but be impressed. It's difficult to imagine a situation where she's *not* the most hyped-up member of the group.

"The cab can't hear you," Shaun laughs.

Ophelia elbows him in the ribs and he grunts.

"Hey, where did Johnny and Erin get off to?"

"Hotel," Damien mutters, in between puffs on his cigarette. "They wanted to bang it out one more time before Erin went home."

"It's called *making love*," Ophelia corrects him, raising her eyebrows in Phoebe's direction. "You should know."

Damien glances over at Phoebe with a little smirk, and she smiles back half-heartedly. The rest of the night had been a whirlwind, with no time to really get a feel for anything after their conversation. He kept buying her drinks, spending the whole time fawning over her, clearly as some kind of apology. As the hours dragged on Phoebe felt less and less like they had a handle on things, less like they actually resolved anything. Falling back to the same old patterns.

The worry sits in her gut, twisting tighter and tighter, weighing her down more with each passing second. It gets hard to breathe, hard to speak, hard to focus on anything but the downward spiral. They agreed to wait until morning, when their heads would be clearer, when they could say what they really needed to say, but she's terrified it won't go the way either of them wants.

When she was growing up her parents fought often, viciously but quietly. They shut each other out, sometimes literally shutting doors in the other's face, but more often simply freezing each other out for days on end. One time, on vacation to the Grand Canyon, they didn't speak for two whole days. Phoebe and her brother were always the go-betweens for them. It was infuriating, but it also built up a pattern of behavior in the two of them. It's only been in recent years that she's realized just how fucked up it all is, but knowing often isn't enough. Patterns are hard to break.

The cab pulls up to the curb and the four of them hop inside. Shaun sits in the front and Ophelia takes a window, with Phoebe and Damien jammed in beside each other, awkwardly trading smiles a couple times before drifting off into their own little worlds. Phoebe stares out the window as the cab takes off toward the hotel, trying and completely failing to get her mind off the inevitable conversation. His pinky rubs against hers and that rock in the pit of her stomach gets heavier. She knows what's coming, and she knows that she's going to be up half the night worrying about what to say. Her head keeps swimming, one chaotic thought bleeding into the next as Shaun and the cab driver chat.

"So, I'll just say it: I've never driven rock stars around before!"

"Well, we promise not to be too rowdy," Shaun chuckles.

"Maybe *you* do," Ophelia remarks with a grin. "I can't be contained."

Phoebe feels ice rushing through her veins, making her fingers and toes frigid while her chest and face heat up, and Damien leans over, clearly sensing her discomfort.

"You okay?"

She nods, silent.

"I love you," he whispers.

She forces a smile.

"I love you too."

The words come out clipped even though she doesn't mean them to. Damien's gaze clings to her, his brows knit together.

Are you sure?

The two return to their silence as the cab speeds through the city. Phoebe takes in the flashing lights, the sound of horns honking, watching as people stumble along streets full of boisterous laughter. The knot in her stomach twists and tangles into an even larger mass as she sees the hotel come into view. Shaun offers the driver a couple of wadded up bills, and he happily accepts as everyone piles out. Ophelia clings to Shaun, practically swinging off him with glee, and Damien seems prompted to reach for Phoebe's hand, but he pulls back at the last second as they reach the doors.

"Sorry," he murmurs under his breath. "Forgot, rules."

This time, Phoebe offers a small smile.

"It's okay."

It's always okay.

The ride up the elevator is quiet. Shaun and Ophelia snuggle up against each other, sharing exhausted kisses as Damien and Phoebe stare straight ahead. Shaun glances over at them as the elevator comes to a stop.

"Still keeping it secret, huh?"

"Yeah," Damien rasps, his jaw clenched.

Phoebe nods and Shaun smiles.

"Cool, cool. You two are stronger than me, that's for sure."

Damien stumbles a little and catches himself as the doors open, chuckling under his breath. Ophelia waves to the two of them as Shaun opens the door to their room, winking at her mischievously as she follows him inside. Phoebe smiles to herself and shakes her head, nearly bumping into Damien who's stopped in his tracks. He's frantic, looking around with his hands in his pockets.

"Ah, fuck, where..."

"What?" Phoebe asks.

"Lost m'key."

She sighs, "Damien, come on..."

His eyes flash with anger. It's brief, but it's there.

"I don't want to do this right now, Pheebs," he snaps.

She can feel the adrenaline shoot through her, a little too ready to push back. This is the other type of fight her parents would have, more active but just as cruel, where every little thing that goes wrong turns into ammunition to use against the other person. Of course none of it matters. Any other night she'd probably just laugh, he'd make a joke, and everything would be fine. Instead, her brain is screaming at him, how could he fuck this up, how hard is it not to lose a goddamn key?

She takes a breath.

"It's fine." she whispers, digging into her purse and pulling out her own key. "I've got mine. We're good."

Damien doesn't say a word as he stumbles inside and kicks off his shoes. They make a dull thunk as they hit the wall, and Phoebe instantly feels that same irritation spike again. She keeps herself cool as she slides off her own boots, just as his arms snake around her waist. His lips brush against her ear.

"Hey."

She doesn't move.

"Hi."

He lets out a haggard sigh, loosening his grip.

"Pheebs, come on."

"What?"

"Talk to me."

She wants to, but it's not right. Nothing they say right now will help. They might not even remember it in the morning.

"We can talk when we both have a clear head."

He groans and she turns around, her eyes narrowing.

"Damien, I'm serious."

"I know, I know, it's just... 'don't go to bed angry,' right?"

"I'm not angry, are you?"

"Seems like you are," he mumbles.

She takes a deep breath to steady herself as she looks up at him.

"I'm not angry, Damien. I just think we need to sleep on this. We can talk about it in the morning." She raises a brow. "Like we agreed to?"

He nods, a disappointed expression trickling across his face.

"Yeah, 'kay."

There's something new in his eyes, fear. It's strange to see in a man who's usually so sure of himself. She places her palm on his chest and gives him a fragile little smile.

"I promise it's fine, but we really need to sleep, okay?"

The two of them lay in the darkness, with only the sound of each other's breathing to fill space between their lingering tension. Damien's large frame wraps around her, his arm sliding along her waist, hand splayed out across her belly. He kisses her shoulder, and then the back of her neck.

"You're still my girl, right?"

Phoebe squeezes her eyes shut, tears coming on without warning.

"Yeah," she chokes. "I'm still your girl."

She half-expects him to climb on top of her. It's been an effective solution, using sex in place of communication, because it's easy. It's familiar. But the thing she's anticipating never comes. Damien wraps himself around her, and all she can hear is the steady sound of his breathing as he fades into sleep.

Tomorrow, she's going to shut down the whole idea of going public, at least for now. By the time they're ready, after the tour and everything is said and done, it'll be fine. She can even tweak the timeline, implying they really got to know each other after the article got published. Maybe in the studio, maybe just randomly meeting again in New York. At a party or something. She can make it work. No one has to know.

It will be *fine.*

She can dodge Brian's questions, and they can work out a story for the media. Damien is an expert in that arena. They can do this. It'll be okay.

Phoebe struggles to swallow, her throat is ragged.

She'll take out the really personal details from her article, shift the focus off of Damien so it doesn't look like she's some googly-eyed teenager who's fucking the frontman.

She gently lifts Damien's arm off of her. He rolls onto his back and huffs before turning all the way over to face the wall, a soft snore spilling from his lips. Her toes sink into the carpet and she pushes herself off of the bed, heading for the bathroom. Her head is spinning, the *room* is spinning. She's sweating. Her body is trying to push the poison out of her system. She can taste it in the back of her throat as she kneels down in front of the toilet. She takes a deep breath, lurching as she empties the contents of her stomach.

She flushes the toilet, splashing her face with water from the sink before stumbling to the floor, resting her head on her arm. All she can taste is vomit tinged distinctly with juniper. She closes her eyes.

"Fuck."

She runs through her affirmations again. It'll be okay. She's smart. She can work around this. They both can. She won't lose her job. She won't lose–

"Pheebs?"

Damien's voice is a little shaky as he lingers in the doorway.

"I thought you were asleep."

"Heard you ralphing in here."

She laughs.

"Ralphing, that's– Yeah, sorry."

"S'okay," he mutters, rubbing his eyes.

"You need the bathroom?"

"Nah, just wanted to be sure you were okay."

She nods.

"Too much gin."

Damien stumbles to the counter, knocking some things over in the dark.

She's fought so hard to keep them a secret, for that chance to be normal. As normal as anyone could be in these circumstances. But she knows that they're in a bubble, insulated by this tour that's nothing like real life. So what comes after this? How do they navigate the next storm if they can't even see it?

Damien fills up a glass with water and hands it to her, their fingers bumping together. They share a little laugh before she downs it, immediately feeling her body swell.

"Sure you're gonna be okay?"

"Yeah. I'm coming back to bed, I just need another minute."

He nods, crouching down and kissing her forehead.

"I love you."

They're in this strange state of limbo, both of them still too fucked up to properly say what needs to be said. He fills a glass for himself and stumbles out of the room, hitting the doorframe with his shoulder on the way out.

"I love you too."

Leaning against the countertop, she makes a mental inventory of all of the things she's afraid of, all of the ways that this could go wrong. Tomorrow, she's going to say them all out loud, one by one. They'll talk it all out, figure it all out together. They'll make real promises and find solutions. And it'll all be okay. They'll be okay.

All they have to do is make it through the night.

Angie

THE CRAWFORD HOTEL

Phoebe's been up for hours, her hangover clinging to her as tightly as it can, unwilling to let go as she tries to focus on anything but the chaos of the previous night. She's thrown on a pair of his boxers and one of his shirts that hangs loosely off her, barely covering her hips. She takes a long drag of the last of her cigarette, letting the smoke seep out from between her lips before crushing it in the ashtray.

"Pheebs."

Damien's rasp of a voice hits her eardrums and her whole body stiffens.

"We gotta talk about this."

He looks so rough she could laugh out loud. It's strange to see him in such a different light. Any other morning she would have said that he looked rugged, unkempt but compelling, but now all she sees are red-rimmed eyes and pure exhaustion.

"Yeah," she nods, getting up from her chair. "We do."

He clasps his hands in his lap, eyes cast down as Phoebe joins him on the bed. She reaches for his hands. Maybe being closer will help.

"Look, I want to do this again. Sober, this time." He chews his lip, his expression completely vulnerable. He looks like he could break any second. "I'm *really* sorry about last night."

It would be the easiest thing to shrug it off. He was just drunk, they could forget all about it and move on, but there's been something nagging at her since she woke up this morning.

"It wasn't right."

"I know, I know I fucked up. That's why I'm apologizing."

She shakes her head, struggling to find the words.

"You bulldozed me, just pushed right past all our problems. You've been doing it since things between us started to get intense."

She sighs.

"Since we met, really."

"What do you mean I bulldozed you?"

He's actually much calmer than she expected him to be.

"You come up with your own plans for how we'll handle things, do whatever you want when we're out together. You make all the decisions, and you do it without talking to me."

"Phoebe–"

"You did it last night. You got up on that table and practically told the whole bar we're together."

"I was drunk!"

"That's not an excuse! When you do stuff like that, when we've explicitly talked about keeping quiet, being careful, you're telling me that you don't respect me."

She breathes in deeply, trying to center herself. It doesn't need to be a big blowout or a fight. It just needs to be clear.

"I know that you love me, Damien, you've made that obvious. I also know you like to be in charge. You want to make sure every little thing goes right, to take care of it all for the both of us, but it doesn't work that way. You have to share that responsibility with me. I need to know my input gets respected."

He looks confused, and Phoebe tries to get her bearings.

Be honest. Be clear.

"I'm not saying that your feelings don't matter, but your feelings have *dominated* this relationship. I think it's time to make room for mine as well."

He nods.

That's it, just nods.

Phoebe feels like she's hanging off of the edge of a cliff. She needs him to say something, and he's just staring at her.

"Damien, please say something to me."

She's waiting for the eruption. The anger. The defensiveness.

"I didn't– I didn't realize I was doing that. I was just so fucking happy last night. With you, with the whole Johnny and Erin thing, that I didn't..."

"Think about me?"

He puts his head in his hands.

"I've been trying to tell you about how scared I am over and over again, that we need to take this all more seriously."

"But you kept Chris's phone call from me. And those photographers."

"And that was my mistake," she admits. "I should have pushed harder, but I did try to tell you. I tried when we were in Phoenix, and you said we could talk about it later. I tried again at the restaurant, too, but you just had more pressing things on your mind."

He sniffles, wiping quickly forming tears away with his wrist.

"So... is that it? You're breaking up with me?"

She's stunned. Where did that even come from?

"No, Damien, that's not what I'm saying at all. I'm trying to get you to listen to me when I'm telling you how I feel! Why would you think I was breaking up with you?"

"This is just... it's the part where people leave."

He sounds crushed, still bracing for a wound that's not coming.

"Damien, I'm not ending things with you. I *love* you." She leans in close, squeezing his hands. "I need you to understand that."

"I'm sorry, I– I didn't mean to make this about me–" His head drops, resting on her chest. She can feel him shaking as he tries to slow his breathing.

"I get it," she whispers, running her hands through his hair. "This is good. We need to get everything out on the table, right? This is healthy."

He laughs, still sniffling a little.

"I guess I've never done something this healthy before."

Phoebe smiles as she cups his face in her hands.

"I promise, it'll all be okay. We'll get through this as long as we communicate. We work together."

She leans forward and presses her lips against his in the silence. His hand drops to her waist and he pulls her toward him so that she's forced to climb into his lap. She can feel a beat of time pass by where she's completely happy to let all of their problems melt away, but as it passes she drops her head with a wry smile.

"We're doing it again."

"What?"

"Trying to fix things by having sex." She straightens up. "We have to get through this whole thing."

"I just thought we were done."

"Damien, can you–" Phoebe takes a deep breath. "Please, I need you to take this seriously."

"I am!"

"Okay, well I've laid all of my cards on the table. You know where I'm coming from, now I need to know how you feel about all of this. I don't just want you to smile and nod and say you agree. You told me you were on-board with being inconspicuous a dozen times and look how that turned out."

Damien runs his fingers through her hair with a heavy sigh.

"All on the table?"

"Yes," she replies.

"Okay," he nods. "You're right. I didn't respect our promise enough, and that's going to change. I'll keep us a secret, out of respect for you and for your job. If I fuck that up again, you'll have every right to walk out that door."

A wave of relief runs over her. As long as he understands, they can–

"But Pheebs, even if we do that, we haven't solved the real problem."

She frowns.

"What problem?"

"The end. When the tour's all over. Think about it, what are we going to do when it's done? We both agreed we don't want this to stop, it *can't* stop. I love you too fucking much to let you go, and I know you feel the same way." He smiles, shaking his head in exasperation. "But that's the problem, people *will* find out."

Phoebe swallows, running through her little list again.

"I can fabricate a timeline, make it all make sense. Brian will never–"

"No, you can't. People have seen us, Pheebs. You can't just wish that part away. That asshole Chris knows, that guy in Phoenix who saw me with you... this is going to get out, sooner or later. I know how this tune goes, all it takes is for a few people to talk to each other."

It's all stacking up like a pile of bricks on her chest.

"We need to get ahead of it," Damien says softly. "Your plan to make up a timeline and try to hide us behind a bunch of bullshit, it isn't going to work out the way you think it is. You work with journalists, and journalists are smart. More importantly, they're nosy, and the way you're writing your article–"

"Then I'll fix it! I can still edit the article, it's not a big deal."

She's floundering, scrambling for an answer that she knows she doesn't have. Deep down, she knew this was an inevitability.

"No, Pheebs."

He sighs, pinching the bridge of his nose.

"I need you to listen to what I have to say. It's not just the way that you're writing about me, all that softness and vulnerability. Sure, there's an intimacy there that you can't just achieve through an interview, and sure people are going to pick up on that, but that's not the problem. Even if you change the article, even if you somehow turn it into a cold and calculated look at the band, people will see your name on it. They'll see Phoebe Miller printed next to an article on Damien Bell and his band, and you know what they'll see next?"

Phoebe rubs the back of her neck, pinching at the skin. The anxiety clings to her like sweat. No matter how much she shifts and wriggles, she can't get away from it.

"They'll see us in the paper, some rag, or even in person at a show. They'll see us together, officially, even if we never announce it. And suddenly your name on that article? It calls everything into question. Your credibility, Titanium's, Brian's... all of it. And it won't even matter if any of it's legit. It won't matter what you wrote. The tabloids will only care about the newest headline, the one that says you fucked me for a story."

Phoebe's fingernails dig into the back of her neck like knives. Maybe they waited too long. Could they have worked this all out earlier if they just came clean? Because he's right. He's right about how her peers would react, and anyone looking for a story. There was no dodging the fallout, even if they managed to stave it off for as long as they could.

"And that's the thing Pheebs, it's not going to be me who gets hit. I'm not going to be the one under public scrutiny, not for long at least. They're going to come after you, and you're not gonna get a chance to tell your side of it."

She leans against him as they let silence retake the room, and for a long while the only sound is their own measured breathing.

"Erin said the same thing. It's what Johnny was worried about."

"Yeah," Damien whispers. "It's what they've been arguing about for years. Look, when this thing with us blows up and hits the press, I'll be there for you, and I'll shield you from as much as I can." She looks up at him and watches a small, but cocky smirk spread across his face. "If that's the way it goes down, the least I can do is punch as many journalists as I can along the way."

Phoebe laughs as she rests her head in the crook of his arm.

"You can't punch everyone."

"I can sure try." His thumb brushes against the back of her neck. "I'll do anything for you Pheebs, I will, but you have to know that putting off the inevitable doesn't solve anything. It does buy us a bit of time, but with every week that goes by we're just giving them more to dig up. They get to call you a fraud, a liar... worse."

Phoebe plays with her dog tags. She hates that he's right.

"I don't know what else to do," she whispers. "Brian's going to kill me."

"He's going to freak out either way. Once the tour is over, as far as your boss is concerned, so is our professional relationship. You move on with your life, I move on with mine. That's what he thinks is going to happen. If we get found out he'll have to protect the publication, and who could blame him? There's a hundred different ways this goes down, and they all end with some stranger telling the rest of the world what our relationship is, what it means."

There's an alternative, at least sort of. What he's wanted all along.

"You still want to go public," she murmurs.

Damien closes his eyes, dipping down to kiss her forehead.

"It's like I said: going forward, if you want to keep this a secret, I'll support that. If you want to go public, I support that too. This is just the problem as I see it, my cards on the table."

She groans, lifting herself up to meet his eyes.

"Damien, can we make a deal? For real this time?"

"Of course."

"The next time something like this comes up, whatever we're doing, we talk about it right away, instead of putting it off until it all explodes."

Damien nods, a sad smile on his face.

"I can get on board with that. I never want to fight like this again if we can help it. Jesus, my parents used to fight so fucking much when I was a kid. I hated it."

"I'll try to be more honest with you, too. I'm sorry I didn't come to you with some of this earlier. You made it so easy to want to push it all aside."

"I get it, this is all new to you. Trust me, even if you've been doing it for a while, some of this stuff doesn't get any easier to deal with."

As they hold each other, Phoebe can feel him still slowly relaxing, his breathing returning to normal. He hasn't fully gotten over his panic from earlier.

"You really thought I was going to break up with you?"

He laughs, shaking his head.

"Yeah, I was so sure. And then we just talked it all out. I feel pretty stupid right about now."

The next words come out faster than she intends, straight past her normal filter of consideration.

"Is that how things ended with–"

She immediately regrets the aborted question.

"Emily, yeah. Similar conversation, too."

She holds him tight, struggling for a moment with what to say next.

"You must have really loved her."

He sighs.

"People were starting to get suspicious, it was a few months on, and she... well, she couldn't take the heat." He nods to himself, a silent affirmation. "I understood, even back then. It's fair, you know? I met her on the road at some bar on a day off, and she got swept up in everything so quickly. It started out as a fling but it just built and built and built. This... whole thing, the cameras, the press, the fans. It's not for everyone. She had a life, a normal life, and she went back to it."

"Do you still talk to her?"

"Saw her right before we left for the tour. She's dating some stock broker, working in fashion now." His smile is warm, genuine. "She's happy, and I'm really glad for that. Me, I was fucking miserable when we broke up, and after that I just kind of figured I'd end up alone. I don't think we were built to be under a microscope all the time, and I can't be mad at anyone who wants to avoid it."

Phoebe nods. Even Johnny and Erin had a rough time making it work, and they may as well have been star-crossed lovers.

"There's really not a lot of space to breathe."

"Definitely not," he chuckles to himself. "Some people say it comes with the territory. Who the fuck knows, maybe they're right and we're all just a bunch of whiners."

In the tiny amount of time she's spent involved in it, even just thinking about it, Phoebe's found the entire thing absolutely draining. She can't imagine what it must feel like full-time.

"I think it's the way we put people on pedestals that's the real problem. God help you if you want to avoid the whole thing, because then? Well, you're probably a freak, and they dig even harder."

"Yeah, you don't get the space to be a human being. It's a real killer for relationships sometimes." He grins. "In my personal experience at least."

It clearly haunts him, but it's his normal now. Just another consequence of the job.

"I'm sorry I scared you," she whispers.

He shakes his head with a shrug.

"This is my baggage. It's like I said, I was just preparing myself for the worst."

"Well, you don't have to anymore." She pushes him down onto the bed, pinning his hands above his head. "Because it's not happening with us."

"What are you up to, sweets?"

Somehow even the gentle purr of his voice is enough to set her off. She places gentle kisses on his cheek, down his neck, and nips at his collarbone.

"Making you feel better."

"It's good medicine, doc, but I thought we had rules for this sort of thing."

"This is all within the rules. We fought, we talked it all out, and *now* we get to have the makeup sex."

He laughs.

"Ohhhh, see I had some of that mixed up! I'll remember for next time."

Phoebe hums as she feels his cock pressing up against her, wiggling her hips and grinds on top of it.

"Really, it's the only good part of an argument."

Phoebe looks at him hungrily, tracing her finger along his chest and down toward his waist.

"Let's say we skip the fighting from now on and just get right to the good stuff, what do you say?"

Maybe it was a little fucked up, but she didn't care. They talked it out, they did what good couples are supposed to do. Now it was time for the reward.

The kiss is soft at first, delicate, saying everything that they've already said and so much more. Their problems are beneath them now, still a present danger, but one they get to safely play above. Phoebe presses harder against his lips, and the softness melts away as she releases his arms and lets them wrap around her. She feels warm. Protected.

He rolls her onto her back, leaving a trail of his own kisses down her neck, sliding low and dragging her boxers down to give her a sloppy bite on her inner-thigh. One of his hands wanders beneath the soft fabric of her shirt and her eyelids flutter. He's memorized her body, exactly where to touch her to make her melt.

"How do you want it?" His voice is still raspy from a rough sleep.

"Softer today," she breathes. "Just Damien and Phoebe."

"Just what I was hoping you'd say."

Phoebe feels the goosebumps rushing down her body, her breath hitching in her chest as he tugs at the hem of her shirt.

"First thing's first, this has gotta go, babydoll. I don't want anything else between us today."

She giggles as he lifts her up, helping her shed her shirt and tossing it casually aside before he pushes her back onto the bed. He slips the boxers the rest of the way down her legs, moving himself on top of her. He pushes the dog tags aside, biting down softly on one of her nipples as she can feel his cock playfully pressing against her lips.

"Damien, please."

He stops, his body hanging directly above her.

"Please what?"

"Ugh, don't make me– No teasing, just please fuck me," she begs.

His eyes are bright, his body lit by a small sliver of sunlight that spills in from the cracks in the curtains.

"I want to warm you up first."

She nods, pushing his hair back with one hand and forcing his head lower and lower until his mouth is hovering just above her hips. Phoebe closes her eyes as one of his hands links with hers, and she quivers at the sensation of the soft bites along her thigh. She holds herself still as he licks a long and truly agonizing line up the center of her cunt, ending with a playful flick against her clit. Phoebe's legs wrap around him like ribbons as she releases his head, pulling herself even closer. Damien doesn't waste any time, wrapping his lips around her clit and sucking gently but firmly.

"Damien– Oh Fuck!"

The sensation is addicting, a fire consuming every thought in her head as he devours her in turn. She begins to moan, louder and louder as his tongue slides and swirls around her clit at a carefully measured pace. The sheets rustle and shift beneath her body as he pushes her, closer and closer to her climax until she's right there, her muscles coiled and ready to release, her breathing heavy as she strains against him.

And then it all stops, and all she's left with is that deep ache and the sound of her own heart hammering in her ears.

"Fuck!" She wails. "Damien!"

She can feel him pull away before crawling over top of her, his arms caging her in. His eyes are intense, digging into hers as he stares her down like a starving animal. His fingers find the chain of the dog tags around her neck and he twists them, gently in his hand.

"You're desperate, aren't you?"

She nods.

He licks his lips.

"Tell me how badly you need me."

She glares up at him, grabbing one of his wrists tight in her hand.

"Damien, if you don't start fucking me right now, I'm going to throw you on the ground and do it myself."

A big smile spreads across his face.

"I love a woman who knows what she wants."

"Then shut up and fuck me!"

He gets up on his knees, grabbing a condom from the nightstand and rolls it onto his cock, playfully dropping the used wrapper on her stomach before sliding back down.

"Aw, we're not fighting again, are we?" He begins to push inside of her, and Phoebe takes a breath, relaxing her body as he pushes her lower lips apart. She's so wet that he could just slide right inside of her, but he doesn't. The pace is agonizingly slow and she loves it. He brushes his knuckles against her cheek, a devilish smile on his face and a glint in his eyes. "Because this doesn't *feel* like we're fighting again. Not to me at least."

"You're *such* an asshole."

He presses his forehead to hers.

"I know, it's why you love me."

"Mmm. True."

Her eyes flutter shut and her legs clench tighter around his waist as he pushes deeper. Damien kisses her on the forehead as he tests her limits, bottoming out as slowly as humanly possible just to torture her. Phoebe's mouth hangs open as she lets out a ragged groan.

"You can take it, sweetheart." He grins. "This is what you wanted, isn't it?"

He doesn't even wait for a reply, starting to pump his hips as he captures her in another kiss, fiery and sweet all at the same time. She rakes her fingernails down his back, leaving deep red marks behind as he fucks her, the two acts equally slow, equally deep. He was right, it's just like she wanted. Her limbs feel like they're made of jelly, and she quivers beneath him as he starts to rock his hips, bumping up against her G-spot with each stroke. Her legs rest up against his shoulders, pressed close enough together to make everything even more snug.

It's like she's desperately trying to find an anchor, to lock herself to him with no chance of escape. Her breathing gets even more erratic, with little whines slipping out of her mouth as Damien leans forward, his lips pressing against her ear.

"Perfect," he whispers. "You're being such a good girl."

Their bodies move in tandem, and Phoebe feels nothing but passion and love. That either of them thought this could *just* be sex seems crazy to her now.

"Faster," she pleads. "I'm so close."

"You're gonna come for me?"

"Yes, yes, please watch me come!"

Damien leans back as he begins to buck against her faster, each thrust slapping his body right up against her swollen clit. The pressure building in the pit of her stomach is overwhelming, and the headboard thumps against the wall as the sound of their muffled moans fill the room. Her cunt clenches around him and he cries out as he leans into her; she clings to him like a life raft in a storm as she feels the thick ropes of muscle in his back straining beneath her touch.

"I'm so close," she wails. "I'm– Oh fuck! Damien!"

"I can't–" His voice breaks, each thrust somehow harder and deeper.

A wave of heat rushes through her, trembling as her fingernails rake down his biceps. She cries out as she feels Damien's hips slam to a stop with one final push. He comes with a rough and ragged grunt, grinding against her in a desperate and impossible bid to push even closer together.

The room is almost silent as he collapses, with only the sounds of their heavy breathing filling the void as she holds him tight. She kisses his shoulder, his neck, his cheek, and Damien begins to shudder with laughter.

"Well, It's safe to say I hate fighting, but I *loved* that."

She snorts as he lifts his head, rubbing his nose giddily against hers.

"Me too," she agrees, staring into his eyes.

It could work. They could make it work. She'd figure it out. She had to.

"You need anything?" He asks. "Water? Food? Coffee?"

She grimaces, noticing for the first time that day just how hungry she is. The whole process was exhausting. She's spent, but it's been worth it.

"I might have to go for all three."

Damien grins.

"For my girl? Anything."

Songbird

The Crawford Hotel

"Oh! Oh! Look at this!"

Damien's pointing at the TV, cranking the volume as he takes a big bite out of his burger. He landed on Revolver's earliest music video, apparently still getting airplay on MTV even after all this time. He kisses her on the temple and wraps his arm around her.

"They made us shoot this at like 5:00am," Damien snorts. He gestures to a shot of the band getting out of a limousine, every member dressed like they're in a bad Poison cover-band. Suddenly, the shot shifts to a mob of fans who look so exhausted that even calling them 'fans' felt like a bit of an overstatement.

"Why do they look so, uh..."

"We had maybe two fans at this point!" He hangs his head as his shoulders shake with laughter. "The label had to pay people to be there for the shoot, and half of them didn't even show up. They had to do these weird edits to make it look like there were dozens and dozens of people but I don't think we could have had more than ten." He leans forward, pointing directly at the screen before turning back and beaming. "Here, look, you can see this guy in like five different outfits in the video! Keep an eye out for him, I remember Johnny was so fuckin' embarrassed."

Phoebe snorts, shaking her head.

"Everyone starts somewhere, right?"

The band looks so much different than they do now, none of them having a clue how they wanted to present themselves. Or maybe it was just the studio trying out some really bad gimmicks. Regardless, they were clearly enjoying the moment, just a bunch of kids on TV for the first time. She glances over at Damien who's beaming with pride as he bobs his head to the music.

"You know, this video isn't so bad," he chuckles.

"I like it. It has a lot of heart."

"Johnny wants the film burned, you know. Still petitions the studio from time to time."

"Aww, no! I think you guys look cute."

"Cute?" Damien jumps to his feet, raising an eyebrow to match his impish smile. "Rock stars aren't cute, that's what you're here for."

Phoebe pushes him away, struggling not to laugh.

"Oh god, Damien, that was so cheesy!"

"It was not! It was a great line!"

It doesn't matter where they are, or what they're doing, Phoebe feels at home when she's with him. Even in their most chaotic and fucked up moments, it's worth the work to fix things. To stay together.

"You feel better? About the whole thing last night?" His smile hasn't faltered, but she can tell it's still a sensitive subject. He really did think she was going to get up and leave. He was so afraid.

"Yeah. It felt good to get that stuff out."

"We really needed it," he agrees.

There's still sadness lingering in his eyes and Phoebe tilts her head, silently trying to pull the next sentence out of him. Her fingertips brush against his bare chest and he grasps her wrist, his hand slipping under hers to cradle it as he kisses her fingers.

"I'm sorry I was such a dick, Pheebs. I wish I could have–"

"No more sorries." She leans over and rests her head on his shoulder, snuggling up as close as she can. "I'm outlawing them."

"Outlawing?!" He laughs. "You're really taking charge, aren't you miss Miller!"

She smiles to herself as she feels him relax against her.

"It's all good, Damien. We're good."

"Okay," he breathes. "But you'll think about what I told you, right?"

She nods her head slowly.

She's been avoiding thinking about it all morning.

"Yeah. Of course I will."

"Promise me," he says softly. "You can't just backburner this, Pheebs."

"I know," she whispers. "I just… I need time."

"And I can give it to you, as much as I can squeeze out, but…"

She looks up at him, dressed for the show tonight. There's makeup smeared underneath his eyes, his hair wildly tamed; he's supposed to look aggressive, but all she sees is the man who fell to pieces at her feet. Not once did she expect to see him broken as he was back then.

"Nevermind, I'm just rambling. You get it."

She runs her fingers through his hair.

"Thank you."

He kisses her, first softly on the lips and again on her cheek, and once more before breaking away.

"You're sure you don't want to swing by before the show?"

"That's the tough part of being on a paid vacation with my rockstar boyfriend, every once in a while I have to actually get some writing done."

She'd let herself fall behind on the article, over and over, and this would be the perfect time to prove to them both she could make it work. She'd force it into whatever shape she needed to get them safely through this process.

"I want to get a rough draft sent out to Brian and re-work some stuff. You know, punch it up and get everything into shape."

"Oh, so you're cutting the part about my huge cock after all? That's fine, I guess. Can't have folks getting too jealous."

She throws her pillow at him, nearly knocking what was left of his burger onto the floor.

"What's wrong, I thought you liked talking about my cock. Should I be worried? Has something changed?"

"Just keep talking it up. I might have to remove it and bring it back to the office as evidence."

"Whoah, okay, okay, I surrender!"

At least a quarter of the article is finished, with a mountain of notes and transcriptions sitting next to her typewriter. She's amazed she found time to work at all these last couple days, but tonight she wants to see if she can hammer out the frame, a solid draft. She'll pull back, be more objective. She'll present a more removed view of Damien and the band, a safer one. No one'll be able to tell.

Suddenly, Phoebe sees Damien recoil out of the corner of her eye.

"Ugh! God! Fuck that!"

She cranes her neck and just barely makes out a crumpled pile of leather pants, his eyes bugging out as he leans in to take what must be the second big whiff. He gags.

"When's the last time you cleaned those?"

"Wait, you're telling me you're supposed to clean them?"

His eyes are bright, well-matched with his classic shit-eating grin. She knows it's bait, but it's fun to take.

"Damien Bell, that is so disgusting, I wish I knew your middle name so I could sound even more disappointed."

"Ah, well we can't have any more secrets. Damien James Bell, at your service."

She smiles, glancing off to the side.

"James... I like that."

"So in the name of complete and total honesty: what's yours?"

He pulls a Mötley Crüe t-shirt over his head. There's a big rip in the front, carefully placed to perfectly highlight his abs of course.

"It's Lynn." She pauses. "It's actually my mom's middle name."

"That's a cute one. You like it?"

She shrugs.

"I'd like it more if my mom weren't so..."

He chuckles.

"Believe me, I get it."

Damien strides toward her, cupping her face in his hands.

"You *are* coming to the show, right?"

"Wouldn't miss it for the world."

He presses his lips against hers for a delicate kiss and she can't help but think back to their first time, way back in that dressing room in California. Back then they had built up such intensity, so much tension sitting between the two of them, that the second their lips met it was like a bomb went off; it all but obliterated her. But this was different, like an all-consuming wave that could crush her in an instant but crashes around her instead, leaving her safe and warm in the center.

Damien breaks the kiss and lets out a soulful sigh.

"Fuck, I wish I could just stay here with you."

"Mmm. I think you'd be a *particularly* bad influence."

"You're right. I have to give the genius her time to work," He pulls away, but hesitates. Just as he opens his mouth to say something else, there's a knock at the door.

"Yeah?" Damien calls.

"Car's downstairs, bud!" Johnny's voice cuts in through the wood and the door handle jiggles dramatically. "Hey, it's locked for once! Good for you!"

Phoebe chuckles, shaking her head as Damien pulls a face.

"Phoebe Miller, are you taking precautions?"

"Someone has to, you're a hot commodity you know."

"I'll get it one day," he replies, pausing to shoot her a quick little wink on his way out the door. "See you soon, babydoll. Don't be late!"

With the click of the door, Phoebe peels herself off of the bed and heads straight for her typewriter. Her fingers wiggle in the air, snatching the paper out of the platen and resting it beside her. She'll start entirely from scratch, see how far she can get. Hell, maybe inspiration will strike. She feeds a new piece of paper through the machine, tweaking each setting to her liking, and takes a deep breath.

"Objective," she whispers. "That's all it needs to be."

She sits there, fingers hovering above the keys for half an hour. Once in a while they fall, a clack or two ringing out before she stalls again. The TV is buzzing too loudly, the wind rustling the curtains is aggravating; everything's set up exactly right to ruin her focus and spoil her cool.

She stands up and paces around the room, adjusting everything, creating the perfect environment. She even considers calling Janis, but Phoebe knows she'd just say the same thing Damien did.

"The tabloids will only care about the headline, the one that says you fucked me for a story."

She shuts her eyes and takes a deep breath, as though that act alone could push the right words from her mind onto the page.

When I landed at LAX, I never expected...

She falters.

"To fall in love," she mutters. "Jesus, you can't write that garbage. It's..."

The most honest thing she's written? She snatches the paper out of the typewriter again and feeds a new piece through, smacking herself gently on the forehead.

"You *can't* write that. Come on, Pheebs, try again."

Her fingers strain on the keys, itching to write. This is always the worst part in the process, knowing that there's a damn good story nestled in her brain that she just can't tell. She grasps absently at her bag, finding a pack of cigarettes and jamming one between her lips.

She lights it up, taking a long drag as she rocks back and forth in her desk chair, each creak a punctuation mark on her own lack of progress.

"Maybe start with a vague description of Damien," she mumbles. "Might be easier that way?"

Her fingers find the keys again, and before long they're flying.

Few musicians have been as mysterious and avoidant of the press as Revolver's lead vocalist, Damien Bell. When I first landed in LAX to meet the band, I was convinced the story that I'm about to tell would follow an expected formula. That I would meet a man of few words with a disdain for the press, who wanted nothing more than to–

She groans, clutching her head.

It's fucking impossible. Her throat tightens as she stares at the page, and dread begins to fill her like half-set concrete. Damien was right. He was right, and she was running out of time. She sniffles, tears stinging her eyes.

Don't you dare cry.

The only thing that keeps repeating in her head are Damien's words.

"...Even if you change the article, even if you somehow turn it into a cold and calculated look at the band, people will see your name on it. They'll see Phoebe Miller printed next to an article on Damien Bell and his band, and you know what they'll see next?"

"Us," she sighs.

She can't write around it. She can't avoid it.

Her eyes fall on her suitcase, lying on the floor and surrounded by their clothes. Her vision blurs with her tears. She knows what she wants: No more secrets, no more lies, no more hiding. Just the two of them together. And if she can't have that...

Phoebe pushes her chair back and walks to the nightstand, pulling the phone book out of the small drawer. She rifles through it until her finger lands on the number, cradling the receiver against her shoulder as she puffs on her cigarette. The phone rings and it rings and it rings.

"Denver International Airport."

"Hi, I need to book a flight to New York."

"Yes ma'am, and when would you like to leave?"

"As soon as possible," Phoebe replies.

She hears a hum and some clicking on the other end of the line.

"I have one going out tonight at 9:00pm."

She looks over at the clock. 6:00pm.

"That's perfect," Phoebe replies.

No matter how much it hurts.

Dedicated to the One I Love

DAMIEN

He's pacing back and forth, Ophelia's drumsticks in his hand and his heart in his throat. He checks the clock hanging on the wall while Johnny and Shaun sip at their beers and Ophelia does her makeup. He should be excited, every gig is supposed to bring a new thrill after all, but as the clock ticks down to showtime his brain begins to spin out of control. All he can think about is Phoebe walking through that door, and why it hasn't happened yet.

"Hey, where's Pheebs?" Shaun has to have noticed the nervous pacing.

"Back at the hotel," Damien replies, trying to play it off like it's nothing.

She was okay this afternoon. They were okay, weren't they? He'd never had a fight quite like that before, and he'd never resolved one. Who knew communication really was the solution. He must have missed that memo.

Take a breath, man. Calm the fuck down. She'll be here.

It's her job– this whole thing is her job. And she loves it. He's never seen her bail on a gig before, even the couple times early on when they'd butted heads. Even when he was certain she was going to take the next plane back to New York.

She intrigued him from moment one, the journalist he had been reading about for nearly a year finally had a face, and a cute one at that. He planned to be on his best behavior for her, some kind of schoolboy desire to impress her. Maybe she would think he was cool instead of just a clown who hurled beer bottles off of hotel balconies.

Turns out it was harder to keep that going than he thought, but it ended up not mattering. At first, he kind of liked the way he made her jump and scurry away like she was afraid to spend more than a couple minutes near him. It was that old instinct kicking back in and that inherent mistrust of people in her profession, but it all changed so quickly. He loved how she stood up to his bullshit, how they made it all work, and now all he wants is to see her walk through that door.

Shaun snaps his fingers in his face.

"Yo, space-case, how is it way up there?"

He blinks.

"Where'd you go, man?" Shaun laughs. "Getting cold feet so soon before a show? That's not like you at all."

"No, I'm good. I'm just–"

"Five minutes, lady and germs!"

Troy's booming voice takes over the room, with even Ophelia giving him her undivided attention. He surveys the group, nodding and gesturing at nothing in particular as if he was running down an invisible checklist, before his eyes land on Damien.

"Well well well, Mr. Front Page," he pauses, glancing around for a moment before leaning in close. "Where's Miller?"

Damien sighs, going through the same song and dance again.

"She's still back at the hotel."

Troy frowns, running a hand through his hair.

"What is she, sick or something? We need pictures and, I dunno, whatever she writes in that little notebook. You didn't piss her off did you?"

Damien huffs.

"She said she was gonna be here, so she'll be here."

He can't keep the irritation out of his voice. He's so anxious he can barely think straight. Is she still pissed at him? Did she decide this was all too much and just bail? On them? Where the *fuck* is she?

Troy holds his hands up in mock surrender.

"Chill out, Bell. Worst case scenario she's a little late. You're a professional, and believe it or not, sometimes professionals perform without their girlfriends cheering them on from backstage."

"She really will be here, Damien," Ophelia assures him. The reflection of her eyes are locked on him as she finishes applying her makeup. "You guys were good after last night, right?"

"I thought so," he mumbles. "Now I'm not so sure."

"I need your head in the game, kid. No more dramatics, this is another big show for us." Troy points emphatically at each of them. "That goes for all of you."

Ophelia sighs, her eyelids fluttering as she barely keeps her eyes from rolling out the back of her skull.

"You say that every night, and we always deliver."

Damien hangs his head and gently smacks the drumsticks against his thighs. He feels a clap on the shoulder and glances up to see Troy flashing his best smile, dropping the hard-ass manager act even if just for just a minute.

"You need anything, kid?"

He shakes his head.

"She'll be here, and she's gonna be disappointed if you're just moping on stage, right?"

Damien nods, and Troy gives him another quick pat on the back before checking on the others. Moments like these remind Damien why he sort of enjoys Troy having a stick up his ass most of the time. It lets you know when he really cares about something.

He twists his thumb ring back and forth over and over again until the metal feels like it's heating up his skin. Maybe he should call his parents and tell them about Phoebe, about how he's finally found someone. They'd like to hear it, to hear that he's met someone to confide in. Anything to feel something else. But it's a stupid idea. Not enough time.

"Three minutes, guys. We're making our way to the stage whether Princess Miller shows up or not."

"Sullivan, I swear, I'm gonna pop you one," Damien growls.

Troy swerves left and right, tapping Damien on the chest a couple times as the rest of them get to their feet.

"Come on, Bell. You remember jokes, right? You love 'em!"

Ophelia snatches the drumsticks from Damien's fingers and gives him a little boop on the tip of his nose.

"She'll be here."

Damien nods, burying the nerves and mounting anxiety under a deep breath. Troy is right: they've got a job to do, and maybe the crowd will give him the buzz he needs.

"One minute!" Troy shouts. "We're leaving all the moping at the door!"

"Let's put on a fuckin' show," Damien whispers.

He slings his arms around his friends and the four of them head for the stage. He can hear the crowd chanting their name over and over, and that incredible electricity sparks in the back of his brain, rushing down his spine and lighting up his frazzled nerves. There's only one thing in the world that makes him feel like this, and he relishes it.

As they make it to the steps Troy grabs him by the shoulder, letting the rest of the band take the stage ahead of him.

"You're gonna kill it tonight. You know it, I know it. Fuck, listen to them out there. They sure as hell know it."

Damien only grins.

Up on stage the lights hit him right in the eyes, but it doesn't matter. He could do this gig blind if he needed. Shaun's at the front, hyping up the crowd as Ophelia settles in at her drum kit. Johnny takes a sip of beer, tossing him another bottle. Damien downs the whole thing in seconds and the crowd erupts.

"Denveeeerrrr!" He bellows. "How the fuck are ya tonight?!"

He glances to the side. She's still not here.

His heart begins to race as the absolute crush of noise reaches a new level.

"That's what I like to hear! Let's start this fuckin' show!"

So what if she's not here. She loves him. She's not going anywhere. And hell, maybe they'll make enough noise she'll hear it all the way back at the fucking hotel.

Ophelia thrashes against the drums as Shaun's guitar kicks into high gear, and suddenly Damien's on autopilot. Joy and elation course through him as he sings every word as clear as if he was singing right to her. He thinks about the way she looks at him, the dorky little smile she gets on her face when he makes a stupid joke, or the way she slips between doe-eyed wonder and confident control. This could all fall away, his whole career. He could tumble into complete obscurity and lose everything, but it wouldn't matter so long as they fell together.

Damien slides back down to earth as the song transitions into the bridge. He saunters toward the back of the stage to guzzle some water, and Troy throws him a quick thumbs up from the sidelines.

"You're on fire, Bell, keep it up!"

Damien waits another few bars before launching back into the chorus. He can barely bring any of it to mind, but it doesn't matter. The words are just pouring out of him. He gets up close to the crowd, sliding on his knees and soaking it all in. Everyone's desperate to reach him. They grasp at his jacket, screaming his own song right back as they claw at him with a strength that always catches him off guard. These are the moments he dreamed of as a punk kid in Brooklyn, all of it sprung to life from his blank lyricless pages. He can't imagine what his life would have been like without his band, his music, and everyone who made him who he is.

But in the moment he knows for certain he'd let it go for her.

The crowd refuses to relent as their first song cascades into another, and another and another, but after a while the magic starts to wear thin. Every song affords a couple moments to check for her, but every time he's met with empty space.

He just wishes he could talk to her.

With the final notes of their last song ringing in the air, the audience's banshee-shrieks reach their apex. He smiles, covered in sweat, his hair sticking to his face as they all take their bows. It might just be their best show yet.

"Thank you, Denver! You've been fucking amazing!"

It just doesn't feel right without her.

Backstage, Troy is on him in a heartbeat, clapping him on the back. He's all smiles, with only a bit of the usual business mixed in.

"You did good, kid. Great, even!" He gets a little closer, dropping his voice a bit. "But you were distracted out there, sure things are good with Miller? Nothing I need to know about?"

"It's fine Troy, I just wanted–"

A loud voice echoes from the hallway and grabs his attention. It's one of the security guards.

"Nah, no way you're getting back there."

He rushes for the entrance, but Troy steps in front of him, putting his hand on Damien's chest.

"Settle down, pretty boy. I got this."

As Troy disappears around the corner, Damien is nothing but nerves. The crowd's still screaming behind them, and he can feel the pressure mounting with each passing second.

"Damien! They want an encore!"

"Come on, man, they're throwing shit on stage!"

He glances back at his bandmates, throwing out a vague and irritated gesture. He couldn't care any less what the crowd wants at this point, and he turns back just in time to see Troy round the corner, clearly a bit annoyed.

But there she is.

"So where the hell have you been? You missed the whole show!"

"I just need to talk to–"

"It can wait. They're going back on stage any minute now.".

"Sullivan, you are out of your goddamn mind if you think I'm going back on when there's a beautiful lady here just for me."

Troy rubs his eyes, any will to fight long gone with the crowd's applause.

"Alright, alright, you two got five minutes, tops!" he growls.

Damien pulls her aside, his chest tight and his face still hot with sweat. She looks up at him with those beautiful honey-colored eyes. He can barely stand it.

"What happened?" He asks. "Where were you?"

"You were right," she whispers.

Damien's brows knit together as she takes a breath, steadying herself.

"Pheebs, you're freakin' me out," he laughs. "What are you talking about?"

She flings her arms around him, and he jumps a little in surprise at her kiss. When she pulls away, a smile tugs at the corners of her mouth, a little scared, but hopeful.

"I'm going back to New York."

Damien's stomach twists, panic flooding his body. She can't leave.

"Oh god Damien, no! It's not what you think. I'm coming back!" She obviously sees the fear in his face. She can probably even feel his heart threatening to smash out of his chest as leans against him. "I need to tell Brian everything about us, on our terms. I need to set things straight."

Damien's whole body relaxes as the relief pours over him. He cups her face in his hands, his thumb brushing against her cheekbone. She wants them to be in the drivers' seat. To take control of the narrative. All of the possibilities run through his head as he stares into her eyes.

"What if he says no? What if he fires you?"

"It doesn't fucking matter anymore. I can sell the story to Kerrang, Rolling Stone, anyone. I have the experience, the connections, and I've done the work. Anyone would kill to get their hands on this story, so if Titanium doesn't want to keep, it they can go fuck themselves."

He captures her in a kiss made up of all of the fire and passion he can muster, thinking back to the first couple days when she was too terrified to acknowledge how he made her feel and he was too stubborn to tell her how quickly he fell. He flies back over all their time up until now, living in the little bubble of the tour, pretending it would all work out on its own. But here she was, taking the reins.

"I'll call you every day you're gone."

"I'm gonna be there for like a day." She chuckles, taking his hands. "Damien, you don't have to worry. You're going to see me again. I'm going to finish this story, because that's the job, but the job's not what's most important."

He can tell nothing's gonna stop her.

"Let me come with you. I can ditch the show, we can go right now."

She smiles, just a little sadly, and shakes her head.

"No."

"Why not? We can move some shows around, just let me be there for you."

"I have to do this alone, it has to come from me and only me. Besides, *you* have a whole stadium worth of fans who're clearly still losing their goddamn minds."

Damien pulls her closer, relishing the warmth of her body against his.

"I can't do it without my girl," he whispers.

Those lips, those eyes, her cute little nose that crinkles whenever she thinks something is really funny. There isn't a single part of her that he doesn't love. But she knows him too well, and only laughs.

"You've done it before me, and you can do it again."

His throat tightens the second he looks into those big, honey-colored eyes. A smile flickers across her face.

"Make me proud, sweets."

Damien snickers and gently boops her on the tip of her nose.

"I see how it is, got a new badass attitude, ready to take on the world, and now you're stealing my nicknames?"

"Deal with it, tough guy."

The chanting is getting louder and louder. This crowd might just storm the stage if they don't get what they want.

"You got one minute, Bell!" Troy calls.

Damien caresses her hand as they start toward the stage.

"You're really doing this huh?"

"Yeah," she sighs. "I really am."

Johnny, Shaun, and Ophelia disappear, met with riotous screams, whistles, and applause. Damien takes a few steps toward them before glancing back over his shoulder. He points straight at her, his arm outstretched and a big smile on his face.

"Just a day or two? I'm betting you're gonna miss me the second you walk out those doors."

She shouts something to him he can't quite make out as he takes the stage, the crowd going ballistic as he grabs the microphone.

"Well, well, well. If it isn't Denver." He leans out toward them, a sea of hands reaching up in vain. "A little birdie told me you guys might want an encore."

The crowd may as well be an impenetrable wall of sound, but even with all their eyes on the stage, on him, all he can think about is her.

And there she is, just off-stage, smiling ear-to-ear.

"Well Denver, we're starting off with a bang 'cause I've got something brand new for you tonight! This one's called Babydoll, and just between you and me, it's dedicated to one *very* special girl!"

To Be Continued

Damien and Phoebe's story will continue in Dollhouse: A Rock Star Romance

Acknowledgements

I don't even know where to begin. I started writing this book in June of 2021 during the pandemic as a way to keep me from going off the deep end during grad school. It's been a long, difficult journey with a lot of ups and downs.

And I have some people to thank:

My parents for always encouraging me to be creative, and who told me to always follow the road less travelled. It's taken me to some strange places, but I'm forever grateful for your guidance. You'll probably never read this book, but know that I love you. Thank you for instilling a love of music in me at such a young age. It's one of the reasons why I wrote this. Thank you for always being there, and thank you for never giving up on me.

My *incredible* partner who took it upon himself to help me edit and restructure this book. I **literally could not** have done this without you. You have been so encouraging, helping me develop and get better as a writer, and I fucking love you more than I could possibly say. I'm so thankful that you came into my life when I least expected it and I'm grateful for you and your wisdom and humor every single day.

To the people who read this book when it was in its very early and very chaotic stages. Your support, enthusiasm, and overwhelming love for this story is what inspired me to turn it into a book. Thank you all *so* much.

My Patreon Patrons, *you* helped to create this book! You helped me buy the formatting software I needed, pay for a cover artist, for marketing tools and software, etc. I cannot thank you enough for having my back and supporting me.

This is going to sound weird, but thank you to the city of Portland where *NINE* chapters of this book take place. I knew I had to set at least part of this book there. Portland was the place my partner and I got engaged, and it will always be so special to me.

To the Sugar Club. Thank you for being wonderful friends, and for helping me challenge myself and be a better writer.

About the Author

Thea Lawrence is a writer and former PhD student living in Ontario, Canada with her partner of nine years. Her passions include horror movies, naps, Marvel, and all things Halloween. When she's not writing, you can find her watching vampire movies or looking for something that she's misplaced.

You can check out her website, or find Thea on social media:

Instagram: thealawrenceauthor

TikTok: thealawrenceauthor

Website: thealawrenceauthor.com

Upcoming Titles

Books by Thea Lawrence:

Heathens: A Vampire Mafia Romance (Blood & Bullets #1)

Dollhouse: A Rockstar Romance (Revolver #2)

Upcoming Titles:

Swipe Right: An Age Gap Romance

Ravenous: A Phantom of the Opera Retelling

Nightingale: A Vampire Why Choose Romance

Black Mass: A Vampire Mafia Romance (Blood & Bullets #2)

Afterglow: A Fake Dating Romance